A
TREMBLING
UPON ROME

A TREMBLING UPON ROME

A work of fiction by

Richard Condon

G. P. PUTNAM'S SONS · NEW YORK

Library of Congress Cataloging in Publication Data

Condon, Richard.
A trembling upon Rome.

Bibliography: p.
1. John XXIII, Antipope, 1367–1419—Fiction.
2. Church history—Middle Ages, 600–1500—Fiction.
I. Title.
PS3553.0487T7   1983   813'.54   83-3131
ISBN 0-399-12834-4

Printed in the United States of America

Second Impression

For
Hilary Hazlewood Jackson

"If the future and the past really exist, where are they?"
—St. Augustine

CAST OF CHARACTERS

Measured from the birth of Baldassare Cossa in 1367, the events of this work of fiction occurred over six hundred years ago. To heighten the effect of the story—as this is a novel and not a history text—the vital statistics of two of the characters have been altered.

FRANCO ELLERA (1355–1424), a slave of the Cossa family; later cardinal-deacon of Santa Amalia di Angeli (1411); accessory to the murder of King Ladislas of Naples; attended Council of Konstanz; husband of Bernaba Minerbetti, lifetime companion of Baldassare Cossa.

NICOLO COSSA (1342–1412), duke of Santa Gata, conte di Troja, signore di Procida, and marchese nel suo Libero de Protonotari Partecipanti; head of the Cossa family based on the island of Procida, Bay of Naples, pirates and marauders for four generations; father of Pope John XXIII.

BALDASSARE COSSA (1367–1419), archdeacon and chancellor of the University of Bologna, 1390; senior private chamberlain to Pope Boniface IX, 1396–1402; cardinal-deacon of Saint Eustachius, 1402; commander of the combined armies of Florence, Bologna, and the Papal States and *legate a Latere* to Bologna, 1402–1410; Pope John XXIII, 1410–1415; seller of the head of St. John the Baptist, property of the Convent of St. Sylvester, Rome; sponsor and major partner with Bernaba Minerbetti, principal *ruffiana* (procuress) of the Papal States; cardinal Tusculanus, 1419. Cossa's permanent retainers were: FRANCO ELLERA (above), COUNT ABRAMO WEILER, physician, FATHER GUBBIO FANFARONE, chaplain, GEOFFREDANO BOCCA, master cook, and LUIGI PALO, enforcer.

PIERO TOMACELLI, a Neapolitan; bishop of Santa Grazia di Traghetto, 1386–1389; Pope Boniface IX, 1389–1404; second pope of the Great Schism.

BERNABA MINERBETTI (1363–1420), prostitute, mistress of Piero Spina, 1379; principal *ruffiana* (procuress) of the Papal States, 1403–1420; wife of Franco, Cardinal Ellera.

PIERO SPINA (1354–1418), a Sicilian; protonotary apostolic at the Vatican, 1379–1402; cardinal of the Church of Santa Mobiliare, 1402–1418; attended the Council of Konstanz.

GIAN GALEAZZO VISCONTI (1351–1402), duke of Milan, dominant force of northern Italy; husband and first cousin of CATHERINE VISCONTI, mistress of Pope John XXIII.

KING LADISLAS OF NAPLES (1379–1414), sponsored by Pope Boniface IX, enemy of Popes Alexander V and John XXIII, "protector" of Pope Gregory XII; a syphilitic womanizer.

COSIMO DI MEDICI (d. 1464), at the ascension of Pope John XXIII became the prime banker of the Catholic Church throughout Christendom; was the behind-the-scenes organizer of the Council of Konstanz; employer of the marchesa di Artegiana; son of GIOVANNI DI BICCI DI MEDICI (d. 1429), founder of the Medici Bank, whose headquarters were in Florence but whose branches were in all principal European cities.

DECIMA MANOVALE (1371–14??), mistress and aide de camp to William Turton, chief of staff to Sir John Hawkwood, 1383–1387; a *ruffiana* in Rome, 1387–1399; leading *mezzana* in Rome, 1399–1401; joined the Medici Bank 1400; was made marchesa di Artegiana by the Emperor Wenzel in 1400 through intervention of the Medici; mistress to Gian Galeazzo Visconti, 1400–1402; mistress to Cardinal Cossa, 1402; remained his mistress when Cossa became Pope John XXIII in 1410; principal organizer of the papacy of John XXIII and of the Councils of Pisa and of Konstanz in Medici interest; attended (and disappeared from) the Council of Konstanz; mother of four daughters, all courtesans: MARIA GIOVANNA TORETON, later mistress to Cosimo di Medici; MARIA LOUISE STERZ, later mistress to John of Nassau, archbishop of Mainz, then to Sigismund, king of Hungary, king of the Romans, and overt organizer of the Council of Konstanz; HELENE MACLOI later (simultaneously) mistress to Pierre, Cardinal d'Ailly, confessor to the king of France, and Jean Gerson, chancellor of the University of Paris; ROSA DUBRAMONTE, later mistress of Piero, Cardinal Spina, later mistress to Pippo Span, the count of Ozoro, a general of the Hungarian armies. Manovale was a political technician, the ultimate power broker, who worked for commissions from the Medici Bank, Pope John, and others.

THE COUNCIL OF PISA (1409), was called to dissolve the Great Schism of the Church, in which two popes, Gregory XII and Benedict XIII, reigned simultaneously over Christendom; assembled by a decree from the cardinals and prelates of both obediences and attended by 18 cardinals, 4 patriarchs, 10 archbishops, 70 bishops, leaders of 190 monasteries, 300 abbots, 200 masters of theology, the generals of the Jacobins and the Cordeliers, and the representatives of Oxford, Paris, Bologna, and Prague universities. The council deliberated, then formally dissolved the schism by deposing the two sitting popes, electing Alexander V as the single pope.

SIGISMUND (1368–1437), son of Charles IV, Holy Roman Emperor, margrave of Brandenburg (1378), king of Hungary (1387), king of the Romans (1411), king of Bohemia (1419), later Holy

Roman Emperor (1433), crowned in Rome; advocated the end of the Great Schism of the Church for pious political reasons; prime founder of the Council of Konstanz.

MASTER JOHN HUS, confessor to the queen of Bohemia, professed Church reformer, accused heretic, burned at the stake at the Council of Konstanz.

JOHN OF NASSAU, archbishop of Mainz (1370–1422); first elector of Empire; the warrior-prelate who was the richest churchman north of the Alps and a supporter of John XXIII at Konstanz.

PIERRE D'AILLY (1350–1420), bishop of Cambrai (1390); cardinal (1410); a principal candidate for the papacy (1417); most persuasive advocate of reform at the Council of Konstanz; confessor to the king of France; the richest churchman in France; political enemy of John XXIII; "protector" of Helene MaCloi.

LOUIS, DUKE OF ANJOU; the KING OF ARAGON; FREDERICK, DUKE OF AUSTRIA; LUDWIG, DUKE of BAVARIA; the MARGRAVE OF BADEN.

NOBLE ROMAN AND ITALIAN FAMILIES: Colonna, Orsini, Savelli, Este, Gaetani, Capocci, Stefaneschi, Annabaldi, Visconti, Montefeltro, Malatesta, Alidosi, Manfredi, and Ordelaffi.

THESE POPES: *popes before the popes at Avignon*—Celestine V (1294), Boniface VIII (1294–1303); *popes during the schism*—Urban VI (April 1378–October 1389), Boniface IX (November 1389–October 1404), Innocent VII (October 1404–November 1406), Gregory XII (November 1406–July 1415); *popes at Avignon during the schism*—Clement VII (September 1378–September 1394), Benedict XIII (September 1394–July 1417); *popes of the councils*—(Pisa) Alexander V (June 1409–May 1410), John XXIII (May 1410–May 1415); (Konstanz) Martin V (1417–1431).

THESE CONDOTTIERI: Sir John Hawkwood, Muzio Attendolo Sforza, Paolo Orsini, Facino Cane, Ugo Cavalcabo, Franchino Rusca, Ottobuono Terzo, Alberico da Barbiano, Carlo Malatesta, Chevalier Macloi, Albert Sterz, Andrew de Belmonte, William Turton.

THE COUNCIL OF KONSTANZ (1414–1418): 33 cardinals, 5 patriarchs, 47 archbishops, 145 bishops, 93 suffragans, 497 clerical princes, 24 auditors and secretaries, 307 religious schools, 217 doctors of theology, 366 doctors of canon and civil law, 171 doctors of medicine, 900 *magister artium* and licentiates, 5,300 priests and scholars, 24 papal secretaries, 16 papal gatekeepers, 12 papal beadles with silver rods, 60 other beadles, 132 abbots, 155 priors, having combined households of 32,254 people.

plus

KING SIGISMUND, 2 queens, 5 princely women, 39 dukes, 32 princes, 141 counts, 71 barons, delegations from 83 kings, 477 imperial towns, 352 princely towns, 1,924 knights, 2,700 servants of nobility.

plus

1,263 prostitutes, 16 apothecaries with shop, 77 goldsmiths with shop, 1,408 merchants, gracers, furriers, blacksmiths, shoemakers, innkeepers, artisans with shop, 24 royal heralds, 1,700 pipers, trumpeters, fiddlers, other musicians, 432 vestment laundresses, 41 barbers, 16 jugglers, 294 pickpockets, 11 lottery operators, and 218 professional gamblers.

plus

Approximately 90,000 tourists each year, who traveled from all over Christendom to see a running event on such a scale as had not been witnessed in Europe's history.

LED BY A SNAKE OF SCARLET CARDINALS, BY
WHITED PATRIARCHS AND PURPLED BISHOPS IN
CHANTED UNCTUOUSNESS, LAWYERS ALL, LURCHING
AND SWAYING TO THE CLINK OF ASPERGILLA, POPE
JOHN XXIII, BENEATH A BLOOD-RED MITER BORDERED
WITH WHITE, BECAME THE CENTER OF A HOLY
PROCESSION AND WAS FOLLOWED BY ARCHBISHOPS
AND ABBOTS, ATTENDED BY GREAT NUMBERS OF
CLERGY, BY FLORENTINE BANKERS, MILANESE
GENERALS, VENETIAN TRADERS, AND PISAN, PERUGIAN,
AND PARMESAN BUSINESSMEN, BY THRONGS
OF CITIZENS, ALL PROCEEDING TO THE CHURCH OF
SAN PIETRO MAGGIORE AND, AFTER THE SACRAMENT
HAD BEEN ADMINISTERED, SAT UPON A GOLDEN
THRONE SO THAT ALL MIGHT KISS HIS FEET.

PART ONE

PART ONE

Chapter 1

I am Franco Ellera, who has been the chamberlain, companion, bodyguard, and counselor to a pope. I became a cardinal of the Universal Church as a service to my master. I was born a Jew, I have lived as a Jew, and I will die a Jew. My master's lifetime is over, my own is nearly done. The Church accused my lord of a catena of crimes—heresy, simony, murder, sodomy, and fornication—when he was merely a man who put power and its sensuality foremost among the things that people need.

His story must be told to raise up his memory so that his life may be seen for what it was, an achievement and an adventure. His place is among the great men of his time. We lived among them and beside them: the kings, the popes, the cardinals, and the great soldiers. I knew Cosimo di Medici well, and Sigismund, king of Hungary, king of the Romans, king of Bohemia, and the marchesa di Artegiana. I knew the great cardinals d'Ailly and Spina. I supped with the woman who rid this earth of King Ladislas of Naples. I knew the warrior-archbishop John of Nassau and the duke of Anjou. These people were the keys to the kingdoms of earth in our time.

The estate of a pope has no peer, an emperor follows him and a king is correspondent, a high cardinal next in dignity, then a king's son, an archbishop his equal; a duke of the blood royal; a bishop, a marquis, and earl co-equal; then a viscount, legate, baron, suffragan, and mitered abbot, down through doctor of divinity and protonotary to master of chancery, parson, vicar, and yeoman of the crown, to worshipful merchants and rich artificers, gentlemen well-nurtured and with good manners.

But a pope is supreme. The apostles said, "Behold here are two swords," and the God of Christendom replied that this was enough but not too many. He who denies that the temporal sword is in the power of Peter wrongly interprets the word of the Lord when He says, "Put up thy sword in its scabbard." Both swords, the spiritual and the material, are in the power of the Church; the one, indeed, must be wielded for the Church, the other by the Church; the one by the hand of the pope, the other by the hand of kings and knights, but at the will and sufferance of the pope. The ecclesiastical power is verified by the prophecy of a Jew, Jeremiah, who said, "See, I have this day set thee over the nations and over the kingdoms"—and the other things that follow. Therefore, if the earthly power err it shall be judged by the spiritual power; if the lesser spiritual power err, then it shall be judged by the greater, a pope. A spiritual man judges all things, but he himself is judged by no one. Every human creature is subject to a pope.

That is how the Christians were all taught that it should be. But that is not how the mockery of time saw it happen.

Baldassare Cossa, my master, a great *condottiere,* the eldest son of the feared pirate family of Procida, creator of the papacy of Alexander V, friend of kings and Cosimo di Medici, the scourge of Ladislas and thus the savior of Italy, the shatterer of the Great Schism of the Church, the beloved of countless women and ruler of Christendom, which is the world of men, became Pope John XXIII.

I was born in Hamburg in 1355, twelve years before my master. Our city, with others in the league, served as an intermediary between Western Europe and the East—as did Italy. But the Italian East and our East were different things. Their East was older and richer. Ours was in the process of colonization. Russia, if one could call it that and not Western Tibet, for the Mongols ruled there, was in a state of primitive barbarism, covered with forests and fringed by a sea rendered inaccessible by ice.

My father, a cannoneer, was killed at Helsingborg defending the league against Waldemar IV. I was ten years old when my mother, with about thirty other young German widows, took me aboard a Hanseatic cog in a convoy of six cogs and two escort ships, to sail for the island of Sicily where husbands were waiting for them. When we were well into the Mediterranean Sea, two ships of the Cossa pirate fleet attacked us. Our cogs were sunk. My mother drowned. I remember her well and I love her to this day. I was pulled out of the sea and thrown like a fish into the bottom of a boat. I slept there until I was flung ashore, dragged to a warehouse, and locked in, alone and frightened. That is what I remember about my origins.

In time, I was told that I was the slave of Baldassare Cossa, the eldest son of the duke of Santa Gata, whose pirates had drowned my mother. All of the German women who survived were sent off to the slave market at Bari to be sold. My mother escaped that disgrace.

Baldassare Cossa, my master, was five years old. I was seventeen. The duke gave me my new name. I had a serviceable and honorable name, Franz Heller, which my family had defended throughout time, but to the duke I was nameless. He said at my Christian baptism ceremony, which was laid on to entertain his crew ashore, and which I could do nothing to prevent, "Ellera means ivy in the Italian language, and this Franco Ellera will cling to my son."

All the Cossas had been pirates for three generations, marauding from the two-mile island of Procida in the Bay of Naples, which they possessed entirely. I was happy on Procida. They were kind, hearty people, who lived out their good health on top of their skins. They ate constantly and well. They made love without shame.

The two peaks of Vesuvius rose into the perfect sky due east of us. Sometimes it sent up columns of smoke, which the Cossas told me was proof that there was a hell. It was such an *Italian* claim to make. They had murdered my mother yet insisted that we were looking all day at the proof of hell.

The Cossas were large-scale pirates, putting to sea in two great war galleys. *La Palazzina* was eighty feet long, with an overall breadth of nineteen feet amidships. Its oars were arranged on two levels. It was fitted with two masts and lateen

sails, and was manned by a hundred oarsmen and fifty soldiers,
all of whom had been sworn in on the Gospels. Its poop was
protected with fortified towers and, at the bow, there was a
castle equipped for offense and defense. With the second Cossa
galley, three carracks, and seven smaller craft, the Cossa strong-
hold at Procida numbered 766 people, counting sailors, rowers,
and fighting men, with land-based chandlers, armorers, agents,
scribes, spies, merchants, slave masters, priests, nuns, wives,
and children. Baldassare Cossa's father, head of the family, was
not only a Neapolitan duke, but also the holder of four baronies
in the Kingdom of Naples. His titles, conferred upon his family
by popes and kings, included conte di Troja, signore di Procida,
and Marchese nel suo Libero de Protonotari Partecipanti, as
well as duke of Santa Gata. Baldassare Cossa was his heir.

My five-year-old master instructed me to call him Cossa. He
never changed those orders. His father told me, "He has no
mother. I could have found a woman to raise him but clearly
God meant him not to have a mother so I prefer that he be raised
in the company of fighting men. That will serve him better as he
grows older. You will be in charge of him."

My work was to see that Baldassare Cossa was clean and that
he worked at his studies. Our teacher was a young priest named
Father Fanfarone, a very stupid fellow, who had good Latin and
no interest in religion whatsoever. He had become a priest because he was so lazy. We learned Latin, Italian, history, writing,
numbers, and singing. I had a magnificent voice. Cossa had a
fair voice. He was young.

Cossa taught me the Neapolitan dialect. I taught him German.
He was only a child but, as he grew, I was diligent in my attendance on him. I was certain to be courteous, glad of cheer, quick
of hearing in every way, and ever on the lookout for things to
do him pleasure. In the morning, against my lord's rising, I took
care that his linen should be clean. I would hold out to him his
tunic, then his doublet, while he put in his arms, then his vamps
and socks so that he should go warm all day. I would draw on
his socks and his hose by the fire and lace or buckle his shoes,
draw his hosen on well and truss him up to the height that suited
him, put round his neck and on his shoulders a kerchief, then
gently comb his head with an ivory comb and give him water

wherewith to wash his hands and face. This and more I would do for him from the time he was five years old until his death long, long years after. He knew from the beginning that I was his slave but, through our lifetimes, never treated me as other than his true friend for, as I was kind and good to him as a child, he was kind and sweet and good to me as a man.

The duke of Santa Gata's captains taught us the arts of war, on land and sea. I was included in this instruction so that I might protect the boy wherever he went. On our third raiding voyage aboard *La Palazzina,* when Cossa was ten years old (I was twenty-two, very big and strong, and as tall as any soldier in the crew), the ship we attacked, a Dutchman, had a company of fighting men waiting for us in its hold. They put up a bitter fight before that prize was taken.

I stowed Cossa in a deck locker while the fighting swirled all over the ship. A swordsman backed me across the deck. As we fought I tripped going backward. He rushed in to kill me. I was in bad trouble. Cossa stepped out, struck a dagger into his back, had the coolness to pull out the knife, then stepped back into the locker, a classical exercise for a boy that young. He saved my life that day, and he would save it again. How much I wanted to be like him.

In 1379, when our education-at-war was as complete as a going business had the time to make it, his father told Cossa that he had been awarded an appointment to the University of Bologna to study law.

The molten sun bore down with heavy heat upon the shed that was the port captain's office on Procida when Cossa and I stood before the duke's table, myself two paces to the rear of Cossa. The duke said, in a voice like chains falling on stones, "Piero Tomacelli is our man in the Lateran Palace. It was he who interceded with His Holiness, Pope Urban, to get you the appointment to Bologna. Over the years we have paid Tomacelli a lot of money to keep us well with the Church and to guide the throne of Naples to view our business benevolently."

He smiled with that enormously pleasing family smile that burst out of the saturninity of Cossa faces to win anything they chose. The duke had a magnificent smile, but his teeth were old.

Cossa's smile until he was an old man was a really beautiful thing to see. His teeth were perfect—white and even. It was said of Attila the Hun that he was one of the most charming men in history. Cossa's smile, in the same sense, seldom meant what it seemed to convey, which was loving regard, open honesty, and an entreaty for sincere friendship.

"I have written to your uncle Tomas in Rome," the duke said. "He will arrange a meeting with Tomacelli. Don't waste time trying to flatter him or to fool him. He is the complete Neapolitan who I hope one day you will become. Now—Baldassare— hear me well. As you excel at Bologna, Tomacelli will be watching you from Rome. As your excellence assures him of your promise as a lawyer, Tomacelli will be plotting for you, and advancing your cause with the pope."

"But we worked hard to excel at arms," Cossa protested. "How can that serve me if you make me become a lawyer?"

"Wait and see," the duke said. "Do you think you know anything outside Procida? You are going from a life of freedom to a totally dominated life. So did every other successful man. Never forget that the Church has run all the lives in Europe for a thousand years. The Church didn't get where it is on theology, my son. The hierarchy of the Church is a hierarchy of lawyers. Rich bishops, princely cardinals, and sainted popes—all of them are lawyers." He got up suddenly. "The carrack is waiting for you at the quay. It will take you, the escort, horses, and some gold to the mainland. Tomas is waiting for you in Rome." He embraced his son and held him closely. He stared at me intently and spoke to me over Cossa's shoulder.

"He can go to any heights in the Church if he learns to think like the rest of this family," he said.

Chapter 2

Our carrack plowed across the Gulf of Gaeta, cutting through the August heat to the mainland at Terracina, where we unloaded horses, food, gold, and men. Cossa's armed escort (of which I was in charge) were the companions and servants of his lifetime, but casual servants, not so close to him as I was. Father Fanfarone, always referred to as his "chaplain," was Cossa's favorite priest, because Fanfarone had so little interest in religion that he never annoyed Cossa with urgings that he confess or attend mass—and because he was so blissfully stupid. He was a fairly good forger and was assigned to keep up a cheerful correspondence with the duke in Cossa's name and writing. The duke had decided that a chaplain within Cossa's permanent household would create a most favorable impression upon the university prelates who would report student progress to Rome.

The second man in our entourage, as far as I was concerned, was Geoffredano Bocca, the master cook of the Cossa fleet. His bracioline made with beef, ham, breadcrumbs, and parsley were the finest sausages I have ever eaten and within me was the sausage-eating compulsion of hundreds of thousands of frozen Germans. I tell you that when he laid out layers of wide noodles, with alternating layers composed of that same compelling bracioline in minced form, then added his own secret sauce, then hard-boiled egg and two kinds of those cheeses which have made Italy the triumph of body and mind that it is, then sprinkled that with what he *said* was just grated cheese but which anyone who has ever tasted it knows was the powder of a master alchemist, I renounced once again—it happened every day I ate Bocca's cooking—Germany and all of the world except Naples. Before each meal he cooked for me he would say to me with that mysterious smile, "I am going to put something secret in your food. I will not say what it is but after you eat it you are going to be able to do things like you have never done them before."

The third man was a silent physician from the Adige (which the Italians consider as being far to the north!), Count Abramo Weiler, a healer who was bound to the Cossas because of his ruinous compulsion for gambling. The duke cured him by taking him aside and telling him that he would kill him if he ever gambled again. He said whether he killed him himself, on Procida, or in Naples, or whether he had to send men to kill him wherever Count Weiler chose to gamble, he would disembowel him and leave him to die in terrible pain, alone. Weiler told me that he totally lost interest in gambling after that, but he still continued to calculate the odds on almost everything, even if only in his head.

The last man, deservedly so on any list, was Luigi Palo, who did Cossa's (our) dirty work. He carried the title of Cossa's squire. He was a villain who would steal, maim, traduce, procure, or kill for Cossa, a specialist humbly offering his specialties. The duke had reasoned that during the ten years Cossa would study at Bologna he would occasionally meet people who would offend him gravely. This being certain, given Cossa's particular character, the duke did not want it to happen that Cossa (or I) should take any revenge personally, for that could go against Cossa's record in Rome—so Palo was sent along as the surrogate avenger of affronts and to undertake any necessary task that might be damaging to Cossa's honor.

The members of Cossa's permanent party were, on average, ten years older than Cossa, but he was the leader. Dr. Weiler was oldest, Cossa youngest; Father Fanfarone, stupidest, Cossa, the wiliest; Bocca, most garrulous, Cossa, most laconic; Palo, cruelest, Cossa, most deadly. How would I rate myself

against Cossa now that I have graded the others? I was the most
serious, Cossa the most devious.

We rode into Latium, Fanfarone complaining about his back-
side all the way, through Cisterna di Latina to Velletri and Al-
bano to Rome. We rode through a land that had settled into four
social divisions—just as in Germany—knights and their retainers, who lived in castles or keeps; merchants, artificers, trades-
men, and their dependents, who filled the towns; farmers, who
lived in wattled huts under the protection of their lords, spiritual
or temporal; and the clergy. The world was divided into un-
counted but gigantic masses of Christians and Mahometans
with, here and there, pockets of Jews. The knights, merchants,
and farmers took their places by right of birth and inheritance.
The clergy had to work their way up by the devious rules of the
Church.

When we reached Rome I, as leader of our party (Cossa
wasn't aware of that, but his father had put the entire expedition
in my charge), sought out the house of Cossa's uncle in the Via
Artanis, off the Tiber across from Vatican Hill. Rome was a
collection of shanties, thieves, and vermin. The Black Death had
reduced its population by one-third, to 17,000. The city was
wracked with factional strife among the Colonna, Orsini, Savelli, Gaetani, Capocci, Stefaneschi, and Annabaldi families. As
we rode along the river on our first day, on a guided tour of the
city by Cossa's uncle Tomas, we saw wolves wandering near St.
Peter's. "If this is Rome," Cossa said, "Bologna must be only
a clearing in the forest."

"Bologna was a city when Rome was a village," his uncle
said. "Rome looks like this because it has lived off the papal
interests like a mendicant. The whole population has allowed
itself to depend on the hordes of pilgrims and litigants the papacy brings to Rome."

Tomas Cossa was a one-eyed man who had been a sea captain
in the family business, but whom the duke had judged to be too
smart to stay at sea, there being plenty of other men to do his
job. Tomas was a ruffian who was burned to dark leather by his
lifetime in the sun. He had a hanging left eyelid that had
frightened many people before he had killed them. His voice

was coarsely hoarse from drinking Greek olive oil. He was the Cossas' chief intelligence agent and employed dozens of sub-agents in the seaports of Germany, France, England, Spain, and North Africa, to locate and evaluate shipping destined for the Mediterranean. He passed this complex information to the Cossas on Procida. Knowing when and where, the Cossa ships would sail out and plunder these ships. Tomas was probably responsible for my mother's drowning, but he was a Cossa and death meant nothing to him. Baldassare Cossa was the same, throughout his life. He killed at will but he offered his own life as forfeit if he failed. The family trade must have brought all the Cossas to that view.

Chapter 3

The popes! The cardinals! The bishops! The Curia! All because of the Jews and Constantine. Christianity was the religion of a Jewish sect who saw themselves as the true Jews because they thought God had granted to them the right to bring the saving work of the people of the Old Covenant to a conclusion because they thought they had found the Messiah. The other Jews merely referred to them as "the Nazarenes." Questions of agonizing urgency began to bother this sect, but the biggest question was whether Christianity should supplant Jewish orthodoxy or remain distinct from but closely linked with the Jewish community, its synagogue, and its traditions. By the third century, Anno Domini, by their counting, they were regarded as a heretical sect by other Jews. These Christians, disowned by the Jewish people, at last, three hundred years after their leader had died, called out to convert the whole of mankind to their Lord's message, in order to survive. Then the whole thing, the entire misunderstanding, was made legitimate by a politician's accident.

It is almost impossible to believe that because a politician, Constantine, claimed to attribute his cavalry victory at the Mulvian bridge to the God of the Christians, who had been nurtured so feebly in Rome by a handful of renegade Jewish fanatics, we must now suffer hundreds of cardinals, thousands of bishops,

and tens of thousands of indolent priests and monks, in all of
the arrogance of their plump wealth: It is almost enough to shatter the spirit. But the shrewdest of all the politicians, Constantine, on October 28, A.D. 312, became the Father of
Institutional Christianity, in the crass version by which we now,
in the fifteenth century, know it. He rigorously enforced its dog-
mas and doctrines across the face of Europe, although he himself did not bother to become a Christian until he had fallen into
a coma and the eager priests baptized him on his deathbed.

That about sums up Christianity, in my humble opinion. It has
changed a great deal since then, but if they didn't know they had
a good thing when they were Jewish, I mean, as my father told
me, why try to improve on the real thing? How could a few
centuries, more or less, be expected to accomplish anything
except to make the countless executives of the Church worse?
Worse they became, believe me.

By the time we made it that far through our lives to get to the
Vatican Palace, Christianity had become a complicated, complex, big business. Bishop Piero Tomacelli, the Cossa family's
unofficial representative to the papacy, worked only at night in
the new papal palace on Vatican Hill, near St. Peter's. He was
the curial officer in charge of the administration of the *Rota
Romano,* preparing cases for appeals to the pope from all over
Christendom. His department, the *audientia litterarum contra-
dictarum,* had maintained diligent files over the centuries. It
examined and ruled on objections and exceptions to appeals.

At midnight on the day after our arrival, Tomas took us to the
Vatican Palace for a private audience with Bishop Tomacelli,
the expensive friend of the Cossa family. Tomacelli was the
blandest man I have ever met or seen. He was tall, elegant, and
handsome; of a noble Neapolitan family, although not of the
Cossa family's rank. He was ten years older than Cossa, which
made him two years younger than me. "Tomacelli is not over-
learned," the duke had explained to us, "but he is courteous
and affable and certainly knows where the money is."

The luxury in which the bishop lived impressed us deeply. I
could see Cossa shivering with the pleasure of imagining how

cardinals must live. Seeing Tomacelli, a young man, covered
with jewels and fine clothing, surrounded by so many servants
in such an opulent setting must have settled the matter of Cossa's entering the Church in his own mind. It had never been real
to him before. The Church was the place for sandaled dolts such
as Father Fanfarone but this—this was living! I would have to
agree with him, if living without women is living.

"How I long to see Naples again," the bishop said. "But you
and I, by our service, Baldassare, must put that past behind us.
You have been chosen by His Holiness to study at Bologna, to
transform yourself into an instrument of the Church." Tomacelli's voice rode upon exquisite Latin, although a few years later,
after I had perfected my own, I didn't rate it so highly. He was
striking a bargain with Cossa.

"There is no career that can equal what the Church can offer
to a brilliant young lawyer," Tomacelli said. "Canon law is the
skeletal structure of the Church. It is the oil that has been
rubbed into her by her lawyers, keeping her agile for more than
a thousand years."

We crossed the bridge of Sant' Angelo at about one-fifteen in
the morning. The horses were lively in the night air. Cossa was
still excited by the audience. "Did you notice his shoes?" he
asked us. "At first I thought they were painted on his feet but
after a while I saw that they were made of silk."

"Shoes?" I said. "What about the furniture? How about the
paintings?"

"Yes!" he said. "And I thought to myself that Margaret of
Durazzo, ruler of Naples, cannot have better than that. Where
are we headed, Uncle?"

"Your father told me to put you on a woman," Tomas said.
"That's where we're going."

"A woman?"

"You'll like it, my lord," I told him.

"You've mounted women?" he asked me with astonishment.

"Well, after all, I am twenty-five years old," I told my thir-
teen-year-old master.

"Who?"

"A couple of your cousins."

We clattered through the night streets past the closely packed houses of the *burgo,* with their gables and sloping roofs facing the streets, most of them made from pilfered Roman ruins. Tomas stopped us in front of a two-story house that had an outside marble staircase to the upper floor, in the street of the Blessed Sta. Denisetta di Grellou. There was a small garden in front of the house with one olive tree, one fig tree, and one apple tree. Tomas led Cossa up the outside stairway. Halfway up, Cossa stopped him. "What's her name?" he asked.

"What do you care?"

"I have to know the name."

"Bernaba."

"Bernaba what?"

"Are you going to marry her or just wrestle her? Her name is Bernaba Minerbetti. She comes from Bari, the pope's home-town. She's so new to Rome that hardly anybody knows she's in business. You are lucky—she is a beautiful little piece with a lot of life in her. The reason you are going to get to have her at this time of night is that her protector—if you can imagine a fellow who thinks he has bought a whore all for himself—is a Sicilian protonotary apostolic named Piero Spina, who works the night shift at the Vatican."

"I wouldn't want her to be too much of a whore," Cossa said.

"She'll be whatever you want her to be," Tomas told him. "That's her business."

Tomas knocked at the door at the top of the stairs. They waited. "Why is she taking so long?" Cossa asked.

The door opened. A tiny, dark, very pretty sixteen-year-old woman, wearing a sheepskin and holding a guttering candle, opened the door. "Where you been?" she said. "You got me all horny waiting for you."

Tomas patted his nephew on the shoulder. "I have a virgin for you," he said to the girl.

"Ah, Uncle Tomas," Cossa said. He didn't want to say that he had screwed many of his cousins, because one of them was Tomas' daughter.

Tomas pushed him and the girl pulled him inside the door. It closed on my upturned face at the bottom of the stairs.

Tomas went home. I fell asleep in the garden waiting for Cossa to finish. Several hours later I was awakened by a racket above me. Cossa told me later what had happened. He and the girl fell asleep in each other's arms after he had done four or five times what she had found out he could do quite well (and he spent the rest of his life perfecting it). They came out of sleep the same time I did, like stones from a catapult, when the door splintered open and two violent men broke into the room.

The girl sat straight up. "Spina!" she yelled. It was the protonotary apostolic who was paying the rent. Cossa told me Spina's eyes were popping out of his head with the outrage of the horror of his personal disgrace. He had been conditioned to react this way, he was a Sicilian.

"*Sfregia!*" Spina shouted.

The girl moaned like the night wind.

"*Sfregia?*" Cossa said blankly.

"He's going to cut up my face!" the girl shrilled, moving backward and upward in the bed. "No, Spina! This is only a boy. He is from my village. He is my *brother,* Spina. He had no place to sleep."

Spina took out a knife. He moved slowly around the bed toward the girl's side, motioning to his companion to move in on Cossa. The other man took out a knife and moved toward Cossa. By this time I had made it to the top of the stairs. I banged the companion over the head. He went down. Cossa, naked, had leaped out of bed, picked up a heavy wooden chair, and charged at Spina, holding the chair before him like the horns of a fighting bull, running over the top of the bed to crash the chair into the soft front of Spina's head and knock him to the floor unconscious.

"*Do* something!" the girl yelled, as if we had just been standing around. "He is a Sicilian! He will hold a *trentuno* to get his revenge! Oh, shit, and I just set up business in this town."

"What's a *trentuno*?" Cossa asked.

"He will come back here with thirty men from the Vatican and they'll rape me one after the other."

"Impossible!" Cossa said.

"You have destroyed his honor and he brought his own witness to see it," Bernaba keened. "Listen—he is the most rabid *kind* of Sicilian. It could even be a *trentuno reale,* a continuous rape by seventy-nine men. I won't be able to work for two weeks! Then he will burn the house down. Oh, shit, those poor people downstairs.''

"Get dressed," Cossa said. "You'll come with us.''

"Where?"

"Bologna."

"Over the mountains? Where it *snows*?"

"If you want a *trentuno reale,* then stay here.''

"Ah, shit."

Cossa scrambled into his clothes. I kicked both men in the head to make sure they stayed unconscious. Cossa wrote a note.

"Get me a pin," he said.

"What are you writing?"

He took the pin from her and knelt beside Spina's broken face. He pinned the note to Spina's chest. "It's in the best Latin," he said, grinning, and, as I said, he had such a smile that the girl, despite all the trouble she thought she was in, had to smile as if somebody had handed her a gold florin. "Listen to this," Cossa said. "The entire male family of Bernaba Miner-betti have just performed a *trentuno* upon every orifice of your body. You have lost your honor. We are revenged.''

"You knew my name!" the girl said with immense pleasure. "But that really does it. Spina will spend the rest of his life trying to avenge this.''

"Let's get out of here," I said.

We left Rome with the escort one hour before dawn. We reached Bologna four days later without incident. The year was 1379.

Chapter 4

As we were riding north I said to him, "Your father wouldn't like it if he knew that, on our second night in Rome, you made an enemy of someone in the Vatican."

"It being the second night in Rome had nothing to do with it," Cossa said. "The fact that I was there on my second night in Rome is my father's fault. He wanted me to have a woman. As for making an enemy in the Vatican, the man came at me with a knife, so he must have been my enemy before I could be his. You might as well blame my uncle Tomas for not taking me to an ugly girl who had no friends."

As you can see, it was always difficult to talk about serious, moral things with Cossa, because the nature of his mind resisted them.

"Was she kidding about snow in Bologna?"

"Well, in the winter, sure."

"And I suppose the dialect is different?"

"Why not?"

"How's the food?"

I shouted to Palo, the fellow Cossa's father had sent to Bologna to get everything set up for us. "Hey, Palo! How is the food in Bologna?"

"You are not going to believe it until you taste it," Palo yelled. "It is like ninety times better than Neapolitan food."

"Well, they have snow so they should have better food,"
Cossa said.

Aeneas had not crossed into Italy, Ascanius had not built Alba
nor Romulus Rome, when Bologna was already one of the no-
blest towns in Italy, and the chief Etruscan city north of the
Apennines. It extended as far as the foot of the Apennines,
flourishing and fruitful, abounding in vineyards and olive groves.
Unpolluted by marshy vapors, its soil was fertile, producing
more than enough for the people of the plain. Water was brought
into the city by the Canale di Reno. The city was famous for its
square towers even more than for its arcaded streets. There
were more than 950 towers, for the most part built of wood,
often within five feet of their neighbors. The upper stories of the
houses projected over crooked, narrow streets, the more preten-
tious made of brick decorated with terra cotta. There was no
marble.

Bologna, ancient on the Aemilian Way, was at the intersection
of four provinces: Lombardy, the March of Verona, the Romagna, and Tuscany. It was the point at which the great lines of
communications between the northern entrances of Italy and its
center converged. Students of the law from Norway to Greece
who were to take their places in power throughout Christendom
became our friends there.

The University of Bologna was the most famous center of
learning in southern Europe. Its rivals were Oxford and Paris. It
taught the codification and administration of the laws on which
the Church had survived for a millennium. It ignored theological
speculation. Religious thought, which would have been only an
illusion to these fledgling canon lawyers, had no substance. Theology was theoretical. The law took its substance from the material opportunities it represented. The student lawyers would
graduate as doctors of canon law then go on to become prelates:
bishops, archbishops, and cardinals of the Church, stoically unaware of the spiritual side of the extraordinary complex they
served, yet preserving and extending it by the attributes of their
legal practice.

By banishing theological speculation from its curriculum, the
university also banished all heresy to which such speculation

gives rise and extinguished all interest in the purpose and meaning of the religion the young lawyers were being trained to serve.

The scholastic year lasted from the tenth of October to the end of the following August. We needed to write no lies about Cossa's scholastic accomplishments in the letters I dictated to Father Fanfarone for forgery into Cossa's hand. Cossa became renowned as a scholar.

Bernaba had brought her own money and a small collection of jewels. Spina had been generous. She thanked Cossa for his offer of hospitality in the same spacious, well-furnished house that we occupied, which Palo had found, four streets from the university. She told us she had to leave to get her business organized. "It's always hard to get started," she said, "but I did it before and this looks like a pretty lively town."

"You need a manager," Cossa told her.

"A pimp?" she asked without resentment.

"Watch your language, Bernaba," I told her.

"Then what does he want to manage?" she asked. "Am I a singer?"

"I have introductions to a lot of important people in Bologna," Cossa said. "After I establish myself with them, I could introduce them to you."

"What do you get?"

"Information."

"No money?"

"Information is money."

"Then you won't take my money?"

"You're goddamn right he won't take your money," I told her.

"I didn't say that," Cossa told her smoothly. "Franco Ellera said it. This is business. You are a talented woman at your kind of work. I'll put up the money to set you up in style—see what I mean? It's like my father fitting out a ship for raiding. We'll agree on how much you earned in Rome and I'll allow you that much free and clear. But I'll take fifty percent of whatever you make over that, because of my investment and my key introductions, which will, after all, set you up in business in a strange town."

"What about trouble—you know—complaints, noisy drunks, and women-beaters."

"We have Palo for that."

"It sounds all right to me," Bernaba said. "I will need all the protection I can get. But I'm not clear on what kind of information you want."

"That will develop naturally," Cossa said. "Let's concentrate on the business side for now. Like maybe you could add two or three more hot-looking *cortigiani* to your stable. We would finance that and protect their operation under you and take twenty-five percent of what they make. You provide them with our money and our muscle—and a nice place to work— and divide the other seventy-five percent with them."

"Cossa, hold on a minute, here," I said.

"What's the matter?" he had the arrogance to ask me.

"I want to get something straight with you. This has nothing to do with fitting out a ship for your father's business. Even if it did—I would still say that to make money from the business that drowned my mother is better than living off the shame of a woman who rents her body to men for the uses of their filthy lusts."

"Filthy?" he said indignantly.

"Shame?" Bernaba said with shocked astonishment. "I am eating now! I have a place to live and I had that before I met the two of you."

"This is not personal, Bernaba," I said. "I want to be sure that Cossa understands something important."

"I do understand," Cossa said. "We were cast into these roles. I am the son of a line of pirates. You are the son of a woman whose fate was to drown on a ship that my father took, because, of all the women aboard those ships, about two hundred women, only three of them drowned, so that was their fate. Bernaba was poor. You heard her. Until she went into her business as a courtesan, she didn't have enough to eat or maybe even a roof. We saved her from mutilation in the course of her work, yes, but we cost her a valuable client. So we owe her something. If we do nothing, if we turn her out upon the streets of a strange city, would that be right, when you know we can help her? But, and this is the important point, Franco Ellera, the moment we help her on a large scale, then she is obliged to give us a share in that business."

"I'll count it when I see it," Bernaba said.

"It will work," he told her. "You will be a rich woman as long as you remember that I have nothing to do with any of this. Franco Ellera will be your contact. Franco Ellera will run Palo. We never had this conversation. If I am ever connected with this, a *trentuno reale* will be nothing to what will happen to you."

Bernaba yawned theatrically.

"You understand me?"

"Yes. It makes a lot of sense."

Bernaba moved into a very comfortable house that I found for her in Castelleto Street, where was the market for caviar-eyed Cyprian women who were forbidden to live near churches or monasteries. From what I have seen, at closest quarters, of churchmen and monks, it would have represented too much wear and tear on the girls. The street was named after a celebrated brothel in Venice at the end of the Rialto Bridge, which I saw later on. Ours was better.

Cossa, who was exactly like his father, could never see anything wrong in anything that produced money. If, for example, two thousand people lived in a forest that grew many hundreds of kinds of medicinal plants of benefit to mankind, and if the forest contained dozens of animals and maybe insects that were the only food for those people, and Cossa or his father had a good money offer for the wood, they would cut down the entire forest immediately and feel it had been a good transaction. They knew instinctively that one of the things about a lot of money is that it eliminates moral nagging instantly. They were just as direct about the pursuit of power. Cossa was committed to spending ten years studying law because, if he excelled at it, he would be invited to enter the doorway to power through the Church.

Chapter 5

The university was a key to Cossa, and not merely to scholastic achievement. Thousands and thousands of students had flocked there since it had been established, but Cossa was (possibly) the only one who exploited *every* opportunity. He became scholastically accomplished and he won scholastic honors while he was turning over in his mind how the university worked and how he could use it to move his career along.

Within the university was the Universitas, an association in the world of learning that corresponded to the guild in the world of commerce—a union among students possessing common interests to protect and advance. By the beginning of his fourth year at Bologna, Cossa dominated all of the cisalpine student unions—which included his own Neapolitan-Sicilian group as well as the Lombards, the Tuscans, and the Romans—and several of the transalpine unions, by his bribery of the rectors who governed each union. I handled the direct bribery. Palo handled the threats. This, in addition to the amazingly personal information that Bernaba and her *cortigiani* amassed for him every night about the many powerful citizens of Bologna, gave Cossa early standing with the City Council and an important identity within the local Church, which, in turn, reflected his growing eminence in its reports to Rome.

Cossa had his own money, never used, from his father. He

had a substantial income from Bernaba's business. But he made a lot of money by organizing and supplying protection for the gambling houses of the city, called *baratterie,* and he bribed his way to eminence with that.

The *baratterie* were scattered throughout the city. They offered dice, draughts, knucklebones, and skittles. Cossa had Palo form troops of street fighters from neighboring towns and villages, to begin quarrels in the gambling houses, which led to violent brawls, which broke up the *baratterie.* In each place, I would go in after the second time it happened, bringing with me outrage and sympathy and gradually working out a system that guaranteed the owner total security from such disturbances, if he paid the fees.

Cossa took only fifty percent of this weekly income. Palo and I got fifteen percent each and the rest was divided among the troops. No one could connect any of these illegalities to Cossa. He was the model student, the most promising lawyer in the student body. He was certain to rise in the Church.

The amazing thing was that the climate agreed with all of us but, most of all, it agreed with Cossa. "I feel like working here," he said. "I can do twice as much work, and the food is so good that I may never eat a pizza again."

"You don't miss Procida?"

"I miss the freedom. But what is freedom if it doesn't get you anywhere? I found out here, in Bologna, that I like to work. It is clear in my head that if I work I am going to have the same freedom, but I am also going to be one of the people who tells the other people what to do."

I grinned at him. "That's one thing you don't need," I said. "Since you could talk you've been telling people what to do."

Nearly all the servants of the royal and ducal courts—the diplomats, the *consiglieri* to great nobles, the architects, and the entire tribe of lawyers—were ecclesiastics. The civilization owed its development to canon law and its elaborate system of written precedents and codes, its judicial evidence, and its established procedures. The tie that bound the Church and the Law was Latin, the language of all educated people throughout Europe.

I speak Latin very well. Not as well as Cosimo di Medici but better than Cossa, who coarsened every language he spoke with a brutalizing Neapolitan accent.

Bishop Tomacelli, Cossa's sponsor at the Vatican, however, was the ultimate Neapolitan, so he had the ultimate accent. He was so devious as to be almost invisible. He was consecrated as a cardinal in 1384, and thereby was in a position to encourage the Bolognese government's appreciation of Cossa's gifts, by making sure that Cossa was invited to the only three dinners that he gave, as cardinal, in Bologna, over a two-year period, at which Cossa was seated at his right hand.

When Tomacelli was elected pope on November 2, 1389, taking the name of Boniface IX, Cossa consolidated all that good will and saw that the word was spread among the politicians of Bologna that he was the new pontiff's "nephew." When a pope acknowledged someone as his nephew it was always his illegitimate son. This made Cossa more powerful in the city.

Gliding forward into his papacy with smoothest affability, Tomacelli reinstated the cardinals whom Urban VI, his predecessor, had ejected, and set to work to win the temporalities of the Church.

Boniface must be explained, because he was the gateway to Cossa's career, making possible Cossa's highest rank, his great power as a condottiere, and his earliest riches. He brought Cossa together with the nineteen-year-old Cosimo di Medici. That friendship was Cossa's ultimate fulfillment, positive and negative, and the substance of his immortality, because, when Cossa was dead, it was Cosimo di Medici who commissioned Donatello to design, for eternal placement in the Baptistery at Florence, Cossa's tomb, which will honor his memory forever. Cossa, in turn, realized Cosimo's father's dream of consolidating the finances of the entire Church in one consolidated banking account, which they will retain forever, you may be sure. Cosimo di Medici loved Cossa. He respected Cossa because he had had to use him so badly in his secret way. I think that speaks well for Cosimo. Other men, having used Cossa like that, would have had to detest him.

As soon as Tomacelli was made pope, he welcomed the overtures of the throne of Naples, which had paid him a fortune over the years, sending a cardinal to Gaeta to anoint and crown the new, young King Ladislas. From that day hence it was the policy of the king of Naples to support the pope at Rome, without question, ignoring the other pope at Avignon.

Boniface sat down most agreeably with the noble families of the Papal States: Este, Montefeltro, Malatesta, Alidosi, Manfredi, and Ordelaffi. He convinced them that it would be to their best advantage if they acknowledged his overlordship. Then, with ineffable bland patience, he persuaded Rome itself to abandon republican independence and to admit his full domination. The Vatican was fortified. The Papal States were rearmed and fully reinstated to their former strengths.

Although Boniface was one of the most successful popes ever to fill the chair of St. Peter (from an executive standpoint, for he took an enfeebled Church and remade it into a magnificent piece of machinery), his success required much money to reach fruition—more money by half than the Church had. There was a pope commanding separate allegiances at Avignon, in France, Clement VII, exacting his dues and tithes (and more) from his part of the obedience of Christendom, and there was Boniface IX at Rome. The deep schismatic wound of the Church had a mournful history. The popes had been in France for eighty-four years, but the actual schism that had produced two popes simultaneously had begun with Urban VI, Boniface's immediate predecessor.

I am not an ignorant man, as you have seen plainly since the beginning of this narrative. One would have immediately supposed that Cossa was highly educated and that I was untrained. But I educated myself. I used books. I studied Cossa's books and I insisted on being the only one to drill him in his studies, because, had I not educated myself, he would have outgrown me and even such small influence as I had with him would have been wholly diminished. But besides knowing the law, without being privy to its honors, I was more educated than Cossa because the only history he cared about was military history and whatever Church history he required to get his diploma.

I devoured history. Everything about history depended on money. It was the money that made the history, so I tried hard to understand money, while not expecting to get any of it. Cossa, having so much of it, never had to study money. He took it for granted, and no matter how much he had, he always needed more of it.

Chapter 6

If there is anybody within five thousand miles of where I am writing this who hasn't heard about the schism in the only Church they'll ever have, I don't believe it. Maybe if I wrap this manuscript well and hide it in a good place, somebody will read this story a hundred years from now and maybe they won't remember what started the schism, which split their Church in half and was also very bad for business.

This is how the schism happened and how the papacy was moved from Rome to France.

In 1292, when Nicholas IV passed into God's fullest grace, there was a deadlock in the Sacred College for twenty-seven months before his successor could be elected, and even then only by a cruel trick. There were only nine cardinals left in that college and only three of those were independent, the others were either Orsini or Colonna. Pope Nicholas had been an Orsini. The Orsini would not accept the loss of the papacy, which the Colonna were determined to take away from them, and you may be sure that the three remaining cardinals were unwilling to offend either of these families that had willfully scattered murder throughout the streets of Rome.

The cardinals disputed who should be elected pope until the plague came to Rome, then they withdrew to the mountains of Perugia, still deadlocked.

One of the neutrals—a cardinal who was neither an Orsini nor a Colonna—was Cardinal Gaetani, the greatest canon lawyer of his time. He was a cold, pinguescent man who towered over everyone (though he would not have towered over me, had I been there). He carried his weight as daintily as a hippopotamus, with eyes like knives, the determination of an assassin, and delicate hands.

To break the deadlock, in his own devious way, Gaetani told Malabranca that he had received a "letter of fire" from a holy hermit, Peter of Morone, which prophesied the vengeance of God upon all of them if a pope were not soon elected.

This was July 1294. Malabranca was a *very* religious fellow. He took the forgery Gaetani had handed him with devout seriousness. He prayed. He contemplated, then, on the fifth of July, he summoned the handful of cardinals, read them the letter he believed had come from the holy hermit, and as he demanded a vote instantly, he was so carried away by his own visions that he cried out, "In the name of the Father, the Son, and the Holy Ghost, I elect brother Peter of Morone." The deadlock was broken by the logic of demonstrating to Colonna and Orsini alike that neither of them needed to prevent the other from winning.

Not that the cardinals of either family bothered to make the journey to the new pope, to kiss his feet as every tradition of the Sacred College required. But, since it is only the villain of every piece who is certain of what he wants, Cardinal Gaetani did go the Abruzzi to pay his homage. With him were the king of Naples and an enormous following of ordinary people. In a bleak cave in the Abruzzi mountains, Gaetani told the holy hermit that he had been made vicar of Christ on earth. The confused, frightened old man, who had never seen so many people in his life, nodded to the statement, because Gaetani had bellowed at him from that great height, in those rich and beautiful scarlet robes covering that barrel chest and hogshead belly, commanding that Peter would now nod his head to signify his acceptance of God's glory. Emaciated, hardly understanding Latin, much less the condition, Peter accepted the rulership of Christendom filled with mortal terror because he would have to leave his cave. He refused to go to Rome. He would rule from Naples. At Gaetani's suggestion he chose the name Celestine V.

From that day forward Gaetani served his pope as his lawyer and soothed the pope with a replica of the hermit's mountain cell, which he had recreated in the Castel Nuova, which had become the Lateran Palace of Naples.

Celestine belonged to an order that was called the Spiritualists, which now brought terrible pressure upon him to bring pure love to the world. Gaetani saw to it that the tough, cynical bureaucrats of the Curia jockeyed around the new pope.

Gaetani's consideration in duplicating Celestine's cold, wet mountain cave within the Castel Nuova was a hidden speaking tube he had installed in the ceiling of the cell. Deep in the night, while Celestine prayed for divine guidance, Gaetani sat at the working end of the tube and, in sepulchral tones that soared out of that great belly, warned his pope to abdicate the throne or face the flames of hell. After agonies of nights of this, the poor old man turned to his eminent lawyer, Gaetani, for advice on how such an abdication could be arranged. Piously, Gaetani piloted his client's request through dangerous legal shoals.

The news leaked out. There was an uproar. Along with his consuming fear that if he didn't get out before he died he would be damned to an eternity in hell, Celestine had to cope with the ferocities of his fellow Spiritualist monks, who knew the abdication would prevent the long-awaited reign of eternal love and take away from them their new privileges. They stirred up the populace of Naples until the king, afraid that the capital of Christendom would leave Naples as a result of the abdication, battered upon the old man to change his mind.

Celestine pretended to reconsider while Gaetani's legal machinery ground on, but fifteen weeks after his coronation the miserable, addled old man summoned his last consistory and read out the prepared deed of renunciation to his cardinals. Slowly, to favor his old legs, he descended from the throne and stripped himself of his imprisoning robes.

Gaetani was elected to the papacy ten days later, as the compromise candidate, taking the name of Boniface VIII. His first act as pope was to order the arrest of Celestine, whom he sentenced to imprisonment for the rest of Celestine's life.

Boniface VIII was consecrated and crowned at St. Peter's in Rome. He witnessed the archdeacon throw the scarlet robe over him, confer his papal name and declare, "I invest you with the Roman Church." Boniface was seated upon the *sedes stercoraria,* a true night commode, so that all would see that their pope was demonstrating what was said in I Samuel 2:8, "He raiseth up the poor out of the dust and lifteth up the beggar from the dunghill to set them among princes."

Boniface had burdened himself with many "nephews" to allay his agony as a spiritual ruler, which was—although the papal range was greater than any king's—that he was denied the right to transmit his power and his possessions to his children. He acquired rich cities and contiguous territories in the name of Gaetani. One-quarter of the revenue of his reign was poured into buying these. His dynastic ambitions began to shove the great families to one side. Inevitably he had to come up against the Colonna, who ruled what they owned from the hilltop city of Palestrina, twenty-two miles east of Rome.

The Colonna took their case against Boniface to the common people, instilling the belief in the populace that his election could not have been legal because it had been secured by the people's loss of heaven on earth, when Pope Celestine, chosen of the Holy Ghost, had been displaced by him. They might have won with that, but Stephen Colonna raided and sacked a column of the pope's gold, which was being sent to Caserta to buy yet another city for the Gaetani dynasty. Boniface, almost insane with rage, jailed two of the Colonna cardinals. The Colonna offered to return the gold, but Boniface wanted not only Stephen Colonna but also to install papal garrisons inside the chief Colonna cities. To the Colonna, papal garrisons would be Gaetani garrisons. At dawn the next day Colonna heralds posted manifestos that attacked the legitimacy of Boniface's election all over Rome, leaving one tacked to the high altar of St. Peter's. That evening Boniface issued the bull *In excelso throno,* which expanded savagely upon the injuries the papacy had received at Colonna hands. It excommunicated the two Colonna cardinals and every member of the cardinals' branches of the family unto the fourth generation. Boniface charged them with heresy, and by putting them beyond the law, identified them as legitimate prey for all who could overcome them. In mid-August he extended this to include all the Colonna. In November he proclaimed a religious crusade against the Colonna, using money from all over Europe, which was intended to finance the Crusades in the Holy Land, to buy the Knights Templar to crush the Colonna strongholds. The Colonna women and children were thus to be killed or sold into slavery. By the summer of 1298 all the Colonna cities had fallen except Palestrina. Boniface offered a pardon for everyone if they would yield the city. When the Colonna agreed and surrendered, Boniface destroyed Palestrina. It was not a token destruction, such as the demolition of a short section of the city's wall; it was razed to the ground, and the hideous Roman ritual of the plow and the salt was reenacted to leave the place eternally barren. The Colonna went to France in exile.

Then, at the crest of his power as "father of kings . . . ruler of the world," to demonstrate his power over princes, Boniface forbade the king of France to tax the French clergy.

The French king took this stricture so badly that he forbade the export of all money to the pope. He forbade foreigners to live in France, which excluded members of the Curia. Warming to his task, he called an Estates-General to charge the pope with infidelity, loss of the Holy Land, the murder of Celestine V, heresy, fornication, simony, sodomy, sorcery, and idolatry in a list of twenty-nine charges, all of them of the sort employed when some faction wants to rid the Church of a pope, many of them quite true. The only weapon Boniface had was the solemn excommunication of the king of France, which would release the French people from their allegiance to the king. The publication of this fatal bull was planned for September 8, 1303, from Anagni, the pope's summer palace.

The bull had to be stopped. It could have stirred up cataclysmic turmoil in France. The king sent William of Nogaret and Sciarra Colonna into Italy, where two thousand troops had been raised to storm Anagni and to drag Boniface to France to be tried on the twenty-nine charges.

Anagni was the capital of the Gaetani family, as Palestrina had been the home and capital of the Colonna. Somebody inside the city opened the gates to Sciarra Colonna and two hundred men. With drawn sword, Colonna raced into the papal palace to find Boniface, now almost eighty, seated on his throne clad in his robes, with the three-tiered tiara on his head, cross in one hand, and the keys to St. Peter's in the other. If Sciarra was shaken by this serenity he did not show it. He told his men to strip Boniface naked. Sciarra jammed the tiara down over the pope's eyes and, knocking him down, had his men drag him by the feet across the stones and down a granite stairway, to be flung into a narrow, lightless dungeon where Sciarra ordered the men to urinate on him. They left him locked in there to fight off the rats. Two nights later the people of Anagni expelled the French and rescued Boniface. It was six days before he could travel. He reached the Vatican on the eighteenth of September and died twenty-four days later. The Church was never the same again, thank God. Benedict XI was elected pope after him, but he died within ten months. What followed was a relentlessly bargained conclave that took eleven months to elect Clement V, who was Bertrand de Got, archbishop of Bordeaux, a man who had never set foot in Italy and, as it turned out, never would. He was controlled by the king of France.

Clement V was crowned at Lyons in November 1305 but there were many bad omens. During his procession he was thrown from his horse, a wall fell on him, and a rare jewel in his crown was lost. One of his brothers and ten barons lost their lives under that wall. He settled at Avignon, finally, in 1309, and was succeeded by six French popes, who, at the will of the French king, remained in France. The Church was still under a single papacy, three-quarters of a century away from the schism, but it wasn't until 1377, seventy-two years later, that the papacy returned to Rome, when Gregory XI went to Italy to save the Papal States for the Church and died suddenly in Rome, probably poisoned.

Of the sixteen cardinals in his College, eleven were French, four were Italian, and one was Spanish. The city magistrates warned the cardinals that their lives would be at stake if an Italian pope were not elected. The Romans were desperate lest the papacy should return to France. They had become poor people in an Italian country town that had grass growing in its streets since their big business had been moved to Avignon. They had missed out on the profits from about two million pilgrims to Rome since Clement V was elected, and the French had gotten all that money. As the cardinals entered the upper story of the building to hold their conclave, a prodigious electrical storm came on. The wild-eyed Roman mob, well rehearsed by the money they might lose forever if the papacy remained outside Rome, pressed upon the cardinals on their way into the building, screaming for an Italian pope, chanting, *"Romano, Romano volemo la papa, o almanco Italiano!"* There were thousands of them, and while the conclave deliberated, it must have been able to hear the mob bellowing outside. Drunken rioters forced their way into the lower room and set fire to it. They shoved lances through the ceiling into the conclave room above, and when three cardinals came out to parley they were threatened with being torn to pieces if they didn't elect a Roman or, at least, an Italian.

The conclave chose the safest pope—Archbishop Bartolomeo Prignano of Bari, a Neapolitan who had been vice-chancellor at Avignon. He was a small, fussy man who disapproved of everything, but most of all French curial extravagances. At Avignon, he would fling inkwells at the walls in frustration, yelling that the cardinals were turning the Church into a pawnshop. Prignano took the name of Urban VI. His sanity slipped its leash when this petty bureaucrat realized that the awesome, unknowable duties of the papacy had fallen upon him. The insanity came only a short time later. He was the swift choice of the cardinals, but some Church histories say that Prignano had been forced upon them by the murderous mob. That was not so. Prignano had been one of their Curia through the old days at Avignon. When he was consecrated all of them gave him homage and got many favors from him. The guardian at Castel Sant' Angelo had strict orders not to give up the keys to the new pope until six cardinals still at Avignon consented and those six ordered that the keys be placed in Urban's hands. There was not a single objection or hesitation or dissatisfaction with the election of Urban VI until he held his first consistory and attacked the cardinals with ferocity, screaming at them in street Neapolitan, venting his spleen, accumulated over all of his years in the chancery at Avignon, against their simonies. He told them there would be no more shares in the *servitia* for them, an impossible condition for cardinals, because it attacked their right to an as-

sured, unearned income. The *servitia* was equal to one-third of
the income of all of the bishops in Christendom. At the first
consistory he singled out each cardinal in turn, reviling them
individually and by name. He cited the instances of their corruption. He limited their food and drink. He forbade their acceptance of pensions, provisions, and gifts of money.

Of course, he doomed himself. One by one the cardinals left
Rome and assembled at Anagni, a fated and fateful city for the
papacy. The same College of Cardinals that had just elected
Prignano now met and declared the election null and void on the
ground that they had been coerced into electing him in fear of
the violence of the Roman mob.

It seems hard to believe, but they elected a brute named Robert, cardinal of Geneva, to the papacy, he who was called the
Butcher of Cesena because he had ordered his troops to put
three thousand women and children to the sword because they
objected when his transient soldiers raped sixty women. The
Butcher took the name of Clement VII, whereupon Urban VI
excommunicated him, then he excommunicated Urban, and the
Great Schism of the Church had begun. There were two popes
who ruled Christendom simultaneously, Urban in Rome, Clement at Avignon. The Cossa family's advocate, Piero Tomacelli,
succeeded Urban as Boniface IX.

As I said before, much money was needed to restore the
weakened Church, so Boniface undertook the sale of offices and
benefices. The ordinary income, such as Peter's Pence, was
grossly insufficient. Papal expenses were higher than they had
ever been. In addition to a pope's usual duties—fixing points of
doctrine and discipline, granting dispensations, confirming benefices, and maintaining manifold external relations with foreign
courts—he had an immense amount of work to do as the ultimate spiritual and temporal court of appeal.

If an order on any papal matter was given, a minute had to be
made, a bull or other formal order executed, and an office copy
of it transcribed. These things I know well, because Cossa was
in the thick of them. It followed that the pope had to maintain
an enormous staff within the Curia in addition to the officers of
his own household.

Boniface IX accepted the Church's fate. He did not flinch from prostituting the spiritual to the temporal. Boniface reaped enormous wealth for the Church from the Jubilees of 1390 and 1400. In 1350, the period between Jubilees was reduced from one hundred to fifty years by Clement VI. The period was still further reduced, to thirty-three years, the length of the life of Christ, by Urban VI, who appointed 1390 a year of Jubilee. Boniface reduced the period to ten years.

Under his rule simony reached its great climax. He multiplied the sale of indulgences. It was useless for a poor man to appear before a papal court of law. Income for the Church was sought from each and every source. Everything, even a signature, had to be paid for and if, after the first man had bought a place on the ladder and a second man made a better offer, the second offer was accepted also, the second grant was antedated and the first man lost his place. Any and all income for the Church was sought. Although gorged with money, to his dying day Boniface was never filled. He piled tax upon tax, graft upon graft, simony upon simony. He taxed the Papal States, demanded fees for appointments and annual dues from those ordained to political office. He appropriated the entire income from benefices and brought all benefices under papal patronage. He appropriated the property left in the vast estates of cardinals and bishops when they died. There were special taxes for alienation from holy orders, for the creation of new orders and congregations, for personal honors and promotion, and for any other privilege.

Boniface's fiscal policies were typical of his country at the time. Italy was sunk in vice and violence. Man cast about frantically to achieve his own destruction. There was little devotion in the Church. Money was the deity. The laity had no faith, no piety, no modesty, and no discipline of morals. Men cursed their neighbors. Most men's hope had failed them for the sins they saw in high places.

Chapter 7

In the eighth year of Cossa's studies at Bologna, when he was twenty-one years old, something happened that changed our lives forever.

At Bologna, I preferred to sleep in the hall outside Cossa's door. We had had a letter from Cossa's father with news of everyone at Procida, which always elated Cossa (and me), so we had had a little party, drinking wine and reading the letter over again and again, with Cossa remembering two stories for every name that his father mentioned in the letter. Therefore, I was sleeping well (however alertly) when Bernaba sent one of her girls, Enrichetta, a luscious thing with a body like a pasta statue, to tell me to come at once to Castelleto Street. Enrichetta and I went out into the black night, moving through alleys to avoid patrols, and, on the way, I will never forget it, we did it standing up in an arcade. I am still convinced that Enrichetta was in love with me during the time it took her to turn the trick.

Bernaba took me into her room and locked the door. She seemed awestruck to me, a condition that I had thought to be unattainable by this dear woman. "Franco, listen to me," she said, almost piteously eager to shift whatever she knew to somebody else, "I have a papal agent drunk in there, Giovanni Brisoni, the papal pawnbroker. In wine, the truth—right? Well, he told me that a shipment of gold has left the Vatican. It will pass through Bologna in three days' time on the way to Venice."

I didn't understand what she was implying. I didn't make the connection.

"Franco! For Christ's sake! A mule train carrying sacks of gold made to look as if they were sacks of grain. The soldiers are dressed like farmers. They are so sure the ruse will work that the escort is even smaller than it should be."

"How much money?"

"Two hundred thousand gold florins. What do you think I wet my pants for?"

"Where does the pope get that kind of money?"

"You can have fifty guesses. Why are you still standing there? Run and tell Cossa!"

"He's asleep."

"Are you an idiot? Have you forgotten Cossa's family profession?"

I made the connection. I am slow but I am thorough. I questioned her about the strength of the escort, the routing of the shipment, the number of mules in the train, its route and departure time from Rome. Bernaba had all the answers. I left through a window into an alley and went back to Cossa's house by the shortest way. Cossa was quite interested when I awoke him and gave him the information, which was not startling considering the amount of money involved.

"Twelve men is a lot of protection," he said. "But I'll have surprise and night on my side."

"Our side," I told him.

"Round up ten of Palo's regime," he said. "Tell them nothing except where they are to meet me."

"Where?"

"One mile south on the road out of the west gate. One hour from now."

"Only ten men?"

"With me it's eleven," he said.

"And I make it twelve."

"You're not going, Franco Ellera. And Palo isn't going. Some of our lads won't survive tomorrow night. They will take the gold to where I'm going to hide it but after that I'm going to have to kill them all because there will be a gigantic reward out from the pope. So you stay out of it."

"You mean you would have to kill me?"

"For argument's sake, isn't it logical? Listen to me, the pope is going to go half-crazy with rage about this. Two hundred thousand gold florins? He may order the torture of everyone in the Papal States to find out who stole his gold. Who can hold out against an expert?"

"Cossa, you don't *need* that money."

"Two hundred thousand gold florins?"

"You'll have to wait until he is dead before you can bank it or spend it. They will keep looking for that money as long as Boniface lives."

"Franco Ellera—I am surprised at you," he said to me tenderly. "Where would my family be if they had taken this attitude? Sure, money is important for its own sake, but what puts one set of people over all the others is their boldness in taking the money. Of course everybody reaches a point where he doesn't really *need* money. As you point out, we have two going businesses here, but we have them only because of a bold approach to making a good business. You want me to be a bishop, right? Do you think we have enough money to give to Boniface to make me a bishop? Not yet, we haven't. So I've got to think like a bishop. I've got to grasp the chances of my life boldly and, really, Franco Ellera, even a philosophy student would reckon two hundred thousand gold florins as worth a big risk."

"This is a big mistake, Cossa. This can put us right into prison if it doesn't get us killed. Don't do it. This can undo your whole life. Put it out of your mind."

"I am going to take that money. That's enough. No more talk."

"I am more scared of your father than I will ever be of you and he made me take a solemn oath to protect you. If you won't listen to reason I am going on the raid."

Palo's men, led by a reliable brute named Venta, made the rendezvous on the south road as Cossa had thought off the top of his head. I gave them his new instructions. They rode out ahead of us going south-southwest. Cossa and I rode southeast for thirty-four miles and bought a small holding in the name of Carlo Pendini, to the south of the mountain village of Castrocaro, from the agent of the duke of Urbino. There we again met

Venta's men and made our final plans. We studied the terrain between Acqualagna and Fossombrone. On either side of the lonesome road there were harsh gray hills, scarred with gashes from a millennium of erosion. The sparse fields gave up such a hard living that few farmers would reach for it. The fields were so untended and rocky that they were indistinguishable from the mountainsides.

Our appointed meeting with Venta and his men was at the opening of a gorge four miles south of Fossombrone. Steep slopes bracketed the main road to Bologna for about four hundred yards. "This is sweet," Cossa said. "It is like one of Papa's coves." To him it would be no different from raiding a merchant ship. That night he waited with five men at the south side of the pass, which ran roughly from east to west. I waited on the north side with Venta and the other five men. It was a very dark night.

Cossa worked with a handled German boar spear. It had a sharp ten-and-a-half-inch blade tip with a hole just below it for a transverse bar to prevent deep penetration so the spear would come out easily. In the other hand he had a Sienese dagger with a nine-inch blade that was notched to entangle and snap an opponent's blade. His raiding crew was spaced out on either side of him and I could see them as the torchlight of the train came into the gorge. Each of the men carried a poled halberd, a combination of a spear and a battle axe, five feet long, which gave footfighters a better chance of winning when they fought men on horseback. We would attack on foot.

Cossa had had the men dig an eight-foot-deep pit across the width of the road. They covered it with light tree limbs, leaves, and heavy dust. The train would fall right into it in the night.

The heavy procession of mules and men moved behind four mounted soldiers, then the mules, then more soldiers. What were probably a captain and a sergeant rode on either side of the train. With a wild scream Cossa led his charge down the slope as the leading horses and soldiers fell into the road trap. Cossa hacked at the legs of the horses who were half in, taking one leg off and sending the rider forward into the pit, where one of our lads bashed his brains out. My crew attacked the legs of the rear-of-column horses, running the riders through as they fell. The terrible sounds of the screams of the horses, the fearful shouts of the guard and the muleteers, and the shrieks of pain and fear were only to be expected from such an action. I worked my way forward along the smashed column while Cossa worked his way back. When we met we were drenched in blood, but within a few minutes every member of the train's escort party was dead. The only survivors of both sides were Venta, Cossa, two of our lads, all of the mules, and me. The gold was intact. We dragged the bodies of all of them, with the horses, into the wide, deep road pit, and shovelled in dirt to level it off. We took the gold to Cossa's new holding at Castrocaro.

The lads were exhausted from the emotion and exertion of the slaughter. They moved mechanically as they lowered sack after sack of the heavy gold into a great hole that they had dug earlier at the small holding. He was gentle with them, encouraging them with soft promises as they shovelled in the earth to cover the sacks of gold. When half of the deep pit had been filled, when their heads appeared just over the top of the pit, Cossa nodded to me and we struck hard with the edges of the shovels at the backs of their heads, knocking them flat into the hole. Cossa leaped into it and ran them through the hearts and throats with his German spear. He climbed out so wearily that I reached down and lifted him out. We took up the shovels again, covering everything in the pit with soil, leveling the ground up to two inches of the top of the pit, then Cossa turned to the low stack of turf rectangles that he and his men had earlier stripped so carefully off the ground, and began to lay them back in place while I went to the shed and lifted up the heavy tombstone we had brought from Bologna, and carried it across the ground to embed it at the head of the newly dug common grave. It said:

HERE LIES
THE FAMILY OF
CARLO PENDINI
TAKEN BY THE PLAGUE

"That should keep any ghouls out," Cossa said.

"See?" I told him as we stumbled off to our horses for the ride back to Bologna. "You couldn't have done it without me."

Chapter 8

The duke of Santa Gata attended his son's graduation from the University of Bologna. Cossa was twenty-three years old, a leading student of his class, the most potent factor in the university life of his time, and a figure within Bolognese politics. He was seated in the magisterial chair, the book of law was handed to him, the gold ring was slipped on his finger, the lawyer's biretta put upon his head, and he was pronounced a Doctor *Utriusque Juris*. He had entered an order of intellectual nobility that had as distinct and definite a place in the hierarchical system of Christendom as the priesthood or the knighthood. The duke, smiling the family smile, expressed his enormous pleasure that Cossa was now ready for his life, and told us that Pope Boniface IX had named his brilliant son archdeacon of the University of Bologna and chancellor of the university (from which Cossa had graduated about eleven minutes before). "It was his own idea," the duke said. "He summoned me to an audience and he explained that as an archdeacon you would be starting your career in the Church as a prelate, no less. Naturally, it wasn't free. I had to pay one hundred florins for such a benefice, which you and I will share equally after you have paid me back the hundred florins. You should be able to earn that back in the first two years."

With the greatest of ease, Cossa made the job earn the money back in the first eight months. He made administrative changes. No one could be graduated without his consent. He controlled all examinations and their results. Only he had the power to confer the licenses without which graduates could not teach or practice law anywhere in the world. He reorganized all university systems, beginning with lodgings for all students. He instituted a chair-leasing tradition in the classrooms, a "head tax" upon each student, and annual fees for "materials and certificates," examination fees, and a charge for "the review of graduation applications," as well as a final fee for the processing of licenses to practice. The Curia allowed him to keep thirty-five percent of all the money he collected on a semiannual basis and, at the end of his first year as archdeacon, Cossa received the congratulations of the pope for the fine work he was doing to increase university standards. At the end of the second year Cossa instituted a "field privileges" system, which permitted senior students to gain experience in drawing wills, land deeds, and contracts to be certified by the chancellor's office after the payment of a graduated scale of fees to the university. His executive ability, as well as the audible appreciation of the Church for his leadership, bound him even closer than before to the Bolognese City Council.

Mysteriously (we thought at the time), the Medici bank in Bologna let the council realize that Cossa came from "a famous family of warriors" in Naples and, within a short time, he was appointed as a deputy commander, under the old duke of Este, of the Bolognese military, such as they were at the time. Cossa won fame as a soldier for his leadership of the successful massacre at Rocco di Estia, which eliminated a pocket of troublemakers who had refused to pay taxes. Cossa enjoyed leading troops. He was as good at it as he was at everything else, because his secret was that everything he did was important to him when he did it, before he did it, and after he did it. The Church, wars, and women were the fields within which he exercised this talent.

I have had many opportunities to talk to Cossa over the years about the feverish nature of his relations with women, and essentially, our debate all came down to this. I would point out to him—for instance, after he became pope—that love was God's and that the proper place for fornication and sodomy, with its burden of sin, was marriage; they had not been designed for constant promiscuous pleasure. I reasoned with him within the tenets of his own religion (which was not mine) that every golden moment of the Christian existence had to measure up to the profound philosophical preconceptions and prejudices of its founding fathers. Using the trick of his sweet smile—which, even though I fully understood its uses, I could not resist—he would answer me that, because religious and secular law were practically one tissue, the "morality" of sex had become embedded in religious law. Having created guilt and blamed it on Adam and Eve, the founding fathers of the Church saw that the easiest way to remind people of their guilt was by putting restraints on all human pleasures. He told me, patiently, that the "morality" of sex was, therefore, an important factor in social control. He admired the founding fathers for having had the genius to separate sexual relationships from all other human relationships, then to give sex a permanent stain of inner-felt unholiness. But, he said, God—or nature—has a far stronger influence over us than the ambitions of clergymen, and God insists that the most important act of our lives is to reproduce ourselves. This desire to do the right thing in God's eyes is so strong in us—certainly in me, he said, it may be different with you Germans—that it cannot be overcome by slanted doctrines from covetous minds.

He became angry with Bernaba during the first year he was chancellor, because she said that he should allow her to send women to him, as he most certainly had received carnally other wives and daughters of Bologna, and that he should stay away from Castelleto Street because it just didn't look right for a man of his dignity, an archdeacon as well as chancellor and therefore a promising prelate of the Church, to be seen by students entering and leaving a whorehouse. They got into a hot argument over that. Bernaba was a woman of strong character and she recognized no difference between herself and Cossa—or anyone else. Cossa told her to run her whores and keep her advice to herself so she called him a stupid donkey and he told Palo to take her outside and beat her. Palo started to get her but I stepped on his feet and when he fell down I stumbled over him somehow and fell on his head with my knees, somewhat heavily. Bernaba enjoyed it but it made Cossa more angry.

"Listen," I told him, "Bernaba is one of the oldest friends we have. We don't want anyone—particularly Palo—getting the idea that he can beat her." I stared at him until he got the point. At last he smiled and said, "I'm sorry. I just lost my temper. It's been a long day."

She ran across the room, put her arms around him and gave him a big kiss. "Just stay out of Castelleto Street," she told him. "I'll send you all the women you can handle. You're the chancellor. You have to give a good impression."

They were pals again but years later, when I married Bernaba, she wanted it to be our secret. "Listen, Franco," she said to me, "Cossa thinks you are only alive to serve him. He would break all the furniture if we told him."

"My God, Bernaba," I said. "How can I keep a secret from Cossa?"

"There is one easy way to do it, Franco. Keep remembering that he is capable of sending me to his father to be sold in the slave market at Bari. He is a nice man. But why should he know?"

I must explain how I can write down this history of my friends —or autobiography, depending on how you see it. It would be too easy to allow my own life to dominate this narrative. But this is Cossa's story. I have the feeling that Church history isn't going to deal well with Cossa, but we have to remember, for all his gestures of action, Cossa was a fatalist who allowed things to happen to him. Villains are never like that. Villains always know what they want and they move to get it. There were villains on every side of Baldassare Cossa, and not all of them inside the Church.

I have known Cosimo di Medici almost as long as I have known Cossa. Cosimo was three years younger than Cossa. Boniface IX was ten years older than Cossa and I was senior to all of them. Cosimo is a banker so he doesn't talk much unless he needs something, or if he is plotting something, but he has told me plenty. After I became a cardinal everybody wanted to tell me everything they knew. It's a kind of bragging on their part. The ones who knew the most about things that should be buried deep in the ground were Decima Manovale and her four daughters. The daughters told Manovale and Manovale told Bernaba.

Bernaba was my wife for nearly thirty years. She is dead now. Bernaba was in a business that gave her the keys to a lot of closets. Some things she didn't tell me until the year she died. She wasn't concealing anything. Whatever I asked her, she told me. Most of the people in our lives are gone now, and I knew everything she knew about them before I wrote this book.

For example, Decima Manovale. When Cosimo's father began to take an interest in Cossa, Manovale told Bernaba about it. That is so long ago that, at the time, the Medici was only the third-ranking bank in Florence, after the Bardi and the Albizzi. The Bardi were ruined by loans they made to the English crown. The Albizzi favored the rich. So the Medici had no choice but to go after the business of the middle classes and the poor, and that wasn't easy. Cosimo's father is the most ambitious man in Europe. His son was just a son when he started in the bank and he didn't really make much of himself until a good while later. By that time, they were the biggest bank in the world. Giovanni di Bicci di Medici worked every corner. He operated farms, manufactured silk, traded with Europe, Russia—and Islam, which was against the Church law—but his ruthless ambition was some day to become the banker for the Church.

Cosimo di Medici told Decima's daughter Maria Giovanna that his father had this obsession with Church banking from the day when he found out from some country bankers in Cahors that the papal treasury at Avignon had eighteen million gold florins and seven million more worth of plate and jewelry on deposit with them. Gold florins were the most desirable currency in Europe. One gold florin was worth three and a half English pounds, and old man Medici probably considered all of it to be family money because it was named after the Republic of Florence.

Cosimo di Medici's father's one overwhelming desire was to attract the Church's banking away from the different Sienese, Roman, Venetian, and foreign banks into one central depository of all Church income and capital, controlled by him, because he believed that those other banks didn't understand how to use the power of such an opportunity.

The Church was the great industry of Christendom. Its bankable deposits flowed not only from the Vatican but also from the bishops' sees and religious orders, and from the obediences of the princes who were dependent upon the Church, and that meant all of them. The old man used to get furious, Cosimo told Manovale who told Bernaba who told me, because nobody seemed to see that the Church income and capital should have been centrally organized.

Giovanni di Bicci di Medici had another, invisible advantage. The papal tax-collecting organization naturally favored Italian employees, for this established and maintained the predominance of Italian banks throughout Europe. Even business in and around the North Sea and the Baltic was largely financed by them. He kept repeating to his son that if one bank had *everything* the Church deposited, any pope could be made content, even happy, and the bank therefore could prosper beyond anything any banker, except Giovanni di Bicci di Medici, had ever dreamed of. With a few happy popes leaning on every see, every prince, every religious order, to bank with one single bank's branches—which would be conveniently located everywhere— a banker could have a really flourishing business.

Therefore, Cosimo di Medici's father was always redrawing his mental maps to try to create new alleys or highways that could lead to financial influence with any pope, however casual the approaches might seem to be. That explained the Medici interest in Cossa, a young churchman on the way up who might provide some levers.

The Medici banking branch in Bologna gathered and passed along to the head office in Florence raw information, even gossip, about what was happening in the city. The Medici were keener than most governments on intelligence operations. The Bologna branch routinely reported the new organization of whores and the *barrateries,* but their operations were so expertly shielded (by me) that, at first, the Medici weren't able to find out who had created the whole thing. But they kept trying. Florence was interested in people who had an instinct about money and knew how to make it. It took the Bologna branch a long time to find out that Cossa was the man. Luigi Palo probably took some money to tell them.

When Cosimo's father knew a mere law student at the university—and a student of *canon* law at that—was responsible, he was so impressed that he told his son to work with the Bologna branch on building up a running file on Cossa. Cosimo had to find the right man at the Vatican from whom to buy Cossa's record, and the man just happened to be Piero Spina, then still a protonotary apostolic (who was still searching for Bernaba and the man who had broken his nose, even though he had no idea who he was), which could put people in awe of the combinations God plays with.

When the Medici read the Vatican file they had two sets of information, not exactly matching. The Vatican file said Cossa was a prize student who had a future in the Church, that he was the eldest son of the duke of Santa Gata, and, interestingly to old man Medici, from a line of pirates and slavers. They put this together with the information about organizing the whores and the gambling houses and his bribery of the rectors, which created local political influence, and they liked what they read. So, they instructed their branch manager in Bologna to have a quiet conversation with Bolognese city councilmen, reminding them that Cossa would be the next duke of Santa Gata, an impressive matter to politicians, and that Cossa should be considered as one of the duke of Este's commanders of the Bolognese military. Therefore, and not at all as mysteriously as Cossa thought, it happened that while continuing as chancellor of the university (and with the permission of Rome) Cossa became a *condottiere* leader while Cosimo's father continued his plotting to move him into the Vatican. The invisible can cast long shadows.

One afternoon while Cossa was working out a series of complicated positions in a fleshy pile with Enrichetta and two new girls from Lucca, a letter arrived from the pope, summoning him to Rome. He lost all interest in completing the coilings within the coilings. When the women had gone he said to me (I had been keeping notes on and sketching the more impossible couplings), "Read this. What the hell can he want?"

"He wants to promote you."

"It doesn't work that way, Franco. If he wanted to transfer me upstairs I'd get word from the bishop here and the bishop of wherever they're sending me."

"Correct. Except that the bishop who is going to get you

outranks the bishop here. What is the pope? He is the bishop of Rome.''

"Jesus," he said, "suppose they have worked out who took the gold from them at Fossombrone?''

"How could they work it out? It went into a hole at Castrocaro. How could they trace it to you? And if they did, they'd have a squad of soldiers pick you up, they wouldn't send you a flowery letter.''

"I'd hate to walk into a trap.''

"Cossa, please! Don't pretend to have suddenly discovered that you have a conscience. Who do you want to go with us?''

"Leave Father Fanfarone here. He might be arrested as an enemy agent if he ever fell into conversation with a real priest at the Vatican. Bocca, of course—but only Bolognese and Venetian food. No Neapolitan food. Palo stays here to protect the business. Lay on a bodyguard. We'll leave tomorrow morning.''

Chapter 9

In his lifetime—beginning with his cousins on Procida—Cossa
seduced three hundred and seventeen matrons, virgins, widows,
circus performers, and nuns that I know of. That figure does not
include courtesans, excepting my wife. He was a healthy man
who had a natural view of women. The way Cossa looked at it,
he needed everything he got.

Out of the three hundred and seventeen only two were important to him, involved with him mystically and emotionally. We
met the first woman on that journey from Bologna to Rome to
see the pope.

As we rode away from Bologna that day in 1393, Cossa kept
saying he was tired, which meant he was still worried about
whether the pope had found out who took the gold. When we
arrived at Perugia, about halfway, he was welcome, as the chancellor of the University, to stay at the house maintained by the
duke of Milan for official travelers. He told me to take care of
the horses, to have my dinner with whom I chose, and to call
him at dawn for the journey to Rome.

The next day he told me what happened to him after that. He
had gone into the garden to consider the best time to take the
gold safely out of the ground at Castrocaro when he heard someone close by call him by name. He turned and saw a beautiful
woman with commanding red hair, whose eyes, he said, were

painted with lust. When he left her bed at dawn the next day (because I personally pulled him off her), Cossa was insane with love. When I finally forced my way into the room after exhorting him through the door, pleading that the pope was waiting for him, he was dressed, wearing chest armor, with weapons strapped to his person, so that even if he were to be overcome with the need to mount the woman again it would be too painful a possibility for both of them. But it became even more of an impossibility for him to separate from her without one more go, so he tore off the armor and loosed his manhood from its cradle of chainmail and leaped upon her again with such incredible speed that I had not the time to stop him; thrusting and grunting while she cried out as if in excruciating pain, which I knew could not be the case.

As soon as they ceased their shocking agitations—I do not mean that I was shocked by what they were doing, but I was shocked by the extent to which they were doing it—I pulled him off her, probably because I was not an Italian. As I lifted him away I yelled into his dazed ear, "We must travel, Cossa. As it is we will scarcely make it." He kissed the lady's tattered mouth and left the room.

We were two hours on our way, with Cossa riding along staring like a sheep at the horizon, when he remembered some terrible omission. He tried to wheel his horse, but I grabbed the reins. "I don't know her name!" he wailed. "We must go back! How will I ever find her again?"

"Wherever she was going, she has gone," I told him. "I will send a man back to talk to the innkeeper. But wherever she is headed, she doesn't have an appointment with the pope."

He actually began to weep. He moaned that he couldn't live without her, that I didn't understand—things like that—while I kept him riding a good distance ahead of the escort lest they discover what a fool he had become.

We reached the Lateran eighteen minutes before Cossa's appointment. A Guards captain took Cossa into the palace. Boniface only did business at night. It was an unusual meeting, Cossa told me. The pope was engaged in quarterly accounting audits and apologized that he wouldn't be able to give Cossa much time. He said he wanted from Cossa an estimate of the costs of raising an army of mercenaries for Bologna. Mercenaries, the slogging *condottieri* of Italy, fought all of its wars. Boniface instructed him sternly never to forget that most of the funding would come from the Council of Ten in Florence. "Be aware that a small part will come from our Papal States," Boniface said, "and we expect you to keep our forced contribution to this project to a minimum. I expect you to make up for our financial losses by doing a considerable amount of looting and hostage-taking."

"Me?" Cossa asked.

"The duke of Este has gotten too old to lead troops," the pope said, "and, as the Florentines will be paying the bulk of the costs, they insist upon choosing the commander, and they have chosen you."

"Who are we fighting?" Cossa said.

"I don't need to tell you that this is not to cause a shift in your loyalties, Cossa," Boniface said sternly. "It is only a temporary campaign to contain the lord of Milan, to get him out of Bologna, to keep him out of the Papal States, and to thwart his ambitions for the conquest of Italy."

The lord of Milan was Gian Galeazzo Visconti. The Visconti had been rulers of Milan since the end of the thirteenth century. Their power was so established and their reputation so great that they had been able to rise from the status of Lombardy bandits and hired lances to intermarry with the royal houses of England and France, and with the princes of Germany. When Galeazzo II died in 1378, his heirs were his son, Gian Galeazzo, and his brother Bernabo, as ruthless a ruffian as anyone had ever had for a relative.

Bernabo worked plot after plot to get rid of his nephew, but without effort the nephew managed to detect and defeat these deadly schemes. In perfidy and dissimulation the young man was more than a match for his uncle.

All at once, Gian Galeazzo became absorbed in devotion to the Holy Spirit. He visited churches, rosary in hand, spent hours of devotion before statues of saints, and tripled his bodyguards. In May 1385 he let it be known widely that he was going to pray at the shrine of the Madonna del Monte at Varese, near Lake Maggiore, which was within his uncle's territory. His bodyguard was commanded by Jacopo dal Verme and Antonio Porro, pitiless men.

Bernabo Visconti and his two sons joined Gian Galeazzo at the shrine. Nephew and uncle embraced each other tenderly. Gian Galeazzo held on to his uncle tightly and gave the order, in German, to murder his relatives. Thus did Gian Galeazzo Visconti become the head of the Visconti family and the sole lord of Lombardy.

His wealth exceeded that of the Holy Roman Emperor who shivered in dripping northern forests (and from whom Gian Galeazzo bought the title "duke of Milan" in 1395, for one hundred thousand florins). When Gian Galeazzo made war he hired the best *condottieri*. When he made peace he told Europe he had dismissed his generals but kept them on half-pay on the condition that they ravage only the lands of his enemies and leave his own untouched. He conquered Padua and Verona. He ruled Bologna. By 1386, the vipers of his blazonry were hoisted over most of northern Italy. He wrested Pisa away from Florence. In Italy, aside from his firm ally, Venice, only Florence, the Papal States, and Naples were not possessed by him. It was a matter of desperation to him that they fall before him. He prepared for the attack for two years and made no effort to conceal his intentions.

"Your real career is in my hands," Boniface told Cossa. "Remember that."

"I am only the servant of Your Holiness," Cossa answered.

"I tell you that the Florentines have asked for you because you should know who is putting the wine in your glass. They say you are almost a Bolognese." He looked at Cossa suspiciously, then smiled. "What do they know of Neapolitans."

"It is all a mystery to me, Holiness."

"I doubt that. The son of Giovanni di Bicci di Medici is waiting for you in the anteroom. His name is Cosimo, a lad of seventeen or eighteen years. He will assist you in this compilation and our people will see to it that you have ample working space with sufficient scriptors, correctors, abbreviators, and counters. I want your report in five days. We will meet here again at four o'clock next Thursday morning."

The pope swept out of the room attended by a chamberlain

who held up a sheet of numbers under papal eyes as the two of them walked away from Cossa.

Cossa found Cosimo di Medici to be a wonderfully agreeable young fellow to whom nothing seemed to be a problem. Cosimo was drawn to Cossa. He told his father that he had been entirely right, that Cossa was the kind of up-and-coming Church executive that they had been waiting for. Though my wife never agreed with me on this, I thought that Cossa and Cosimo even looked like each other. They were both middle-sized with pronounced noses and rosy-olive complexions. They both had receding hair and beautiful teeth. Cosimo, then and now, was the graver of the two, but after all he was a banker, and the more professionally kindly. Cossa had his extraordinary smile and behind everything he did was a permanent sardonicism as befits a man whom God has absent-mindedly placed in the wrong niche. Cosimo appeared to be the gentler but he believed, more strongly than Cossa, that states are not ruled by *pater nosters*.

Together they turned out a solid plan. Even Cossa's uncle Tomas was impressed. The plan explained how the *condottieri* would be recruited, armed, fed, and deployed, and how much it would cost to turn Gian Galeazzo back to Milan.

We went back to Bologna. Using Este's army, Cossa moved harshly to clean out any pockets of treason within the city. Bologna was a part of the state of Milan; Gian Galeazzo's fief. Cossa wrested away the possession of the citadel. He seized all the strong towns that surrounded Bologna and strengthened the line of the Papal States immediately to the south. He moved so boldly and with such force that Gian Galeazzo did not march to retake Bologna, and more time was bought when Florence and Bologna struck a military alliance with the king of France.

The real proof of Cossa's success was in the speech that Cosimo's father made before the Signoria of Florence, which said, in part, "There is so much worth in this man, Cossa, for having from his boyhood applied himself to letters and, having worked so that he became not only a celebrated orator and poet but a philosopher also—he turned his mind to other matters—he made himself master-at-arms to a city where he is now esteemed as one of the first soldiers of Italy.'' Of course, Giovanni di Bicci di Medici was justifying the cost of Cossa to Florence when many other soldiers would have done the job as well, but sponsoring other soldiers wouldn't have promoted Cossa toward that place where he could realize those enormous gains for the Medici.

When he had secured Bologna, the Medici's poet-philosopher, Cossa, was recalled to Rome by his pope to become one of his three private chamberlains. The night before we left I said to him that he was about to begin his career at the pinnacle of the Church, at the right hand of its pontiff. I told him that the time had come to forget soldiering and politics and to begin to think of God.

He said to me, ''Do you think, Franco Ellera, if there were a God there would be any need for the complexities of this Church? If God were anywhere, he would be within man, don't you think? But instead we are given a counterfeit of this glorious friendship, styled by cold popes and bishops whose only work has been to build a cage around their God who should not exist —if he exists at all—by virtue of his omniscience and omnipotence, to live in such a cage. God is the sublime idea of man. The Church is an expanding corruption of functionaries' tangled, haphazard rules, which define religion, not God. Religion is only political bargaining for souls of which they have no knowledge. But God, if he existed, would be subjective, infusing all selves, the selves that are both heaven and hell, reward everlasting.''

Chapter 10

Cossa was placed at the pope's right hand, at the heart of the apostolic chamber that administered the papal finances, Boniface's most urgent interest, in that it yielded income that was about three times the income of the king of France.

The chamberlains worked wherever Boniface worked or slept —at the Vatican Palace or at the Lateran—in three separate eight-hour shifts. Cossa worked at night, from midnight until eight in the morning. The second chamberlain, a somber Sicilian, Bishop Luca Salvadore, worked in the day to execute the papal decisions taken at night. The third chamberlain served from four in the afternoon until midnight. He was Piero Spina, formerly a protonotary apostolic. Spina handled the legates and ambassadors of foreign princes. He breakfasted with the pope every afternoon at four. He set the pope's appointments, but Cossa had the place of power.

As senior chamberlain, Cossa was placed to keep an eye on bishops everywhere in Christendom. He could, when he chose, warn them when they were likely to be transferred and earned a rich crop of first-fruits from this when he intervened with the pope to prevent changes of diocese that would have been costly or inconvenient for the incumbents. Sometimes, the threatened transfers existed only in Cossa's imagination. He had come to Rome a wealthy man. He became wealthier. The money he won was invested fruitfully; it is my experience that whatever Italians earn, they save.

The sale of indulgences was at fullest auction cry in Boniface's reign. In 1300 Boniface VIII had granted full remission of sin (*plenissimam omnium suorum concedimus veniam peccatorum*) to every penitent pilgrim who made his confession and who visited the churches of St. Peter and St. Paul in Rome.

Pilgrims overran the city that year. Their gratitude was so profitable that the period for the Jubilee was reduced from one hundred to merely fifty years by Clement VI, in 1350. Then it was shortened to thirty-three years, piously noted as the length of the life of Christ by Urban VI, who named 1390 as the Jubilee Year. Cossa's patron, Boniface IX, was anointed in time to reap the fruits of that Jubilee, which brought in such enormous returns that he immediately extended its privileges to the following year. He really knew how to strip an artichoke. Cossa helped him. He was pretty good at it, too. He provided the "statistics" on the bands of armed men who lurked along the roads to Rome to rob and rape the pilgrims, thus reducing papal receipts. Respectfully, and with the circumspection which His Holiness valued, Cossa recommended that "if the pilgrims are prevented by these outlaws from coming to us for grace, we must therefore take it to them—for payment." On that advice, Boniface ordained that all pilgrims who were unable to travel to Rome, but who could make the pilgrimages to certain shrines in Germany, would be admitted to the same indulgences as those who had traveled to the Eternal City—providing that they paid over to the Vatican the expense that the longer journey would have entailed.

The plan met with universal approbation in Germany. Boniface shared the proceeds of the pious economy with the emperor, Wenzel, and with the lords of Bavaria and Meissen. Cossa's foresight had increased Jubilee income by thirty-one percent. The pope gave him a large ruby ring to show his appreciation and, covertly, the emperor and the lords paid over to his account, at German branches of the Medici Bank, the combined princely sum of six thousand gold florins.

The day all three new chamberlains began their tours, Boniface gave them breakfast (at 4:00 P.M.), a working breakfast, and laid down the basic rule of the operation, which was mainly that if he were resting, he could only be disturbed if at least two out of the three of them could agree that it was necessary. He made sure they understood. "No cardinal has that right. The Curia and the Sacred College have been told that together you are an extension of our own being, aware of our requirements and immovable where our comfort is concerned."

The chamberlains chewed politely and waited.

"You were carefully chosen. Spina is known throughout Rome as the most devious man in the Church, an astonishing feat. It is said that he can think the same thought four ways at the same time, which bespeaks the caution we require in all things. Luca Salvadore is our financial wizard. He will send out our decisions across Christendom to get the money back. Cossa is a *condottiere* general, a tested negotiator, and a man of much cunning who will sit with me at all appointments and confirm my judgments."

After breakfast, Luca Salvadore remained with the Holy Father while Cossa and Spina strolled in the gardens to become acquainted.

"You seem to have had a bad accident with your nose," Cossa said.

"Yes. A freak thing. When I was a lad my mother asked me to get a traveling case down from a high shelf and it slipped and came down on my nose."

"It must have been damned painful."

"One forgets such things. I must say you are the first to have shown enough interest to ask about it."

"It wasn't just idle curiosity," Cossa said. "I thought I could help. I have a cousin who is a surgeon. He does wonderful work with the men of my father's fleet."

"How kind of you, Cossa. You know—I have the feeling we have met before."

"I don't think so. I certainly would have remembered it. Of course, it's possible. We are both southerners—countrymen."

"Southerners, yes," Spina said. "But not countrymen. Sicily is a separate place."

Chapter 11

As chamberlain, Cossa tried to steer the papacy's growing business toward the Medici Bank, or at least he took credit for it when Cosimo di Medici, with a few other Florentine magnates, was invited to the Vatican to talk money with the pope. That turned out to be an important meeting, for all of us; not for what happened during—nothing much came of it—but for what happened after.

Cosimo later told Cossa that he had been sexually aroused by thinking about the possibility of the bank getting so much money. After the meeting, as he was being escorted out of the palace with much deference by a captain of the Papal Guard, a mustached Swiss named Ueli Munger, from Winterthur, near the German border, Cosimo asked him where he could find pleasure in Rome. Munger winked at him, a startling effect from such a martial figure. "There is a new *mezzana* in Rome," he said. "A very handsome woman, herself. Big, you know what I mean."

"Is that so?" Cosimo said, adjusting his clothing.

"She set up a new house ten days ago. She has sensational girls. And they are also cultured. No whistling or catcalls when you go upstairs at Signora Manovale's."

"You mean a *broth*el?" Cosimo asked him.

"Oh, no. Don't get me wrong, sir. Signora Manovale is a

broker, not a *ruffiana*. She is an intermediary—you know, a *mezzana*—between very beautiful, if lonely, women and the men who sometimes feel they need pleasure. It is all very high class, believe me. You can dine there, just talking to some beautiful woman, or you can listen to music or poetry or you can fuck. It is *the* meeting place right now, sir. Very refined and *very* expensive."

I had been there. I wasn't married when I was in Rome with Cossa. Bernaba, who later became my wife, had given me a written introduction to Signora Manovale, which I had composed and written myself, reading it back to Bernaba, who had never learned to write. I never stayed with any of the courtesans Captain Munger spoke about but I had a good thing going with the doorkeeper, a very sincere nymphomaniacal sort of a woman.

On slow nights I sat around with Signora Manovale and her daughters, because Manovale was a good personal and professional friend of Bernaba's and Bernaba always wanted the best for me. As I did for her, of course, but it wasn't the same, if you catch my meaning. I never knew Manovale when she was a *ruffiana* but I think that is the key to her character. A *ruffiana* doesn't only deal in women, she sells love potions and sometimes these potions are poison because that is what happens to love sometimes and women would go to her to pay for the poisons and Manovale would sell them. To become a successful *mezzana* she had had to acquire polish and this tended to conceal what she was. One might think that this would change her character, even her appearance, but Manovale was the most extraordinary woman of her time; of her century. Manovale could not be measured by any usual standards. No one's ambition, including Giovanni di Bicci di Medici's, ever looked so high.

"It sounds charming," Cosimo said to Captain Munger. "Perhaps you could assign a man to guide me there."

"Give me a few minutes," Captain Munger said.

The captain was having a low-pitched talk with a young priest when the other Florentines in Cosimo's party emerged from the palace. Their escort, bringing the horses, arrived at the same time to meet them. Cosimo told them that he must part company with them. "I am going to call on a beautiful lady who has several beautiful friends," he told them, "if any of you would like to come along." Only one man, Count Giuliano Rizzo, took up the invitation, but he had enjoyed so much of the pope's wine that when the hostler handed him up into the saddle he kept going right over the top and landed heavily on the stones on the far side of the horse, which put him instantly to sleep. Rizzo was *not* a banker, but later became a cardinal.

Cosimo and his bodyguard mounted their horses. The young priest led the way out of the palace courtyard, across the bridge over the night-laden Tiber and into the city, running barefoot ahead of them. They clattered on for about twenty minutes, then came to a halt before a handsome building. The priest ran to its massive door and knocked on it heavily. My friend, the doorkeeper, opened the door, dressed in pantaloons and a tailed coat, a mockery on such a figure. The priest went to her and spoke into her ear. She told me later that even she knew what a Medici was. She bowed to the men, still horsed, and went into the house, leaving the door open, for which Signora Manovale gave her proper hell the next evening.

The young priest bade Cosimo dismount. Cosimo told his men to return for him in three hours, then turned to the entrance as the *mezzana* filled the doorway. She was dressed splendidly. She was a blonde who had become blonde, my friend the doorkeeper told me, by cutting the crown out of a black hat, putting the brim on her head and arranging all her dark hair upon it for exposure to the sun for weeks and weeks. She was a vividly beautiful woman who was not quite thirty. She had the art, for all of her life, of seeming to stare directly at whatever was the greatest strength or weakness of a man, whether that was his money, his conscience, or his weariness.

"Cosimo di Medici!" she said fondly, making the name a declarative sentence and conveying a prodigious sense of reunion. She gazed at him so longingly that he could have been standing upon all of the money in the world. Cosimo walked forward but the young priest was close enough behind him to jostle him, so di Medici put a small gold coin into his hand.

Signora Manovale curtsied as Cosimo came into her house and asked him what his pleasure would be as my friend closed the door behind them.

"Some simple food," he said. "Some wine. And perhaps some company."

She took him up a marble staircase and left him with two young attendants who she said would bathe him. She returned to the main floor and summoned a female butler, ordering supper for two for the gentleman who was waiting in her own apartment. "Send Maria Giovanna to me," she said.

She sat and looked into the woodfire, her bold, high cheekbones almost concealing her sea-blue eyes. Her wide, full mouth smiled with the pleasure of her thoughts, showing her small, very white, cat teeth.

Upstairs, the two silent maidens eluded Cosimo when he tried to bring them down. He was bathed, massaged, and titillated, if that is possible to do to a banker. They dressed him and vanished as soon as there came a knock upon the door. Tables of food were carried in. Behind them came Signora Manovale and a young woman so startling in her beauty that Cosimo, in his elevated state, thought she must be the most thrilling woman he had ever seen. "I offer you this repast, my lord," Manovale said, "as I offer you my daughter."

Cosimo gasped.

"She is the jewel of my collection," Manovale said. "At fifteen, she is more learned in the women's arts than anyone in Rome—or in Florence. She is the perfect concubine—a concubine, not a courtesan. Do you like her?"

He nodded, flushed.

"She is for lease, my lord."

"Lease?"

"Let me tell you about her." Manovale sat in a chair beside him so as not to distract his attention from Maria Giovanna, who stood before him in the clear. "She is a linguist, which is something more than being merely a mistress of tongues," Manovale said lewdly. "She is a musician and a profound astrologer. She can read and write in Latin, Italian, French, German, and English, and converse upon all of the classical or current subjects, weightily or frivolously. You observe the beauty of her face. I

cannot describe to you the beauty of her body. But these things
are not for rent, my lord. Maria Giovanna is for lease.''

On the spot, Cosimo convinced himself that this young
woman could take over all of his important business entertaining
in Florence. He was betrothed to marry but it was impossible
for his wife to do what this young woman could do for the bank.
This family is a secret weapon, he marveled to himself.

''I will have this lease,'' he said.

The following morning Cosimo signed a written lease, which
provided for Maria Giovanna's companionship in Florence or
wherever else he might specify, a clothing and jewelry allowance
for her of seven hundred florins a year, an agreement that she
would be provided with a small but elegant house to be freely
held by her, in her name as her property, with an emolument of
two thousand florins a year, payable quarterly in advance, and
that the money be deposited at the Medici main bank in Florence
as a joint account in the names of Maria Giovanna Toreton and
Decima Manovale, payable only in gold florins.

When the deal was struck Cosimo said to Manovale, ''Now—
perhaps you and I can come to some arrangement.''

She pretended to misunderstand him. ''But I am not a courtesan, my lord,'' she said. She told Bernaba that she could not
see the shape of her future just then, but that she could feel its
presence and it had the thrilling smell of money. This was Cosimo di Medici who had just leased her daughter. To carry away
what his family had would require more men than even she had
known in her lifetime.

''After this day,'' he said, ''I shall hardly need a courtesan
again.''

''You don't need me to write love letters for you.''

''We can be useful to each other. It is tiresome for me to have
to travel to Rome so often on banking matters, yet people I
could send in my place are not sufficiently—ah—sophisticated
to understand the sort of persuasion that might be required. You
have a feeling for such things. I want you to be our bank's
special representative in Rome.''

''Business?''

''Very much so.''

"Business is money."

"How much?"

"A tithe."

"Not possible. I don't want you to negotiate for me, I want you as a persuader."

"Try me as a negotiator. I shall work for nothing for three months so you can measure whether I am worth a tithe."

"Only my father has the authority to do that. Perhaps you would like to meet him—at the bank in Florence." His father took a longer view than anyone else. He went for the golden florins, not for nice customs and traditions.

Mother, daughter, and Cosimo left for Florence the following morning. Both Decima Manovale and Cosimo di Medici were part of a mutating European spirit which was turning itself away from power by force toward the more reasonable yet deadlier channels of holding power through manipulation. They used force when there was no alternative. They were a century ahead of their time. That they had found each other so relatively early was an immense circumstance for both of them. For the time left to them together, they would think in parallel with each other, anticipating the clink of money and the exertions of power, each able to operate in places and with people whereof the other could not.

Chapter 12

Decima Manovale was born in 1371, four years after Cossa's birth, eight years before Urban VI became the vicar of Christ and slipped his leash to cause the Great Schism in the Church. An important figure in Manovale's story is Sir John Hawkwood, the great *condottiere,* who was knighted in the field by the Black Prince in 1356. Hawkwood was one of the most powerful hired lances of Italian history.

After the Treaty of Bretigny, in 1360, when he became one of the hundreds of surplus captains, he formed his own company of mercenaries and moved southward from Burgundy along the Rhone valley to the papal capital of Avignon—one free company, that is a company whose men elected their leaders, among a horde of sixty thousand mercenary soldiers. They had all heard about the papal riches and they had decided that, all together, they could scoop it all up before moving on. Avignon, to those soldiers, was a museum displaying samples of the booty that was waiting on the other side of the Alps. Avignon was a miniature Italy that glistened with the wealth of the south. The city was packed with merchants, goldsmiths, weavers, musicians, astrologers, prelates, pickpockets, whores, and forty-three branches of Italian banking houses. The papal court was so opulent that cardinals' mules wore gold bits. You can imagine what was gold on the cardinals' whores.

A great river of money rushed into the papal palace from every corner of Christendom, in the form of tributes for annates and media fructus, the *spoilia,* visitation fees, dispensations, absolutions, tithes, presents, sales of places, papal loans, taxes on bulls, and benefices. For forty-five groschen the king of Cyprus secured permission for his subjects to trade with the Egyptians. There was a graduated scale of prices that permitted the laity to choose their confessor outside their regular parish. The pope could change either canon law or divine law, but the divine law was changed only if there was enough money; money could buy anything, deliver any manner of permission to the petitioner.

For a king to carry his sword on Christmas Day—150 groschen

To legitimatize illegitimate children—60 groschen

For giving a converted Jew permission to visit his parents—40 groschen

To free a bishop from an archbishop—30 groschen

To divide a dead man and put him in two graves—30 groschen

To permit a nun to have two maids—20 groschen

To obtain immunity from excommunication–6 groschen

To receive stolen goods to the value of 1,000 groschen—50 groschen

Avignon might have been a freebooter's dream of a city to be sacked, but it had the strongest fortifications in Europe. Pope Innocent contemplated that vast encampment across the river and decided to pay the mercenary armies to persuade them to go away, preferably to Italy. He included a plenary indulgence for all of them, as a part of the price, which wiped out a teeming population of sins.

Hawkwood's White Company, so named because they kept their armor shining, was hired by Pisa to defend it. Hawkwood invented the designation ''lance'' as a system of accounting for troops in Italy. Lances fought on foot. With two thousand of them in the field, a thousand page boys called *ragazzi* held the horses at a safe distance in the rear. Two men held each lance, standing in units of twenty or thirty lances, balled together like porcupines. When these defense/attack units broke the enemy, the *ragazzi* would run forward with the horses so that the men within the lance could take up hot pursuit, hoping to take prisoners who could be held for ransom.

The murderous complement to the lances were the longbowmen on their flanks. A good archer with an English longbow could loose six arrows a minute; a superb one could have a sixth arrow in the air before the first hit the target, shoot twenty a minute, and kill at two hundred yards. It was the secret weapon of the White Company, because the longbow was exclusively an English weapon, and was irreplaceable in Italy.

The White Company was organized much as were other companies of the time, an observation which is relevant to Decima Manovale's story. Hawkwood's chief lieutenants in the field were Andrew de Belmonte, an aristocratic Englishman called "Dubramonte" by the Italians, and Albert Sterz. The key figure after Hawkwood was the company treasurer, William Turton, to whom the Hawkwood clients paid over the agreed costs for defense. "Toreton," as the Italians called him, ran the money, the paperwork, and the intelligence system and he needed a large Italian staff. He was also Hawkwood's lawyer, diplomat, and banker. Manovale says he was a beefy man, very tall, with very red cheeks and an insatiable lust early in the morning. She said if she really wanted something from him she was always careful to ask in the afternoon or over she'd go. He liked very young women, between ten and fourteen. After that it was hard for a woman to hold his attention.

Turton acquired Decima Manovale, tenth child of sixteen children, when she was twelve years old, from her father, for five florins and the agreement that he would teach her to read and write. She was a healthy, handsome child, so that when she was thirteen, she had her first child, called Maria Giovanna Toreton then, late the same year, her second child, Maria Louise Sterz. Her third was Helene MaCloi (by Chevalier MaCloi, chief of staff to the duke of Anjou), born when Decima was fourteen, and Rosa, fathered by Andrew de Belmonte, was born the following year. Decima learned to speak Latin and the languages of the four men who had fathered her children: English, German, and French, which she taught to her children.

Children born out of wedlock were commonplace and accepted. Decima worked on at Turton's headquarters while she took care of the children, learning how to run wars, conclude treaties, direct and collect intelligence, and judge men. She got an understanding of power and the necessity for its ruthlessness when she was very young. Cossa didn't know the first things about power compared to Manovale, but as I have said, he was a passive type, a very Italian kind of a fatalist.

When Decima was sixteen, and Turton never went near her for diddling even in the early morning, but listened to her notions when it came to business, Hawkwood left Tuscany, Decima's homeland, and sold the company's services to the lord of Padua, in the north of Italy. Decima took her children to Rome. She knew Turton would be glad to see her go. He had his eye on a nine-year-old girl whose father had been sending her into the camp with firewood.

Turton was Hawkwood's treasurer of wars. It was he who had negotiated the contracts for Hawkwood's captains, which provided for their pay, their "regard" or extra reward at the rate of thirty gold florins for every thirty men-at-arms for each quarter-year's service, for the division of booty, with Hawkwood (and Turton) receiving twenty-five percent of that, and for the sharing out of the ransom money for prisoners of every station, and he really understood money. Hawkwood had organized war in Italy on the English system and it paid highly, win battles or lose battles.

Turton was fond of Manovale, and felt responsible for her (and her four children). He saw to it that each of the fathers of the children, including himself, contributed one hundred gold florins to the Manovale traveling fund and, in addition, he gave her seven cups of pure gold from the loot stores, three valuable tapestries, and five good rugs. Manovale had enough capital to support her family well for the next four years.

Although she was beautiful and accomplished and, I am telling you, if you think about spectacular, stately women, it would be nearly impossible to conceive of a woman who was more beautiful up to the moment I last saw her, and although there wasn't much else for her to work at to support her four small children, she refused to become a courtesan. She became a *ruffiana* instead. She dealt in women, boys, potions, poisons, fortune telling, and stolen goods, and she prospered.

Later, when they could understand, she told her children,

"You were sired by great men. The strength of their characters and mine have joined to form your characters. Had I become a courtesan it could have been said that we could not know who your fathers were, so varied are the seeds that are scattered over a courtesan's fields, until it is nearly impossible to know whose seeds took root." She trained and raised her daughters to be courtesans. The first two helped her to teach the others.

Such young women were called courtesans because they were the companions of the *cortigiani,* the courtiers at the courts of Italy. They had been raised from the street title of whores by an official government designation of *meretrix honesta,* or "honorable whores." Courtesan was a title for the convenience of their patrons, usually men of station but always men of funds. Whore would have been a gratuitously rude label for the companions of such esteemed men.

Rosa, the youngest, became a courtesan when she was thirteen. Her youth and virginity, both endlessly extended by Mama, were not her only attractions. Like her sisters she could read and write, sing, paint, think, wear clothes and jewels, and play musical instruments. Mama's central commandments to Rosa and her sisters were as The Words that had tumbled out of the burning bush to Moses.

"A whore is not a woman," Manovale taught them. "She is a whore. It is what you make of the work and not the label that counts. We are the ants who hoard up the summers of our beauty and our art against the dread winter. Woe to the one who has no brains, for that is where the art lives. You must be able to burst into tears while a man is taking his pleasure from you, tears without reason, enough to make him stop what he is doing —that is the great test of the art—to beg of you why you weep. You answer with broken words and sobs. 'I cannot make you love me!' you tell him, or words to that effect, 'that is my fate, a life without your love.' Of course there are many variations, but the men swell with pride that a woman is lovesick for them. Occasionally, you must weep when they arrive so that they will believe you weep for joy at seeing them again. Love is not for us. Oh, as a caprice, yes—here today, gone this afternoon. Neither is lust for us. She who keeps drinking never feels thirsty. But all of the best of it can be yours in this life if you dress yourself becomingly and are always ready and cheerful, hardly ever laughing outright, which shows teeth and gullet like a street whore, but cultivating a sweet and attractive smile because you are a woman of quality. As the men come to you, you will entertain them cleverly and never play dishonest tricks on them. You will never drink too much—men detest that in others—nor will you stuff yourself with food.

"My dearest, talk if you feel like talking but only when you are with your family. When you are with the man who engaged you, please, I beg of you, talk no more than is necessary and, when it is time to lie down, do nothing roughly or carelessly. Work to captivate your lover and make him love you more. And remember! It is not enough to have beautiful eyes and lovely hair. Only your art, which is your brain, will pull you through. The difficulty is in keeping lovers, not in getting them. Only make promises you know you can keep, nothing more, and whatever other good opportunity comes your way, never shut your door in the face of the one who is entitled to sleep with you. You must swear an oath daily that you will take many little baths as often as you can, then wash and wash again, for if there is loving advantage in giving oneself to many, the least we can do is to stay clean."

When Rosa was discovered by the tenebrous Piero Spina, Mama's own place in the carnal garden had long before been transplanted from the *ruffiana* parterres to the sunlit terrace of the *mezzana*—mistress of the latest love songs on the lute and viola da braccio, writer of elegant love letters for her clients in the best Latin, French, or German, and brilliant at transactions that made rich old men believe it was they who were being placed within the proximity of seemingly unattainable beautiful women. She moved her family into a small palazzo in Rome to make comfortable the wealthy churchmen, rich businessmen, and *condottieri* generals who were her clients from all over Italy.

Touchingly, Spina's discovery of Rosa had been made to happen in a church. Selective church attendance was the best advertising for a courtesan. It showed off her beauty as well as her clothes and jewels, which were tributes to her desirability. Young and poor men jostled each other outside church doors to watch the women enter, preceded by pages and menservants, surrounded by supporters, while still more servants closed in at the rear. In May 1400, on the feast day of Santa Grazia di Traghetto, all the space between the altar itself and where the cardinals were seated was occupied by courtesans, including Rosa.

Previous to setting his hooded eyes upon Rosa, Spina had made his carnal discoveries at night, prowling the streets wearing disaffecting cloaks and huge disguising hats to move into the beds of the women his agents had put aside for his pleasure while he carried out his endless search for Bernaba Minerbetti. It was not in any way that he was ashamed of his desires (or of Romans' becoming aware of them), but rather from his devious conviction that his right testicle must never know what his left testicle was doing. Since the night Bernaba Minerbetti had deserted him, disgracing and humiliating him, he had been searching for her. He was prepared to spend the rest of his life searching for her because she must pay for what she had done to him. She had not returned to Bari: His agents had sought her out there and found nothing. She must be in Rome. He had paid for her and had not yet finished with her. He had vowed to inflict *sfregia* upon her if she went with another man. It was his duty to his honor, to his being a Sicilian, to accomplish that vow. He roamed the streets at night looking for her. When he saw Rosa, that did not change the need to find Bernaba Minerbetti and to ruin her face, but Rosa could fill other needs. He would maintain her. An occasional arrangement at first was best for testing these women, he sensed. It was not a matter of sampling, but of character. Also, he had refused to establish any courtesan under his permanent protection because he could not live with the idea of unseen people attempting to get her to get him to do things for them. Even after spending most of my life around churchmen I can still say that I have never met a man as devious as Piero Spina.

Decima Manovale taught her daughters to search for their clients' oddnesses, weaknesses between man and woman, so, when Rosa was brought together with Spina, she acted out convincing terror at the possibility of being known to Rome as a prelate's lover because then it could be bruited about that she

was a courtesan, which he knew she was not. NO! And he was
to tell her nothing of his life, for women were weak and their
tongues wagged. She would place her long, silken hand over his
mouth when he offered her as much as a good evening, because
why did she need to know anything except her love for him, or
to feel anything but the madness that came over her when he
touched her? She always wept when she returned to him and
when they parted.

Because Spina had persevered all of his life in never telling
anyone his inner (or outer) thoughts, or what he was doing, had
done, planned to do—because he had been unable to trust anyone until this dear little shepherdess had wandered into his life
—he had to tell her everything. Spina became an extraordinary
source of information for Manovale.

"Never cease exploring the vastness of self-doubt and uncer-
tainty within your clients," Manovale instructed her daughters,
"for these lead to gold and power. Great wealth is the source
of friendship and praise, of fame and authority, in the individual
as it is in the prosperity of the state. A family must erect and
decorate buildings, possess beautiful books, much power, and
fine horses."

Chapter 13

The day after her arrival in Florence with her daughter and Cosimo di Medici, Signora Manovale, feet together, hands in her lap, eyes (frequently) cast down, sat in the Medici house in the Piazza del Duomo of Florence, facing Giovanni di Bicci di Medici.

Behind the senior Medici, beyond the windows, were the almost imperceptibly rising walls and dome of the cathedral, which the city of Florence intended to be grander than any yet built. Cosimo sat soberly at his father's right hand, thinking pure thoughts, no doubt.

"When my son told me of his plans for you," the father said to Manovale, "I rejected them. At least I thought I had, but my son and I think alike, I have trained him so, and your possible usefulness—women are not usually such useful objects—began to emerge as I studied your dossier. I asked old Turton, the *condottiere,* to come to see me. He remembers you as what he called, 'the most promising soldier on his staff.' What do you say to that?"

"I knew him, of course. He was a kind man. He taught me so much of what little I know."

"About war?"

She shrugged. "About war." War was for men. "Mainly about how to gather intelligence and how to use it."

"I will pay you ten gold florins a month."

Manovale told Bernaba that she tried not to laugh, but she couldn't help it. She laughed, rocking in her seat, holding a handkerchief to her face, with her left hand holding her side. She laughed with disappointment that was almost the equal of despair. She laughed at the waste of her time. When she was able to regain control of herself, she wiped her eyes and said, "And, of course, you would expect me to give up my business as a *mezzana* to work for you?"

He looked at her steadily. "We misunderstood each other," he said, "I offered the ten gold florins a month during the first three months in which you offered to work for nothing."

"Ah. Such a difference."

"Signora—we have been after a piece of northern business for almost four years. Church business. Church business is important wherever it is to be found and this happens to be a large piece of business involving the archbishop of Mainz who will go to Rome to see the pope in one month's time. There is French Church business, which is also important, and we have learned that the bishop of Cambrai, who is the confessor to the king of France and a close adviser to Pope Benedict, will go to Rome to see the pope on most secret business in three months' time. We must always remain several steps ahead of the other banks— here and elsewhere. Is all of this comprehensible to you so far?"

She smiled.

"Let us discuss the bishop of Cambrai, Pierre d'Ailly, a greedy fellow. He has the look of a sleek house rat and he has served almost as many sides as there are in France. He supports anyone from whom he can gain, short term or long. When I spoke of Pope Benedict as being the pope at Avignon, that usage could seem to oppose our pope at Rome. Well, we are bankers, and there are two popes in this world, but Benedict is shut up in his palace at Avignon, defying the French crown. He is a very stubborn man who wants to be independent of the French king. The bishop of Cambrai, our same Pierre d'Ailly, will go to Rome for him—as secretly as possible, of course, to discuss with Boniface the sharing out of certain benefices in Poland, Hungary, and Greece. These are open territories and both popes feel they should share in them. Piero Spina will be the Pope's negotiator. Do you know him?"

She nodded.

"How well do you know him?"

"My youngest daughter is his mistress," the signora said.

He smiled at her for the first time. "Now, then," the banker said, "working on the theory that you can be useful to us, we will propose that friends of ours in Paris work on d'Ailly's lust for comfort and pleasure by offering to arrange for him to stay at your house in Rome. No one must know he is there, you understand. The pleasures, however unusual they may be, must be brought to him privately, you understand. His weakness with women has to do with talking. He makes classical conversation with beautiful women—beautiful *young* women, and such conversationalists are hard to find."

Signora Manovale made her eyes opaque. "What about that northern business you have been after for so long," she asked pleasantly. "The archbishop of Mainz, is it?"

"May we feel secure about d'Ailly?"

"What do you want from d'Ailly?"

"Well, I know what I want in a limited sense. I want those benefices in Poland, Hungary, and Greece to be sold by whichever pope is involved with our bank. But there could be a larger opportunity there. Pope Benedict is breaking away from the king of France. He therefore must keep his money, sooner or later, independent of French bankers. We would like to be his bankers."

"Please tell me about the archbishop of Mainz."

"He is John, count of Nassau, archbishop of Mainz, as unordained as the rest of them, a ferocious warrior, and the richest churchman north of the Alps. If he can be induced to bank with us to the exclusion of the other bankers, that could lead to the banking business of all the electors of the Holy Roman Empire —because he is the first elector—as well as the kings and princes of the north and the businessmen who seek their goodwill."

Manovale returned to Rome and called her daughters Maria Louise and Helene to her. "The time has come for our first great harvest," she told them. "The rewards of our years of work are about to be reaped. I shall set you each a refresher course of studies. You, Maria Louise, are going into great riches to live

among your father's people, the Germans, as mistress of a war-
rior-count who is also the archbishop of Mainz. Helene goes to
Paris, to her father's France, as the mistress of the richest
bishop in France. Maria Giovanna is at the side of a rich banker
in Florence. We will be one entity that will interchange information in order to rise and to continue to prosper.''

John of Nassau, archbishop of Mainz, arrived at the Manovale
house in Rome, a long string of a man who resembled a famished
eagle. His face was scarlet, his eyes shining black, his hair pre-
maturely white with streaks of brass. I knew him well, not then
but later, and cultivated him for Cossa. He was charming when
one was alone with him, or when two or three other men were
present, but he became offensive as soon as there were women
in the room and impossible if the women were pretty.

He came to the Villa Manovale dressed in blood-red ecclesiastical garments worn under polished battle armor. He wore
spurs to the dinner table. He stared at Manovale's body as if it
were unclothed. She felt encouraged in her task.

"You *are* the Medici representative in Rome?" he asked
mockingly.

She smiled at him. She allowed the smile to begin gently then,
with experienced control, she slowly increased its heat to lasciviousness.

"I understand," he said.

On the day after his arrival, a papal messenger brought an
invitation to the archbishop suggesting that he join His Holiness
at dinner at two o'clock the following morning at the Vatican.
Unwilling to consider going to bed only to be reawakened, the
archbishop asked Signora Manovale if she would lay on a
"merry luncheon" at ten o'clock in the evening before his meeting with the pope.

The signora invited Paolo Orsini, the contracting *condottiere,*
so that the archbishop would have someone with whom he could
talk shop if he chose. She brought in the famous actor, Aleghieri
Melvini, and Giovanni di Gianni, a man who controlled the grain
in Rome and who was a new client of the Medici Bank, recruited
by her. There were women to set these men off but, seated at

the archbishop's left, speaking in both Latin and German, was
Maria Louise Sterz, whom the signora introduced only to her
guest of honor, who was soon so delighted with her that he made
it clear to the others that he wished to speak to no one else at
the table.

John of Nassau remained in Rome for eleven days, six days
longer than his original intention. He saw the pope once again
and spent all of the rest of his stay with Maria Louise. When she
was absent, seeing her dressmaker, she said, her mother comforted the archbishop with fine wine and soon established a relationship for him with the Medici Bank. She assured him that
the Medici would be so honored to have his account that they
would immediately open a branch in Mainz for his convenience,
as well as, she was hopeful, for the convenience of the considerable banking business of the Church in Swabia, and for the
bank deposits of those dioceses that neighbored the archbishop's jurisdiction and looked to him for protection from the Teuton and Polish princes. His Eminence, archbishop and count,
wanted something from her, so the matter of which Italian bank
held his money was of little interest to him. Therefore, when the
count of Nassau left Rome, the signora had made a banking coup
that delivered over five hundred thousand florins each year to
the new Medici branch at Mainz and twenty-five thousand gold
florins to Decima Manovale, at a commission of five percent,
which had been instated immediately by the bank when she
produced the business.

Chapter 14

The archbishop of Mainz departed from Rome at the head of his troop of six hundred horsemen, with his household of 192 people, and with Maria Louise Sterz, whom he had leased from Signora Manovale at terms no more strenuous than those she had secured from Cosimo di Medici for Maria Giovanna Toreton.

That night, the bishop of Cambrai arrived in Rome after his journey from France. He had traveled with only ten men. I worked with d'Ailly several years later. It was a cheerless task, like trying to touch a man by addressing his reflection in a mirror. He was a smart fellow who had seen everything and had done everything. He never lost sight of himself.

Manovale received him in the company of an exclamatorily attractive young woman of fifteen, whom she introduced as Mademoiselle Helene MaCloi. Everyone spoke in French. The two women dined with the bishop that night and soon he and Mlle. MaCloi were into a dense discourse, which excited the bishop. He drank much wine and insisted, when the evening came to an end, that the young woman take him to his bed.

Each day at one o'clock, Piero Spina (disguised) came to the house, a few minutes before luncheon was served for two in the bishop's apartment. Each day Spina remained with the bishop until 4:45 P.M. They met for three consecutive days. Signora

Manovale observed and listened to their conversations through a gallery slit high up in the room and reported them by courier to Cosimo di Medici.

After Spina left each day, the bishop napped until seven o'clock, after which he bathed and exercised. When he dressed for the evening's dinner with the two ladies he did not don ecclesiastical robes but wore a fashionable knight's surcoat made of fabrics of great sophistication and garments that were extremely short and padded with a mighty codpiece. His hose were laced to his upper garments. Buttons ran in long rows up and down his arms. As he gazed longingly into his looking glass he combed his hair in radiation from the center of his crown, with the line in the back dipping well below the hairs that were the bangs cropped on his forehead. He wore the long, pointed shoes that his king, Charles VI, had forbidden his subjects to wear because they made it impossible for the wearer to kneel in prayer. By the time he was well-scented, Mlle. MaCloi was waiting for him with her mother in the large salon. There, they discussed French literature: *Guillaume de Dole;* the idealistic conception of human love as portrayed in *Roman de la Rose,* and Gautier de Coinci's *Les Miracles de la Sainte Vierge.*

Dinner was served on a balcony overlooking an inner garden where the bishop said that not anywhere in France, not even in Paris, had he encountered a woman who so combined beauty with intellectuality, who not only understood the true culture but had the ability to *listen,* as did Mlle. MaCloi. "I am too old by far for such things," he said, "but were I not, I should have to say that I have lost my heart to you."

"We love with our minds, you and I," the young woman said fervently. "Although," she added, blushing skillfully, "you have not allowed it to stop there."

"Oh, I can race for a bit, but then I am exhausted," the bishop said. "Such a body as yours requires constant worship."

"But your mind is an instrument of prodigious skill at love-making," she protested. "When you fill my heart with the poems of Eustache Deschamps and Guillaume de Machaut, fighting the battle of realism against idealism, you are wooing with the strength of youth for the love of all women."

He patted her absent-mindedly. "I must leave for Paris," he

said. "I have lain awake nights plotting how I can take you with me yet still know that you will be served well with love in those years that lie in wait before me like brigands."

"It is a problem for the mind," she said gently. "Therefore, you will find a solution."

"I have done so," he answered softly, reaching out to hold her hand, oblivious to the presence of Manovale.

"Please—tell me."

"I hesitate."

"But—why?"

"It is unorthodox."

"You aren't capable of a flawed solution—is he, Signora?"

"Let us hear him," the signora said.

D'Ailly smiled ruefully. "When I was chancellor of the University of Paris," he said, "I had a student who was so brilliant in his kindness, and so generous with his intelligence that, when I became a bishop of the Holy Church, I went to the king and persuaded him to name this student in my place as chancellor."

"That is friendship," Helene said.

"It is my history," d'Ailly said. "Because I desire to have you near me—for the rare quick race and for the ecstatic talk and response, I am proposing that, for long enduring love-making as well as for the fulfillment of minds, you allow yourself to be shared by my student, the chancellor of the University of Paris, Jean Gerson."

"In the same bed?" she asked shyly.

"Sometimes. Sometimes not. But could such a paradise be possible?"

"Mademoiselle MaCloi is my daughter, My Lord Bishop," Manovale said.

"What? My dear woman, how titillating."

Helene rose. "You two will need to talk," she said.

"Does your mother speak for you?" the bishop asked blandly.

"She speaks for me." Helene turned to leave the room.

"Wait!"

Helene turned back to him.

"Before your mother and I may speak," the bishop said, "I must know where your heart and mind rest."

She stared down at him, silent for several moments, then she spoke to him alone in a low, caressing voice saying,

> Slender, lovely, darling friend,
> When shall I have you in my power?
> Were I to sleep with you one night
> And give you love's kiss,
> Know it: I'd have such desire
> To hold you in another's place,
> If you'd promise me to do
> Everything I'd want you to.

"From *Estate ai greu cossirier!*" the bishop cried.

Manovale made Bishop d'Ailly a profitable variation of her daughter-leasing deal. Later that evening, when Mlle. MaCloi was packing for her departure for France with the bishop on the next morning, the signora and d'Ailly arrived at a banking arrangement whereby, for the payment of a quarter-tithe to the bishop, and for another quarter-tithe to be paid into the account of Pope Benedict XIII in a branch of the Medici Bank to be opened at Perpignan, all of the funds received daily from that part of his Christian obedience which was outside France would be deposited in the same Medici bank.

Four months later, in the autumn of 1400, Manovale was summoned to Florence to meet with Cosimo. "My father is *enormously* pleased with your work. This new business with Perpignan and Mainz is entirely in the direction of fulfilling his most cherished dream."

"How happy that makes me, my lord," Manovale murmured.

"He has extraordinary plans for you. He wants to establish a branch in Milan and in Pavia and he wants the state of Milan to put its money there. A war is coming."

"Good," she said blandly. "When Milan goes to war against your own Florence and the pope, Gian Galeazzo will need to find a lot of money. Where better than from our bank?"

"You will be introduced to Gian Galeazzo Visconti, duke of

Milan, with safe conducts from the king of France and from the Emperor Wenzel, Gian Galeazzo's patron. To establish you as closely and as favorably as possible to the duke of Milan—he is a colossal snob—and you are a woman who will be made the more, ah, credible for such an adornment—for a certain, ah, sum, which my father has paid to him, the emperor has conferred upon you the title, if not the estates, of the marchesa di Artegiana. My dear Decima! You are now a marchesa and there are letters patent to prove it.''

"My lord Cosimo!" Manovale said, clutching her throat in wonderment and awe. She was overwhelmed for the only time in her life. A peasant woman who now—Holy Sweet Mother of God!—she was not only a marchesa, she was on her way to becoming a rich marchesa!

"Don't get it confused, Decima," Cosimo said with soft amusement, "the title is only a banking tool. You will have to take Gian Galeazzo from this point onward and make him see what is best for all of us. There will be danger. If he misunderstands your purpose he will have you executed as a spy, be sure of that, but if you can persuade the duke to bank with us and to give up Pisa to Florence—peacefully—my father will advance your share of all future work to a full ten percent.''

She smiled at him blissfully, happier than she would ever be again.

"Our agents are at work in Mantua, Perugia, and Siena, getting them ready," Cosimo told her. "We will appear to be the allies of the pope, even to financing his military expedition when it happens sometime—perhaps a year or two from now. When you have Gian Galeazzo ready, you will give him those cities, delivered from within, in exchange for Pisa's going to Florence. When he has those cities of the papal states, Gian Galeazzo will be ready to move south to take Rome, then Naples. He needs to be able to think that he can do that.''

Becoming a marchesa changed everything for Manovale. I know it changed life for my wife and me. We were still her friends but we saw her in a different light. It hardly seemed possible that she had been a *ruffiana* and a *mezzana,* that I had thought of her as Manovale, never as Signora Manovale, that she had run whores and had dealt in the bodies of boys, mixed potions, sold poisons, handled stolen goods, and told fortunes. Her title changed everything but the woman herself. She continued to be as she always had been: aristocratic, noble, serene, and ruthless.

Chapter 15

Pope Boniface IX believed in a one-man Church, as far as possible. He did not have the patience to be hampered by too numerous a College of Cardinals, for example, and it was a pope's right to appoint as many cardinals as he wished to name. It was more economical and efficient not to have to provide for them than to have to haggle with them, ending by refusing them their expected shares in the Church's revenues. Of the thirteen cardinals who had elected him to the throne of St. Peter in 1389, only five were still alive for the Jubilee of 1400. To replace those who had died he raised only four priests to the College, all able men: Henricus Minutulus, whom he used constantly as a roving papal legate; Bartholomaeus de Uliarius, especially assigned to the court of King Ladislas of Naples; Cosimo de'Migliorati, (afterwards Pope Innocent VII), whom he used as ambassador between Gian Galeazzo Visconti, duke of Milan, and the Republics of Florence and Bologna, and Piero Spina, his bent-nose Sicilian chamberlain, who became adjudicator among the several disputed territories of the Papal States.

Baldassare Cossa was awarded a red hat in the same ceremonies that created the other new cardinals. It was very early in the morning, shortly after dinner, when Boniface told his protégé that he was to be made a cardinal. As His Holiness solemnly explained the significance of the cardinalate, Cossa told

me he found himself remembering the lost beauty of the prodi-
giously sexual woman who had bedded him so single-mindedly
in Perugia, nine years before. As his influence at the Vatican
had grown, he had been able to institute consecutive efforts
toward finding her, meaning that I was given the job of looking
for her, but, wherever I looked, no one had known her. She had
vanished. It was as though Cossa had imagined he had been with
her, excepting that I was his witness that she had once existed.
She had a lovely natural perfume. I can smell her still.

Cossa despaired that she had escaped him, such a beautiful
woman, with long red hair, pale skin, large green eyes so filled
with eager lust, as I remember them, that no one, having once
seen her, could cast her from memory. Cossa said he had to
force himself to listen to the pope instruct him about the cardinalate.

"Because you have no knowledge of theological matters,
Cossa," Boniface said to him, "you have not been ordained and
have spent your life as a lawyer—we are going to explain to you
what are the duties and the rewards of our cardinals. Our work
has its two arms—the Curia, which is all the offices that deal
with administering our papacy, and our pastoral mission—apart
from running Rome and the temporal requirements of the Papal
States. We need this complex machinery for, as the papal monarch, we not only claim the ownership of *all* islands, but are also
the feudal lord of many countries. As general overseer we are
entitled to depose princes, release subjects from their oaths of
allegiance, confer crowns by making kings, and dispose of territories. It is in our powers to order the dispatch of troops in
support of a ruler, or we can prohibit further military engage-
ments. We can order the preservation of the legal systems of
invaded or conquered countries or transfer one kingdom to another. By the same powers we are entitled to annul certain laws,
such as the Magna Carta in England, on the ground of interfer-
ence with royal power. Our papacy acts as a court that ratifies
treaties between kings and countries, hence we have the right to
prohibit trade where necessary.

"The cardinals are, of course, a part of this. That is, and never
fail to remember this, as much a part of it as we permit them to
be. Originally, it was the clergy and the people of Rome who

elected the pope, but gradually the defects in that system were adjusted until the Third Lateran Council in 1179 issued the decree that stated that all cardinals of whatever rank were to be the equal electors and that, for a valid election, a two-thirds majority of their votes was required. And there you have the only function of cardinals—to elect a new pope. And that is where their freedom of decision ends, for at the moment of a pope's election and his own acceptance, he and he alone has the governing power. Often popes are not even ordained priests, let alone consecrated bishops. Sometimes months pass before a pope is ordained or consecrated." Boniface leaned forward toward Cossa for emphasis. His voice grew softer. "Let that demonstrate for you the nature of the papal office. It is juristic. It is executive and it is administrative before anything else. You are about to enter the Sacred College, which is, usually, made up of seven cardinal-bishops, twenty-eight cardinal-priests, and eighteen cardinal-deacons—which will be the rank that you will hold. The head of all the cardinals is the cardinal-bishop of Ostia, who consecrates the pope and anoints the emperor. By custom, and in varying degrees, depending upon the policy of the sitting pope, the cardinals participate in all sources of curial income, as well as sharing in Peter's Pence. This is because the cardinals form 'part of the pope's body,' a concept modeled on Roman law, which laid down the same intimate connection between Roman senators and their emperor. By constant adjustment to new contingencies, our vast machinery functions out of the resilience and continuity of a slow evolution that reaches back across the centuries, founded upon order and based upon law."

Thus, in February 1402, when he was thirty-four years old, Baldassare Cossa was created cardinal of Saint Eustachius, a cardinal-deacon who had never taken holy orders but who was a first-class army commander and a very good canon lawyer, and who had a definite talent when it came to diverting a gold florin from the purse of the faithful.

Chapter 16

On July 14, 1402, Bologna passed again under the sway of Gian Galeazzo Visconti, duke of Milan. He held Padua, Perugia, Bologna, Siena, and Pisa. He had Florence surrounded. When it fell, he would march to conquer Italy.

The Florentine delegation reached Rome almost as soon as the first dispatch came to the pope about Bologna. They were men who were somber with anxiety as they sat down to luncheon at one o'clock in the morning at the Vatican. When the servants had withdrawn, the pope invited Cosimo to speak his mind.

Cosimo told of Gian Galeazzo's preparations in Pavia. He concluded the report by saying that his committee, representing the Dieci and the Signoria of Florence, wished to make recommendations that they hoped would be welcomed by His Holiness.

"Why not?" the pope said.

"It is our opinion, Holiness, that Baldassare Cossa should lead the papal forces that the money of Florence, Mantua, and Parma will finance."

"Well, you liked his work the last time," the pope answered.

"Yes. As well, we propose that you make Cossa your legate to sit in Bologna. This would provide proper proportions of risk for Gian Galeazzo, while lending a stateliness to the alliance, including France, against the duke of Milan.''

The pope sighed. ''Cossa is so useful to us in his work here, but I will do as you wish. Cossa is a valuable man to all of us.''

He spoke the truth, of course. But he underestimated it by perhaps a thousandfold, if Cossa's value to Giovanni di Bicci di Medici were to be measured. The Medici Bank considered that it had done a slick piece of business that night. They were one step closer to pocketing Holy Mother Church as a valued banking client.

Chapter 17

The plans of the papacy and the Florentines had to be changed again. On September 3, 1402, Gian Galeazzo Visconti died of the plague at his castle of Marignano. His loyal *condottieri* scattered across northern Italy, taking for themselves whatever pieces they could of Gian Galeazzo's rapidly disintegrating dominions, or, failing that, simply selling their services elsewhere. His widow was left with the difficult job of saving what she could from the ruin, as regent for her son Giovanni Maria, then fourteen years old.

In Rome, Cossa prepared his defense of the Papal States and his counterattack into Visconti territory. On the twenty-seventh day of May, 1403, the Milanese troops at Bologna were reinforced. On the second of June, commanding an alliance of such *condottieri* generals as Carlo Malatesta and the constable, Alberico da Barbiano (both of whom had, until his death, been in Gian Galeazzo's pay), Cossa took over from Nicholas of Este, marquess of Ferrara, as commander of the papal armies. Cossa was the pope's legate to the city-state of Bologna as well. He arrived with his force before Bologna's walls on the ninth of July and ordered his army to dig in to besiege the city.

In the third week of the siege of Bologna, Cossa worked at a field desk deep within his besieging army of 16,000 men, 4,000 horses, 7,300 camp followers, 177 priests, 59 spies, and a musical group of general entertainers from Rimini, which was taking in money hand over fist. Word had been confirmed that Jacopo dal Verme, one of the few *condottieri* generals still loyal to the Visconti, was preparing to relieve the city, marching from Padua. Cossa ate the meal that Geoffredano Bocca had prepared for him, then played cards with me for about a half hour.

"The change in the drinking water gave me the runs," he said.

"What do you expect," I said, losing the hand.

"The water is better in Rome. It is the only thing that is better." He dealt the cards out rapidly as if he were doing required exercises.

"You'll get used to the water here."

"I know. But it's kind of a shock to know that there are animals in the drinking water in a great place like this and not in Rome." He won two more hands, then turned in for the night.

I made a bed at the entrance to his tent and went right to sleep as always. Some time later a gentle hand shook my shoulder. I opened my eyes and had the surprise of my life. It was the doorkeeper at the old Manovale place in Rome. "What are you doing here?" was the first thing I asked her, then the real question came to me. "How the hell did you get here through the lines?"

"How do you think I got here? I rubbed the lads a little. Franco, listen to me. This is important. My mistress, the marchesa di Artegiana, has to talk to the cardinal. Believe me, it is very important."

"Who is the marchesa di Artegiana?"

"Didn't you hear? She is Signora Manovale! The emperor made her a marchesa!"

"Mano*vale*?"

"Franco, we can't talk here all night. She is waiting out there and some patrol might come on her and stick a sword into her just for the fun."

"All right. Okay. Bring her here."

The doorkeeper, her name was Michela, went back into the darkness, then reappeared in a few minutes with Manovale—that is to say, the marchesa di Artegiana.

"Franco!" she said softly, putting her arms around me and

kissing me full on the lips, rubbing her crotch into mine as if we were long-time lovers. I had shaken hands with her a couple of times, but no more. "How wonderful to see you again." It was nice, and skillfully done. She let me go and stepped backward only slightly. "I have information that can change the war," she said. "I must talk to the cardinal."

"Are you really a marchesa?" I asked her mockingly.

She nodded solemnly. "The emperor honored me," she said simply.

I went into the tent to awaken Cossa.

"Franco Ellera! For Christ's sake, it is still dark!" he said.

"There is a woman here, Cossa," I said urgently. "Very beautiful. Very rich. She passed right through our lines and no one stopped her. It must have cost her a fortune. She came right to this tent. She knew the right tent. She is unarmed. I made sure of that. She wants to talk to you. She says she has information that could change the war."

"Beautiful *and* rich? Send her in in ten minutes."

When Cossa was dressed he opened the flap of the tent and motioned to me. I passed in the marchesa, a tall, hooded figure, and left them. The doorkeeper and I got back to old times, and her hips had never lost their skill.

This is what happened inside the tent from the first moment Cossa ever met Decima Manovale. It is exactly as Cossa told it to me.

The marchesa threw back her hood and Cossa was axed by her beauty. She was tall, large, and deep-chested, having a cap of odd-looking golden hair, very white skin, which was dusted with sun spots, and large deep-blue eyes that came up like stars behind her high cheekbones. Cossa was astonished at her commanding beauty. He stared into her face and she became imprinted upon his mind and spirit. It may have been the light, a wood fire, and two candles. It may have been the fault of his transformation from the half-death of sleep into a place that becomes as a dream, because the strange beauty of the woman had a bewitching force upon him. Cossa had forgotten his army and his rewarding Church. He had forgotten the woman who had felled him at Perugia. He had almost forgotten his ambitions. He stared at her like a country boy peering from behind a barn as she dropped the cloak, showing him the strong, white outline of her shoulders and the rising, half-concealing bodice above a shimmering green dress.

"Your Eminence," she said with a Pisan accent, speaking as if she were unaware of her effect upon him. She reached for the hand that hung at his side, lifted it and kissed his ring. Returning the hand to its limp place, she said, "I am the marchesa di Artegiana, at your orders."

Cossa came to himself again. He pulled her down upon a bench and sat close to her, smelling her, touching her on her arms and hands. "Why did you come here?" he asked her.

She held his hand loosely, caressing the soft flesh under his wrist, and peered out at him from over the tops of her cheekbones like a sniper working high up from behind a rock, let her lips slacken into an expression of sincere lust and began contemplatively, "Last year, Gian Galeazzo, duke of Milan, died in my arms, of the plague. A huge comet appeared in the sky as he lay dying. 'I thank Heaven,' he said, 'that the sign of my recall appears in the heavens for all men to see.' Gian Galeazzo is dead, Eminence," she said in a soft, provoking voice, "and most of his *condottieri* have abandoned the Visconti, and now the duchess and her sons have lost control of Milan itself. They are walled up in the castello in Milan, besieged, and they are powerless. You need not defeat dal Verme, or take Bologna, you need only march on Milan with your army. My people have already seen to it that if you march by Reggio and Parma, they will greet you as their liberator. In Milan, the duchess will tell the city to come to terms with you because the wives of your generals are her sisters."

"How do you know these things?"

"I was close to Gian Galeazzo. My department ranked with that of Francesco Barbavara, who ran his chancery, and now runs the duchess'."

"Your department?" He leered at her, giving it lewd meaning, as if he were startled that a department that called for lying on her back with her legs spread wide, with her knees lifted, could have ranked with Barbavara's.

"It is right that you mock me," she said, "but I ran his agents, who supplied political information from all over Italy and Europe. I ran his agents in Aragon, Burgundy, Germany, and twice among the Turks. I ran his agents at the court of Sigismund, king of Hungary, and close to Wenzel, the emperor." Cossa believed her story, but I didn't when it was told to me.

"What did you learn about me?"

"That you adore women. That thoughts of coupling are on your mind most of the time."

He showed her what a Cossa smile really was.

When she stood away from Gian Galeazzo's corpse she had seen what she must do, she told Bernaba later. She had secured Milan for the Medici Bank, but if the papal armies conquered the north of Italy because Gian Galeazzo's talisman was not there to ward them off, then all that good work, and her tithe, could go to waste. Better to protect the new Milanese deposits by persuading the commander of the papal armies to transfer the money of Bologna and of all the cities of the Papal States into the Medici Bank along with Milanese florins. She was now established at the Medici Bank as being entitled to a full tithe. She had advanced Giovanni di Bicci di Medici's plan to secure all of the Church's banking. She saw that she must go to the papal army's commander as soon as she had some lever, some useful gift of information for him. The commander would have to be grateful to her. He would have to cooperate with the Medici Bank.

That the commander turned out to be a wiry, compact, elegant ruffian who was a cardinal amused her and stimulated her the more.

"Where will you go from here?" he asked.

"I go with you, my lord, to aid in your conquest."

He put his hands into her bodice and lifted out her breasts. "Better your conquest than anyone's, dear lady," he said.

Cossa left a token force at the gates of Bologna to remind the occupying Milanese troops that their work was over. He rode through the cities between Bologna and Milan taking cheers. A peace was written with the Council of Milan. The pope instructed Cossa not to include his allies, the Florentines, in the peace, after they had expended eighty thousand florins on the war, because he had learned that "a Florentine bank" had financed the Visconti in making the war and he did not wish, either, to have to share Cossa's loot and ransom money with them. Despite this betrayal, the Florentines showed no rancor against Cossa, because the marchesa di Artegiana had confirmed to Cosimo di Medici that she saw qualities in Cossa that could be fortunate for the bank, so Giovanni di Bicci di Medici extolled Cossa eloquently in his speech before the Signoria, the council of Florence.

PART TWO

PART TWO

Chapter 18

Cossa was besotted with the marchesa. I had seen him almost as insanely affected years before when we had left the red-haired woman on the bed in Perugia and I had made him ride on to Rome, but he was older now and, after the stint at the Vatican, a far more worldly man, who anyone would have thought would be less paralytically susceptible than the marchesa revealed him to be. He wanted her at his side at all times. He could not keep his hands off her. He could stare at her for embarrassingly long moments, as a hen stares at a white chalk line on the ground. He heaped jewels on her. When the temperature dropped he ordered furs to be brought to her. He was on her and in her like an unbalanced satyr, moaning, talking brokenly. I must have lost two hours' sleep every night because of the noises he made on that woman.

He told me he felt as if he were two people. One of these was pulled helplessly into the orbit of the woman from Perugia, the other knew it belonged to the marchesa forever. "I still think of that woman whom we left in Perugia, Franco," he said to me. "There has never been a day or night gone that she was not vividly in my mind. Even when I am upon the marchesa and almost frantic with the love of her, I think of the woman whom I left in Perugia. She is with me now. She will probably always be a part of me and I rejoice for that, but the woman who commands my soul is the marchesa di Artegiana. She consumes me. She is in my mind and in my bones and yet—even I know that she is but one of the two women of all of my life. I will never see her again, that woman in Perugia, but she lives for me while the marchesa blinds me like a sun."

"It could be worse," I said.

"How could it be worse?"

"Well—it could be four women. Or ten. But at some point you would have to start to lose track."

He glared at me. "How would you like me to have Palo cut your balls off?" he snapped.

When Cardinal Cossa concluded the papal treaty with the council of Milan, at the moment he was alone in the command tent outside Milan's walls, Carlo Malatesta spoke to him. He was one of Cossa's generals, called "the best and most loyal of his race," a man who was married to a daughter of Bernabo Visconti, making him a brother-in-law of the late Gian Galeazzo Visconti, duke of Milan. Cossa had respect for Malatesta as well as affection. They greeted each other warmly and, to honor the day, Cossa bade him sit and drink a glass of wine.

"What brings you here?" Cossa asked. "I am happy to see you, always."

"Your Eminence—there is a matter—that is, you may know that my wife's sister is Catherine Visconti, widow of Gian Galeazzo."

Cossa nodded.

"She has asked me to ask you for an audience for her. She is a sensible woman, after all she is a Visconti, so there is no possibility of embarrassment for you. And may I also say that Francesco Gonzaga, lord of Mantua, who was one of the council with whom you have just made the treaty, who is also married to yet another sister of Catherine Visconti, there are nine in all, adds his own petition to mine that you grant this request."

"My dear fellow! Of course. I would be honored to meet such a great lady."

"Then she will come to your tent tonight, Eminence."

"Out of the question. That would be intolerable. I will, of course, go to her."

Malatesta cleared his throat. "That would be indelicate, Eminence. As you have just concluded a treaty with Milan without conquering it, the Milanese would be offended if you entered the city."

"Nonetheless," the cardinal said, "I did conquer them and I will not permit the widow of a great man to be humiliated by having to come through a military camp to see me. Please—you, yourself, and Gonzaga as well, if he wishes, will escort me to some little-used way into the city and take me to where the lady waits. I will dress myself as the Milanese dress. No one will notice me."

"The duchess wishes to meet you alone, Eminence. I will send you Gonzaga's own man to take you to her."

When Malatesta had gone, Cossa asked me what I thought it was all about. "It sounds a lot like she wants to get laid," I said. "Some widows are like that."

On the following night, three hours after darkness fell, Cossa's guide came to the tent and I searched him for weapons. When the cardinal-general, dressed as a civilian, rode with the man toward the city walls, I followed them silently.

When they reached a secondary gate I caught up and the three of us were passed through by the guard. The streets had been emptied by curfew. "She is in the citadel," the guide told them. When we reached the door of the high, windowless tower Cossa dismounted. I secured his horse and settled down to wait.

The man unlocked the door. Cossa entered and the door was closed behind him. When he returned four hours later he was an utterly different man. He was very pale, as if he had slept with giant bats who had drained him of blood. He appeared to me to be about fifty pounds lighter and he wore a silly coltish grin. He told me what had happened after the tower door had closed.

He faced a spiral staircase ascending into darkness. He climbed the stairs. A few minutes before he reached the top a door opened above him and light fell upon him. He kept climbing, then, at the top, entered the open door, closing it behind him.

Before him, in serene repose, sat the delicately ravenous woman who had occupied his mind since the night in Perugia when he had been an archdeacon and she had seduced him, the woman for whom he had searched until the marchesa di Artegiana had emptied him of the dream. He reached out for her as if he were stretching out to grasp an apparition. She was solidly real.

Long after, while she lay in his arms, she told him her story dreamily. She said that, in 1380, her father compelled Gian Galeazzo to marry her. She was twelve years old. She lived with Gian Galeazzo, her first cousin, at the palace in Pavia, the great fortress-palace that his father had built into the north wall of the city. Although her husband was a stranger to honor, she said, he was devoted to art and scholarship. He was secretive. He loved the silent gardens and the woods that stretched away on the other side of the Ticino. He was already a widower but he had to put away his private grief because having no male heir gave temptation to his rivals. Before they were married—because it would have strengthened his position against her father—Gian Galeazzo was negotiating a secret betrothal to a Sicilian princess, but her father made sure that wedding did not take place. Gian Galeazzo was then completely at her father's mercy, and her father had little mercy.

Gian Galeazzo would not come near her bed because, perhaps, he felt nothing for her, but she thought it was to reassure her father that there would be no male heirs.

She told Cossa she could see her husband from the tower at Pavia as he paced with his leopards in the garden, plotting how to rid the world of her father. He had to kill her father, she said. He wanted to rule Milan alone. But more than that he wanted dominion over all of Italy and to do that he had to get at the undivided resources of Milan. So he killed her father and her brothers, then made his triumphal entry into Milan as the people shouted, "Long live the Count of Virtù! Down with taxes!" His coup was so well-planned that the Pisan government voted its congratulations on the same day and Pisa is 140 miles away.

"As soon as he was ruler of Milan he made me pregnant with my first son," she said. "I am telling you this so that you will see that a woman can only find safety under the protection of a great man. You are more of a man than my husband was. He was timid. You are a lion. I can see now that everything he held is going to fall into shards. There is no strong control, such as you would bring to Milan, and his generals grab territory to make up for lost booty and pay. Facino Cane is finished in Bologna. You finished him. He will carve out his domain in Piedmont. Ugo Cavalcabo has seized Cremona. Franchino Rusca took Como. Ottobuono Terzo took Parma. Brescia has gone to the Guelphs and your friend, Carlo Malatesta, will hold Rimini.''

"Well,'' Cossa said, "that is how history is made.''

"Not Visconti history!'' she said fiercely. "We hold what we have killed to get. Hear me, my cardinal, my general, my beloved—together, you and I, by combining Milan with Bologna, we could hold all the power. City by city we would add Perugia, Siena, Padua, Parma—on and on—back to where Gian Galeazzo had taken us before he fell. Then we could consolidate the power and breed the money and you—if you wished—could force them to make you pope, whatever you wanted, and whatever the Viscontis wanted, you could have.''

He lay silent. He was confused. The marchesa rose dimensionally in his mind so vividly that he felt her beside him. The two women were different but they were very much the same. A very few nights before and on this night he had discovered two great lights of women. The marchesa di Artegiana and now, again, this wanton, filling his heart and his mind, were destroying his purpose as a soldier and a cardinal. In their different ways, or perhaps it was the same way, they were offering him kingdoms. He did not want to be pope but Catherine had touched his deepest ambitions when she had told him he could be the conqueror of Italy—if he would agree to relinquish his cardinalate and shame his father. It came to him that, if he had not thought of such an escape, another one as useful would have taken its place.

He had already led armies. He would never accept the papacy. It was entirely possible, and certainly in keeping with her family's character, that this woman would have him killed after he had got everything back for her, but more than that, more than anything or any other reason, he knew, as his mind clogged with desire, that he was the total captive of the marchesa di Artegiana and he did not want to be freed.

As I have always said, Cossa was basically a passive man. All the fatalists are.

"I am a cardinal of the Holy Church," he said to her as his answer. "I am the servant of His Holiness, Pope Boniface IX, whose armies I lead. Let me take the time to consolidate the papal claim upon the Papal States and let me think about what I could bring to the alliance you propose, dear lady, and then, please God, we will meet again."

He told me all that and I believed him. It was in keeping with his character, for what he was really saying was that he wanted to have time to think about all of it, then to come to a decision, but he did not tell Catherine Visconti that and he wasn't sure if he could do that. He asked me bitterly why an entire qualifying list of particulars had to go wherever the women went, why they could not just do what everyone wanted to do, make love until they had exhausted themselves, then see how life would turn out.

I was aware of the two women who walked with Cossa from every day after that. They seemed two entirely different women to me, the one who had been born a high aristocrat but was a slut, and the other who had been born a slut but became a high aristocrat. I thought about them for a long time because they were bringing so much force to bear upon Cossa. In the end I saw that they were both offering him more money and more power, that Cossa wanted those things and nothing else, but that he was, within himself, timid. He believed he needed both women to help him to get what they all wanted, so he was able to deceive himself mightily.

Chapter 19

After Cardinal Cossa secured the peace in Milan he returned to Bologna, on September 1, 1403, spending the night at the monastery of the Crociari outside the walls of the city. He made his triumphal entry into Bologna in the morning, by the Porto San Mammolo, to pass along streets adorned with colored cloths and silks, embellished with the arms of the Church, the city, and the legate, to the cathedral. All the chief citizens and most of the populace came out to meet him, a long-adopted Bolognese. Hundreds of gleeful people ran to greet him with cheers of *"Viva la chièsa!"*

The procession was led by a *carroccio* drawn by four bulls and hung with scarlet trappings fringed with gold. Above the cart floated the banner of the Church and upon it stood eight doctors of law and eight knights, to whom the legate presented scarlet robes. The city ancients came, then the magistrates with their attendants, with much music.

Baldassare, Cardinal Cossa, entered the city on prancing horseback as befit a supreme commander of the papal *condottieri*, with a scarlet canopy, richly fringed and lined, held over his head by four young nobles acting as his grooms. There surged within him the wish that there might be some instant painting made of the entire scene and that it might be sent as instantly to Procida to cause his father to marvel at his son, commanding general of the papal armies and a cardinal of the Church.

At the city gates, to the sounds of trumpets and drums, the keys were handed to him upon a golden salver. Orations and verses in Latin and in the vulgar were proclaimed. Boys dressed as angels, singing shrill hymns, lined the streets to the cathedral and became his escort to witness his welcome by the bishop and the clergy.

To the extent that he had established the righteousness of Boniface IX in restraint of the ambitions of Milan, so did Cardinal Cossa, *legatus a Latere,* seek to control the morality of Bologna when he decreed that its prostitutes and its gambling houses operate only under paid license. Further, he undertook programs to strengthen the city's walls, ordered fortresses and citadels in the Papal States to be repaired, and all connecting roads to be mended. He dismantled the citadel at the San Felice Gate and erected a defensive castle at the Galiere Gate. The licensing of prostitutes allowed Bernaba to pinpoint the working locations of all new competition unknown to her, and allowed Palo to send his regimes in to discourage such competition. The licensing of the gambling houses, as well as the women, brought in money to the state, in which Cossa also shared out of the pope's share, thus increasing his income from both areas by about nine percent.

Otherwise, when he was not busy with defenses and taxation, he spent his time with the marchesa di Artegiana. He was besotted with her, bemooned by her. He sat silent and gaping as she would instruct him in the ways of power as if she were the Empress Livia and he a shepherd boy from the hills. Her mind dominated his, and he was as possessed by her body as she instructed him in its usages as well, teaching him new and startling sexual doxologies. She was learned about money and about politics and he soon came to accept what she suggested as durable law. When she explained public health to him, he built a large, covered sewer for the city, raised the flooring of the muddy, perpetually damp piazza, and paved the entrance to San Petronio. He built for Bologna but he had to force these benefits upon the people. He had to force them to understand that mod-

ern advantages could only be purchased with increased taxation
so that the loans from the Medici Bank that made all of the civic
progress possible could be repaid so that greater loans could be
extended.

Cossa knew he was a far-seeing governor because the marchesa, and her admirer, Bernaba Minerbetti, never ceased reminding him of the heroic work of state administration that he
carried alone on his shoulders. The Bolognese wanted it both
ways: They were proud of their up-to-date defenses, their im-
proved public health, and other modern comforts, but they
would not stop keening over the taxes that paid for the benefits.

Counseled by the marchesa, Cossa introduced a strict system
of sales and excise taxes—legal and legitimate—to be shared
with the Curia in Rome. A tax of fifty percent was imposed on
wine. Taxed bread could only be bought at appointed shops.
Gamblers, jugglers, goldsmiths, and acrobats were taxed, but
moneylenders and courtesans were exempted. Cossa became
unpopular. He raged about the ingratitude of the people while
counting his share of the taxes. City magistrates, council members, and the nobles were taxed at the same rate as everyone
else. He taxed even the outlanders who came to the city with
safe-conducts from outside rulers, and if the more powerful and
rich citizens complained that an arrangement should have been
made to exempt them from such insistent taxation, Cossa made
them into examples. Did Mantua, Padua, Parma, or Perugia
have sewer systems? he would exhort them. Were those cities
the headquarters of a papal army, which spent its pay there? Let
those who would rather suffer without such civilization move to
Mantua or Parma and pay less taxes.

While the contracting companies that were controlled jointly
by Cossa and the marchesa won the contracts for the city improvement schemes, the marchesa saw that they delivered
value. Also, while Cosimo di Medici had insisted that Cossa
accept a quarter-tithe (soon increased to a half-tithe) on the
expanded banking business that the civic projects and the presence of the papal army had created, and although Cossa partici-
pated heavily in the income from Bologna's courtesan business,
and in the branch businesses Bernaba had established in Siena,
Perugia, Mantua, and Parma, and while his share of the income

from the gambling houses was large, the bald fact was that Cossa gave *value* for his services to the cities of the Papal States, which was how he looked at it. He was probably right. What is money compared to strong public defenses, government-inspected whores and tightly supervised gambling houses? The quality of the wine might have suffered from the river water the wine merchants added to it to make up for the taxes, but people got used to that.

If Bernaba was surprised to find the marchesa di Artegiana turn up in Cossa's bed and at his side for most waking hours, she did not show it. At the first chance, when Cossa was busy elsewhere, she went to visit her old friend. There was much laughter, talk, and wine.

Soon the marchesa warmed to her subject and she outlined how Bernaba might set up a network of courtesan operations throughout the cities of the Papal States under Cossa's protection—the sources of women, how Palo might be instructed to set up protection, the organization of information at each point of sale and how a network should be formed to get the information back to Cossa in Bologna. It was not only a wonderful Sunday afternoon, it was profitable, and it formed a lasting bond between the two women, so much so that, overall, when Boniface IX died on October 1, 1404 (to be succeeded by Innocent VII), Cossa had been able to deposit 102,000 florins to his account in the main Medici bank in Florence, as a result of his stewardship of Bologna and the Papal States.

As soon as Boniface died the volatile people of Rome rose in revolt. The Colonnas demanded the return of the ancient freedoms and rights to the city, meaning that they and the other great families wanted a larger share of what Rome earned. There was so much civil turmoil and bloodshed that King Ladislas of Naples, whose astuteness and craftiness the Visconti themselves might well have envied, marched on Rome and had himself appointed as the rector of Campania and Martina for five years. He permitted the Colonna to ally themselves with him and—most disastrously to hopes for an end of the papal schism—induced Pope Innocent to promise not to agree to any plan for the union of the Church that did not include the recognition of

Ladislas' title to all of the papal realm. This was a fatal bar to the accommodation of the claims to the throne of Naples by his kinsman, the duke of Anjou, and thus made impossible the co-operation of France to end the papal schism, which had yoked two popes upon the world—Innocent VII in Rome and Benedict XIII in Perpignan, after he had defied the authority of the king of France and had moved from Avignon. Ladislas' army so enforced the peace of Rome that he was recognized as Protector of the Holy Roman Church when Pope Gregory XII was elected pope on November 30, 1406.

Gregory was an old man with many "nephews," and Ladislas, who intended to rule Italy, surrounded him with a heavy presence. To prepare for his conquest of the Papal States, which he saw as merely a bloodless transfer of power, Ladislas prodded the pope to remove Cossa from the command of the papal armies and to issue sharp public rebukes upon Cossa that he was keeping more than his share of papal income and withholding it from Rome.

Cossa was ready for an extended argument until the marchesa explained the facts to him. "Why should an old man, new in the papacy, carp about these petty matters when—over all of the years you have served—the papal Curia, the *experts* on taxation and the proper rate of cash return to the papacy, have never complained about you? Look who stands astride Rome, Cossa. Whom do you see?"

"I don't follow you, Decima."

"Ladislas! Look at the size of his army occupying Rome! Ladislas means to shunt you out of the way, as if you were some scribe in the Vatican, and to take over the command of the papal armies, then to rule Italy from Naples. What happens then? Do you flee or are you the timid servant of an old, confused pope?"

She had received an urgent letter from Cosimo di Medici that morning. He had laid the peril out before her.

"What do you think will happen to the banking relationship we have with the Church in the Papal States if Ladislas is allowed to dictate to the papacy?" the letter said. "Ladislas means to remove Cossa and if Cossa goes we will lose hundreds of thousands of gold florins of cash deposits from the Papal States. Our planning to take over Church banking will be ruined.

You've got to light a fire under Cossa. Since he is in no position to throw Ladislas out of Rome, he must be made to understand that he must defy Gregory.''

"You think that is what Gregory has in his mind?" Cossa asked her. "You think the pope would turn on a cardinal, on me? Listen, I bring them more money than all of the rest of Italy put together. Are you telling me that the pope would take a chance with an adventurer like Ladislas?"

The realization came on Cossa so fast that he was incensed by the thought. He imagined he could hear his father tell his uncles that he had always been afraid that his son's success had been based on luck, not ability. "I tried to put the boy into a safe niche where he could have a good living as a lawyer for the Church and now look at him—he posed as a soldier, as a *ruler,* but when a real soldier ordered the pope to call him to heel his luck collapsed with his courage.''

"What can I do?" he asked her. "I am the papal legate. Gregory is my pope, just as Boniface was my pope. I have to take orders. I must submit Bologna and the Papal States to Ladislas if that is what Gregory commands. What else is there to do?"

"What are you saying, Cossa?" she shouted at him. "You are a Neapolitan so you are awed by the king of Naples. Forget it! The only people who have anything to say about this are the people whose trust you have accepted—the people of the Papal States and the Bolognese.''

"If I defy the authority of the pope then anyone has the right to defy my authority. Gregory is the *pope*. He isn't a man to me, he is my *pope*.''

"Then help him! Do you think he *wants* to give away the Papal States to Ladislas? Do you think he *plans* to kill this goose with its golden eggs, which you have made so plump for him? What do you think an old man can do when he is surrounded by Ladislas' army?"

"Well—ah, I see, all right. Then it is Ladislas who oppresses me.''

"You are a *leader,* my lord. You are the cardinal, and the general, and the administrator to all of these people *after* you are the servant of the pope but, nonetheless, you owe all of them equally the salvation of your defense. When you summon the emergency meeting of the Bologna council and explain the peril that threatens their destruction, you will tell them that they must *order* you to refuse this deadly threat to their rights, even to their lives, which will make this foreign tyrant their master. I can hear your eloquence as you warn them that Ladislas will bring them double the taxation if they force you to accept the pope's command. My God, it will make you the most popular figure this city has ever known."

His jaw stiffened. "All right. I have made up my mind," he said. "I am going to summon an emergency meeting of the council and get this thing settled."

With the wholehearted support of the people of Bologna, Cossa resisted the pope's orders. He cast himself adrift from the papacy, knowing well that Gregory would reward him well when Ladislas was driven out of Rome. Just the same, for insurance, he was going to see to it that the Curia got better and better shares of the benefices and necessarily increased taxation, for only by reminding the apostolic chamber that he, Baldassare, Cardinal Cossa, was making such increased income possible could he enable it to persuade the pope not to replace him as *legate a Latere*. He would be walking on the crumbling rim of the crust of the Church if he did less.

Chapter 20

The marchesa di Artegiana was fonder of Cossa than she was of other men. Cosimo di Medici was not any part of such feeling, they were mutual extensions of each other. By the quality and nature of her life, men and women, excepting her daughters, were much the same to her. Sex, having been her grist for most of her life, was neither momentous nor interesting to her. It was her work, and there could be neither romance nor sentiment about it or about any other of her relations with men. Nonetheless, Cossa was a special man to her. The simple brutality of his ambition and the harshness of his greed comforted her. Cossa was as natural a leader as she had seen in a lifetime of hundreds and hundreds of men, including Hawkwood and Turton. The benign confidence and respect that other leaders, important men of the highest distinction, gave to him and that the masses of people gave to him had strengthened and polished his own lust to lead. The Medici had singled him out as being capable of being elected pope. She was Cossa's keeper, for the Medici, so she was expected to put him upon the throne of St. Peter. When she did there could be no end to the money. Her tithe would become an ocean of gold from a bottomless source and, because she would have made it clear to Cossa that it had been she who had won the crown for him, she would also share in his share of the fortunes that were waiting to be made by him. She would be somebody. She would have lived up to and exceeded the title the Medici had bought for her, and as her next step up the ladder, she intended to be made a duchess, with each of her daughters being named a countess.

If the marchesa felt love (a difficult conception to understand), excepting always the love she felt for her daughters, it was for status. She had waited and worked for it very long, working her dignity and self-respect to the bone to get it. It had eluded her for a long time, until the night Cosimo di Medici had come to her house for the first time. When she thought about the struggles to get within striking distance of the money, she felt momentarily exhausted and empty and she felt a wistful romantic need to fill Cossa's consciousness with all of herself. She dealt with that aberration by knowing that it was the men who were the romantics, that the women of all time had only been trying compassionately to give the men what they needed so badly, that glorious mirror-sense, that achievement of looking into another's heart and seeing oneself with the eyes of the adorer. Not that Cossa was much of a romantic. His experience with women had been constant and compulsive, enjoying the physical profits of one body then moving on to the next. However, as she worked with him, as she managed him and he became more dependent on her, she sensed his deepening need for her approval, and she knew that when he finally recognized that need he would need to call upon love, the blank-eyed mopery of romantic love, to build the echo chamber lined with mirrors for him so that as he yearned for her he would be self-fulfilling, to be able to penetrate his own dreams of self by projecting them upon her so that, by her sighs and her sheep's eyes, she would make him more adoring of Cossa. That was the man's way. It didn't seem possible, but that was the way they wanted it to be.

She would need to build him up to love slowly so that it would be the more lasting. It would be what she would want when love occurred to him, and it would be useful to her.

In a relatively short time, a pitiably short time, she thought, Cossa conditioned himself to become obsessed with love for her. Even he was aware of the willfulness of this but he had reached a plateau on his long climb. The power he carried with him kept increasing in its weight until some unconscious race memory he possessed, as all other men possessed it, told him that he must find someone worthy enough to be allowed to admire the power and himself. He pined for her when she was away from him and sighed over her when she was near.

Nonetheless, he had to be sure she was worthy. He lived with her in the present, reflected her into the glass of a fanciful future, and brooded about the possibilities of her past. She was the marchesa di Artegiana, but what did that signify? Who had been the marchese who had brought her to that title? Where were her lands? Where did she go when she told him that she must make the long journey to visit her daughters, who she said were in Florence, in Paris, and in Mainz? When he gradually made it clear to himself that he knew nothing about her, that made him fearful. He only knew she had come to him from the duke of Milan and he knew that she had been the duke's lover, but where had she been before that? What experience could have trained her to achieve such a man as that? She told him that she was an associate of Cosimo di Medici and Cossa had been careful to have Cosimo confirm that, which he did with detached admiration and relish. He had asked the marchesa about Cosimo.

"What about him?" she said. "I am fortunate enough to be paid a small commission from him for bringing new business to his bank."

"That is all?"

"Cossa! He is in*tensely* married! Besides it was I who brought him together with his only mistress."

"What about Gian Galeazzo?"

"Whomever I met before I knew you should be meaningless to you. All I really can remember about Gian Galeazzo now is that he would have taken Rome and Italy were it not for your power against him."

"The plague was the power against him."

"No! You were in his stars. I saw you there. Gian Galeazzo was guided by the stars. I served him in many ways but what he believed was my real power was that I could read his stars, and his fate was there to be seen. You were there to be seen. How else do you think I knew to go to you, if I had not seen it in Gian

Galeazzo's stars, the stars that foretold that you would keep him planning in Pavia at the center of the plague."

"So you arranged his death with astrology?" he said with mockery, himself greatly confused again.

"Cossa! Who can know who will survive any plague? I ate the same food, drank the same wine, breathed the same air, but I survived it while it killed him. His generals survived it but we were only the appendages of his power. I served him well and he was so grateful that he gave me an estate in Perugia to house me and my family."

"Why did not your husband, the marchese, provide a house for his family?"

"Ah, my dear—he has long been dead and that was in Germany."

"A marchese in *Ger*many?"

She made an impatient sound. "He was a margrave. Would you prefer me to call myself the margravine di Artegiana in Italy?"

"Artegiana isn't a German noun."

"All right! I will insist—since you insist—that you introduce me as the margravine die Koenigskuenstgewerbler!" She bugled her indignation so forcefully that he barked with laughter.

He brooded most about her when she went away from him on long trips, which she said were to visit her daughters. While she was away he threw himself into a frenzy of activity to block anxiety from his mind about what she might be doing.

To force her out of his mind and to fill his time, he moved against treason inside Bologna, ferreting out plots within plots, which always led to Nanne Gozzadini, a man to whom intriguing was as nourishment. Cossa put Gozzadini's brother to death but the succeeding plot exposed Cossa's own trusted captain, Vanello da Montefalco, so he had to die. Cossa drove Gozzadini out of Bologna to Rocca di Cento, where Cossa ran him to earth. Gozzadini's own son, Cossa's godson, was taken to the plain in front of the fort where Gozzadini hid. Cossa stood beside the boy and called out, "Gozzadini! See who is here! It is your only son, Gozzadini. Shall he live or die? Come out, Nanne. Surrender the fort or I will kill our little Gabbione, the son of your heart."

There was no answer. When a quarter-hour was gone, Cossa smiled sadly at the small boy, Gabbione, shrugged, turned to Luigi Palo, who was holding the boy, and said, "Cut his throat."

Nanne Gozzadini fled to Ferrara. The populace of Bologna sacked his palace at Cossa's orders. Bologna had peace.

As if in an exchange of justice, on the night following Gabbione's execution Cossa was stricken with ague and fever. He was fearful that his troops would hear of this and judge that God had stricken him because he had put the boy to death. While he was rational he ordered me to keep everyone out of his tent. He swooned into a coma. The marchesa di Artegiana had been in Florence conferring with Cosimo about means to consolidate the bank's growth in Bohemia. She returned to Bologna to be told by Bernaba that Cossa was dying. The marchesa went into Cossa's tent in the blackness of the early morning with her satchel of herbs and potions. She and I bathed Cossa and I am not ashamed to say that I could not stop weeping. She held the limp body in her arms and slowly fed a hot, black liquid into him. When he had taken all of it she told me to go and rest. "We can do nothing but wait," she told me. "He will sleep untroubled now. You are spent by your days and nights of nursing him. I am fresh. Rest while I wait for him here." I had been awake for two days and three nights. I hardly had command of my senses. I went to a tent and fell into sleep.

At least two years passed before I knew what happened between Cossa and the marchesa that night, but I sensed that something was wrong, so I sent Bernaba to the marchesa to learn the story. This is what happened.

At dawn Cossa came awake in a frantic flight from the demons that pursued him. He came awake screaming, "Smash their heads, Franco Ellera, be quick!" He struggled against the marchesa, putrid with fever.

"Where are you?" she whispered to him softly.

"Castrocaro!"

"What are you doing?"

He described the night of the pope's gold, the screams of the horses, the blood, and the confusion as if he were reading from a huge mural on the wall of his mind.

When I returned to Cossa and the marchesa in that battle tent he was pale and silent, but he had no fever, and the marchesa said that in two days he would be well enough to ride back to Bologna.

Chapter 21

Cossa recovered in moody silence, resenting the joy he took from the marchesa because he could not be sure that she was worthy of the monument his love had built around her. In dark flashes, he showed her his fears by his endless questioning, seeking to know the things about her that he had decided must be shadowed by guilt and sin. She ignored his morbidity. She continued his education concerning the world he had never seen, unraveling the politics of Europe for him. She told him how Wenzel, the deposed Holy Roman Emperor, was a drunkard and a murderer, how he related to his brother, Sigismund, who was in love with mirrors and every woman, and how they both related to Rupert, poor Rupert, king of the Romans. She took him through the stories of the two popes, then went on to the king of France and the University of Paris. She made clearer for him the allegiances of Ladislas of Naples and Carlo Malatesta, lord of Rimini, to Pope Gregory XII. She traced for him the positions of the Spanish, the English, and the Germans to the papal schism, and she made him see that he, himself, was only a provincial warlord when he could be a part of the great world.

He could not hear what she taught him. The more she taught him about Europe the more he had to find somehow an intimate knowledge of her past, which had brought her to such a familiarity with all of these people. In the spring of 1408, when she left Bologna again "to visit my daughters," a tour that would keep her away from him for four months, he called in Bernaba and told her that she was to find out everything about the marchesa's past.

"Why don't you ask her yourself, Baldassare?"

"She could lie to me."

"Why would she lie? She loves you. She came to you of her own accord, a grown woman. Whatever happened to her before she ever met you can have no meaning to you—why should it? It is done, and if she would have changed whatever she did because one day she would meet you, she could not know that she was going to meet you. Baldassare, hear me. The marchesa di Artegiana is a woman of great character."

"Then all you need do is to confirm that for me, Bernaba. We are not gossiping. Find out the truth and bring it to me."

Bernaba told me about it. She was worried. "He's not himself, Franco," she said. "I mean he is out of his mind. What am I going to do?"

"We'll wait. Maybe it will pass. I agree he is out of his mind on this subject."

Cossa did not see Bernaba again for two months, then he called her to the palace and demanded a report from her. She asked me what she should do. I wasn't much help. "Stall him," I told her. "Just keep him off balance until the marchesa gets back here. She knows how to handle him on things like this, and if we tell him what we know about the marchesa, he is going to blame us for knowing about her and not telling him before, and for telling him now, *and* for how terrible he is going to feel when he has the information he thinks he wants. And he would probably never forgive us."

"It is very difficult, Baldassare," she said to Cossa. "There is so little to go on."

"Are you flouting me! She is intimately connected with the princes of Europe—in Mainz, in Prague, in Florence, and in Paris."

"Well! I had no idea you wanted *that* extensive an investigation."

"I must know all about her!"

"It will be very expensive."

He took her by the shoulders and shook her. "Have you become stupid? Or are you deliberately trying to misunderstand me? I am the ruler of the Papal States of Italy! I have given you an order!"

"If you knew it was going to take all that time and travel," Bernaba said stubbornly, "how could you expect the answers in such a short time?"

"All right. I will put Palo on it."

"I don't think you want that, Baldassare. If I do it the information will be safe with me, whatever it is or may be, but if Palo does it—well, he is Palo."

"So you do think she is concealing something important. Why should there be anything to conceal? This is a routine state investigation. As her cardinal, I seek only to prevent the remote possibility of any censure by putting her true past on the record."

"Ah, well, then," she said. "If it is only routine and for the state perhaps you should put Palo on it."

His expression became deadly. "You refuse to do this?" he said.

She could read his eyes and his face. She knew he was ready to kill her or to have her killed by Palo. She sighed. "I will do it."

"Good."

"I need time."

"How much time?"

"People will need to be found and bribed. I'll have to travel. The marchesa is a brilliant woman and if she chooses to hide her past, it is possible that—"

He struck her heavily. Very slowly she regained her feet and stood before him again, betraying neither her hurt nor her hopelessness. He struck her again, then he smiled at her, that wonderful smile. "You have ninety days," he said, "beginning now."

Bernaba had stayed out of sight for almost a month when he summoned me to demand news of her. I was heavy and sullen.

"In this whole world," I told him, "we don't have another friend as good as Bernaba. But you not only struck her, you sent her on a wild goose chase. Where is she? What do you care? She could be dead."

"I am a prince of the Church!" he shouted. "I will not be talked to in this way by a slave. Are you a part of this conspiracy, or are you pleading with me to bring Palo into this, who will rip out eyeballs to get at the truth? I have had enough of this! I am going to send Palo after Bernaba."

"Cossa?"

"I will send you to the slave market at Bari!"

"Cossa," I said to him, "I think that you have become insane or you would never say such things to your friends. I think you believe that if you can learn terrible things about the marchesa, true or not, you can break some spell you think she has put upon you and make yourself her master. But after you find out the worst you want to know, even if you are reduced to having Palo deliver it to you as a fabric of lies, won't you wish you were dead?"

"Franco, my friend, forgive me, please forgive me. But I have to know about her."

"Then ask her."

"How can I ask her? What can I say—are you a spy for Ladislas? Or—what was your life before you gave your body to Gian Galeazzo? Do I ask her—since you sold Milan to me so easily will you just as easily sell me and the Papal States to Naples?"

"If that is what you want to know then that is what you must ask her."

Cossa slumped into a chair. "I could lose her."

"If you will not ask her yourself then only Palo can find out for you. After Palo is through with her either she will be dead or you will banish her. She will be gone from you. And just as desperate as you are before me today you will be more desperate trying to find her again. But if you must know, then you, yourself, must ask her—at least, that way, there is a chance for you, Cossa."

Chapter 22

The marchesa found him in the tower room of the palace. His face was gray. A sheaf of papers lay on his lap. He looked up at her hopelessly as she came into the room as if, despite his love for her, she had forced him to destroy her.

"Cossa! Are you ill?" she asked.

"I *know,* Decima. I know everything about you. You sold whores in Rome. You dealt in boys with degenerates. You told fortunes as a heretical witch, made charms and amulets, and sold poisons to vengeful women." He leaped to his feet, scattering the papers. "Don't deny it!"

She stared at him with such contempt that he almost lost the certainty of his judgment. "How can such things matter to you?" she asked him.

"How? You dare to ask me *how*?"

"You have taken money from the whores of Bologna for almost fifteen years and from the whores of the cities of the Papal States for almost four." She stared at him with distaste.

"Bernaba told you that! It is a lie! I helped her when I was a student and, out of gratitude, she set up those women to get me information to advance my position."

"You took money from whores."

"I was a boy!"

"You still take money from whores but you aren't a boy, you are a prince of the Church."

"We were talking about you, not me."

"We will soon, of course, Cossa. But not yet. Let us talk instead about the night you murdered sixteen men to steal the pope's gold."

"Franco Ellera!" he screamed in pain.

"No."

"No one else living knew that."

"Oh, yes, they did."

"Who?"

"You."

"Me?"

"Last winter, when you were dying of fever after murdering that little boy at Rocca di Cento, you told me everything. You ranted in my arms because, you told me, the men you had killed had come back to murder you."

He held up his hands to make her stop speaking.

"I said to myself," the marchesa went on, "that if that were the kind of man you are then that must be what drew me to you. What else could the son of a pirate know to do? What else could be expected of a general of *condottieri?* I saw that if you believed you owned a part of those whores you had to take money from them because that was your share, as you saw it. You didn't need the money, but that is how a pirate or pitiless *condottiere* would think. Everything is a share in the loot that costs human bodies. You came from the sea. The pope's gold convoy was no different to you than a convoy of poorly armed merchant ships. You took the pope's gold, then, as a natural conclusion for a brutalized man, you killed all the witnesses, your own people, because you feared the pope's vengeance. That explained everything to me, but it changed nothing. You are still a whoremonger and a pimp. You are still a thief and a murderer, which is rare enough work for a cardinal of the Holy Church. But we are what we become, Cossa, not what we think we are."

His eyes became opaque with pain, trying to blind himself to this vile knowledge of himself. He wanted to find just enough light to show himself to himself as he had always seen himself. Deadly things lurked beyond such light. Because he could not shut out the truth of how she saw him and how he must now see himself, he began to weep, sitting with his face clutched in his hands, so he confessed to me.

She knelt beside him and stroked his head. "I would have told you anything you wanted to know," she said to him. "If I couldn't conceal my life from myself, how could I hide it from you whom I love?" He reached out blindly to touch her cheek. "Come," the marchesa said, "it is night. I have traveled a long way and I have been too long away from your arms." She had traveled over the mountains from Florence where Cosimo di Medici had told her that his father had decided that the time had come to get the papacy for Cossa. Giovanni di Bicci di Medici's plan was now the plan of the marchesa di Artegiana, because she was expected to execute it. She had had to be severe with Cossa about his boyish anxieties. He had to be lifted into his saddle and sent off to his glory. There was a lot of money to be made.

Chapter 23

Cossa told me where, thinking about it, his mind turning like a prayer wheel ten thousand times, he had allowed his life to take a wrong turning. Where it happened, he thought, and of course he was wrong, was one winter's night when he was in bed with the marchesa at the Anziani Palace in Bologna. The eternal rat moved across the bedchamber where a single, foot-thick, half-spent candle burned at the center of the room, twelve feet away from the foot of the bed. Its melted wax piled up at its base like heaps of fallen angels. The bed stank of him and it mingled with the smell of the blind sanctity of the candle and the marchesa's faint smell, like sea moss.

She must have felt the golden hawk of her ambition, which was always perched inside her, fly in upward spirals across her chest, higher and higher from deep within her, until it was a nearly imperceptible thing in her sky, but from such an elevation as that it could see everything in the future. She listened to Cossa's hoarse, shallow breathing gradually subside. She turned toward him, brushing his arm with her breasts, and whispered into his ear, "You can be pope."

His answer was a thick, contemptuous grunt.

She waited, thinking of the enormousness of the room and of the rooms around it, all nested into the size of the palace she had taken. She willed him to answer her.

"There are already two popes," he said.

"The treasure of the Italian people is the papacy, Cossa," she said harshly. "The French have their university. The English have their kings. The Germans have the Holy Roman Emperor. The Italians must have their popes."

"They have Angelo Corrario whose ancient body is called Pope Gregory XII."

"He is Ladislas' servant! We have a pope who cannot even hold Rome because he is eighty-one years old. And de Luna, the other great pope! De Luna composes *his* ancient and tiny body—his dapper, tidy, neat, and tiny body—in Perpignan. He is Pope Benedict for the Spaniards and the Scots."

She got out of bed with one lithe movement of her long legs and pulled a fur robe over herself, a powerfully made, tall, blonde woman of thirty-seven years—youthful, with cheekbones like kneecaps and a large, soft mouth against porcelain skin. I can see her carnal glory with my mind's eye. She strode around the bed and pulled a stool close to it at Cossa's side. She looked down at his shut eyelids, rectangular upon his square, brown face. She leaned over, close to him, and spoke to him. "History has changed itself, Cossa," she said. "The people of Italy speak different languages, eat different food, and think differently from the people of the other nations, excepting that they all want an end to this long, ruinous papal schism."

He grunted.

"Do you know what this schism is doing to business in Europe, Cossa? How it is devastating the politics of the nations? Money and the power of the Church are being thrown away instead of increasing by a steady expansion of business. And, with the strength of the papacy split into halves, the nations are being ruled, more and more, by the princes. Not by popes. Not by the businessmen, who understand what is best for all. This weakening must stop. You must stop it. You must dissolve the schism by uniting the Church under one pope and seize the power that is being scattered across Europe."

"I have enough power," he mumbled.

"Power? You run a principality made up of a handful of puny city-states. You can have Europe and all its riches, don't you see that? You—their pope—can hold the balance among those opposing princes. Italy is divided by mindless armies. Germany is shattered by the warlords. England and France bleed each other, always at war with each other. One strong, shrewd pope can use all that separateness to keep them all forever off balance and peaceful.''

Cossa rolled over and propped himself up in the bed to face her, confused, as always, by her intense talk of politics. "A pope has only illusory power," he said. "He has a handful of troops. He rules a hierarchy and a clergy who are trained only to say mass, hear confessions, and extract money from the faithful, but he doesn't rule Christendom. He has no contact with the people and if he rules at all then he rules only in some symbolic way."

"Not in *some* symbolic way," she said urgently. "That is the *only* way he rules. That is what sustains the domination of anybody over anything, the mystical symbolic way alone has any meaning, and who has more symbolic meaning than the pope, who rules with the symbolic power of Christ. Cossa, that is the *lasting* power."

"Get into bed. You will be cold. You will make me cold."

"Listen to me! All the princes have is the force of arms, and when a prince dies his successor must start that force of arms all over again, or lose his place to stronger men. But when Christ died who were his heirs? The popes! A pope is the vicar of Christ on earth! The papacy is the greatest receptacle of power in history. What is power to you, Cossa? The control of men's bodies or the eternal dominion over their wills and dreams? Liberate yourself! You live for power but all of your life you have believed that power was only force. Force is temporary. Real power lives on as a great symbol in the single continuing mind of the people, nourishing the faith of the ruled in their rulers. The Church is the chalice of power from which the great popes drink. To deny the right of the popes to rule would be like denying the right of Christ to rule."

"You don't think Christ ever existed as the Franciscans say he did?" Cossa asked her sarcastically.

"Cossa, I am only a woman. You are a cardinal. *Some*one laid down the truths that men have shown they want to live by. People may not be able to absorb history but they can absorb symbols. The people who are ruled have shown that they want to hold to the symbols that they were told Christ had given to them. Christ promised them eternal life. A pope is the guardian of the gates of that eternal life as promised by Christ. That is *power,* Cossa! That is what will scatter the princes, what will rally the world around you."

"All that is just theory, Decima."

"Look back on the popes in our memory! They were strangers to Christ's promises so they became political princes. But if *you* seize the papacy, which is withering away before our faces in the heat of this newly found nationalism, if you *enforce* the power by proclaiming your allegiance to Christ's promises as popes were meant to do, then you can return the princes to where they belong in history—as vassals of the Church again. In the hierarchy of the Church you are very near to being an associate of Christ, Cossa! He is the symbol of the greatest power over the people. Take the power, Cossa!"

Cossa thought that the last they had seen of Christ was when Boniface IX, the master money changer, had personally driven Christ from the temple. As a *condottieri* general, Cossa knew that Christ was an ineffectual figure. But he knew what the papacy was and how it worked and what fortunes could be made from the throne of St. Peter. His muscular sense of greed developed greater curiosity.

"How will you make me a pope?" he asked.

"By a supreme council of the Church."

"Such a council may not be held without the authority of the pope."

"What authority, Cossa? Which pope? There are now two popes and this council must be called so that there will be only one pope."

"The Church is not a College of a pope and some council. It is the congregation of the faithful in the unity of the sacraments. That is basic canon law. The Church was built upon Christ, not on popes."

"Ah, at last you take my point, Cossa. The popes symbolize Christ, you admit at last. And now we have two used-up rival popes who are begging for the princes' support against each other, and are therefore obliged to surrender the Church to the princes. Italy is desperate. The body of the living Church will be hacked to pieces by the princes. As we may soon see, *friars* will control both small parishes and great cathedrals, the benefices of popes. Cossa, hear me! Call a council, which is the voice of the Church, because the alternative will destroy everything."

"What alternative?"

"False councils, which the princes will assemble. Estates-General. A terrible beginning of anarchic government by separate fragments of the population of Christendom—government of the people by the people themselves. Not stable papal authority and containment, nor even the iron rule of princes, but rule by the *people,* who are as hostile to the princes—with whom the Church can at least *deal*—as they will most certainly become to the popes."

"This is something I must think about, Decima."

Her eyes hardened with her heart as she thought of Cosimo di Medici, actually believing, in all of his own purity, in his sense of devout deity, that all one needed to do was offer the papacy on a platter and the nominee would reach for it eagerly and gratefully. This provincial bandit of the Church needed to be made more aware of his position on the games board. It was a mistake to set him up as the Adonis of my desiring love, she thought, because that makes men, who are naturally lazy, lazier. She would need to chill him down if they were to get anywhere with the greatest opportunity she would ever be offered by God or by man in her lifetime. "No, Cossa," she told him, "you don't need to think about it," she said. "I spoke of you in Germany to the electors. They share my view that you are the man who could end the schism. They want the schism ended because only the pope in Rome can consecrate their Holy Roman Emperor, ruler of Germany. They are seven men—the three great archbishops of the Rhine: the archbishop of Mainz, arch-chancellor of Germany; the archbishop of Cologne, arch-chancellor of Italy; and the archbishop of Trier, arch-chancellor of Burgundy, those three representing the German Church. Then the king of Bohemia, cupbearer of the emperor; the count Palatine, who is grand seneschal; the duke of Saxony, who is grand marshal; and the margrave of Brandenburg, who is grand chamberlain—seven men whose single reason for collecting is to elect the king of the Romans who will be crowned as emperor by one single pope. I was with d'Ailly and Gerson in Paris and they—and remember they are French—agree that you are the single figure in the Church around whom the Gallicans can rally to end the schism if the reform of the Church will follow immediately. Florence holds the same views and, with Spina as the pope's ambassador to Naples, that means my daughter, Rosa, is there, and she can prepare Spina to prepare Ladislas to take his armies into the field against you so that while the prelates pray and orate for the end of the schism at our council, it will be you who will be defending the Church against a mortal enemy in whose interest it is to continue the schism forever because, with the world behind one pope, not split among three, he could never conquer Italy.''

"You talked about *me* with strangers? As if I were some boy you were trying to find a place for?''

"They are not strangers to me. They are pivot men in Europe who have investments to protect. What have you suddenly imagined happens when there is a need for a new pope, in this case one unified papacy? Do you think that the people who run Europe do not confer with one another so that the man most suitable to them be chosen?''

"Aaah—get into bed.''

"When we have this settled.''

"All right! It's settled. A council will be called.''

"Where?''

"You must have thought about that.''

"Pisa, I think. I was born in Pisa.''

"Pisa, then. Now—get into bed.''

"When will you call the council?''

He closed his eyes and lay very still to prevent his anger from dissolving the erection that had grown upon him because he had been staring at her beautiful breasts and at the sanctuary within that V of black hair above a passage that must be made of writhing snakes and gripping chains contained by catapults. He said, ''The two schismatic popes must be advised that a council is to be called.''

"Neither will answer.''

"I will also need time to assemble quorums of the Colleges of

Cardinals from the schismatic Curias. They will send out proc-
lamations of the convening of the council and set its starting
date. If everything works out, the council will meet in one year's
time."

She stripped the fur robe from her body and stood over him.
"Ah, God," she said, "there has never been such an exciting
man as you," then fell upon him.

Chapter 24

At the end of my life—I am nearer the end than the beginning—in these calm, late-autumn days, I have been befriended by the marchesa's daughter, Maria Giovanna. She talks to me for hours as I sit in the garden at Cosimo's great house, doing my needlepoint. She remembers her mother and her sisters. Yesterday she remembered the exciting days before the Council of Pisa.

In the sweet summerlike October of 1408, Rosa Dubramonte was twenty-two years old, the youngest of the four daughters of the marchesa di Artegiana. She had a passionate nose whose thrust was surrounded by a lascivious face of certain beauty, all supported by a professionally effulgent body. Maria Giovanna was the most womanly of the daughters, Maria Louise the most cunning, Helene the most vividly intellectual, but Rosa was the most intelligent. She thought her way through life's illusions and sensations and would accept none of them, unless at her mother's command, and unless it gave her good reason. Rosa had a mind that could herd mice at a crossroads, the Irish abbot, MacMahon, had once said of her.

She rode with an escort of six armed men from the establishment of her protector, Piero, Cardinal Spina, through a countryside of vineyards and olive groves. Among the vineyards there were trees, including a great number of pomegranates, which punctuated the distance with vivid color. She rode under a broad scarlet straw hat, wearing slippers embroidered with pearls, and a light yellow riding cloak over a lime-green Chinese silk dress. She was traveling from Naples to a family conference in Perugia, which had been called by her mother. Her manufactured blondeness flashed in the wine-light of the lantern sun, which hung at the eastern edge of the world. She would soon be with her family. They were almost across the valley, which was more than a thousand feet below the Etruscan walls of Perugia. Little of the town could be seen, but soon the climb would begin up toward its frescoes, up the steep road that looped through the olive groves.

The marchesa's house in Perugia was set beyond the Prior's Palace near the eastern wall of the city, standing at the end of a straight tree-lined drive whose entrance was flanked by stone figures of Juno and Venus. The main building was in two stories, built partly in travertine, partly in Assisi limestone, with red and white marble from Bettona. It had a fine entrance doorway with a round arch that was richly decorated by the Sienese artist Shanon Philippi, and in the lunette was a statue of St. Ercolano, patron saint of Perugia, holding the hand of St. Catherine of Pisa. There were lower recessed wings on either side of the central building; each end of these was flanked by curved buttresses. The whiteness of the architectural rhythm was emphasized by the stands of tall cypresses behind it.

Within the house the *piano nobile* was divided into rooms for each of the marchesa's daughters, each with a cove ceiling, arranged around a cruciform hall. Behind the house, at the garden end, which was the top of the cross, a square salon had been formed from which a line of rooms extended to the left and right along the garden. The walls and ceilings of these rooms into the salon were decorated with frescoes by Giacomo Ricardo Blaca, painted at the zenith of his powers. Each fresco, a masterpiece of *trompe l'oeil,* made each room appear to have been placed within open arcades overlooking the marchesa's native Pisan countryside on a perfect summer's day. Level valleys soothed beneath blue-tinged mountains with vineyards, olive groves, and chestnut trees offering shade and peace.

The main room was placed at the base of the cross. Here Blaca had achieved a supreme triumph of illusionistic painting, in which an enormous figure of the marchesa, clothed in colored silk, soared across the painted sky in a vastly calming composition, with the imagined heavens around her filled with a host of cherubim flying or seated upon banks of clouds, all of their small figures in the likenesses of the marchesa's daughters as babies.

On the walls of the great rectangular room were four life-sized portraits on each side, the Blaca frescoes depicting the same infants grown into the glowing beauty of their childhood, all trooping away from the garden entrance; but, as they came nearer the main door, they were each seen as having grown into youthful maturity, striding out to find precious moments of their lives. It hadn't been like that in their lives but it gave them joy to see that that was how Mama wanted it to be remembered.

The family assembled at noon in the main room, all crowding around the marchesa, who had arrived last, from Bologna. All of them were fashionably turned out: long, close-fitting laced or buttoned dresses with short-waisted bodices and wide, low V necks with wide belts under the arms and breasts. The border of the marchesa's skirt was gay with brocade. Each woman wore a small, fashionable dagger at her girdle. They pulled chairs into a small circle so that the girls could face their mother.

"Frederick of Austria sends you *special* greetings, Mama," Maria Louise said. "I had no idea you were up to something with him."

"I can't tell you what it means to me to see all of you together," the marchesa replied blandly.

"And how wonderful to have a few days away from the insatiable Spina," Rosa murmured.

"It isn't so much that Spina is insatiable," the marchesa observed, "but that he is so determined to get his money's worth."

"He wears a different disguise each time he does it!"

"Rosa! You know that is necessary so that he may feel that perhaps you are not sure that it is he in bed with you so that he may deny it should you bring it up later. He is a cardinal, after all."

"Really, you don't know, any of you. Spina is so devious that he will not allow a mirror in our bedroom, because if he saw himself reflected in one of those disguises he would have to accuse me of infidelity."

The sisters all exploded with laughter.

"Sometimes I wish I had a lover like that," Maria Giovanna said. "My Cosimo is so careful that he won't make love in the daytime unless the shutters and blinds are closed and the curtains are drawn. Oh, don't misunderstand, please. He is merely very, very careful about everything."

"He has a great deal to be careful about," the marchesa said. "What is happening in Paris, Helene?"

"Never mind Paris. Paris will keep. Please, Mama, why are we all here?"

The marchesa smiled a dangerous smile. "We are going to end the schism in the Church," she said, "and elect Baldassare Cossa as the one, true pope. And we are going to be richer and more influential than ever before."

"Have you told Cosimo we will end the schism, Mother?" Maria Giovanna asked.

"It was his father's idea and they will finance everything so that, when it is done, the Medici Bank will be the only bankers for the Church, which will make them the richest bankers in the world. And this time we are going to have a real share in the action—a tithe of the bank's share and a tithe of Cossa's share as pope."

Her audience was unable to speak, or perhaps they were counting. Helene found her voice first. "No woman has ever negotiated such fees from her protectors," she said with awe.

"Mama is the greatest courtesan who ever lived," Rosa said proudly.

"Oh, Mama!" Maria Giovanna cried, "you are the idol of all womanhood."

"Where do you begin with such a task?" Maria Louise asked, "and how do we fit into it?"

"You are the keys to it," the marchesa said. "As Cosimo has pointed out, Cossa controls the support of the canon lawyers, the theologians, and the juridical faculty at the university. They are going to publish and justify—before the fact—the decision of the cardinals of both obediences to call a council of the Church."

"Where will it happen?" Helene asked.

"Pisa. Everything is right for Pisa on this. It is close enough by sea from France and yet it is Italy, close by Florence for the convenience of the Medici. Right now, Cossa is organizing the Bolognese jurists to lead an embassy to Florence to secure their agreement for a council at Pisa. Cosimo has everyone prepared in Florence. Helene will need to engage the University of Paris to persuade the king to intercede with all the princes of Europe to announce their neutrality toward the present popes."

"Yes, Mama," Helene said.

"When the two popes are neutralized and left without any partisan support, they can be backed into supporting our council for the election of a single pope. What about that, Helene? Will the university take the position that only a pope may call such a council or do you agree with us that one may be called by a congress of the cardinals from both obediences?"

"I think it is safe to say," Helene answered carefully, "that the university will advise the king that the head of the Church is Christ, not any pope. The chancellor will hold, I am *quite* sure of it, that only the Church can assemble a council. I shall point out to Gerson that the Council of Jerusalem was not presided over by Peter but by its bishop, James."

"Excellent!"

"I think the principle you want to see applied here, Mama, is that the right of the Church was never abrogated. That right is to be exercised not only by bishops and cardinals but by all believers, who, by reason of their urgent exhortation, possess the right to represent all those who work for the unity of the Church."

"You are *sure,* dear?"

"Well, I am sure that Gerson enjoys the pleasure of demonstrating the superiority of theology over canon law. Oh, it will be *quite* legal to convoke a council without the authority or intervention of the popes."

"Most of the electors will side with Cossa," Maria Louise said. "But that still leaves Rupert, king of the Romans, who supports Gregory, and Sigismund, king of Hungary, who only wants to end the schism and who doesn't hold any opinion on anything for longer than fifteen minutes and particularly if a woman walks through the room while he is pondering it."

"Then we know how to cope with Sigismund," the marchesa said. "But I would prefer to avoid the direct approach right now."

"There is Pippo Span," Maria Louise said. "He is the Hungarian army general who is closest to Sigismund."

"Yes. Rosa would like him."

"Why should I be the one to like him?"

"You know you adore young men."

"Mama!" Rosa blushed beautifully. Rosa was the young woman her mother would have been, her mother often thought. Being a courtesan was a temporary thing in Rosa's mind, like a childish garment that is cast away when it is outgrown. Rosa wanted what Mama believed that she, herself, would never attain. Rosa wanted love—romantic, true, pure, young love. Maria Giovanna wanted power as her lover. Maria Louise wanted property, possessions, and status. Helene wanted to be ravished by intellects, and Mama wanted all of those things and had possessed them all, except love.

Servants brought in hare cooked in a rich sweet and sour sauce of vinegar, sugar, chocolate, and raisins. It was Tuscan food. There were hearts of artichoke cooked with mushrooms and cauliflower in a sauce of milk, butter, and cheese. They drank old red wine made of Sangiovese grapes. The marchesa said, "The Medici must be kept far in the background on this, of course."

Everyone sagely agreed.

"Florence wants one pope so badly," Maria Giovanna said, "that they will agree on Pisa. And I think Gino Capponi is the man to work for the desertion of Gregory by his cardinals. He is only a Florentine, not a Sicilian, but he is nearly as devious as Spina."

"And Benedict?" the marchesa asked.

"He has problems," Helene said, "seven of his cardinals have already left him. He is a difficult, stingy old man. An eighth cardinal has just disappeared. The ninth died. The tenth, Louis de Bar, who told me all this, has returned to the court in France. Only three cardinals are left and Benedict doesn't trust one of them."

"Cosimo's father must know that, of course. That could be why he has chosen to act. What will Benedict do?"

"De Bar says he will raise up five more cardinals. He wants eight for his grand council at Perpignan."

"*His* grand council?" the marchesa asked indignantly. "Cosimo's father must have known about that, as well. Why are people so secretive? When will *his* council happen?"

"November, de Bar thinks."

"Then we can't hope to be first. So we must be the biggest. By all means, Maria Giovanna, help Gino Capponi to persuade those old men to desert. You are so good with old men."

"Yes, Mama." Maria Giovanna wanted to be all the things her mother was. She wanted Mama's instant brutality, the impatience of her greed, the sensations of her lusts, and her knowledge. Maria Giovanna often dreamed of hearing her mother's last will being read, to learn with exaltation that Mama had left to her her soul.

"What of Ladislas' new war?"

"The new war will help everything," the marchesa said contentedly. "It will show Cossa as the strongest of all of the cardinals, the only actual defender of the Church, out on the field of battle risking his life while the rest of them ponder the schism in Pisa."

Chapter 25

The tiny, stately, neat-as-a-button Pope Benedict XIII descended with grace and splendor from the Castle of Perpignan to the Church of Sainte-Marie-la-Réal to open his grand council on November 15, 1408. His nine cardinals were present with four patriarchs, three archbishops, thirty-three bishops, and many prelates from Gascony, Savoy, and Lorraine. Had there not been a royal prohibition on attendance at the council there would have been many more from France. Some did come, in disguise to elude the guards set to stop them on the roads. Including the foreign ambassadors there were fewer than three hundred people present. The pope himself celebrated the mass, the Dominican bishop of Oleron preached and King Martin of Aragon was the Protector.

The first and second sessions were ceremonial but, at the opening of the third, Benedict rose and spoke on the importance of ecumenical councils, regretting that the Babylonian confusions of the time prevented him from calling one while he was under the domination of France. He had assembled this council, he told them, to reform the Church and to terminate the unfortunate schism. He explained that in order to refute the lies that had been spread against him he had written a full account of all of his works up to the date, which Cardinal de Chalant would now read.

It took from the third session to the ninth session to get through the accounting.

On November 21, the pope asked for the advice of the assemblage as to his future conduct toward the resolution of the Great Schism, feeling that he might safely trust this with them, inasmuch as the majority present were as Spanish as he was. The answers were supposed to be forthcoming on the twelfth of December but, due either to the difficulty of the question or to the long deliberation necessary, there was no reply until February 1, 1409. By that time, most of the members attending the council had departed. Only ten were left. They resolved that Benedict was free from all reproach for heresy or schism but that he should send a delegation to the Council of Pisa empowered to effect his abdication in case of the removal of his rival, Gregory XII, for any cause.

The tiny, ancient, outraged pope answered them. "I shall do none of these things," he said. He threatened to imprison Cardinal de Chalant, who led the delegation, where he would never see the light of the sun again. In his reply to the world at large, and in particular to the delegations from Pisa who offered him safe-conduct for thirteen months, he threatened to excommunicate anyone who took any measures to his prejudice or who dared to elect a new pope while he was alive.

Again, at the New Year, 1409, the king of Naples maddened himself into a warlike intensity, urged on by Cardinal Spina, who called for the protection of his pope, the cardinal having been urged on by Rosa Dubramonte as her part in the marchesa's plan. For a handsome consideration, and to Cossa's consternation, Pope Gregory had transferred a deed to the Papal States to Ladislas and the king now had to attempt to take possession of the holding before reaching out to grab Florence and Pisa. He massed an army of ten thousand cavaliers and a large body of foot soldiers in December to march to besiege Baldassare Cossa at Bologna.

Cossa had turned them back by March, but Ladislas' army kept Cossa pinned down, preventing him from attending all but the last three sessions of the Council of Pisa. Nonetheless, the council was well advised, daily, of Cossa's sacrifices in their defense. They knew because the marchesa, her daughters, and her agents told them that only Cossa's bravery and brilliance as the greatest soldier in Europe stood between them and their humiliation by a bloodthirsty king.

The lovely old city of Pisa was under Florentine control, so anything that would bring money into the city was welcomed by the Medici. The Pisan Duoma was one of the wonders of the world. Where could there be found so fitting an edifice for the meeting of such a council? Giovanni di Bicci di Medici marvelled.

After the war with Florence, which followed the transfer of the city, by Gian Galeazzo Visconti, to the Florentines, six thousand Pisans had joined Ladislas' army, so there was plenty of accommodation for the congress of the spiritual and lay worlds. Embassies from England, France, Bohemia, Poland, Portugal, and Cyprus attended. The entourages of the dukes of Brabant, Anjou, Burgundy, Austria, Lorraine, and Holland were there. Almost every kingdom in Christendom was represented, excepting those of Scandinavia.

There were 14 cardinals in Pisa on the day before the council opened, and 4 patriarchs, 10 archbishops, 70 bishops and the representatives of 80 more, the leaders of 70 monasteries in addition to 120 who appeared by deputy, 300 abbots, and 200 masters of theology. The universities of Oxford, Paris, Bologna, and Prague were represented, together with the generals of the Jacobins and the Cordeliers. Of the more than 600 ecclesiastics who were present, two-fifths were French. The benevolent and guiding hand of Baldassare, Cardinal Cossa was apparent over all of them as the marchesa and her agents reached out to all of the holy men spreading his messages, intentions, wishes, and all positive interpretation of these.

On the morning of March 25, 1409, the council assembled at the Church of St. Martin, south of the Arno River. Arrayed in their albs and copes, crowned with white miters, the cardinals and prelates formed in procession and moved, lurching and swaying with lawyers' solemnity, across the Ponte Vecchio until they turned off to the Piazza degli Anziani. Skirting the archbishops' palace, they reached the cathedral, which had been completed nearly three hundred years before. On the long seat at the level of the great altar sat the cardinal-bishops, the cardinal-priests, and the cardinal-deacons. Behind them was the picture of Christ painted by Cimabue. Facing the cardinals were the royal ambassadors who were prelates. Behind them, on both sides of the nave, glorious with their layers of black and white marble, were the seats extending down to the door of the church for prelates in order of their seniority. Stools were provided for envoys from chapters and convents.

When all had taken their places the Mass of the Holy Spirit was celebrated by the aged cardinal of Palestrina. The council was opened.

After the second meeting, after the prelates knelt with their heads to the ground, miters before them for the length of the *Miserere,* after the deacon and subdeacon read the litany, after a prayer from the cardinal of Palestrina, they rose. The cardinal of Saluces, habited as a deacon, read the Gospel. The *Veni Creator* was sung by the entire assembly, kneeling, then they put on their miters and took their seats. The business of the council had begun.

The presiding cardinal deputed two cardinal-bishops, two archbishops, and two bishops to discover whether the popes, Benedict XIII and Gregory XII, were present at the council. Accompanied by notaries they went to the doors of the cathedral and called out to Pedro de Luna and Angelo Corario in Latin and in the vulgar, demanding that they appear at once either in person or by their fully empowered proctors. The call was repeated three times without result.

The two popes defaulted again on the third and fourth summonings at these sessions.

Chapter 26

While the council deliberated in sanctity, day by day, the marchesa and her apparatus entertained its cardinals, archbishops, and bishops by night. Spina was Pope Gregory's legate to the court of Naples, but Rosa visited with Maria Giovanna in Pisa to help out with the pleasuring. They used Mama's "little house" in Portogiorgio, using Giovanni di Bicci di Medici and his son Cosimo as their set pieces for the entertaining, prelates always having been comforted by the presence of bankers.

Helene had rented a small house adjacent to the quarters of the French delegation to the council. In Paris, in January, she had come to an agreement with Pierre d'Ailly that, if Cossa could organize the council to give him the papacy, Cossa would make the bishop a cardinal in return for d'Ailly's active support. To establish his goodwill under the agreement, d'Ailly made an eloquently powerful appeal, before Pisa was convened, for a general council of the Church, which was heard across Europe from his sounding board of the Synod of Aix. He was a gifted orator and he asserted that, since the Church had both a natural and a divine right to its unity, it could and *must* call a council without papal sanction. D'Ailly, confessor to the king of France and treasurer of the St. Chapelle, was one of the richest churchmen at Pisa, a magnet who drew cardinals to Helene's dinner parties. At more than one of these dinners d'Ailly said to the engaged and thoughtful cardinals, "This schism has been a form of civil war within the Church and there is not a churchman today who does not cry out for its end. This council is the means to end it, to be sure, but when the man is named by you as the unitary pope to bind up the wounds of Christendom, he must not be a pastoral pope. He must be a lawyer, an executive, and a trained fighter who can weave the Church into one whole piece again and he must be a strong, determined man of experience with battle to be able to quell the partisan feelings among Christians."

When he was asked who such a man could be he would grow thoughtful, stroking his beard. "I would say there is only one such man," he would answer. "Baldassare Cossa, who, even now, is beating away the threat of Ladislas so that we may complete the business of this convention."

Each of the marchesa's daughters had different spokesmen for Cossa on different nights—and there was not a night throughout the entire session of the council that each of them did not entertain strenuously. Rosa read to six cardinals, two archbishops, and four bishops a letter from Cardinal Spina, which she had written herself, but with which Spina seemed to consecrate Cossa as "the savior of the Church who waits for our call from the field of battle to do his duty." Cosimo di Medici called upon the cardinals for European stability, which had not existed since the schism had fractured the body of the Church. "The scourge of schism can be driven from that body," he would tell dinner assembly after assembly, "but what have we gained unless the new pope, alone upon the throne of St. Peter, is able to marshal the powers and weaknesses of the organization of his Church into one seamless garment. That takes a strong man, Your Eminences, a soldier rather than a pastor, an executive rather than a theologian."

Maria Giovanna or the marchesa would lift Cossa's name into a dinner table conversation and Cosimo would seize upon it, brandishing it like a flag, telling them that "Cossa understands the problems of business. Cossa is a student of finance. Cossa is the only tailor we have to sew up the ragged purse of the Church."

If prelates were firm and continually vocal in the cause of Cossa's candidacy, the marchesa made certain they knew that Cossa would not forget such advocacy and that, when it was in his power, he would reward real support with red hats. By this she moved such key churchmen as Alaman Adimar, archbishop of Pisa, John of Portugal, Lucius Aldebrandinus, and Guillaume Fillastre to look for Cossa's gratitude. Large amounts of Medici money were spent. Splendid gifts were made: Henricus Minutulus, a Neapolitan cardinal, was given two Irish stallions and six blooded brood mares from France. Francesco Ugoccione of Urbino, cardinal-priest of the Sainted Quatro Coronati, was given a set of female triplets from the western highlands of Ethiopia. De Anna, Caracciola, and Maramaur preferred to accept future benefices in return for their votes for Cossa.

I was neatly split in half by Cossa and the marchesa. I spent half my time in Pisa—Bernaba was doing an enormous business there, the marchesa wanted me to attend at least part of every party she or her daughters gave, attend behind screens and at concealed listening posts so that I could hear everything that was being said and done on Cossa's behalf and then report all of it back to him in the field.

Cossa listened to my reports with his fullest attention and sometimes he would sigh and say, "I don't know how the Church ever came to be seen as a spiritual organization."

Chapter 27

Cossa and I had the war to fight. Ladislas' army would press north and we would fling it south again. During one such afternoon in the field Cossa's forces separated eleven units of lances from the body of the Neapolitan army and demolished them, smashing heads as if they were summer melons. The heat of the battle was succeeded by a damp, cold night. Cossa fell ill. His chest and arms became so weakened that he would not move himself and seemed to be at the point of death. I held him down, and to prevent the whole camp from knowing our most guarded secret, I had to bind Cossa's mouth with a cloth, so much did he rave on about dead men and the pope's gold.

The illness lasted in diminishing force for three days, then, at last, he could travel. I took him to Siena where he was waited upon by the count of San Severino and Moergeli, the famous Swiss herbalist. When Cossa felt strong enough again, we picked up the advance of his army, which was following the Neapolitans. We traveled to Radicofani, then crossed by way of Abbadia and the town of Piano where, in a green meadow, the people made them shelters of brushwood and received the cardinal with cheering and rejoicing. He gave them his blessing from horseback then rode on to Acquapendente, then to Bolsena, which had been a populous town before it was destroyed by Hawkwood. Only its rich soil, the convenient lake, and its position on the road to Rome had saved it from complete destruction. As we rode toward Orvieto, I told Cossa about what he had babbled in his sickness. Cossa said, "It must be that we live in many places at once. What you tell me I said is so real to us that I must have been there as I said it to you here in a delirium."

The next day we came to the rocky mountain, which was about six stades high, rising in the middle of a valley. The plateau on top was about three miles around. Cliffs, none less than twenty ells, were its walls. Ladislas had hit the town five days before, leaving half-ruined towers and crumbling rubble, but the church of the Blessed Virgin, inferior to no church in Italy, stood intact in the middle of the city with its walls and floor of varicolored marble, its wide, high facades filled with statues, whose faces stood out from the white marble as if alive. Cossa led his men to the episcopal palace where he went to bed at midafternoon and slept until midnight.

I sat at Cossa's bedside until he awoke. "They have a pretty good cook here," I told him. "He's no Bocca but he's better than anything we've had since we left Bologna—whenever that could have been."

"I'm not hungry," Cossa said. "What else?"

"Four women are staying here. They're not town women. The kitchen people say they just came in here yesterday and took over. They've been throwing a lot of money around."

"Women?" Cossa said. "Alone?"

"They're alone inside this palace, if that's what you mean. They have a troop of soldiers in the north courtyard, maybe fifty men."

"Well, I woke up too late to do anything about four women, but at least the idea makes me hungry. Tell the cook I'm coming down."

In the anteroom before the dining hall, Cossa found the duchess of Milan seated on a sofa facing the door as he entered. Two ladies-in-waiting were standing behind her; one was beside her on the sofa.

"Good evening, My Lord Cardinal," the duchess said, and at that moment the ladies withdrew from the room. Cossa stood still with astonishment. All at once, again, he was bewitched by the demanding sexuality of the woman. The inexplicable feeling returned to him, which he had spoken to me about that afternoon, about separate places, or separate worlds, which the human mind is capable of inhabiting simultaneously with other places. Surely each time he saw this woman he had left reality behind? Hallucinating under the power of the loose lasciviousness of her mouth and the feverish glitter of her eyes and the way she seemed to offer her body and withdraw it at the same instant. They had had only two encounters before tonight: sixteen years before in Perugia, six years ago in the tower above Milan, and she was still compellingly sensual, even if time and the Visconti blood had left hawk's marks on her face.

"The world has stopped," he said.

"Of the two times we were together, only once was it an accident," she said. "Now again, as the last time, I had to talk to you."

"Speak quickly so that we may return to our destiny," he said.

"When it was confirmed to me by Filargi, the archbishop of Milan, that the Council of Pisa was on the verge of electing you as their pope, I was so distraught that I swooned away for two days. I could not believe that you would allow such an imprisonment to happen to you."

"You could not believe that I could be pope?" he asked.

"I could believe in an instant that all the world was capable of pressing upon you to make you agree to be pope, but I could not find it within any sanity that you would accept giving your life over to saying endless masses, to mumbling perpetual benedictions morning and night, to wrapping yourself inside the stink of sanctity."

"I do not see it that way," he lied.

"You are a man, and you are a great soldier. There is nothing more for you to be."

He tried to make light of it, but the words that she rained upon him began to shake him. He had never thought of the papacy except as a business, but what she said it was was what it had been even for Boniface—even for Boniface. They would ordain him and he would spend the rest of his life within a cloud of holy

incense disputing with old men about the number of angels on a
pinhead. They would demand that he confess to them every day
so that he could be purified to accept communion every day. He
could not contemplate that. He had too little to confess, perhaps
merely something like never telling his father about what rested
in Carlo Pendini's grave, and too much time left to waste it on
ecclesiastical nonsense.

"You loved me," she said. "Your body said you loved me.
We have a greater destiny together than the papacy."

"My bones creak," he said. "I am lame with gout."

"We can rule Italy."

"I have come upon you too quickly tonight. I can only think
of one thing, one close, passionate thing—not shadows in the
distance."

"My Lord Cardinal," she said with urgency. "If Pisa dis-
solves this schism—if France agrees to go along with that sacred
notion—they will be intent only upon the reform of the Church.
What you desire from a papacy will be ignored. When they elect
you, they will do so believing that they control a model pope—
a disciplined lawyer and soldier who by their special conjuring
will have been transformed into a devoutly religious pope, stroking away the Christian disappointments of Europe. You, a man
trained to dip his hands into the treasure chests of the Church,
a man to whom lust is far more natural than piety, will have to
turn your back upon your life. You would move and speak only
as they told you to move and speak. Your freebooting days will
have been done."

He stared at her, his desire for her building higher.

"My lord, hear me." Her face hardened with her will. "I offer
you command of the Milanese armies. They are still loyal to me,
commanders and troops. My sons are being prepared to show
their disloyalty and to go along with ambitious men who are not
Visconti. You are being backed into a corner. Deny the Council
of Pisa their choice and you will be cast into a corner of oblivion
within the Church. You need what I have. I need what you have.
We will share everything. You will cast out the interlopers and
you will retrain my sons to be what their father was. Ruler of
the north of Italy you will be, and ruler of more than that if you
but choose it."

"Leave the Sacred College?" he said. "Give up my place at Bologna?"

"Cossa, I speak to you of *real* power. You will leave nothing. You will give up nothing. We will lay down the terms of the existence of the Church and if you wish to be first among the cardinals, they will confer that upon you to win our favor. You will be the temporal ruler of Italy. And that is your true meaning. Combined with the gold of Milan, and with the force that it can buy, you will tell them what it is you want, not the other way round."

His mind began to soften. He almost had agreed, mindlessly, with the marchesa and Cosimo because his father had imprinted upon his purpose long ago that he was being sent away to become a lawyer so that he could go to great heights in the Church. He had put the two outsides together, sides which were in no way any part of him, and he had accepted the bankers' dream of a merchant's world because the marchesa had sold it to him.

If he were to accept the papacy he might as well agree to become an alchemist or a werewolf. But he needed time to think about the destination that this woman was offering to him. They would become intertwined if he agreed. There could be bitter troubles in that. Besides, if he told her right now that he would accept what she offered that would be the end of love-making for this night and perhaps for the many nights to come.

While she lay asleep in the darkness before dawn the next morning, he crept out of her room, dressed, woke me and was out, riding off at the head of his lances before she awoke.

Chapter 28

The marchesa di Artegiana went from Pisa to join Cossa to brief him on what had been accomplished on his behalf at the council. It was the second such journey she had made since the meetings had begun. She spent an afternoon and a night with him at Montanta, a walled hill town off the beaten way between Siena and Viterbo, protected by cliffs, with its main piazza slanting upward, houses huddling around a church that hugged the skirts of a towering castle where Cossa waited for her.

They were in a room with brilliant, bare white walls. She was a good briefing officer. She reported on the finances—she had insisted that Cossa put up one-fifth of the money needed, "to marry all of them in the enterprise"—then she gave him a tally of his support and opposition among the cardinals, with her analysis of the state of mind of the general council, which, she said, was intent upon Church reform, at least the French were, and they dominated the meeting. She detailed the several current European national positions as these could affect his candidacy and as they could present problems after his election. She delivered head counts of the informal caucuses within the Sacred College, then gave him her own estimation of how the election would go. She told him, last, that Sicily had been rejoined with the Kingdom of Naples. When she had finished she said simply, "This time next month you will be pope."

"You can never be sure of such things," he said dryly.

"We can be sure. We *are* sure. It is done."

"Do I not have the right to change my mind?" he said. "To say, flatly, that if they offer it, I won't accept it?"

"No joking, please," she said. "This is important business."

"Listen, Decima. I am grateful for all you have done on this thing and you can be sure I'm going to see that the money you believe you have lost will be made available to you in some other way. But I have thought deeply about this and I am not the right man to be a pope. I am a soldier, not a reformer. I am a lawyer, not a priest. They want a religious man and that certainly leaves me out. The whole thing, the way you have organized it, is the greatest kind of compliment to you. You have accomplished the impossible, but if I took that job it would destroy me."

She clung to the necessity to appear calm. She felt ill enough to need to vomit, but she had to remain serene and in charge of what they were saying to each other. The expression that went out to him from her huge dark-blue eyes, behind which chaos danced drunkenly, was neither pleasant nor unpleasant. "Have you thought of how what you have just said could affect Cosimo and the other bankers of Europe? Do you have any idea of how this is going to hit the investments of d'Ailly and the king of France and the archbishop of Mainz and all the other people who have bet fortunes on you to have this schism over?"

"I am sorry about that," he said dryly. "Let them make other plans with some other puppet."

"Cossa! For Christ's sake! You will make enemies in the Church whom you will never be able to overcome. There are rich, powerful men waiting for you in Pisa now who expect you to make them cardinals."

"Too bad."

"What are you going to do when they come after you?"

"I'll think of something. I do have a few thousand soldiers, don't I?"

"Cossa—listen to me—no one is *meant* to be pope," the marchesa said desperately. "But when a man devotes his life to the service of his Church so successfully that his cardinal-peers choose him and elect him pope—then he serves."

"Stop playing me like a fish, Decima. We have a business

arrangement. You and Cosimo outmaneuvered and outslicked the cardinals and the princes and the businessmen—who don't give a damn who is pope so long as the common policy is to eliminate the schism. Why not? It was good policy for you and Cosimo. You get a tithe of my share and you probably have a tithe of Cosimo's share and we can be sure that any businessmen who want to do business with the new setup would have to pay you off. Never mind. Cosimo wants the Church's banking. Let me do it my way, let me put my own man in as pope and I'll see that the Medici get what they want. Cosimo's way isn't the only way. I have a better way. You'll make even more money when we do it my way."

She wanted to die. For the first time in all her years on God's earth she wanted to die.

Cossa had been thinking of the alternatives ever since he had left Catherine Visconti. He would need the leverage of an enormous amount of money if he ever expected to achieve a kind of equality with Visconti, then maintain it until he did not need her anymore for the conquest of Italy, and he would never need her to handle the German politicians. Slowly, his plan for wealth, which would get him greater power when he agreed to take over the armies and the fortunes of Milan, had evolved and shaped itself.

"First of all, I would hate to be the reformer who tries to take away from those cardinals and bishops what they have considered to be their own for a thousand years. But a mild pass at reform has to be made. A very religious, saintly, holy man has to be propped up at the top where all Christendom can watch him pray while the reformers are carrying on the usual systematic looting inside the Church. That saintly fellow certainly isn't me, Decima. Or am I wrong again?"

"You mean it. You mean all of it."

"When did I ever lie to you?"

"Who is going to tell Cosimo di Medici?"

"It depends on what you tell him, doesn't it? Look here, my darling woman, because of all the work you've done in Pisa, when I go into that conclave as a voting cardinal, I'll be in a position to name the next pope. Before I make him pope, I'll make sure that he knows who got it for him. We will make a deal. He'll do all the praying and the swaying in the processions and the confessing, while I run the show for him. I will be the first among his cardinals, because he won't be able to operate the Church without me. I will run his Curia and the benefices and be in charge of the taxes. Now are you beginning to follow me?''

He would be his own man instead of being everyone's lackey, Cossa thought, marveling over his own ingenuity. He would not need to take the marchesa's offer or Catherine Visconti's offer. He had always been within tantalizing reach of the papal purses for twenty years. He knew that the man who controlled the pope controlled the papal armies and the pope's purse. The world of the bankers, princes, businessmen, and ecclesiastical plotters would need to rally around him or be punished by his indifference and, through him, the indifference of the new and saintly pope.

"Cossa, you rotten Neapolitan shit of Satan, we almost *killed* ourselves getting the papacy for you! Cosimo has spent tens of thousands of florins on this! He has wrung gold out of all of the bankers of Europe to put you into the papacy!''

"Nothing will be wasted," Cossa answered calmly. "They are bankers. They want money. By going along with me they will get their money and so will you.''

"What do I tell the cardinals?''

"The cardinals and I are of one spirit. I will tell them. Even Spina will welcome what I will tell him.''

She clapped her ivory hand to her porcelain forehead, saying, "The *deals* we will have to unmake! The *arrange*ments that will have to be undone." Cossa knew he had won. He felt kind and loving toward her.

"Who will be pope, then?''

"Pietro Filargi.''

"Milan? That old man?''

"He is old but he was once a holy friar. He studied theology at Norwich, Oxford, and Paris. He was a holy hermit on Crete, then his life took him to Lombardy. He became a tutor to Gian Galeazzo's son, then archbishop of Milan, then cardinal. He is fond of wine and knows nothing of the business of the Curia. He trusts me." Cossa smiled broadly. "And I insist that it be you who take the news of his ascension to him so that all of your future clients will know that you know such things first—before all others—before the inside of the inside. Do you follow me, dear one?"

"Dear one, my ass, you double-crossing, two-faced son-of-a-bitch."

Chapter 29

When the marchesa left Cossa's bed the next morning, she was affectionate and blandly understanding, but as she rode northwards to Pisa her mind was hard and her spirit cold. She had been cheated. A tithe of the benefices taken from Cossa as a first cardinal, no matter how much, was far from being a tithe of Cossa's potential share as pope. Standing at the right hand of a first cardinal was no improvement of position for herself or her daughters. She marked that Cossa's excuses for rejecting the papacy were admissions of weakness.

It was reflexive with the marchesa to exploit weakness. She was determined to control Cossa as *pope* in exactly the same way that Cossa intended to control Filargi. Cosimo di Medici had many rightful claims to realizing an influence over the papacy but even his claims were very nearly invalid compared with the rightness of her own claim, because seeing that all Church deposits went into the Medici Bank was only a part of what she would control when she controlled Cossa's papacy.

When she stopped for the night at Siena she wrote a letter to Cosimo. It was a harsh, blunt report of what Cossa had told her. She ended the letter with, "It is too late to reverse his decision, so fearful is he of sitting on the throne of St. Peter. Filargi will be elected. He is an old, old man. You have my consecrated word that Cossa has not yet escaped the papacy."

When she reached Pisa, the marchesa sent a letter to her dear friend, Cardinal Filargi, archbishop of Milan, asking for an audience. He summoned her to lunch the following day. He was such a hearteningly amiable, crinkly faced, brown-skinned, and toothless old man, she thought. If he had a fault in the world it could only be that he spent half his day at table and maintained a staff of four hundred female servants, all clad in his house livery, among whom were four of Bernaba's failed courtesans, who kept her informed of what was happening, as a matter of habit.

As she entered his dining hall he seemed to be very nearly engulfed by the ministering women. As each did her stint, smiling dotingly, others seemed to appear from out of trapdoors, crevices, cupboards, and crannies to bring more comforts— cushions, wine, footstools, hand cream, sweeties, and cooling fans.

"Praise to God!" the old man cried out from beneath the screens of muffling women. "How wonderful to see you again, my dearest Decima. It is like the wonderful old days in Milan when Gian Galeazzo was still alive, and you and I would lunch so elegantly every Tuesday." Three young women lifted him to his feet and braced him while he flung open his arms to receive her. After the embrace they lowered him into his chair and settled him down sweetly among the cushions.

They lunched on *busseca alla Milanese,* a tripe soup containing cabbage, tomatoes, celery, beans, onions, potatoes, leeks, and crusts of bread, flavored with saffron, sage, parsley, and garlic, sprinkled with cheese.

"When I spent that impossibly cold time at Oxford, then even a colder time in Paris—which is surely the coldest place on dear God's earth—their faces went blank when I pleaded for this magnificent soup to get myself warm again, and I vowed to St. Gregory of Nazianus, the supreme theologian of the Trinity, but a saint who wrote more than four hundred touchingly beautiful poems—just as this soup is a poem to the living—that I would, if I ever returned to the advanced civilization of Italy, start every meal of my remaining days with *busseca alla Milanese.* You and I know what is right to set upon a table, my dear. One of the things we were born for was to be each other's eating companion. After the wonderful soup, I have asked for a *salsiccia Milanese,* eh? Your favorite and mine, am I right? Where else but in Milan would veal be sliced so thinly then filled with such infinitesimally chopped veal, pork, ham, breadcrumbs, and the cheese of Parma—all of it bound together with egg yolk and flavored with garlic and nutmeg, then cooked in butter with a little broth and served in its own dear sauce? Please! We shall drink Virgil's own wine—Rhaetic—red, robust, rich, and rewarding Rhaetic from the hills above Verona, such a pleasant change from the heavy wines of Latium.''

"You will make me fat," the marchesa protested weakly.

"Fat is a phase of life," the cardinal explained. "I was thin then God made me fat but, when he grew tired of seeing me fat, he made me thin again. Always the same five meals a day, the same wines, the same sweets . . . here, here, you lazy girls—the marchesa's glass is almost empty.''

They ate and drank. The cardinal talked on and on, like a sweet bird perched upon the brow of life singing its praises. As suddenly as he did everything else, he said, "Have you come to tell me something, Decima?''

She nodded happily.

"Is it a private matter?''

She nodded conspirationally.

"Lazy girls!" he called to his staff. "Tidy me up then leave us.''

Four liveried young women scrambled forward. Two washed his little hands. A third touched tenderly at his mouth with a soft, damp, scented cloth as the fourth arranged his hair. Then they were gone.

He leaned back and nodded to the marchesa.

"I have just returned from Cardinal Cossa's field headquarters," she said. "He entrusted me with a message for you.''

The old cardinal raised one eyebrow.

"He is aware that the council—and the cardinals—are speaking of him as our next pope.''

"Ah, that is true, Decima. These are times when a man of Cossa's strength is sorely needed.''

"Yes. Oh, yes, Eminence. But he spoke most forthrightly to me. He told me that such expectancies as those of the council alarm him because he is not—as you are—a holy man. He is only a man of action, as he describes his own qualities, and he is painfully worried that his experience and abilities as a Church administrator, after all that long and careful training under Pope Boniface, would be lost if he were to accept the papacy."

"He would *refuse?*"

"He wants only to serve God and his pope, where God has shown him that he is meant to serve, my lord. Therefore, because I have his trust and yours, he has given it to me to tell you that his support—all of it—will be put behind your candidacy."

Filargi stared at her steadily, without expression. His crinkled face with its horny skin made him seem like a gentle lizard upon a rock in the warm sun.

"Cardinal Cossa wants to serve you," the marchesa continued simply. "More than anything else, he wants me to make that wholly clear to you. He offers his services to you humbly, as your first cardinal, as your administrator of the Curia and the Church throughout Christendom, as military protector of your person and of the Papal States, as steward and cherisher of the Church's treasures everywhere, and as the host to your serenity."

Two small tears rolled down Filargi's leather cheeks. "Lazy girls," he called out, "fetch me my jewel chest." Women appeared with an iron-bound chest in moments. He scoured a key out from within a hidden pocket of his dress and unlocked the chest set before him. He opened its lid. It was filled with gold jewelry, which shone blindingly, set with precious stones.

"My lady Decima," he said with emotion, "I ask you to choose the ornament that most pleases you. You have brought to me that which honors all of the dead of my family and which will exalt my spirit to eternal salvation."

The marchesa did not hesitate, did not appear to have considered which jeweled object she would choose, but her *ruffiana's* eye had decided what would be the best thing for herself and her heirs by choosing a gold ring which bore a sapphire as blue as the Virgin's robes, within a setting of diamonds.

"I thank you, my lord," she said humbly.

Chapter 30

The session of the Council of Pisa that was held on Saturday, June 15, 1409, began with the celebration of high mass by Philippe de Thury, archbishop of Lyons. The sermon was preached by the bishop of Novara, on the appropriate text, *Eligite meliorem et eum ponite super solium,* exhorting the cardinals to proceed to the unanimous choice of a good and worthy ruler.

At vespers, the twenty-four cardinals, including Baldassare Cossa, entered the archbishop's palace, 110 yards west of the Leaning Tower, and were there immured to conclave under the guard of the Grand Master of Rhodes and other prelates, not to issue thence until a new pope should have been chosen. Fourteen of the cardinals belonged to the obedience of Gregory, who had been deposed as pope by the council; ten to that of Benedict, also deposed.

Throughout the city, stories of exceptional bribery were rife, that every cardinal had promised riches to the servants of others, that the French court had lavished money, that the cousin of the king of France, Louis de Bar, cardinal of St. Agatha, might be chosen, or the "domestic prophecy" of cardinal de Thury might be fulfilled, or that Simon de Cramaud, patriarch of Alexandria, might at last obtain the tiara for which he had sighed so long and worked so ardently.

Two halls and two chapels were set apart for the conclave. In the larger chapel, cells were constructed in which the cardinals might eat and sleep; the smaller was reserved for discussion and for the election of a pope.

On the first day nothing was done but to settle in with greatest comfort. On the fourth day, after sufficient lip service had been paid to the ambitions of the more earnestly yearning cardinals, the conclave turned to Baldassare Cossa. After this result of scrutiny was announced, the cardinals were accustomed to sit and talk together in case any wished to change his mind and transfer the vote he had given to another, for in this way they could more easily reach an agreement. This procedure was omitted after the submission of Cossa's scrutiny.

Cossa stood before them and answered them. "Your Eminence of Ostia," he said gravely, "your opinion of me, as I understand it, is much higher than my own when you attribute to me any more than the qualities that should be held by a soldier of the Church. I am not ignorant that our own imperfection is far more general. I realize that our failings in these crucial days of schism include a lack of vital religious capacities that evolve out of a life of meditation and prayer, something that has not been my lot in my life of action. These failings must declare me to be utterly unworthy. Therefore, with fallen heart over my weaknesses, which must bar me from ever reaching the glory of the papacy, we must disobey the summons of the Holy Ghost, which was made with your voices."

There was a great outburst of protest in the chapel but Cossa quieted this when he said, "If, following the dictates of your consciences, which seek to heal the wounds suffered from this tragic schism, you will attribute the summons of a single, binding pope to God Himself, you will cast your eyes about you seeking the holiest man among you. That man of holiness whom we should raise up as pope does indeed sit among us. He is Pietro Filargi, Archbishop of Milan and cardinal of the Twelve Apostles. Beyond his precious sanctity, I remind you that he is neither Frenchman nor Italian and is by that freedom alone a healing balm for Christendom. He is known by all of us to be an able man and a most active prelate in the affairs of this historic council. He might not know who were his father or his mother but that will save him from the trouble and temptation of providing for his relatives. He might not be profoundly versed in canon and civil law, as he is a scholar of theology, but it was no ordinary man who could win the confidence and trust of that astute tyrant, Gian Galeazzo Visconti, duke of Milan. Pietro Filargi truly fits the throne of St. Peter, for he is able, saintly, and proven to be incorruptible.''

Chapter 31

The new pope, Pietro Filargi, took the name of Alexander V. The news of his election was received with joy in Milan, Florence, and Bologna, but not in Rome, which was occupied by Ladislas' troops. The election of Cardinal Filargi was also a triumph for France, because both he and his chief adviser, Cardinal Cossa, were devoted to the French alliance, that confraternity of French cardinals, the king of France, and the papacy which managed to prosper so well.

Although the Council of Pisa had deposed Popes Gregory and Benedict and had elected Pope Alexander to end the Great Schism in the Church, there was still much before the council to do. There was the desperate question of Church reform, if the council were to satisfy the hopes of Christendom from Scandanavia to Greece, from England to Warsaw. While the council sat, most of Europe had discussed little else but the reform of the Church but, until that reform actually happened, the multinumerous Church without was ruled by a minuscule handful of the Church within—the cardinals and the Curia without whom nothing could be done that had to be done.

The basis of the Church reform for which the Christian world had clamored for over a century, which the prelates and priests of the Church of every country but Italy had wanted for perhaps a longer time, was substantially this: Reform wanted the elimination of images and pictures from the churches, an end put to the solemnization of new festivals and of the building of yet more sacred edifices. Reform wanted an end to the canonization of saints and the prohibition of all work on feast days. Reform called for an end to simony, not only within the papacy, the College, and the Curia, but also by parish priests who milked their poor parishioners. Because of this churchly vice there were many of the faithful under the ban of excommunication because they were unable to pay for justice. Corpses lay in the field "unhouseled, unannealed, no reckoning made" because relatives could not pay priests for a Christian burial. However, despite the continuing demand for Church reform, the Council of Pisa felt it had done the one thing that was absolutely needful by electing a new pope, and the council made no reforms.

Catastrophically worse, the Great Schism in the Church had not been terminated by the signing of conciliar decrees. Although the council had deposed two popes and had elected one pope, it had not proclaimed in writing to all of the nations and to the people that the schism was over.

This thunderbolt crashed down upon the Church and upon Christendom. To the horror of the world it soon became clear that the council had merely added one *more* pope to the pope at Perpignan and the pope who had fled Rome and now lived under the protection of Carlo Malatesta at Rimini. Incredible to Christendom, it was slowly and agonizingly understood that although most of the prelates of Christendom had labored mightily, all they had succeeded in doing was bringing one more pope into a world already overcrowded with popes.

All three papacies held their individual obediences in a deathgrip while, relentlessly, they collected their dues and tithes, their *spoilias* and *servitias* from the triply split parishes of the world. Although the latest pope, Alexander V, was obeyed by the greatest part of Christendom, Benedict XIII had the obediences of Spain, Scotland, Sardinia, Corsica, and Armagnac. The city-state of Rimini, parts of Germany, and the northern kingdoms were faithful to Gregory XII.

The twentieth session of the council was held on July first under the presidency of Alexander V. This was marked by greatly increased solemnity. Cardinal de Thury again celebrated high mass. The pope pronounced the benediction. Those parts of the service that had formerly been taken by a cardinal-bishop were now performed by His Holiness. The *Orate* and the *Ergite Vos,* instead of being proclaimed by a simple chaplain or deacon, were now pronounced by a cardinal-deacon and the pope was assisted by cardinals of that rank, including Baldassare Cossa, in white dalmatics and miters. After the litany Alexander himself read the remaining prayers and intoned the *Veni Creator Spiritus.* A lofty seat had been placed for him in front of the high altar, and facing him were the patriarchs of Alexandria, Antioch, and Jerusalem.

After the Office had been concluded, the cardinal of Chalant, assisted by three bishops, ascended the pulpit and published the decree that told that the pope had been unanimously elected by the cardinals. A prayer for the welfare of the new pontiff, and of the Holy Church, was then put up and the pope preached a sermon on the text *Fiet unum ovile unus pastor,* signifying that there would be one fold and one shepherd, which was more than slightly in error.

At the pope's order, Cardinal Cossa rose and read newly formed decrees that ratified all the cardinals had done from the third of May. The two Colleges of Cardinals, those formerly of Benedict and those formerly of Gregory, were formed into a single College. Deposed, the two popes had no ecclesiastical supporters, because, as popes, they no longer existed. The next decree related to the reformation of the Church in its head and its members. The pope requested that different nations appoint men of probity, age, and capacity to consult with him and his cardinals in the matter.

Sunday, July 7, 1409, was fixed for Alexander's coronation. The newest of the three sitting popes, assisted by cardinals and prelates in their long pluvials and white miters, celebrated mass, then emerged from the western door of the cathedral of Pisa to the high throne that had been erected on the steps facing the baptistery. The Epistles and the Gospel were read in Hebrew, Greek, and Latin. The triple crown was set upon Alexander's head by the cardinal of Saluces. Then the cardinals, patriarchs, archbishops, bishops, and mitered abbots mounted their steeds, caparisoned in white cloths and trappings. Last of all came the pope on a white mule, wearing full pontificals, with the tiara on his head. The mule was led by Cardinal Cossa.

The procession rode solemnly through the streets of Pisa. The two rival popes were burned in effigy. The Jews, as was traditional, met the pope as he rode and petitioned for a confirmation of their privileges. They presented him with a book of their law, which he was required to throw backward over his shoulder, saying that he had a better law as his guide. Arriving at his palace, the pope dismounted and the captain of Pisa took the mule and its trappings as his perquisite.

On the last day of the council, on the Authority of God, St. Peter, and St. Paul, and on his own authority, Alexander bestowed plenary absolution upon all who had attended the council, and on the servants who had been with them, and this was to avail up to the hour of their deaths.

Chapter 32

Three months after the ascension of Pope Alexander V, after he had organized his own Curia out of nothing, had implemented the arms of the Church—department after department where there had been no apparatus whatever before—Cossa sent me to Milan with a message to Catherine Visconti, asking her to entrust to me her choice of a meeting place in three months' time.

He had much work to do before he could meet with her to settle anything. Early in the new year he led the pope's armies and allied troops under the command of the duke of Anjou into Rome, where he took possession of the Vatican after driving Ladislas south, back to Naples. It had been six years since Cossa was in Rome. Those years had formed him into the greatest cardinal of Urbanist obedience. He had originated and engineered the Council of Pisa, had secured the election of a holy man to the papacy, and was, himself, the power behind the papal throne.

Cossa's accomplishment in recreating all of the machinery at Rome in Bologna had been a vast executive achievement. To begin with, although delegations of city magistrates and leading citizens came to him to plead, with rich gifts, that he persuade the pope to return the papacy to Rome, and although he knew Alexander was much inclined to that, Cossa was against it. He listened to the committees gravely, and accepted their gifts with sensitive regard to their motivation, but he had no intention of permitting Alexander to go to Rome to stand at the mouths of Ladislas' cannon. Also, he had much in mind the many commercial enterprises that he, the marchesa, and Cosimo di Medici controlled in Bologna, which were enhanced by the presence of the papacy and the Curia. It became necessary for him to remind Alexander of his promise, on election, to work for the recovery of the Papal States. Bologna was Cossa's fief so it would have to do for the old man as well. Without further murmur, Alexander settled luxuriously into Bologna with his immense retinue of female servants; holy, happy, and unhorrified.

Alexander was an old man without experience of papal affairs. He never understood that he was a prisoner of the papacy. He devoted himself to holy worship, undertaking every imaginable ritualistic chore and bringing the people of Bologna and all pilgrims with him in his daily exhibitions of belief, which were as much necessary to the collective spirit as was the inner nourishment of its faith, which he also demonstrated. As he lived only to worship his God with the comfort of the Holy Spirit, the Holy Mother, and the saints, he welcomed Cossa's vigor and intelligence and the experience he brought to the papacy with his churchcraft and statecraft. To outsiders, it appeared that a scramble by the cardinals for offices and privileges had begun, but these benefits were stringently controlled by Cossa and shared only with those who had acted in support of his wishes at the Council of Pisa.

Early in March 1410, when he was sure that the machinery of the Church was working smoothly and that the cardinals knew who their master was, when Rome had been restored to the papacy, Cossa slipped away to a palace at Mirandola, between Ferrara and Parma, which Gian Galeazzo had acquired in his labors of some years before. It was called the Castello di Natale as the birthplace of the first duke of Rusconi, and Catherine Visconti had chosen it as an almost hidden meeting place.

She was waiting when he arrived. The servants were dismissed and they made love vigorously before they prepared for dinner. After dinner they began the slow, deliberate process of working out the treaty they would hold with each other.

"I cannot explain how high my heart lifted when I was brought the news that you had rejected the papacy," she said. "I knew that I was saved and that my sons were saved. What enormous courage and strength you had to tell the conclave that you would not accept their summons, and I tell you how much I recognize what you have done for me—for us—so that you may come to our alliance with an open heart."

"My heart is open to you," he said. "We will move Europe, but not until I have seen to my duty to Alexander and have set his house entirely in order so that the Church may function and prosper. There are obligations to cardinals and to princes, which I am obliged to meet but, within six months from this day we will join our intentions, reclaim your sons from those who would subvert them, and begin the expansion of the state of Milan."

"How much money should I have ready for you?"

"There will be a matter of gifts within the Church—no need to persuade the pope so, but each cardinal will want to understand that my own place as a prince of the Church must not be disturbed. The bankers must be given assurances that we will favor them, and that we will not threaten what they hold now, after we begin to expand out into Italy. I think we should remember that there are princes and churchmen at our flanks and backs outside of Italy requiring that we remember them with gold florins. To raise the *condottieri* necessary for the conquest, naturally the state of Milan must pay for that, but the state can do so with loans from cooperative banks until we may realize the returns of war. Therefore, for immediate capital, if you will have twenty thousand gold florins ready in two months' time I will send my man, Franco Ellera, for it."

"And what do you give to our alliance?" she asked.

"No money. I have only a simple soldier's purse," he said with a straight face. "But I have given my chance of the papacy to our dream and, by leaving the pope to join you in conquest, I may be losing my red hat."

They walked slowly along the high terrace behind the fortress-walls of the castle and both were fulfilled by what they foresaw. Catherine had a warrior in her bed once again. Her children could now be safeguarded, and kept from turning on her. She would preserve Milan for the Visconti and be able to grind into dust every commander of her husband's who had turned on her after Gian Galeazzo had fallen. Cossa saw that he could now be certain that he would spend the rest of his life as great *condottieri* general, while showing respect to his father's ambition by remaining a high churchman. He would use Catherine's money to assure that the pope appointed him archbishop of Milan and that no one in the hierarchy would see fit to object to that. He would be rich from the loot of Italy, Baldassare, cardinal-general-archbishop, while he had the marchesa begin to soften up the electors with a view to making him king of the Romans when Rupert was dead. At no point in his considerations of his future could he imagine functioning without the marchesa. He needed her cunning. He could not proceed beyond Italy without her experience and knowledge of Germany, France, Spain, and England. He would need all of her craft to divert Sigismund of Hungary from ideas of competing with him, perhaps going to war against him, to stop him from being crowned Holy Roman Emperor. All of that was in Cossa's mind when he sealed his treaty with Catherine Visconti with two glorious nights in her bed.

He had about as much chance of being made king of the Romans and all the rest of that as he had of being elected as the most holy churchman in all history. He couldn't get enough of the woman so he lied to himself about all the rest of it. He wanted to be Alexander's first cardinal in charge of everything in the Church and that was what he was.

Chapter 33

I was as unaware as Cossa was of the dangers he had created by refusing the papacy. Neither the Medici, his great sponsors, nor the marchesa trusted him any longer. The reasons had to be there to sense these things, then to prove them, then to convince Cossa of the danger, but I suspected nothing. Business was better than ever.

Cosimo di Medici was aware that Cossa had slipped away to a secret meeting with Catherine Visconti because the marchesa di Artegiana had Cossa under perpetual surveillance. His betrayal of all she had done for him to secure the papacy for him (and the Medici) had been a severe shock, because she could not puzzle out who had helped him to arrive at such a wildly destructive decision. She was confident that Cossa, left on his own, would have done as he was told and accepted the papacy, always providing that he got what looked like the lion's share. Someone had gotten close enough to him to tamper with him. Someone had made him what had looked at the time like a better offer.

The marchesa had reasoned her way through the maze. She reasoned that if Cossa had met, secretly or otherwise, with anyone, it would have happened some time during the five weeks between her two visits to him in the field, during the council. Up to that second visit he had been more and more enthusiastic about the plan to make him pope. He had cross-questioned her about the tactics for handling the cardinals and princes in Pisa, frequently correcting the strategy and improving upon it, always having a sure touch for designing bribes. Whatever had happened had happened during that five-week period. The marchesa realized that the only person who would know whom Cossa had spoken to was me.

She knew me too well to ask me such things directly, so she went to Bernaba and explained what Cossa had done to cheat all of them, most of all himself, out of vast fortunes and the papacy. To Bernaba, next to the money involved, the papacy was the crowning jewel of mankind, the highest honor that could ever be conferred and, since she knew Cossa as well as she did, she wanted the papacy for him and even was able to construct a fantasy whereby he, as pope, would become her confessor. She listened to the marchesa's determination that Cossa would *still* one day be pope and, admiring popes as she did, loving her husband and not being able to imagine how high he would rise if Cossa became pope, admiring the marchesa more than any *ruffiana* in Italy, she naturally agreed to get the information.

The marchesa was astonished, not jealous, when she weighed what Bernaba passed along to her from me. Even she thought it was strange that she, a dealer in women all of her life, had never considered the possibility that another woman might be the force that had deflected Cossa from the papacy. When she had sifted through what I had told Bernaba about what they had talked about in that single night which had brought on the great upset in Pisa, she ordered the twenty-four-hour surveillance on Cossa. The barren reports came to her every day but she was a patient woman who knew that, sooner or later, either Cossa or Catherine Visconti would have to make a move.

She talked to Cosimo about it. "After all," she said, "soldiering is his natural bent. The Church is just an acquired talent. But surely he must know that this woman is a Visconti who will have him assassinated as soon as he gets everything done that she wants done."

"Now we know," Cosimo said, "but it's too late. Filargi is the pope."

"It certainly is not too late," the marchesa protested.

"What can we do?"

"Filargi is an old man."

"Well?"

"Old men die. If this old man dies then I say it becomes *your* problem to make sure that Cossa will accept at the next conclave."

"That is too indefinite for my father, Decima."

"Perhaps it can be made definite."

"How do you mean? No, no! Don't tell me." He held up both hands before him in alarm, his face grown pale. "We have never spoken of this."

"I have studied hard on how to bring pressure on Cossa to make him accept. I have worked out the single incontestable solution in this world. You will easily be able to persuade Cossa to be pope."

"How?"

She told him how, and irrevocably, although I did not know it until much later, they became my enemies.

After the day she had brought him the good news, the marchesa had lunch every Friday with the pope at his palace. She brought him delicious gossip from the world, tidbits that her daughters had searched out in all the corners of all the high places in Europe, and the sweet old pope was enormously entertained by the merry innocence of all of it. Gossip was not all she brought with her. She brought powders that she had commanded since her earliest days as a *ruffiana,* when young women had come to her crying for vengeance against a man whose life they wished to put away without suspicion being cast upon themselves. Between the peals of his laughter and the sips of his wine, the marchesa palmed her potions into his drink and poisoned Pope Alexander V unto death. This I know, for I was in the room when she admitted it.

Chapter 34

On May 2, 1410, Cossa and I were in Forlimpopoli, beyond Forli on the way to Rimini, besieging two hundred horse and two hundred foot of some of Ladislas' stragglers, when he was recalled to Bologna because the pope was dying. When we reached the papal palace Alexander was sinking fast. Cossa didn't go into the sickroom to see the pope immediately. On the way to his apartments, he found a committee of senior cardinals was waiting for him in the anteroom. Covered with dust and wearing war gear, he excused himself. I went into the pope's room and spoke to the doctors, then I went to Cossa, in his apartment, and said, "The pope is finished and the word is out."

"What does that mean?"

"It means that couriers have come in to say that Pierre d'Ailly and the duke of Burgundy are on their way from France and John of Nassau is coming from Mainz."

"How did they find out the pope was dying that far away?"

"He's been ill for about three weeks. Now we know he's dying."

"There is something very odd going on here," Cossa said.

"That's not all. Cosimo di Medici is on his way from Florence."

"What do they all want, for Christ's sake?"

"On the surface it's a crisis, isn't it? I mean, in a sense, it's

the natural thing to do. They are running out of popes. They
have to keep up the inventory.''

"Help me out of this gear. Tell those old farts to come in here
in ten minutes. Tell them I'm having a bath.'' As an afterthought
he said, "Every one of them has been bribed to the hairline.''

"After Pisa last year, you should know,'' I told him.

When the committee came in Cossa was ready for them. As
ready as he would ever be, I thought. While he dressed he told
me he was soaked by a premonition of loss, except that he
hadn't lost anything. He said he was trying to think of Catherine
Visconti and the Milanese gold that would buy him all the *condottieri* that would bring him all of the power that would make
him the ruler of Italy then perhaps king of the Romans then
perhaps Holy Roman Emperor. I didn't laugh at him. It was real
to him. But he said that even that beautiful thought wouldn't
stay with him, because he knew the cardinals and the bankers
and the princes wanted to make him pope.

He greeted the cardinals as they entered the room. He apologized for keeping them waiting. They rumbled their ac-
knowledgements. There were four of them: Jean de Brogny,
cardinal-bishop of Ostia, most senior; Antonius Calvus, cardinal
of Mileto; Pierre Gerard, cardinal-bishop of Tusculum; Ladulfus
Maramaur, cardinal-deacon of Santo Nicolo in Cacere Tulliano,
a Neapolitan. They were quite accustomed to having me at all
meetings. Privately, they called me The Witness.

"His Holiness grows weaker and weaker,'' de Brogny said,
"an excellent man in the whole course of his life, gifted in sweetness and prayer. But he has very few hours left.''

"He shines with goodness,'' Cossa said.

"Cossa, in a few hours your Church will need you,'' Maramaur said in the Neapolitan dialect. Cossa stared at him coldly.
He began to feel the stirrings of panic. He had been about to
begin his march upon the conquest of Italy but these old men
were going to insist upon something else for him.

"Soon there will be a conclave,'' de Brogny said. "We must
have the assurance of your consent to your election as pope as
it should have happened in Pisa.''

Cossa sat down heavily. "Please—" he said "—sit down, my friends." He took a deep breath as they remained standing in a semicircle around him. "My reasons are the best reasons," he said. "I am not fit for the papacy. I lack the holiness."

"We will surround you with holiness like high walls," de Brogny said. "We will elevate you as upon a cloud, which will hold you above all on earth, shining with holiness."

"There would be no one to run the Church."

"You will run the Church. The pope. As it should be."

"The Church is in shards," Antonius Calvus said harshly. "At this moment the Church must have a leader who is more a king than a pope. Holiness is the last thing that is required during this terrible confusion of triple schism. We need a strong man who will dispose of the two antipopes where the Council of Pisa and Alexander failed. We need a great lawyer. We need a soldier."

"Elect Caracciola."

"We choose you."

"You are priests," Cossa said, his voice rising as the panic inundated him. "I am a lawyer, not a churchman. I am a layman in all but title."

"All the more reason!" Maramaur said. "They are pressing us for reform! It is a serious thing! Everyone is after reform, from the king of France to the coal mine owners in Silesia and the bankers in Greece. Do we want reform? No, they want it. We have to live with the Church on an hour-to-hour basis but they want reform. Reform for the businessman is the end of the schism. Reform for the theologians is something else, but Church reform we can cope with. We have to have a cunning lawyer, you, to stand them off by effecting compromises. Can a priest be of any use at that? What would we do with a pastoral pope at a time like this?"

"I—please—give me time. I must think about this."

Luca Salvadore, cardinal of Santa Giovanna di Cernobbio, came into the room, stricken. "Alexander is nearly on his way to God," he said.

The cardinals turned away from Cossa and left the room.

Cossa nearly ran through the rooms to the private door, behind an arras, that led to the private staircase leading to the marchesa's "office." She was sitting in front of a mirror brushing her short, darkening hair. "Filargi is nearly gone," he said numbly. "They are pressing down upon me."

"Did you accept?" she asked mildly.

"Accept?"

"Never mind, Cossa. You will be turned around just the same, and without a word from me."

"Bitch! Whore!" he shouted.

"Please make up your mind what you want from me, Cossa. If I speak, you tell me I am trying to force you against your will or—now—that I am a bitch-whore. If I stay silent you scream at me because I must speak about the one thing on which we don't agree. You are frightened. I won't ask you why but you have lost your nerve."

"Frightened? All right! Yes! I am frightened of having to say two masses a day for the rest of my life and being expected to pour out my sins to some smelly Franciscan every time I have an unclean thought."

"You have heard everything I have to say on this."

"What has happened to everyone?" he asked wildly. "Who is going to defend the papacy against Ladislas? Who will lead the armies, run the Curia, bring in the money that every one of us—and the Church—has to have? Those ramshackle wrecks who were just in there making their insane demands to me would be the first to scream if reform cut off their *servitia*."

"Then it's clear, isn't it? They want someone else to handle the fighting while you concentrate on protecting the Church from reformers, and on building up the benefices that have been reduced to so little for them. The popes are now men of peace, Cossa. The days of the fighting popes, the days of Gelasius II and Calixtus, were nearly three hundred years ago."

"What about the war? If Ladislas takes over here what good will a few extra florins be to the cardinals? To keep whatever he can take he will agree with all of the princes to any of their reforms."

"The duke of Anjou will handle those battles. The Florentines and the Sienese will handle the funding to seal off Ladislas in the south. The electors will give you Sigismund in the north to protect the benefices and keep the peace. Italy and the Church will be held together for you, giving you all the room and security you will need as pope, and you will rule.''

"No! I won't be trapped in this! I have other plans."

"What plans?"

"Big plans!"

"Cossa, hear me. If you reject the papacy you won't get out of this alive. If you deny the people who will be knocking down your doors to convince you that you must accept the papacy, then they are sure of one thing, another council will be forced upon us, which will probably elect a *fourth* sitting pope to rule over an even weaker Church. The French will get their reform, d'Ailly will get his red hat, and at that council your desperate supporters will see to it that you are found to be a heretic and they will burn you to death."

"I won't be here for anything like that."

"Listen to me just one more time, for I have counseled you well over the years. I say to you if you decide to mock powerful men who have found it necessary to travel across Europe to make you understand that you are their choice to save the Church in this desperate hour, then you must believe me that your days are numbered."

Chapter 35

The Piazza Maggiore in front of the Anziani Palace looked as if it had been turned into a country fair. Knots of people were everywhere, all across it, in front of the Church of San Petronio and the podesta's palace on the long side. Street bands were playing, courtesans strolled among the men under affected parasols, leading their followers. There were many uniforms of different countries.

We overlooked the huge piazza from the short west side, and I watched more and more of them troop in through the street at the corner of the Portico di Banchi, each one bringing his small contribution to the widening chaos in Cossa's mind.

He received the duke of Burgundy, John of Nassau, Pierre d'Ailly, Count Pippo Span, representing Sigismund, king of Hungary, a delegation of French bankers, his own father and his uncle Tomas, 230 Benedictine monks, a committee of 28 German commercial guilds, 300 Carmelite nuns, 34 officers of the armies of the Papal States, and an international delegation of learned lawyers, at intervals of two hours over the next day and a half, and replied to their urgent proposals with more conciliatory words than he had used to the marchesa. I was there. I listened to all of it.

Anjou and Nassau spoke to him in almost the same words, in different meetings, conveying views as worldly as Cossa's.

"I can name you eight men," each said to him differently, "military commanders who are your equal. I, in fact, am one of them. As for the administration of the day-to-day business of the Church, you have already staffed that with the best people in Christendom. They are the same people who have run the chancellery and the chamber, who have run everything as if they had the memory of God since the year 380 when Christianity was made the official religion of the empire. As you know, the College trusts you to manage their benefices but let us not ever think that every single member of it knows money almost as well as you do. You have everything backward, Cossa. What the Church needs is a *famous* general who is a *famous* administrator and a *famous lawyer,* as well as being a *famous* statesman. It needs a strong man who has the habit of winning. That is why only you must accept the papacy."

Pierre d'Ailly, still bishop of Cambrai, not the cardinal he had expected to be at Pisa, although he knew that Cossa could have compelled Alexander to confer the red hat upon him, spoke out resolutely for the king of France and the theologians at the University of Paris. "What must be implemented is the strong reform of the Church in its head and its members, Cossa," he said. "If there is no immediate reform then we all know that the Gallican Church will go back to Benedict—and we know you don't want that. By bringing reform you can go down into history as a great pope. You have come too far in your career as a churchman to turn back. You can only go forward. Nor can you believe that if you refuse the Church's cry for help you will be able to go anywhere at all."

"What does that mean?" Cossa said with the old hostility.

"I am sure you know exactly what it means."

"All right, bishop," Cossa snarled at him, "tell your people that I have absorbed their words. I am a soldier. I have a horror of being a prisoner of the papacy yet I hear you, I am sympathetic to what you have said to me. Will that do you?"

"Where is that golden future which used to smile upon me every morning as I opened my eyes?" he asked me. "It has turned to brass, Franco. If old Filargi were to remain alive in this palace we could own the world. And if I couldn't keep him alive forever, I could have him stuffed to sit there behind his beautiful, benign smile, a hand raised in benediction. Well, we are not going to wait here and let them spring the trap that will drop me into the papacy. We are going to get out of Bologna and make the run to Milan, as soon as I can turn our Bolognese assets into ready money. Tell our people to prepare—Bernaba, Palo, Bocca, all of them. Tell Ueli Munger to pick a troop of two hundred of the most loyal men in the guard. We'll be safe and back in business in Milan, with one-half of the gold florins in the papal treasury in the chests of our train. I earned that money, so I am certainly entitled to half of it. We'll be back in business. We'll take over this whole peninsula. Catherine Visconti will be beside herself with joy and nothing, nothing and nobody, is going to persuade me to ruin what is left of my life by accepting the papacy. Get them ready."

He went on with his plans, talking excitedly, and looking like the old-time Cossa. He would answer the outcry that the Medici would organize in Florence, Siena, Perugia, and throughout the Papal States by raising an army in Milan before they could try to come to get him. With an army between himself and the papacy, between himself and the Medici and all of their bankers and businessmen, he would use Catherine Visconti's gold to buy back the favor of the College of Cardinals and, in good time, whoever was to be pope would appoint him archbishop of Milan. He thought of that and it brought him sadness because, by walling off the Medici, he would be separating himself from the marchesa, but Catherine had lived as royalty for all the days of her life and she could counsel him on which were the correct political moves. He would be free, a cardinal of the Church and ruler of Italy. He would lead *condottieri* in a force that would multiply and multiply until he was the power of Europe. With Catherine Visconti, her gold, and her army, he could win anything.

That night Alexander made a good end, summoning his cardinals around his bed and saying, "Let not your heart be troubled. I ascend to my Father and to your Father." He commended France and the University of Paris to their care and

said that any decree made at the Council of Pisa had been
founded on justice and integrity, without deceit or fraud. "Peace
I give unto you. Peace I leave with you." Shortly after midnight
on the third of May he died. He had reigned for ten months.

His body was embalmed. While it was exposed for nine days
dressed in sacerdotal robes with gloves on the hands and the
feet bare for the kisses of the faithful, Cosimo di Medici arrived
in Bologna at the head of a delegation of Florentine, Sienese,
and Pisan bankers and businessmen. He asked for a private
audience with Cardinal Cossa, which was granted at once. The
two men greeted each other with warm affection.

"You look ill, Cossa," Cosimo said.

"I am ill." Cossa brought wine. He asked after Cosimo's
father. They discussed the wine; Cosimo was famous for dis-
coursing upon wines.

"What brings you over the mountains?" Cossa asked. "I ask
you this because I know it cannot be what all the rest of Europe
is plaguing me about."

"You mean—that you take the papacy?"

"More than that. They want me to give up the things I do well
to take up the one thing I would do badly."

"Everyone is agitated, Cossa. But I am here with some bankers. We have come to talk about business, which is to say the
peace of Europe. Florence and Pisa are losing fifty thousand
gold florins a day with the schism; Venice, Milan, and Genoa
are just as badly off."

"Time will cure all that."

"Perhaps. But all of us—all of the bankers and the business
people—agree on one thing. The schism must be finished and
we must elect a strong pope to stand for the meaning of the
Church before the world."

"So it all starts over again. It is no use, Cosimo. I will not be
trapped in the papacy."

Cosimo smiled at him as if Cossa had uttered some brilliant
witticism and talked blandly on. "You are probably the only
churchman who can really appreciate just how bad three popes
are for business. A crisis of confidence is sweeping Europe. The
Church is disintegrating. This erodes interlinking businesses.

The loss in real money is simply enormous and all of it has happened because of this schism.''

"Oh, come, Cosimo.''

The banker's face grew hard as he stared into Cossa's eyes. "I am telling you that the business community is in danger. The people who *gen*erate the cash that is passed back to the Church through benefices and *servitia* and Peter's Pence, the people without whom there would be no pomp and luxury, which our mutual customers expect from the Church, have suffered and still face crippling losses. Three popes, three Colleges, and three Curias are an intolerable financial burden, because they separate and isolate three trading communities from one another. If this trinity continues, commerce and banking will be ruined.''

"Why me? Why always *me*? I delivered the Council of Pisa for you. I have seen to it that your bank has gotten almost sixty percent of the banking of the Church so far and within two years I will have gotten all of it for you. Is it my fault that the obediences of Benedict and Gregory refused to take the solemn rulings of the Council of Pisa seriously?''

"They will agree when they know that they are going to get at least some of the reforms they have been demanding for over a hundred years. The pope who will be chosen at the conclave next week must *manage* those demands and carry through just enough reform to make him the one central leader of Christendom. If you lead that crusade for reform—up to a point, of course—I tell you that you will be marching straight upward beyond the papacy to canonization after your death. I, personally, will see to that.''

"That is hardly the way to turn me. Jesus! To amuse me greatly, yes, but you are taking all the precious solemnity out of our discussion.''

"You would mock the saints?''

"Cosimo, you and I are friends. We understand each other. Do you think anyone who learned to run the Church at the side of Boniface IX could bring himself to kill the goose that lays the golden eggs? Not me, surely. Let some priest take over as pope.''

Cosimo smiled ruefully. He shrugged mightily. He sighed heavily. "Well—I tried. If you won't listen then I must accept that." His eyebrows went up as if startled by some new thought. "My dear Cossa," he said, "with all my need to pour out Europe's troubles I have almost forgotten to tell you of your own astounding good fortune. The day I left Florence the bank received an extraordinary conditional deposit in your name."

"A deposit?"

"A really *amazing* amount of gold."

"A conditional deposit?"

"Yes."

"Who made it?"

"Two *hundred* thousand gold florins. An unspeakable amount of money from a client who says that the gold is to be released to you two days after you have been consecrated as pope."

"Who signed it?"

"Someone named Carlo Pendini of Castrocaro in the Romagna."

His hard eyes moved over Cossa's shattering face.

Chapter 36

Cossa sat alone, almost stupefied with shock, feeling as if all the blood had left his body. They had stopped him. If he rode to Milan that night, Cosimo and the marchesa would share all of the gold he had killed so many comrades to get. He could not leave that behind. He could not be mocked by knowing it had been taken by his enemies. Decima, the woman he had loved even beyond his love for Catherine Visconti, had taken the Pendini gold to Cosimo and, cold-bloodedly, they had dropped it on him from their great height, crushing him with it. He could feel bitterness rise from his bowels and into his throat as if it were gall. He had lost a great army. He was trapped in the papacy. He was just another workman of the Medici.

I said to him, "At least you know who your enemies are. Not everyone is that lucky. And you have the power to strike back now that you are doomed to be the pope."

"Who?" he said, as if he didn't know. "How?"

"The Medici. And the marchesa. She brought the gold from Castrocaro to the Medici Bank to be used against you. And they used it against you. You can't give it up so you will be pope. They did it to you then you did it to yourself. Pay them."

"Pay them?"

"Give the banking of the Church to the Albizzi in Florence. Tell them they can have all of the banking if they follow your plan, then tell them how it all works, how the Medici planned to do it. Make them give you two tithes for making them the richest family in Europe.''

"If I did that," he said, shaking his head despairingly, "just as sure as we are standing here either the Medici would have me murdered or the marchesa would."

"Then we must put together a large escort and ride tonight to Milan where the duchess will give you her army to destroy the Medici. Take Florence. Force Bologna to give you the marchesa. Execute her."

"I can decide nothing except that to be pope must be my fate. My father took me away from a business that had been carried on for four generations by the eldest son because he had a vision or a dream that I would be pope one day. Everything has conspired to make me pope—everything."

"Don't mock me, Cossa."

"I do not mock you! I am helpless and I agree they have done me in, therefore all the more do I want to enjoy whatever you have for them that will repay them, even if I will never be able to summon the will to do it."

"You can do anything. You will be pope. You will send a message to the emperor asking him to strip her of her title. Nothing could be worse for her."

"At the bottom of my soul rests a punishment for everyone, which is far worse than that, but I thank you for thinking of how we might repay my enemies. I can't afford even to think of the Medici and Decima as my enemies. I am trapped by them but only they can bring food to my cage." He seemed to drive the despair from him. "That was all settled when I was born. I am to be pope, but what am I going to do about Catherine Visconti? She is locked inside a more terrible cage and she needs me more than I need the Medici."

"That will solve itself. What is important now is—what are you going to do about the marchesa?"

Hopelessness filled Cossa's face. "I am lost to her. She is lost to me because of what she has done to me in the guise of a lover and a dear friend. I shall withdraw from her slowly, waiting for my chance to do to her what she did to me. I will use her body when I need it to reassure her that I have forgiven her and that nothing has changed. I need her cunning now, more than ever before. I need her knowledge of Europe. But I will possess all that from her and, when I do, and when she is standing naked one day, I will repay her for this betrayal."

Late in the night, after Cossa had finally fallen into a troubled sleep, the marchesa came into the room, fully dressed, stained by travel. She shook him awake gently. She was as pale as the moonlight. He came awake instantly and stared up into her somber face. A single huge candle flickered at the center of the room and it cast the marchesa's shadow high upon the wall.

"Cossa, I bring bad news," she said.

He stared.

"My daughter, Helene, has just come from Milan. She caught up with me a quarter of the way to Perugia and I turned back to bring comfort to you."

"What is it?"

"The duchess of Milan has been murdered by her son. Poisoned. In the citadel. The regents have taken over the city."

"No!" he screamed.

"Milan is going to give its allegiance to Pope Gregory."

"Leave me," he said harshly.

"She has been dead for three days or more, and I—"

"Leave me!"

Cossa covered his face with his hands, and turned away from her.

He rolled over in the bed, sat up, and faced her. "I want you to use all of your cunning," he told her harshly. "I want you to devise a way for us to get that murdering son out of Milan and into my keeping. I will give him to Palo and keep him alive through every agony deserved by a poisoner, deserved a thousand times by a son who has murdered such a mother." She held out her arms to comfort him, but he turned away from her again and she left him.

PART THREE

PART THREE

Chapter 37

On Thursday May 14, 1410, the cardinals entered the conclave. They were bricked up in the great hall of the podesta's palace in Bologna, which was surmounted by a square battlemented tower that, since 1245, had been the residence of city magistrates.

Seventeen cardinals went into conclave at ten o'clock at night, their beds arranged in cubicles divided by curtains of fine silk and adorned with flowers and sweet-smelling herbs. The crest of each cardinal was posted outside his apartment. The windows were walled up but small peepholes were left for light. A strong guard of soldiers was posted outside the palace under the command of Malatesta of Pesaro and Nicolo Roberti of Ferrara.

At midday on May 17, the cross appeared outside the palace, signifying that an election had been made. The cardinals issued from the conclave and announced that Baldassare Cossa, cardinal-deacon of Saint Eustachius, was to be the future pope, and that he would take the name Pope John XXIII, Our Most Holy Lord, Bishop of Rome, Vicar of Jesus Christ, Metropolitan of the Roman Province, Primate of Italy, Patriarch of the West, Head of the Universal Church—*Johannus Episcopus servus servorum Dei.*

He was the pope, he thought, when if he had had any resolve

or purpose, he would have moved everything that was essential to his continuance to Milan months before. He would have been with her and would have prevented her murder by the son whom he would torture and kill for having taken away such a woman into the darkness of death, changing history, changing Cossa's life and shortening his own.

Three chamberlains dressed Cossa for his coronation in the large room in the Anziani Palace where Alexander V had died. I stood with Palo, watching the stream of garments being lowered upon him. The meeting in the dramatic circumstances had been my idea, for the effect it would have on Palo, to get through to Palo that there would be a change in business procedures.

As they dressed him, Cossa spoke to us amiably. He was in the best of health, excepting gout, a spare, strongly built man with clear sharp features, dark skin, white teeth, a smile of glorious effect, and the dead, dry eyes of a hopeless man. I knew how he was suffering the loss of Catherine Visconti, but he now sat upon the throne of St. Peter high above all of the people of Christendom and his life had to go on. He had fallen into fatalism at the moment of his election, a characteristic of people from Naples, an earth-quaking zone. He was pope and there was nothing he could do about it, so I was able to force him to get down to business. We spoke in the Neapolitan dialect so that his chamberlains could not understand us.

"Palo—Bernaba will operate her business as she always has and handle her own money as she always has, but you will protect the women and the gambling in Bologna, Perugia, Siena, Reggio, Modena, and Parma. She will recruit the women and run them. You will collect the money and bring it to Franco Ellera. You understand?"

"Yes, Holiness." Palo wasn't simple-minded or anything like that. He was a criminal.

"From today on, Franco Ellera is out of that operation except to get the money from you. I will need him with me. You understand?" He smiled and Palo grinned back at him. Cossa said, "From today on, you get an extra five percent. You are going to be a rich man, Luigi."

"He is a good man," I said, "but he needs to be told what to do. He will get into trouble if he doesn't have someone standing over him."

"He knows that," Cossa said amiably. "He knows he will be dead if he doesn't do the job the way he always did it when you were telling him what to do. Isn't that right, Luigi?"

"I understand everything, Holiness. It is the most exalting thing of my life to execute the personal business of my pope and you can count on me not to fuck up."

"Good," Cossa said. "Am I ready now?" he asked the chamberlains. They bowed. Cossa smiled at them as though the sun itself were blessing them. He swept out of the room, the chamberlains following. I stayed behind to talk to Palo, thumping my forefinger into his chest.

Led by a snake of scarlet cardinals, by whited patriarchs and purpled bishops in chanted unctuousness, lurching and swaying to the clink of aspergilla, Pope John XXIII, beneath a blood-red miter bordered with white, became the center of a holy procession and was followed by archbishops and abbots, attended by great numbers of clergy, by Florentine bankers, Milanese generals, Venetian traders, and Pisan, Perugian, and Parmesan businessmen, by throngs of citizens, all proceeding to the Church of San Pietro Maggiore and, after the sacrament had been administered, sat upon a golden throne so that all might kiss his feet.

He was ordained as a priest on May 23, six days after his ascension. He was consecrated as a bishop on the same Saturday he was ordained priest, in the Church of San Petronio. Cardinal Giuliano Rizzo was deacon.

On Sunday, the new pope celebrated high mass in the cathedral with John of Nassau and Cosimo di Medici holding the basin for him. Nassau was attended by fifty-five cavaliers dressed in crimson and azure, and by eight fiddlers and five trumpeters to play sweet music.

A lofty platform with a cloth of gold was erected in the piazza against a wall of the church. Pope John XXIII was brought out and seated upon a throne and, in the presence of his sponsors, his family, and the multitudes he was crowned pope by his countryman and nephew, his sister's boy, Arrigo Brancacci, a cardinal newly made for the occasion and as inverted and degenerate a young man as might be found in Italy.

The Archdeacon Melvini threw a scarlet robe over Cossa,

conferred his papal name and declared, "I invest you with the Roman Church." The prior of the cardinal-deacons removed the episcopal miter from Cossa's head and replaced it with the *regnum,* a miter modified by two rings to symbolize the papal power in the two relevant spheres, making it a *mitra* and a crown. Archdeacon Melvini intoned to him, "Take the tiara and know that thou art the father of princes and kings, the ruler of the world, the vicar on earth of our savior, Jesus Christ, whose honor and glory shall endure throughout eternity."

The archdeacon gave the new pope a rod, symbol of justice. He girded him with a red belt from which hung twelve seals symbolizing the twelve apostles, a clear demonstration of papalism against episcopalism. The pallium, that sign of episcopal power, was given to him by Melvini while the cardinal-bishops were kept ostentatiously in the background to prevent any suggestion that the pope received any power from any cardinal or bishop. They had only elected him. What a business!

Cossa stared out beyond the crowd and wondered what was going to become of him, he told me late that night. He sat in the trap and thought, I am not the least mad among them but I am a part of the world and the world makes no effort to be rational. Like everyone else I think I am paying attention to my own sanity but—who can tell? What do they expect from me—a man who has learned all he knows at the elbow of the master simoniac, Boniface IX, who milked all of the preferments of all of the kingdoms. I have been drilled not to pass over such opportunities. Cosimo di Medici, a *most* religious man, and the bishop of Cambrai, the archbishop of Mainz, the king of France, the duke of Anjou, and the Sacred College knew everything about me and my philosophy when they all rushed in to lift me upon the throne of St. Peter. Now I am flung, he thought, among the superstitions of avaricious priests, an overwhelming horde of tens of thousands of clerics, bishops, curates, cardinals, and prelates—all laying about among their empty wine bottles, sucking on chicken bones, nourished by the tyranny of Christianity. Here I am, he thought, marooned inside this alb, pinned under this tiara, their pope, condemned to perform like a street actor for the gullible, shuffling and swaying toward my death, gliding toward the Church's promises of forever: chanting and intoning.

Why am I here? I am a *condottiere* who should be out in battle, doing honest killing. But I know why I am here. The woman I trusted betrayed me to the man I believed was my friend who wants me here for every profit he can take from it. They have both declared themselves to be my enemies. I must learn how to prepare myself so that I may destroy them as subtly as they have ruined my life.

The guns of the piazza were fired. All the church bells of the city were rung. To remind the new pope that he was but mortal, tufts of tow were thrice lighted and thrice extinguished before him by six cardinals who warned him as the fire went out, "Holy Father, thus passeth away the glory of the world."

As soon as he was crowned pope, Cossa raised many lower clergy to higher rank in Italy to secure his own majority in any council that might appear, while at the same time he sought to weaken the council he had been forced to call in Rome, because of Alexander's promise to seek Church reform at Pisa, by discouraging prelates from attending. War, of course (and other hazardous conditions), prevented the Council of Rome from convening as scheduled but when it finally met—for twenty-one days—Cossa dismissed the few prelates present and agreed to call another council at "some other time" to discuss the reform of the Church "in its head and its members," which was reform's evasive description of that time. He had far more important things on his mind, he told me. The Medici had just included him in the most important and promising of any of their hundreds of varied business projects.

I said to him, "Sometimes I think you would like to be remembered in history as a businessman."

"They are the leaders of our society," he said blandly.

"Where do they ever lead us," I asked him, "except to the poorhouse?"

He told me what the Medici had offered him; a model business proposition based on grabbing what someone else had developed from nothing. The previous century had brought industrial machinery into Europe on a scale no civilization had ever known. Across Europe, the Cistercian Order had established water-powered mills: factories that were grinding corn, fulling cloth, tanning leather, crushing olives, making paper, and performing dozens of industrial functions. Monasteries between Sweden and Hungary, separated by thousands of miles, had almost identical water-powered systems. The Cistercians worked on a rigid timetable toward maximum industrialization.

"Most of what the marketplace needs comes from these factories," Cosimo had explained to Cossa, "so naturally there are always crowds in front of all of them. Just as naturally, the prostitutes work the same ground for their business."

"Why not?" Cossa shrugged.

"Bernard, the Cistercian abbot, threatened to close the factories because they were attracting that sort of person. He's dead now, but what would have happened to the banking business—all business—if that had happened? Can you imagine this society returning to manual labor after we have achieved such mechanization?"

"Did the Church kill his objection?"

"Yes. But suppose it hadn't? Suppose we found ourselves with some so-called holy pope who supported Bernard against prostitution? Business could have been set back two hundred years." He contemplated Cossa so gravely that Cossa told me he thought for a moment that Cosimo was going to ask him for his stand on prostitution. Instead he said, "You have been a good friend, Your Holiness, therefore, even though it may become the most profitable single proposition we have ever organized, my father and I want to invite you to invest with us in a network of much-advanced versions of these factories—totally independent of the Cistercians—and when we get them going, perhaps you will even want to prevail upon the Cistercians to gradually withdraw from that kind of activity."

"Very clever, Cosimo," Cossa said. He was always willing to take their money but he was never deceived by their cunning.

"We have decided to accept local investment to spread local good will around. The local people will invest fifty percent of the capital requirement. Our group, the prime financing source, will provide the energizing money to establish the network—the first fifty percent, representing fifty shares.

"How much do you want from me?"

"A token three gold florins for three full shares. That investment should earn you close to a hundred thousand florins."

Cossa's smile lighted up the room.

"How much do you put in?" he asked.

"Our bank will receive fifteen percent of the prime holding of one hundred percent—for the basic concept and the energizing money. We are going to treble the number of existing mills in the next twenty-five years."

"How much money will you invest?"

"Bankers don't invest money. You know that," he said reproachfully. "We are money managers. We invest services. We are at the point of forging iron with these mills. My people have acquired the rights to an invention by two Englishmen, which, instead of providing only a rotary movement to drive millstones —as needed by corn mills, for example—a reciprocal motion can be produced mechanically by cams projecting from the axle of the waterwheel, which raises and releases a pivoting triphammer. Can you imagine what it will do for arms sales? Well! It will change the direction of Europe."

Cossa told me that somehow, such a considerable time later, the talk with Cosimo had, more than anything else, driven home to him that he had lost the great dream of Catherine Visconti forever. The fantasy, that adventure which had never happened and would never happen, was over. The chains around his wrists and the fetters around his legs were now driven solidly into the granite of time—where he would be chained for the rest of his life, sentenced by his dear friends to live with their onerous reality. But he also learned, he told me, that each time the Medici, or the marchesa for the Medici, asked him for something and he granted it—always small things at first but growing to the supreme consideration, the total banking of the Church—they gave to him much bigger things in the form of opportunities that brought him more and more money. The marchesa had read in Cossa's eyes and gestures that money was his substitute for courage in the face of what he saw as his helpless immobility. The Medici piled gold, then more gold, on top of his shoulders until he could not strike out at them in vengeance for their betrayal of him for fear of displacing the great load of gold and being crushed by the weight of such courage.

Cossa found that he needed the counsel and support of a wider experience of cardinals. The College was small and diminishing. Four cardinals had died during the first year of his pontificate, four more were in failing health, and two were absent on legatine duty. With the marchesa's counsel, which she assured him had the benefit of her own as well as the Medici intelligence services, Cossa created fourteen new cardinals from the most important men of every kingdom on June 6, 1411.

Only six cardinals remaining in the college were Italians, therefore he appointed six more Italians to join them. Seven were appointed from countries outside Italy. Kings and princes were consulted. John, archbishop of Lisbon, was appointed at the request of the king of Portugal. George of Lichtenstein, who had been bishop of Trent since 1391, was a close friend of Sigismund, so he was named although he was never strong enough to come to Rome to receive his red hat. Gordon Manning, educated at Cambridge, in his youth attached to John of Gaunt (who made him his executor), had been made canon of York in 1400 and dean the following year. He would have been made a cardinal by Innocent VII when Manning became archbishop of York, but the pope was offended by his execution of the previous Archbishop Scrope. Manning never came to Rome to take his place in the College because the king of England could not spare him. Of Manning it was said that he loved not the death of a sinner, but rather he should turn from his wickedness and live.

The three remaining cardinals were French. The first of these, recommended by the king of France, was Pierre d'Ailly. It went down hard with Cossa to name him a cardinal, for the simple reason that he did not like him or trust him, but the marchesa said he must do it or alienate France from his papacy. She pressed him hard and he buckled. She pressed him because d'Ailly was in deadly earnest about Church reform, which the Medici wanted as earnestly, and the marchesa was there to get whatever it was the Medici wanted.

D'Ailly was a politician of the rational sort. He wrote a tractate on physical geography, the *Imago Mundi,* and another against the superstitions of astrology, the *Tractatus de legibus et sectis contra superstitiousos astronomos.* He was an ardent student of divine philosophy, interpreting it after the school of William of Ockham. D'Ailly preached dogmatic theology rather than a gospel of morality and had all of the theologian's fine contempt for canon lawyers of which group Cossa had become the leading representative in the world.

All in all, d'Ailly was a practical man who could recognize the occasional utility of corruption. However, before he would accept the red hat that everyone knew he wanted so badly, he wrote a letter to Cossa pointing out in no uncertain way that it was the duty of the Church to reform itself first—"in justice and morals"—before reforming its members.

Chapter 38

Cosimo and I were sitting together in Mainz after a long business meeting with the archbishop, and he actually said these words to me: "Bankers can do so much for God's world, Your Eminence. If every man had the piety of my father—or even my own compulsion to serve God and his children—what an Eden this Europe would be. That we should be allowed to profit from giving service to God is not surprising, for does not every man who serves God profit in one way or another? But money is both the raw material and the by-product of banking, which our family uses only for good works. The profit that is yielded by our bank is really only the profit of opportunity to serve God and to hope that Europe may prosper too and that this prosperity may trickle benignly downward upon the masses of the less fortunate. This is the natural way to bless the poor.

"For what God has done for my family, we are determined to protect his people from ugliness. My father has shown me that it is a thrifty investment for the bank to give our fine painters their daily lasagna, for example, in exchange for beautifying our city. Sculptors as well, of course. Let our clients come to Florence and be impressed not only with this beauty but by what we must have *spent* to bring these artists to Florence for our clients' pleasure.

"My own feeling, and in this I believe my father concurs, is that the greatest artist we will ever bring to Florence is the marchesa di Artegiana. There is nothing the marchesa would not be willing to undertake for our bank. We are determined to save Europe from the Turks by keeping Europe strong, by building her industry, trade, and commerce, and by preserving God's Church to preserve God's people. There is no nobler aim.''

He believed every word of it. He did not choke on any word he spoke. He was a respectable banker.

Chapter 39

As the months passed and as hourly problems had to be solved, it was necessary for Cossa to lean upon the marchesa for good counsel. She had the vast Medici intelligence organization at her disposal for gathering the information they needed to reach decisions. Cossa seemed to forget that she had betrayed him, but he had not. When we were together he would speak of his wound and would show me how he had forced it to fester there. Revenge has always been the ultimate luxury of Neapolitans and its comfort was so enormously enfolding that they could afford to wait for it. As time went on the necessity for other revenge outweighed his need to repay the marchesa and Cosimo.

Cossa had his obsession to murder the son of Catherine Visconti to distract him from the day-to-day demands of the papacy, and he had the political distractions of the Church to dull the edges of his grief for Catherine, distractions that the marchesa shepherded across his consciousness. A clergyman named John Hus in Prague was disturbing the peace by attacking his archbishop. The marchesa said that Hus was greatly disturbing Sigismund, who expected to inherit the throne of Bohemia, and that Sigismund wanted something done to silence the man, if only to embarrass the present king, Wenzel, who was Sigismund's brother and who supported Hus. The marchesa reasoned that, since Cossa needed Sigismund, the king of Hungary, who could, quite possibly, be the next Holy Roman Emperor, ruler of the largest political unit in Europe, Germany, Cossa had to do something about Hus.

He agreed to read the Curia's file on Hus. The file told him that Hus was a pastor of purity, a man who thought with clarity and who was zealous for the reform of the Church, in fact a man who was heroic in character.

He preached that the supreme aim of religion was to love God absolutely. How could the corporate Church comprehend that? he asked. "They speak only for a political God who exists to be manipulated." He told his congregations that Christianity was the totality of the predestinate, born of God, and that the Church was the mystical body of Christ and the kingdom of heaven, and not a struggle for power between popes and kings, or a ruse to share riches through what they must think of as "God-given" opportunities for taxation. The prelates' determination that the Church be seen and obeyed as a corporation had allowed them a more concrete expression of the early ideas of ultimate authority, but it was no longer the authority of God that they sought, but the authority of popes, cardinals, and bishops that they imposed. He preached that the Church had become a conspiracy of lawyers.

He opposed the priests, who he said were insane when they claimed to create the body of God, exalting themselves above the Holy Mother who gave birth to the body of Jesus, once, while they claimed to do the same by mumbling over bread and wine, day after day, again and again. To create something is to make it out of nothing, Hus said from his pulpit. Only God is a Creator, yet this offends the corporate Church. These evil lawyers have abused the term "to believe," he said. The corporate Church commands that men believe in the Virgin Mary, in the saints, and in the pope. That is wicked foolishness, Hus told them. We must believe in none but God. Of God we should believe all that the Scripture teaches.

He preached to tens of thousands that his sense of duty cried out when spiritual office was bought or sold for money or for favors. That was flagrant abuse by the corpse that was the corporate Church, he maintained.

John Hus' archbishop in Prague was a young noble, a well-

meaning-enough soldier who had been the canon of Prague since
he was fourteen. He had a smattering of theological education,
but not much, because he gave his obedience to Pope Gregory
even after Gregory had been cast down at Pisa. The king had to
force him to recognize Pope Alexander and urgently required
him to declare that there existed no heresy in Bohemia. The
archbishop burned all of Wycliffe's books. Hus protested this
and the archbishop instantly excommunicated him.

Hus was also undiplomatic. He lost Sigismund's support
when, from his pulpit, he denounced the bull of indulgences that
Cossa had granted to secure resources for his war against Ladislas of Naples. Sigismund had permitted the sale of indulgences, so if Hus opposed them he was disobedient to his
king.

Hus enjoyed the constant favor of the court. He was the
queen's confessor. The king liked him. There were many nobles
who would have protected him against pope or emperor. He was
the idol of the Bohemian population and worshiped by all the
pious ladies of Prague. Cossa solved the Hus problem by sending Cardinal Oddone Colonna to Prague to investigate Hus. Colonna accepted many presents of money and jewels from the
archbishop, then himself excommunicated Hus (following the
archbishop's excommunication), but Hus remained a leader of
the reform movement. He denounced pride, luxury, avarice,
simony, and immorality, both of the lay and of the clerical members of the Church. He denounced the clergy living in concubi-
nage or committing adultery. He lashed out at the prelates of the
Church because of their simony. "We should have more people
like this," Cossa said to me. "Just as we should have a few
more plagues. They are an impossibility. When this man became
a priest he took on the obligations of a priest."

Spurred on by the marchesa and numb with his obsessive
thoughts of vengeance upon Catherine Visconti's son, Cossa
issued a bull calling for a crusade against Ladislas of Naples and
Pope Gregory XII. The bull promised indulgences to anyone and
everyone who would contribute to the crusade. Cossa ordered
all prelates, under pain of excommunication, to declare Ladislas
a perjurer, schismatic, blasphemer, and heretic, and, as such,
an excommunicate. A second bull commissioned the indulgence

sellers and excommunicated Gregory XII as a heretic and schismatic. Of the indulgence sellers appointed for Bohemia, one was Wenceslas Tiem, a German, born at Mikulov, in Moravia. He carried out his commission by farming out whole archdeaconries and parishes to unscrupulous collectors, who in turn exploited the people mercilessly. This nefarious commerce in the forgiveness of sins aroused John Hus' most determined opposition. He repudiated Cossa's bulls. He published two treaties that condemned the inciting of Christians against their brethren in a fratricidal war and trafficking in the forgiveness of sins without demanding the basic requirement of repentance. He denied the right of any pope to make war. He proclaimed that only God forgives sins and does so of his free grace to such as are of contrite heart. "Problem people like this Hus are never solved," Cossa said to me. "If I agreed with everything he said today, he would be back tomorrow with new objections. God save us from the theologians."

Such political encounters to one side, Cossa avoided the sacred side of his responsibilities as pope, to a point where he almost stirred up a mutiny among cardinals, the clergy, and the people, for, to them, the visible, ritual religious appearance of the papacy was what mattered beyond all else. He was forced to celebrate mass on Sunday and on holy days but he refused to do more. He confessed himself to no one. His audiences were confined to seeing soldiers and bankers. He slept through the day, as had his master, Boniface IX, and worked at night (rumor said with a woman) until the ripples of outrage became high waves battering at the spirituality of Europe. It was as though he had decided to show his contempt for the papacy that had (somehow) cost him Catherine Visconti, into which ignoble office as the vicar of Christ he had been tricked and cheated. He refused to try to understand his life. I tried to explain his situation to him. "What does it matter to you whether you do these things? It comes with the job. It matters to the people who hired you, I mean to the Italian people and the pilgrims from across the world, the people, the ones who contribute the money to support the Church that pays you so well. When you were a soldier you had to do a lot of things you didn't like to do. When you were a law student you had to do a lot of things you didn't agree with. What is the difference if you don't believe in the things that they expect you to do? It is a part of the job and you must do it."

He refused to listen to me.

"You are the pope, Cossa," the marchesa drilled into him. "You are the shepherd of the people. As the differences between the classes grow, when there is less social mobility and greater growth of violent unrest in the cities, there is a decline in the moral values. People are even losing their faith in the Church. Look at the public immorality. Let that continue and the revenues of the Church will dwindle even more. It is you who keeps saying that the Church is a business and I am trying to tell you what is happening to businesses in the fifteenth century. Get it all straight, for heaven's sake. You are going to have to call a *real* council, as ordered at Pisa. You have to set France against Ladislas. You are going to need the emperor and the princes. So say mass every day. Confess every day. Walk through the streets in holy processions. Hold daily audiences with the people, because you are going to need them, too."

Cossa was unable to lure Catherine Visconti's son to Bologna. Whenever there was a lapse in the problems he had created for himself, Cossa would write to the young duke of Milan in cordial, even warm terms, and tell him how he hoped the young man could join him on this holiday or to be with him for the commemoration of that feast day, but the young man replied by describing the kind of court intrigues he was fighting, how he would be many more months in weeding out his enemies, but saying that when his authority was safe and undisputed he would most happily go to Bologna to visit his pope.

Cossa went on with what he considered to be the work of the papacy, keeping voluminous records of all financial transactions, no matter how small. He held regular auction sales of benefices to the highest bidders; there was no concession that he would not sell. The plenary indulgence field was extremely profitable, particularly in Germany. In fact, he was even able to squeeze gold out of the Italians. He appointed the marchesa as the Church's land agent in Rome, where she handled the sale of eight churches, their contents, and the land on which they stood, to Cosimo di Medici for capital sums. The churches were razed and their contents sold to provide for high-cost housing. His master stroke of cash leverage was the mortgaging of the income of the Church to the Medici Bank, to meet the current running expenses during periods of inadequate cash receipts. The fees for bulls alone in the first year of Cossa's reign as Pope John XXIII amounted to forty-seven thousand florins.

He perpetuated force. War among the cities of Italy became the first ritual of the Church, because as he saw it, in Italy, power was temporal and naked. Even Italian wars became business propositions. The city-states hired weapons and *condottieri* through generals who were no more than labor contractors. Elsewhere, throughout Europe, society was able to organize stable states on national scales, but Italy would not consider doing that because of the example of the Church. He, Pope John XXIII, was the tallest giant on the Italian peninsula, but he was a pygmy beside the rulers beyond the Alps.

The marchesa hammered at him. "Listen to me, Cossa!" she would shout at him. "The diplomat has to take over from the soldier. Only brains count. Brute force is nothing. Only diplomacy can preserve your papacy." Giovanni di Bicci di Medici had given her a blunt assignment. To carry it out meant changing Cossa, which meant that she needed to be more than blunt.

"Sigismund of Hungary supports the papacy of Gregory XII," she told him. "Until we get Sigismund on our side, locked on our side, the papacy and Italy are going to be smothered by Europe."

"What are you talking about, Decima?"

"Look at the papacy! One-third of its former glory, one-half of its former income. Suppose those two old men, Benedict and Gregory, did die tomorrow, what would you win in the face of these strident demands for Church reform? But if you are the originator who brings the pressure that pushes the impecunious Sigismund to the supreme leadership of Germany by making him the Holy Roman Emperor, you will be able to operate as the popes operated two hundred years ago, manipulating the balance of power among the contending kings for the temporal domination of Europe.''

''Oh, yes? And just how do I do that?''

''It will take careful diplomacy. Only the electors can make Sigismund the emperor. John of Nassau is the most powerful of the seven electors. He is first elector and has great influence over the other six. So we must drug John of Nassau with money and churchly honors.''

''I can spare him the honors,'' Cossa said, ''but who has the money for nonsense like that?''

''Nonsense? *Nonsense?* Will you still think it is nonsense if the Medici advance the money? Cossa—consider Cosimo's water-power scheme, the plan for all the factories. Suppose Cosimo decides to invite John of Nassau into the scheme and suppose you send a strong legate to him to hitch together a natural alliance among Nassau, Sigismund, the Church and the Medici Bank—would you still tell me this isn't the thing we must do?''

Cossa sighed with exasperation. ''You are the agent for the Medici, not me. Why ask me?''

''Who will be your legate?''

''I will think about it.''

''The archbishop of Mainz is the same sort of churchman as you are, which is to say he is a blood-and-guts warrior who lives on noise and never says mass if he can avoid it. So you must send someone who understands you sympathetically. Nassau prefers to speak German. So your legate must be able to do that. If you send a cardinal as legate, Nassau would be outranked. But that suits the way his mind works. He is German. He can only look down on people or look up at someone. So you must send a cardinal, a bold man who will do what you tell him and who will be unmoved by Nassau's noisy trappings of wealth and power. We will have a lock on Sigismund.''

''And where do I find such a towering model of a cardinal? Don't you think Nassau knows all the German-speaking cardinals?''

''You are the pope. Create one.''

''Who? That is all I am asking you. Who, for Christ's sake?''

''Franco Ellera.''

His face underwent visible changes from astonishment to awe

to incredulity. "Aside from the fact that Franco Ellera is a Jew," he said, sarcastically, "and a slave, and has never, to my knowledge, set foot inside a church, he is the very man for the job."

"Is he really a Jew?" she marveled. "He was a part of your family."

"The German women on the ships my father took were Jews. His mother was a Jew. The survivors—and he was one—said he was a Jew. Why, Franco Ellera even claims that his father was a Jew."

The marchesa shrugged. "So he is a Jew. John of Nassau doesn't know that."

Cossa struck the arms of his chair with both fists and bounded to his feet enthusiastically. "By God, Franco Ellera certainly *looks* like a cardinal. That oppressive voice! The compulsion to give advice! That constant self-justification and unending self-approval! That white beard! Those haggard, near-sighted, black-bagged eyes! Franco Ellera could have Nassau feeling as if he were some newly recruited foot soldier."

When the marchesa departed through the curtains and down the private staircase to visit with Bernaba and give her the details of the news, which Bernaba told to me years afterward, Cossa summoned me, bidding me to lock the door behind me when I came in.

"What's up, Cossa?" I asked him. "Locking doors? What kind of robbery are you plotting this time?"

"No plot. I've just been thinking about what a long voyage you've made since you were that boy on that raft."

"I didn't get here alone, you know."

"I just welled over with feeling."

"It couldn't hurt."

"Do you respect the marchesa's judgment?"

"She is almost as smart as your father, and twice as dangerous."

"Would you like me to continue to be pope?"

"If you want it. What is this, a catechism drill, all these trick questions?"

"Franco Ellera—really, this is absurd. That is, at first it is going to sound absurd to you, but the marchesa has convinced me that I must make several strong military and political alliances through the electors of the empire.''

"So? Why not?"

"I'm glad you agree. All right. I will put it to you straight. The marchesa is going to Florence to tell Cosimo di Medici that he must go to Mainz, taking with him certain financial opportunities for the electors. She feels that you should go directly to Mainz to get the electors ready for Cosimo's proposals and thereby secure the election of—ah—our candidate as the next emperor."

"Me?"

"You can do it. I know you can do it."

"Cossa! You have a building full of cardinals for things like that."

"The marchesa has thought it all through," Cossa said patiently. "You have great German, almost as good as mine. Your voice and your belly and your black eyeflags are very impressive. When you put on the costume you will be a really formidable figure. You will be taught what to do, never fear—how to act the role of the pope's procurator and what to look for at every turning."

"It will never work."

"Not so. And to make sure it will work, I am going to make you cardinal-deacon of the Church of Santa Amalia di Angeli, at Fribourg. You will be traveling in the robes of your office and with a cardinal's entourage."

"Baldassare! I am a Jew!"

"I know that and you know that. But who else knows it?"

"Well, my rabbi for one."

"Well! He of *all* people will certainly understand—considering our lifelong relationship and the kind of title you are going to get—you'll be a prince of the Church, Franco Ellera!"

"Are you asking me to convert?"

"Why should you convert? I make the rules and if I, the pope, choose to make you a cardinal, then you are a cardinal."

"A cardinal," I said sadly, shaking my head. "With your influence you could have had me made chief rabbi of Bologna."

"A lot of things would have been different if we both had been religious men."

"My uniforms alone are going to cost you a pretty florin. Two kinds of hats, red shoes, white shoes, dalmatics, copes, chasubles, and albs."

"You have the figure for them, Franco Ellera. What counts is that you start promptly. You will have to move fast. Time is everything."

"What about expenses?"

"A generous per diem."

"For the horses, the liveries, the provisions, the bedding, plate, hangings, secretaries—the entire household?"

Cossa nodded. "Absolutely," he said.

"Speaking of my household, do you think Bernaba could go along? The trip would do her good and she could rehearse me in my lines." Bernaba and I had been married for nine years but we still hadn't told Cossa.

"I don't see why not," His Holiness answered. "And we will see to it that you will be welcomed before the gates of Mainz, where your embassy must make solemn entry. You must be met at some distance from the place of your reception by persons of rank and distinction appropriate to your position as a prince of the Church as well as a papal ambassador."

Chapter 40

John of Nassau was the great-grandson of the Emperor Adolf. On October 19, 1396, at the death of Conrad, archbishop of Mainz, John was a candidate to succeed him in the post. The emperor, Wenzel, favored the claim of Joffrid of Leiningen, so a committee of five chose Joffrid to be recommended to the pope. John of Nassau went directly to Rome, paid Boniface forty thousand gold florins, and was immediately confirmed as the archbishop of Mainz and so became the senior elector of the empire.

He also became the open and bitter enemy of Wenzel. Without pausing for as much as a benediction, he established alliances with the count palatine, with the bishops of Bamberg and Eichstadt, with the burgrave of Nuernberg, the margrave of Meissen, and the count of Henneberg, and with the cities of Nuernberg, Rothenburg, Windesheim, and Weissenburg, and organized the downfall of Wenzel.

The reasons that the electors gave for Wenzel's overthrow would not bear close examination. Even though Wenzel was a drunkard and a murderer, they charged him only with having done nothing to end the schism and with betraying the interests of the empire. But his true offenses were that he had opposed John of Nassau's intention to become archbishop and that he had not shared the bribe of one hundred thousand florins that

Gian Galeazzo Visconti had paid to Wenzel for making Gian Galeazzo duke of Milan.

On August 20, 1400, the electors declared that Wenzel was deposed as emperor. On the next day, at the Koenigstuhl in Rense, they proclaimed the count Palatine, Rupert III, king of the Romans, the title that lighted the way to the imperial throne.

I must explain the difference between being king of the Romans and being Holy Roman Emperor. In 1316, Pope John XXII was determined to bring against the Holy Roman Empire, which was Germany, the largest state by far in Europe, the most extreme claims of the papacy. He took the position that, since Christ had invested Peter with the temporal no less than with the spiritual kingdom of this world, it followed that what the pope had given, the establishment of the empire, the pope could also take away; that when the emperor died the jurisdiction of the empire reverted to the pope and that it was for him to appoint a new emperor.

The Germans contended that it was for the electors to choose the future emperor and for the pope only to crown the object of their choice, that in the event of a contested election, it was for the God of Battles to decide between rival candidates.

The claim of the pope was not one that the electors could pass over in silence. They met at Rense and at Frankfurt in 1338 and resolved that the prince elected by them became the king of the Romans without further ceremony, without need for further confirmation. However, it was understood that to become Holy Roman Emperor, the king of the Romans needed to be crowned by a pope at Rome.

Christendom still thought of itself as one society, torn by schism, wars, and internal conflicts, but it also thought of itself, in a collectively aberrant way, as Romans, because no one liked remembering that Rome had fallen a thousand years before and that they, Christendom, represented the barbarians who had pulled it down. The liberal German intellectuals liked to speak of their people as Romans, the *populus romanus*. Germany, where no Roman legion had ever tarried for fear of becoming the principal objects in the brutally pagan German rites, hailed its king as Holy Roman Emperor and continued to elect him,

because it would have been unseemly to allow the throne of
Caesar, which was the temporal lordship of the world, to be
passed on by inheritance like somebody's house. So, a thousand
years after the ancient Romans had vanished from the earth, it
was the custom of Christendom that the Holy Roman Emperor
was a drenched, red-nosed, German princeling.

When the electors deposed Wenzel they created a schism in
the empire to coexist with the schism in the Church. Three men
now contended for the imperial throne: Wenzel, now king of
Bohemia, where he put it about that he was known as Good
King Wenceslas, a local joke; Rupert, now king of the Romans;
and Sigismund, king of Hungary, Wenzel's half-brother. As king
of the Romans, Rupert was already king of the Romans so it
followed automatically that he would be the next Holy Roman
Emperor, but if anything happened to him Sigismund was the
coming man politically—at least he had most certainly become
so by the time I left Mainz.

Sigismund's father, Emperor Charles IV, king of Bohemia,
was said to be the greatest secular ruler of the fourteenth century because he founded the University of Prague in 1348, almost succeeded in uniting the Latin and Greek Churches and,
by his Golden Bull, brought organization and order to the prin-
ciples of election to the imperial throne, thus holding Germany
together. He had three sons: Wenzel, Sigismund, and John. For
them he turned his life's work upside down, emptying it of wisdom. Against his own Golden Bull, which called for an independent succession brought about by the electors he had named, he
gave the imperial crown to Wenzel, then seventeen, and died.

If Wenzel grew into a dangerous, murdering drunkard (which
he did), Sigismund seemed to have consciously designed his life
to be tossed about upon a noisy, random, splattering whirlwind
of events. He had been betrothed when he was a small boy to
Mary, infant daughter of Louis the great, king of Hungary and
Poland. Because of that marriage, Sigismund eventually succeeded to the Hungarian throne. Mary died in 1392 and, on his
return from an utterly disastrous war with the Turks (securing
his place in history by leading the last Crusade, which required
him merely to step across his own frontier to kill the infidel), he
was imprisoned for five months by the outraged Hungarian

barons. He escaped that solely because of Pippo Span's wit and daring, then he was seized by his own brother, messy Wenzel, because he had (also) pushed his way into Bohemian affairs and Wenzel was then king of Bohemia.

In 1390, Boniface IX proclaimed Ladislas of Naples king of Hungary, inciting him against Sigismund, who, although ever-ready to pick up new titles, like potatoes in a field, was passionate about retaining his used ones. Sigismund not only crushed Ladislas at Raab, but also ordered both Hungary and Bohemia to cease paying any money to the papal treasury.

He led a whirligig of a life because he knew he would not be either welcome or safe if he stayed in any one place too long. He traveled constantly with a gaudy escort. He entered towns encouraged by music—large bands or a few fiddlers. He was an unscrupulous royal adventurer whose juggled sense of success was only slightly muted by his second wife, Barbara. She was called The Hungarian Messalina, a formidable combination of labels, and was mightily busy therefore at keeping Sigismund bobbing within the eye of a storm of cuckoldry. Sigismund shrugged that off. He, himself, was constantly being tripped and falling into the arms of passing women.

At one time, after defeating the Venetians at Motta, Sigismund forced their captain to hack off the right hands of one hundred and eighty of his own men and fling them into the sea. Before that, while still the young Hungarian king, Sigismund disciplined some of the Hungarian nobles by calling thirty-one of them into his tent separately, one by one, and beheading them there. The slaughter stopped only because the rest of them refused to enter when they saw the blood of their comrades running out under the bottom flap of the tent. Sigismund almost always did things in the extreme, not only because he had no sense of proportion, but also because he was never quite sure that what he was doing would be viewed as being kingly enough. He was like that in all things.

After Nicopolis, nearly dying of fever, he had himself hung up by his feet for twenty hours to let the sickness trickle out of his mouth while hundreds of his subjects filed past, wondering about him.

His family were Luxembourgers. After he married the heiress

to the Hungarian crown, he began to carom off each succeeding opportunity. Sigismund plowed through his life flush with promise but slow of payment. He lived like a housefly, ever on the move lest some circumstance strike at him. Within his flaccid self he was a creature of flighty impulse and indulgence, yet, at every exterior inch of him, he was a monarch of men—tall, majestic, handsome, manly—with a flowing yellow beard that was turning gray, married to a willfully pagan wife of twenty-two years, a fair and graceful woman, although her face was marred with spots. Each time he strayed from her bed with another woman, she left his for two other women, three men, and a stable boy, but in all this her husband never interfered. His magpie interest was only taken by the glitter of other things.

More than anything else it was his *amour-propre,* somewhat of a lesser thing than ambition, which drove him to seek the respectability of winning his father's place as Holy Roman Emperor, as coequal with the sort of people who had not existed since Boniface VIII. It was Sigismund's intention, when the great day came, not to admit even the pope as his peer. His father had "almost" reestablished the unity of the Latin and Greek Churches. Sigismund took it as his destiny to be hailed as the one man whose leadership would restore the unity of the Church by ending its schism. Sigismund, the most barbaric, ruthless, and left-handed of princes, the grinning knave of German royalty, was obsessed and besotted with the idea of the abolition of the offending schism in the Church.

Sigismund's great shield, his cloak of respectability and instant honor, was the Holy Church. When all else failed he knew that by rushing to its defense—whether to seal off its enemies, or to heal its schism, or to cry out for its reform, attacking its heretics and simoniacs or battling Turks, this was the certain way he knew he could keep his luster from rusting.

To place Sigismund upon the imperial throne suited the first elector, the archbishop of Mainz, who had eliminated Wenzel. Rupert had alienated his support by destroying nine castles in Wetterau in order to clean out nests of freebooters who had been pillaging the merchants of Swabia, Thuringia, and Hesse. These castles, as it happened, were within the jurisdiction of the archbishop and paid full tribute to him. What the marchesa had known before she had proposed my expedition to Mainz was that the archbishop had decided to depose Rupert as king of the Romans. The pope's support of Sigismund would be, for the archbishop, a political coup.

Therefore the marchesa knew that when my embassy train reached Mainz with its household of 128 people, then joined with the mission of Cosimo di Medici, who had traveled with a staff of 56, the archbishop of Mainz was already inclined toward the views we would present. Cosimo was suitably impressed with my explicit authority. So was I. I had learned my part well, but the fact is, I have always had explicit authority, and if I couldn't stare down a little runt like Cosimo, what would be the sense of Cossa's making me a cardinal in the first place?

I spoke only in German to Nassau and in Latin to Cosimo, easily dominating both men with genuinely rumbling dignity at banquets, masses, and other occasions of state, more impressive in my scarlet robes, white beard, and tragic eye swags than any of the candidates for emperor. Thank God it wasn't in Cossa's power to make me emperor. I persuaded Cosimo to allow me to outline for the archbishop the generalities of the tremendous financial opportunity that was about to be offered to the first elector, then at once brought up Pope John's deep thoughts on the erasure of the schism by bringing Sigismund's youth and power into the awful breach. What was wanted, I told them, was that Sigismund should be elected as emperor but, of equal importance, that Sigismund should know well that it had been the pope who had sponsored him with the electors.

A coup of statesmanship was struck. Cossa could believe that he was again preventing the reform of the Church, while at the same time acquiring military protection on his northern and eastern flanks. Cosimo di Medici knew, nonetheless, that this strategy, which he and the marchesa had so carefully developed, would sweep the schism into history, eliminate the three present popes through stringent Church reform, and sustain Europe as a stable place for the sensible conduct of business affairs. I warned Cossa about those two people until I was blue in the nose but he only shrugged and mouthed nonsense like "What will be will be." The fact is, as pope, Cossa was making more money than he had ever made in his life and that was where contentment rested for him. Things like the Medici's determination to bring about structural and religious reform in the Church were indefinite and always far in the future. The only reform Cosimo believed in was bringing about an end to the schism for the benefit of European business. Not only were Cosimo and the marchesa either charming to Cossa—as Cosimo was to him at all times—or pandered to his needs for sex and power, as did the marchesa, but their advice was making him an enormous amount of money. I warned him that it all had to end in our ruin, I told him again and again, but popes have never listened to their cardinals.

Chapter 41

On May 18, 1410, Rupert, king of the Romans, died. The marchesa convinced Cossa that it was of infinite importance to him that the future king of the Romans should bring all Germany under the obedience of Pope John XXIII, whose obedience depended upon the Council of Pisa, whose authority the dead Rupert had opposed and King Sigismund of Hungary had not acknowledged.

The marchesa's daughter, Maria Louise Sterz, transmitted the news to her mother from Mainz when Sigismund was elected king in Rupert's place, saying that John of Nassau had made it clear to Sigismund that it was the sponsorship of Pope John XXIII that had decided the matter in his favor against the candidacies of his two brothers, Wenzel and John, the three men who were the sons of the Emperor Charles IV. Maria Louise advised her mother that Sigismund would send the count of Ozoro, Pippo Span, as his ambassador to Bologna to show his appreciation to the pope.

This was Sigismund's first recognition of Cossa's papacy over the claims of Gregory, whom the king had previously supported, and Cossa needed Sigismund. In return Cossa removed the sentence of closure on the churches of Hungary that had been passed on the April 6, 1404. Intercourse between Sigismund and the Curia was renewed and the possibly heretical acts of Sigis-

mund were indirectly legalized. Bishop Branda of Piacenza was
sent as papal legate to Hungary to arrange for the institution of
a university and to correct certain abuses and abolish certain
privileges that certain bishops had received from Gregory XII.
At the special desire of the king, Cossa took thought for the
creation of new benefices on the borders of the kingdom.

Even before she told Cossa the news, the marchesa sent a
messenger to her daughter Rosa, with Spina in Naples, to tell
her that she must travel at once to Bologna on family business.
Rosa got to Bologna three days before the count of Ozoro.

"Let me tell you about Pippo Span," the marchesa told her
daughter. "He is Sigismund's favorite. Seven years ago, when
Sigismund was seized by his nobles in the Hall of Audience at
Buda, Pippo Span defended him with drawn sword and would
have been killed if the bishop of Strigonia had not thrown his
robe over Pippo's head and declared him to be his prisoner.
Pippo raised troops to free Sigismund. He wrote to the king
constantly in prison. When Sigismund was freed he gave Pippo
a castle and made him a general, out of gratitude."

"Oh, *God*! How wonderful!"

"Oh, yes, dear. He is a really romantic figure."

"But what an odd name."

"He is the count of Ozoro. Pippo is short for Filippo. *Ispan* is
the Hungarian for captain of a district. He has the most lustrous
dark eyes—and such a sweet, shy smile."

"When will I meet him?"

"As soon as he gets here, dear. Did you know, in the war
with Bosnia, when Sigismund became panic-stricken and fled,
Pippo snatched his crown, put it on his own head, rallied the
troops, and won a victory. For that, Sigismund promoted him
to a general of twenty thousand horse. And what is also interesting, he is very rich and *quite* noble—he belongs to an
old family of Buondelmonte—although his parents were quite
poor."

"I am so tired of old men, Mama. It seems as though I have
spent my entire life with old men. How old is he?"

"Oh, *young*. Quite young. And I am sure he will adore you."

A soft flush settled like light rouge under her olive cheeks.
Her loveliness moved her mother because neither of them would
be this young ever again.

"Spina threw himself into a towering rage when I left," Rosa said.

"What did you tell him?"

"I said that you wanted to tell me, to tell him, before the pope could tell him, that you had secured a very special satisfaction for him."

"Well, then. I must think of something. I must speak to Cossa about some benefices that have become available in Sicily."

"I don't know why he carries on like that about me. He is not only old, he is obsessed by a woman named Bernaba Minerbetti anyway. He wakes up in the middle of the night screaming her name."

"*Really?*"

"And he hasn't seen her in almost twenty years. He has such hatred for her that I am sure he loves her."

"Enough of Spina. Pippo Span is not yet forty. He was born in Tizzano, a sweet little town, about seven miles east of Florence—where he is right now. When he was ten, his father gave him to the training of Luca Pecchia, a trader who eventually took him to Buda, where the boy attracted the attention of Sigismund's treasurer, a brother of the bishop of Strigonia, who took him under his protection. He is so bold and dashing! He was at the bishop's palace when he met Sigismund—who is only four years older than he is—and after dinner a discussion arose about raising twelve thousand cavalry to guard the Danube against the Turks, who had just taken Serbia—but no one present, except Pippo, was able to calculate the expense. Oh, he is a *remarkable* young man . . . abstemious habits, a *great* orator—and he speaks languages like Hungarian and Polish and Bohemian as easily as he does Italian and Latin. And he is the closest man to this new king of the Romans."

"Just what is it that you want me to get Pippo Span to get Sigismund to do for you, Mama?" Rosa asked warily.

The marchesa kissed her daughter softly on the cheek. "The pope is going to need Sigismund," she said, "and we need the pope. I will calm Spina so that you may be acquired by Pippo Span and keep him dazzled against the moment when we need him."

"Suppose he dazzles me instead?"

"He will see a beautiful, loving young woman who under-

stands him deeply. He won't know that it is your profession to
understand him, so he will fall in love with you just the way
people fall in love with their mirrors.''

"But what if I love him?''

"Rosa—we know that *can* happen. Why not? Just as he, a
soldier, knows that he can be felled by an axe when he enters
his next battle.''

Rosa saw Pippo Span for the first time from a window of a
building that faced the papal palace. He stood gallantly in a long,
green mantle, which trailed to the ground as he leaped from his
horse, wearing a military hat with lappets falling on his shoulders. She thought he looked directly up at her. She grew faint
with pleasure, then withdrew to her wardrobe.

His Holiness, Pope John; myself, Francisco, Cardinal Ellera;
the marchesa di Artegiana, and her daughter, Rosa Dubramonte,
greeted Pippo Span as he came into the large, gilt-streaked private audience room in the papal palace. As the count looked at
Rosa, the marchesa could see his heart leap into his eyes. His
Holiness introduced the marchesa di Artegiana as a "distinguished visitor from Pisa,'' and her daughter, Rosa, as "my
godchild.''

We spoke of general things, about the weather, the wars, and
King Sigismund, until I mentioned that the count had been telling me that the king of the Romans had been treated harshly by
former pontiffs.

"We may be thankful that is over,'' His Holiness said.

"The king will be very happy to know that, Your Holiness,''
the count said fervently.

There was a small dinner party. I was a weightily impressive
figure to Pippo Span (as I was to anyone), a mountain of scarlet
fulminations who told him about my embassy to the first elector
to plead, for His Holiness, that King Sigismund be awarded the
throne of the Romans for the sake of Christendom. I was superb.
I was getting into the part of cardinal with enormous art. Everyone spoke German as a mark of respect for the absent king, who
had been born in Luxembourg. Immediately after the dinner,
the older members of the party excused themselves—His Holi-

ness to work, for it was well-known that he worked all night;
myself to prayer before retiring, very short prayers perhaps, in
which I would eventually be joined by Bernaba, who was attending to business on the other side of town, made rapturous by my
new status; and the marchesa, who was tired from travel. Rosa
and Pippo were alone.

I watched them through one of the peepholes the marchesa
had had installed throughout the palace. They gazed upon each
other with wonderment. Rosa was inundated by such feelings as
had never reached her before. His voice was deep and rich and
she longed to hear him sing to her. The clarity of his eyes, which
were utterly without innocence, the risk with which he looked
at her, the sensation of his hand touching her wrist, filled her
with the dread of being parted from him when he returned to his
king, wherever that might be, while she lay alone among the
misshapen bodies of old men.

An immense resolve to keep Rosa with him filled Pippo Span.
He would tell her about his wife in Buda, whom he had not seen
in fourteen months in any case, and about his five children. He
decided instantaneously not to tell her about the children, because that could turn her away from him. Perhaps, for a little
while, he had better not tell her about his wife. He ached for
her.

"This is a dream," he whispered to her. "If I kiss you, you
will vanish."

"Kiss me."

They kissed and clung to each other until they could hardly
breathe from the desire they felt.

She drew him out into the night garden. She led him to a
blanket of sweet grass under a tree.

On the night that followed, three hours after midnight, while
the marchesa supped with Cossa and me at the Anziani, they
talked about what progress had been made toward consolidating
the support of Sigismund. "Pippo Span was at my door before
noon yesterday," she said. "I showed surprise. Rosa and I had
been over the matter in the morning. He had important things to
speak about with me, he said. I took him into the garden and we
sat beneath a tree and he said that he loved Rosa so powerfully

that when he thought of living without her he wished to die. 'My
dear count,' I said, 'my daughter is affianced to a Sicilian prince.
Her future is en*tire*ly settled.' He *wept,* Cossa. I did not soothe
him but waited for him to compose himself. 'I know what I
know,' he said. 'Rosa loves *me.*' 'But you are a married man,
Count Ozoro. What kind of life are you offering Rosa? She
would have no place and she would live in fear of the vengeance
of the Sicilian.' 'Rosa will be more than my wife. She will travel
with me wherever I go. She will take her place equally at my
side in the court of the king of the Romans. She will share with
me any honor paid to me, any wealth conferred upon me, as
well as the king's friendship now and when he becomes the Holy
Roman Emperor.' I brought tears to the brims of my eyes to
show that he had moved me. I said to him, 'That may be so
while you live, but what is to become of this young woman, who
will be alone, without even the protection of her honor, when
some foreign mercenary crashes his axe upon your head in battle?' He pledged that Rosa would be protected. I reminded him
that the dead have no voices to command comfort for the living,
feeling that sooner or later he would find the wit to say that
everything could be put down in writing, but his mind had been
greatly slowed down by his lust. He implored that there must be
a way. I said we must have time to think, that he must go away
while we weighed what must be done."

"Is he going?" the pope said yawning.

"He is gone. But he will be back. In the meantime, things
assume their places. Ladislas grows stronger, but Sigismund
begins to exceed Ladislas' strength. We must be ready to secure
his friendship, to make him your protector. Soon we will need
to meet with him. Before that, Rosa will be united with Pippo
Span so that Sigismund may be bent to do what we know must
be done."

"Then we will wait."

"But while we wait I must compensate Spina for his loss of
Rosa. What do you suggest?"

"I will think about it," Cossa said. But when she had gone,
all he thought about was how and when he would be able to lure
Catherine Visconti's son away from his generals in Milan and
cause him to vanish in the deepest cellars of this building.

Chapter 42

The marchesa sent a message to Cardinal Spina, who agreed to meet her at her house in Rome, he needing to travel from Naples, where he was Cossa's listening post next to Ladislas, while pretending to be of the obedience of Gregory, ever-ready to shift his loyalties back to Gregory should the balance of papal power change.

When he met the marchesa in Rome he used a disguise of heavy grief over his loss of Rosa. The marchesa was understanding but she pointed out the certain logic of Rosa's position. "She is so young, just a girl really, while you must be into your fifties, Eminence."

"What a life I gave her!" Spina said. "I made her the centerpiece wherever we were, whether among kings and princes or among the great of the world. Where is she? How could she do this? Where has she gone?"

"She has become very religious," the marchesa said. "She may take vows."

"Oh—no!" the cardinal cried.

"I saw it coming," the marchesa went on, "which is why—when she told me at last that she would leave you—I prevailed upon His Holiness to confer some great benefice upon you, commensurate with your loss of Rosa."

Spina remained expressionless, except for unconscious movements of his hands, which the marchesa had been able to read for many years but which Spina did not know were revealing. "Eminence, the Holy Father wants you to know how much he appreciates the assistance and support you gave to me before the conclave at Pisa." Spina blinked. He closed his hooded eyes tightly as a defense against the unknown. He smiled with his mouth, not disturbing his eyes. Because he did not know what she was talking about, he answered generally.

"When I first knew you, you were not a marchesa," he said.

"When your mother first knew you, you were not a cardinal," she answered serenely. "Are we going to talk business or do you want to gossip?"

"I was happy to be able to help you at Pisa."

"Spina, what makes you so devious?"

"Devious?"

"Boniface called you the most devious man in the Curia."

"How I miss him."

"The Holy Father has been going over records of Sicilian income and I told him I thought you deserved a greater share of it."

Spina opened one hand but kept the other closed; a neutral signal.

"You have gathered up most of the benefices in western Sicily —it is even possible that you own the city of Agrigento—but the Holy Father thinks you should know that the duke of Anjou, the rightful heir to the throne of Naples, has been ceded the entire island by Pope John as a gesture of friendship to France and—although it is a political matter in which he will have to wrest the actual ownership of Sicily from Ladislas—it *might* occur to him to recall the benefices that you hold and to take over all of the benefices on the eastern end of the island as well."

"With respect, Marchesa, the duke's work is not God's work." Spina's right hand struck at his left wrist, symbolically severing the duke from the Church.

"He could have Sicily for breakfast."

"If he can drive out Ladislas."

"I have another plan."

Spina was silent but his hands turned themselves over, palms upward in his lap.

"This is a new papacy, Eminence, a fresh start. His Holiness now holds *all* the Sicilian benefices, including your own. He has offered to redistribute them through me as a gesture of his gratitude."

Spina's hands turned over and closed.

"Or," the marchesa continued sympathetically, "he can redistribute the western benefices to you, then endow you with the eastern benefices, with the understanding that you will share them with me." The last had not precisely been Cossa's plan but the marchesa had always operated on the principle of "if you don't ask, you don't get." "This would be administered by you and shared out equally with me."

"It is a Solomonlike decision," Spina said.

"Be careful when you count out my share, Eminence," the marchesa said. "For as the Holy Father gives out these benefices, so can he take them away."

Chapter 43

Cossa wanted to take in any money that the Church could make possible—as if he believed that the world had forced him to be its pope, therefore the world could pay him well for the indignity —but European politics kept interfering; Church politics refused to go away. I was good at that kind of thing, even the marchesa, herself, said that once, but mainly I used my skills for advising Cossa, who always kept my advice to himself, because if she didn't agree she could get sarcastic, and nobody likes that.

Cossa wrote to all the Christian princes to announce his ascension to the throne of St. Peter, exhorting them to support him against the two pretenders, whom the Universal Council had condemned and deposed. His first political problem as pope was to break down the support and protection that Ladislas and Sigismund, king of the Romans, gave to Gregory XII. He was on his way to succeeding with Sigismund, the marchesa's instinct told her and she told Cossa, but Ladislas could not be turned because Ladislas was the enemy of Italy. Therefore, all advice, including mine, was that Cossa should identify his cause with that of Louis, duke of Anjou, against Ladislas.

Fighting Ladislas was the duke of Anjou's life's work. That was a fact. He had been at it ever since he was a young man. He had invaded the Kingdom of Naples three times to try to win the throne that had been willed to him by Queen Joanna. Ladislas was, once again, preparing to storm Italy. Cossa's only defense against him was to attack him. The only means of attack available was the ambition and universal availability of the duke of Anjou.

Naples had fought its way through a history that was as devious and as unstable as its own nature. In 1262, Charles of Anjou had been called on to expel the Hohenstaufen and won for himself the Kingdom of the Two Sicilies. His cruelty had brought the Sicilian Vespers of 1282. He lost Sicily. Naples alone remained to the house of Anjou. By 1376, the Kingdom of Naples was ruled by the four-times-married but childless Queen Joanna. Her heir-presumptive was her second cousin, Charles of Durazzo, but the papal schism had begun, dividing both Christendom and the royal house of Naples. Queen Joanna went over to the French side against Pope Urban VI.

Charles of Durazzo supported Urban. To defeat Charles' expectations of the Neapolitan throne, Joanna made a will on June 29, 1380, in which she adopted, as her son, Louis, duke of Anjou, brother of Charles V of France, making him her heir in Italy, Sicily, Naples, and France. Charles of Durazzo invaded Naples and captured Joanna. She was murdered. Charles was crowned king of Naples. That duke of Anjou died in the same year as he was preparing an assault to win back his inheritance. Charles was assassinated in Hungary when he went to that parlous country to accept its kingship, which had been offered to him. This left the claim to the throne to be fought for between two boys: Ladislas, son of Charles, age ten, and Louis II of Anjou, age seven. Three times, over the ensuing years, Ladislas occupied Rome, and three times the forces of Louis expelled him from the city. They were at it for over thirty years.

On the first day of his pontificate, the marchesa had letters of recommendation ready for Cossa to sign that urged all lords (spiritual and temporal) to aid the army of the duke of Anjou in the liberation of Rome and the Vatican. Gregory XII had long since escaped the Vatican for the safe protection of Carlo Malatesta, at Rimini. Cossa informed the princes in these letters that he would entrust the duke with a prefecture to extend his facilities for the invasion of Naples, and the duke had set out from France to try again.

In his eagerness, he sailed on ahead with half of his fleet, leaving behind him six other galleys with his horses, arms, stores, and the larger part of his troops and treasure. This deserted squadron was taken by the warships of Ladislas and the Genoese in a sea fight near the island of Meloria. Three of the French galleys went to the bottom, three were taken, and their valuable charges went to the Neapolitans. Only one ship, with fifteen hundred men aboard, escaped and rejoined the duke at Piombino.

At Piombino, the wall-eyed duke, a compulsive talker with a bilateral emission lisp, received an embassy of condolence from Florence. He mounted a black horse, clad in black raiment, and accompanied by his troops, who were dressed in black, made his sorrowful way to Siena where Cossa had given orders for his cordial reception. Greatly cheered by such courtesy, he got rid of the black for everybody, put on red uniforms, very pretty, and rode off to Bologna to see the pope where he was met outside the city by cardinals and citizens.

Neither his pope nor the Florentines would help the duke with money but they both supplied troops.

"It is no surprise to me that the Florentines would refuse to contribute money to my campaign," the duke said spatteringly, "but you, the Holy Pontiff, called out for the liberation of Rome and the sacred Vatican and that is what I have come all this way to do."

"You have come to crush Ladislas forever," Cossa said. "You have come to regain your rightful inheritance as the king of the Two Sicilies."

"Well, yes. I suppose you're right. Oh, well, I can certainly use all the troops you can spare."

The duke engaged the services of Muzio Attendolo Sforza as his general then forgot to pay him. The papal and ducal troops, together with two thousand five hundred men supplied by Florence, deprived by Christian tradition of Cossa's leadership because it had been three centuries since popes had led men into battle, marched off to Rome. What remained of the ducal fleet, seven large galleys and one small one, sailed off to Ostia, the port of Rome, under the command of Cossa's murderous uncle, Geronimo Cossa, now a papal admiral.

Early in January 1411, the ambassadors from Rome, together with the duke of Anjou and his commander of *condottieri*, General Orsini, arrived in Bologna to escort Pope John XXIII therefrom to reign from the Vatican, an intention that had for long been close to the heart of Giovanni di Bicci di Medici and his son. Reigning from the Vatican has a way of legitimizing popes in a way that nothing else can. If only Rome weren't such a dog of a city. I didn't like Rome, but Cossa detested it, it made the marchesa feel less superior because of the old days when she had been nothing but a commoner and, in fact, was unpopular with everyone but Palo, and he wasn't to be allowed to go.

The cold rain was incessant that winter. The prices of grain and other foods had risen to famine rates. It was even a harder winter in Rome where a fox and five wolves had been killed inside the Viridarium and where a shocking earthquake had been preceded by such a storm that the Romans thought their end had come.

Cossa kept getting reports like that and sat out the winter in Bologna. The marchesa was away on her tour of the daughters. By April first, Cossa had placed Uguccione di Contrari in command of the Bologna garrison and prepared reluctantly to leave Bologna for Rome. He was forty-three years old, but wine and the gout had made him the worse for wear.

The College of Cardinals and the entire Curia left Bologna with him, because this time the papacy was returning to Rome permanently. The removals of the combined households of the papacy, the College, and the Curia was a spectacularly complex operation. The pope's own household contained 530 people. The household of *each* cardinal—and there were 11 cardinals traveling in the entourage—numbered about 210 people. The prelates, prebendaries, and clerics who constituted the Curia accounted for an aggregate household of 600 more, all of it guarded by a detachment of 2,000 soldiers: The whole made up a seven-mile-long procession of 7,000 people. In addition to these came the largest population of the holy hegira, 11,060 more people, not as decorative but equally impressive: cooks, provisioners, scullions, children, teachers, quartermasters, blacksmiths, armorers, wheelwrights, carpenters, laborers, entertainers, jugglers, whores, actors, musicians, fixers, scribes, gardeners, lottery operators, and astrologers; service personnel, accountants, couriers, butlers, housemaids; 209 of the nobility of the Papal States who had permanently attached themselves to the papal court—all 18,000 of them swarming across the hedgeless, sun-hammered countryside, accompanied by endless streams of pack-horses and carts that slipped and stumbled beneath their monstrous burdens, which included plate, jewels, gold, sacred vessels and cloths, musical instruments, paintings, tools, weapons, breviaries and books, vestments, linen, pots, pans and cooking spits, an uncountable amount of clothing, and beds by the hundreds of dozens.

On April 11, at the hour of vespers, they passed through the Porta Sancti Pancrati on the Via Aurelia at the entrance to Rome. The following day Pope John XXIII rode through the Trastevere quarter, over the island bridge where the jewelers had their stalls, through the Fields of Flowers and across the St. Peter's Bridge, which led directly to the Vatican. His Holiness entered St. Peter's Church with the duke of Anjou, the marquess of Este, and the cardinals, knelt at the high altar in observed reverence, then ordered that the sacred handkerchief of Santa Veronica be displayed to the Roman populace who had assembled at the Basilica.

Chapter 44

"My dear Decima," Cossa wrote to the marchesa from the Vatican, "Bologna is in turmoil. Bernaba, Palo, Dr. Weiler, and Father Fanfarone have remained there. Can you recall Corrado Caracciolo, whom I once tried to persuade the College to elect as pope? If you cannot do not chide yourself, for few can. His mother may have had a difficult time remembering him and he was an odd child. But he is sweet-natured, much like Filargi, and I wanted a safe place to stand him so I made him my legate to Bologna. I had no sooner left when Carlo Malatesta, that tiresomely devout supporter of Gregory's, entered the service of Ladislas with an army and at once notified, not dear old Caracciolo, but the Bologna city council, that he would open hostilities against them. He advanced from Rimini, ravaging the land as he came, as far as San Giovanni in Persiceto. Caracciolo tried feebly to persuade him to surrender, then he thought of using force, then—because his time had come and for no other reason—the dear old thing dropped dead. It could have been from the fresh air.

"So I must appoint another legate, probably Henricus Minutulus (a Neapolitan), but he can't get to Bologna in time to make any difference. Meantime, Bologna is a state without a ruler. Already conspirators have elected Pietro Cassolini as leader and there was an uprising inside the walls on May 11. Cassolini has made the whole thing into a holiday after that belly-pinching winter. He rode through the streets on a bare-backed horse yelling, 'Hurray for the people and for Art!' and took the palace. The people followed him and they turned out the magistrates and the officials. Eight Ancients and a gonfalonier of justice were elected. Envoys were sent to Venice for corn. All of it was a quarrel with the nobility, not with me or the Church. My captain—you remember Uguccione?—was allowed to remain. Bologna continues to pay its tribute to my Curia. In fact, this 'commune' has stipulated that the city continue to render 'true and due obedience to Pope John.' Then they made their peace with Malatesta and paid him two thousand florins.

"But I am not desolated by such events, which, after all, provide exhilarating entertainment for the Bolognese people."

The marchesa replied from Mainz: ". . . so pleased with how things worked out in promise of Sigismund's loyalty to you, which I must approach indirectly inasmuch as he is off fighting some war with Venice. I am proud of the way you have handled the mess in Bologna. Malatesta must be some kind of religious fanatic. You must find Giacomo Isolano, the doctor of learning who has such a stinking breath on him that you'd better keep the windows open when you meet. Promise him a cardinal's hat if he can overthrow Cassolini's government in Bologna. Isolano has the nobility on his side and it is a certainty that the fools who have taken over have already abused their power. I agree that Minutulus is a good choice for legate, but he must work closely, as a check, with Isolano. But that is just the side show. You must get on with the war against Ladislas.

"There will be no help available for your war from the duke of Burgundy or from Sigismund. Until Sigismund's war with Venice is over he will be helpless. He is *not* a serious man. His mind is continually peeking into mirrors. He preens disgustingly, singing of what a great boy he is, then tripping over his own feet as he chases women. As for Burgundy, a good friend of yours, he is nineteen and just married. Nothing will prise him out of the bride to pull him off to war.

"It appears that there may be peace between the Teutonic Order and the Poles. Both sides are winded and need a long rest.

"Maria Giovanna writes to say that the Florentines are disgusted with the way the duke of Anjou manages wars, which means they are fearful that they will have to pay for all of the troops, but in any event they have *no* interest in seeing any kind of French rule in Italy. *They are about to make a separate peace with Ladislas and will withdraw from their alliance with you and the duke, taking Siena with them.* You will have to dig in with your heels. The duke is penniless. I recommend that you order taxes immediately in Savoy, Portugal, and the islands of the Aegean, which have been taxed too lightly in recent years.

"Each moment that I hear a step outside this house, or a horse galloping up to it, my heart leaps into my throat because I am sure it is a courier from you, bringing me news of you, recreating you before me, in an unsatisfactory way, but it is the only way we will have until I can get my business over and return to your arms. I throb and burn everywhere upon me, thinking of all of you encircling me and possessing me. Please, Cossa, keep me in your heart."

He thought of her, active and vengeful thoughts, but at night when he slept, he dreamed of Catherine Visconti, alive and carnal and possessed by her appetites for him. When he awoke he wanted to return to her again but when he was awake she was gone. He had only the marchesa.

Chapter 45

Ladislas told his military staff before battle that they were lucky that Paolo Orsini was the senior general facing them, "For in that way," he said, "no one can get hurt."

Ladislas was an unstable, red-haired man, of whom it was said that he maintained such a costly show of arms because he was such an arrant coward. He was also an eccentric womanizer who often left the battlefield with armed guards to cover some woman his agents had rounded up after the previous day's fighting. He was keen on very stupid, tiny women who would name the children he gave them after him, as they were told to do.

"It is the Feast of Blessed Maria di Giorgio," he told his staff officers, "and the false pope, John, is probably out blessing the battle standards to give them into the charge of Paolo Orsini, who makes war as if he had contracted to mend a road. Last year, the only time he ever worked for me, he told me he took pride in fighting battles without the loss of a single soldier on either side." The officers roared with laughter. "Three years ago he stopped French troops from following up a strong advantage, telling them that it is not the Italian custom to kill too many of the enemy. The way he looks at it is: The more men who survive, the longer he will be able to hire them out to fight."

"Nonetheless," Arrigo, Count Cipriani said, "we still face Sforza and he is the most formidable *condottieri* general I ever care to oppose."

"Sforza will be facing you, my dear count."

"By God, Sforza has terrible eyes," the constable, Alberico da Barbiano, said.

"It is a sight defect," Ladislas answered. "Anyway, we are in hilly country and they will come at us around the Pontine Marshes toward Terracina. They will camp somewhere near Ceprano, on the bank of the Garigliano, which will be swollen with the spring floods. The river washes the base of the mountain and a village called Roccasecca, which has a citadel. That is where my headquarters will be. We'll fight on the inner side of the river. Sforza will press the attack but Orsini will be exhorting the troops to avoid a battle and eventually, because his money is running out, the duke will listen to Sforza." Roccasecca was strategically placed between Rome and Naples near Cassino. Whichever side won here would win the other's capital city.

At vespers, when the fifteen thousand Neapolitan soldiers were eating their evening meal, the duke of Anjou led his army across the river and fell upon the enemy. Louis de Logny led the van; the marquise de Controne and the seneschal of Eu led the troops that came in at the flanks. They made a total surprise amid the pitched tents and the gold and silver plate laid out in banquet for Ladislas, who was fright-struck.

Hastily, his bodyguard fell into the ruse that had saved him more than once. Six men were dressed and armed identically in the costume and weapons of the king, a breastplate under a royal-blue coat worked with golden lilies and a golden helmet. The king placed Count Arrigo Cipriani in charge of this unit to insure displays of his honor and bravery, and sent them out into different parts of the fray while he changed with frantic haste into the dress of a slatternly camp follower.

A desperate hand-to-hand struggle went on for more than an hour before the Neapolitans lost heart and fled. The slaughter of horse and foot was great. Pope Gregory's legate to Naples was captured. So were the counts of Carrara, Cipriani, Arpino, Celano, Loreto, and others; in all, ten counts, many other nobles, and hundreds of other men were taken prisoner and held for ransom.

By the time the dust had settled, Ladislas had made it to the castle of Roccasecca, which stood on a height above its village.

He was powerless. The duke of Anjou and the papacy of John XXIII had won a great battle. French and Italian troops were pillaging. Much gold and silver plate was captured and the soldiers were rich from the thirty thousand horses they took. The battle standards of Ladislas and Gregory were sent to Pope John in Rome. Cossa rejoiced. The war was finished. Louis, duke of Anjou, would now be king of Naples. Cossa ordered a great procession to assemble to sway its way across the city and back again in which he, himself, the Sacred College, prelates, deacons, and prebendaries took part, dragging the enemy standards through the mud of the streets of Rome while the people shouted, "Long live the sovereign Pontiff! Long live the king of the Sicilies!"

In midprocession, even as His Holiness distributed his blessings of peace upon the multitudes, while rejoicings were at their fullest, news came that Ladislas and the greater part of his troops had escaped the army of the duke of Anjou and that the great victory had been totally reversed.

Cossa went insane with rage as he was forced to mount a horse in midprocession to rush back to the Vatican and the Fortress of Sant' Angelo.

It was pathetic. Had the ducal troops followed up their victory at Roccasecca, they could have captured Ladislas and overrun his kingdom. The war would have been over. Sforza had been in the first wave, then had retired to repair his army while Paolo Orsini came up with fresh troops. Orsini refused to call his men away from the pillaging to pursue the Neapolitans. Orsini, general contractor for day laborers called *condottieri,* did not wish to see either Ladislas or the duke so well off that they could do without his contracting services.

Nonetheless, through the blood of Cossa's rage, it was the responsibility of the duke of Anjou to weigh the merits of his generals and to see that the victory was properly utilized. The duke had thrown away his only chance. He paid for it with the crown of Naples. Cossa was ruined. He would be the first homeless pope, he told me sardonically. He would have to flee Rome when Ladislas regrouped and arrived at the city's gates, no matter how he pretended that could be forestalled. He was outcast from Rome. Carlo Malatesta occupied Bologna.

Take it from me, the disappointment was simply terrible for him because it was so undeserved. His father was an old man. His father and his entire family would not only be disgraced, but would now be held hostage by Ladislas. Cossa reminded himself again and again that he could have been operating the family business in the Bay of Naples, clearing a steady fifty thousand florins a year and letting all these round-assed churchmen do all the striving. His father had been right only up to a point. There was a profitable career to be made in the Church, provided one had the sense not to rise above cardinal. Cosimo and the marchesa had lifted him into this ridiculous job of pope and he had had nothing but trouble from the day he had accepted it.

I was no great advocate of Cosimo and the marchesa, but I didn't agree with him this time. At the right moment, I thought Cossa should put them away and keep them away. But this was an emergency. It was no time for anything but plotting our own survival. "Your father's business has to go out of style," I told him. "Sooner, not later, it will have to be finished because it interferes with business. Who is going to allow his merchandise to be stolen from him on a regular basis? The banks alone will stop it. And don't believe it's better to be a cardinal. You are at the very top of your profession when you are pope. You are higher than that because there is only one of you in the world—under ordinary circumstances. Think of how many kings and princes and chancellors and dukes there are. Furthermore, they represent only people. A pope represents the actual Christian God on earth. How can you beat that? Listen, Cossa—every business has its good seasons and its bad seasons. You happen to have started off as pope in a bad season. But, and it has actually proved out, a bad beginning means a good ending."

He said to me, "I always feel considerably depressed after listening to you, Franco Ellera. You are a bottomless cesspit of advice."

I didn't pretend to become offended. I knew he was almost unmanned by the frustration of being pope and being denied by custom the right to lead his own troops and fight his own wars, free from the excuses of fools such as the duke of Anjou. I sensed that he was far deep into despair because he hated it with the force of a great explosion that people who had claimed to be his friends had betrayed and tricked him into accepting the papacy. The only hope he could hold to was the assurance that, at the right time, he would avenge the murder of Catherine Visconti, but with his Neapolitan fatalism Cossa didn't feel sorry for himself at any time, but he was beginning to feel sorry for the rest of the people on the earth because, the way he felt, they had brought all of this about with their ridiculous superstitions about some God, always hidden from them. "I can feel no mercy for people who allowed, even implored the men who had been popes before me—dunderheads like Gregory, thieves like Boniface, or murderous tyrants like Robert of Geneva—to accept the crown of St. Peter. How could people believe that the procession of grasping cardinals and bishops through the centuries that had gone before could possibly be the custodians of some sacred fire, the knowledge of which was denied to the very people who paid for all those prelates' luxuries?" He thought of Catherine Visconti and all he had lost, making him cherish the marchesa the more because she was what he had left. He sat concentrating purely upon the moment when he would have Catherine's son within his reach and he would demonstrate to him the motions of honest murder, not filthy poison, as he strangled that son and personally, as pope, saw him cast into hell.

When he had rested, eaten well, and changed into a crisp, clean uniform, the duke of Anjou appealed to Cossa for more money to renew the campaign.

"Give you money?" the Holy Pontiff shouted. "I would more quickly arm and provision the feeble-minded and aged of Rome and send them out to take Naples. You are *use*less, you silly cunt! Do you have a glimmering of how useless you are? You can thank God that your parents were royal and that you were born French because if you were one of my generals, I would hang you."

"Take care lest you offend me, Holiness," the duke spattered.

"*Off*end you? I *piss* on you!"

The duke stood haughtily with long, thin, wall-eyed dignity. "I shall overlook this tantrum," he said coldly, "because you are my pope. But I will point out to you that an *Italian* general, from one of your best families, is the cause of this disaster."

"Orsini? Or*sini*? Everyone but you knows Orsini is no general. He is a businessman. He hasn't worked for me in nine years. Don't blame a simple labor broker such as Orsini. If you, yourself, had pursued Ladislas and captured him the last time you wrecked your own chances, or the time before that, or the time again before that, you could have asked Ladislas and he would have told you that Paolo Orsini is an employment agent who seeks to banish the use of all weapons in the conduct of wars because they damage his merchandise. Louis, hear me! I am trembling on the crumbling edge of hanging you so, please, Louis, get out of my sight!"

On August 3, 1411, I conducted the duke of Anjou to his galleys at Ripa Granda. No Roman noble was in his escort. He embarked to Ostia, and thence sailed to Provence. He reached Paris on January 3 and never again attempted to recover the crown of Naples.

In the time he had remaining before Ladislas' army arrived, Cossa prepared Rome and the Vatican for the revenge that Ladislas would take. He constructed a walled-in passage from his palace to the fortress of Sant' Angelo while he raised money by enforced loans from nobles and wealthy citizens. He raised the tax on wine from fifty to a hundred percent a hogshead. He levied a tax on shoeing smiths, horse marshals, potters, and artificers. He altered the value of the currency by issuing more of it than ever before, agonizing that the marchesa should hasten to his side to tell him what he must do.

Before all else, he ordered Palo to kill Paolo Orsini in his bed, but the dog had fled the city and was, even then, probably ruining somebody else's war. Cossa also pondered on how best to bind Attendolo Sforza to his service. He owed Sforza fourteen thousand florins, so he devised a method of payment that would be profitable to himself and pleasing to Sforza. He made the peasant soldier lord of Cotignola, raising the man's native town to the dignity of a countship. Sforza graciously accepted the "payment," then unceremoniously resigned his command and marched off to Naples with his horse and foot. Ladislas gained the best general of his time.

Cossa almost had a stroke over this defection. He had Sforza's effigy hung from a gallows on all the gates and bridges of Rome by the right foot. In the effigy's hand was a scroll on which was written: "I am the peasant, Sforza of Cotignola, a traitor who, contrary to honor, have twelve times betrayed my Church. My promises, my agreements, my contracts, have I broken."

Chapter 46

Ladislas' advance troops, despite the man's immediate excommunication and the crusade Cossa had preached against him, were occupying the monastery of St. Agnes directly outside the walls of Rome. Cossa had no commander he could trust and no marchesa to advise him, and he wondered grimly if Ladislas would dare to put him into prison. Cossa's situation was not only desperate politically and militarily—Ladislas' army besieging Rome, Carlo Malatesta closing off the north of Italy, Naples lost, Sforza deserted, Bologna in revolt, and famine in Rome— but his father, leading the enormous Cossa family, that forest of grasping hands, was waiting for him three rooms away.

"Don't fathers know that they may only be revered when they are far away?" Cossa cried. "And he has brought the whole fucking family with him!"

He sat glumly and allowed me to wind a flannel strip around his throat to suggest to his family that his voice had failed. If he could not talk then he could agree to less.

"You will be the spokesman but you will say nothing, you understand?" he told me. He often spoke to other cardinals as brusquely so I took no offense. I sought to comfort him.

"I understand, Cossa. But this is your own family. Can it hurt if you say a couple of words to them?"

"Please! No advice!"

He breathed unevenly for a moment or two but regained control. "And don't let my father frighten you. You are a prince of the Church. Has the small throne been set up in there?"

"There is even a nice cushion on it."

Cossa stood up. He motioned to me to precede him to the door of the chamber. We went into the corridor, where I motioned to four deacons, dressed severely in black and white, and six of the palace guard, commanded by the graying Captain Munger, in full uniform. The guard led the procession. I wore my scarlet robes. His Holiness wore a white alb. The four deacons closed the rear. The procession moved solemnly about fifty feet down the hall, where its outriders flung open the double doors on the left side. The swaying snake glided into the room. Cossa went to the throne at the far wall and seated himself, a soldier and a deacon on either side of him; I stood where I could command the room.

Cossa postponed his first look at what he expected to be an ocean of Cossas but when he looked up only his father and his Uncle Tomas were standing there, next to a stranger.

"Where is the rest of the family?" Cossa asked blankly in a perfectly sound voice.

"First the blessing, Baldassare," his father said, "then the business."

Cossa glanced at me with bewilderment. I gave him a small benign shrug. Cossa blessed the two old men and the stranger, then chairs were brought in and they sat down directly in front of him.

"Send everyone out of the room except Franco Ellera," the duke of Santa Gata rasped. The pope signaled and the deacons and the soldiers left the room.

"Papa, where is the rest of the family?" Cossa said with some disappointment.

"What you see of your family is in Rome," his father said. "The rest of your family is being held in prison in Naples and all our possessions and fortunes are forfeit unless you come to an agreement with this noble lord," he nodded toward the stranger. "What's wrong with your throat?"

"My throat? Ah. Oh, yes. I am almost recovered. Who are you?" he asked the stranger.

The man managed to bow while seated. "I am ambassador-procurator of His Royal Highness, Ladislas, king of the Two Sicilies, who wishes to extend peace to Rome."

"Peace?"

"Yes, Holiness."

"Did the Swine King of Naples need to expose my father to the pain of such a journey at his age?"

"Your father has exhausted a cook, a courtesan, a cask of wine, and me," the ambassador said.

"Where is the rest of my family?"

"Safe and living in comfort at Ladislas' expense. They have at least a week before the first of them will be killed. But, of course, no one need come to any harm if we can conclude a treaty of peace."

Cossa called a consistory of cardinals to discuss the treaty. It was proposed through me to the Neapolitan ambassador that the king of Naples must acknowledge Pope John XXIII as the only pope in Christendom. To Cossa's surprise, this was received well because a possible ally, the king of France, had advised Ladislas to abandon Pope Gregory and because Sigismund, whom Ladislas feared, had endorsed Cossa.

In Naples, Ladislas assembled a hand-picked council of prelates and nobles, then he declared that, by their advice, he had hitherto been mistaken in believing that Pope Gregory XII had been canonically elected, therefore he forever renounced him and proclaimed the ascendancy of Pope John XXIII with the obedience of all Neapolitan dominions. He volunteered to release all of Cossa's relatives and all captured officers held in captivity in his realm.

"You see?" I told Cossa. "What did I tell you? Every business has its good seasons and its bad seasons."

Cossa, on his side, renounced Louis of Anjou, recognized Ladislas as king of the Two Sicilies, and appointed him grand gonfalonier of the Holy Roman Church. He also was forced to pledge to pay Ladislas 120,000 gold florins and had to give as security for the payment the towns of Ascoli, Viterbo, Perugia, and Benevento.

Ladislas, in his part, offered to repay all the papal revenues that were overdue from the Kingdom of Naples, and he agreed to induce Gregory to renounce his claims to the papacy within three months. If he refused, Ladislas volunteered to send him off as a prisoner to Provence.

In the final haggling, forty-one days after the first treaty meeting, it was agreed that Ladislas would keep one hundred lances for the service of the Church in exchange for his appointment as the legate to the March of Ancona and the payment of fifty thousand florins, a somewhat one-sided arrangement, Cossa thought bitterly.

The treaty was signed on June 17, 1412, a sad, if not utterly disreputable, alliance built with the cement of perfidy and the stones of faithlessness. But John wrote to the marchesa, in Milan, that the advantage was on his side. "I acquired a substantial territorial increase that must acknowledge my obedience," he wrote. "Because of that, and because of the treaty, the price of grain fell in Rome to one-half its former price, something that I had the sense to profit from in the grain markets before it happened."

Chapter 47

To characterize the mockery of the treaty, that winter Ladislas sent Sforza north to close off any surprise aid to Cossa from the Florentines or the Sienese, dispatched the Neapolitan fleet to blockade the mouth of the Tiber, and sent word ahead that, with a mighty army, he was marching to retake Rome. The prices of grain and wine soared again. Cossa made another small fortune, but it became clearer and clearer that he would soon be a fugitive.

Pope John XXIII and the Roman nobles enacted a brief but uplifting tableau when the pope announced Ladislas' imminent conquest of the city. He said unto them, "I place you on your own feet and ask you to act well and faithfully by your Holy Mother Church, not to fear Ladislas, nor any man in this world, for I am ready to die with you for the sake of the Holy Church and the Roman people." His household was fully packed and he was ready to run when he had finished the speech. The Romans, frantic to move him on his way so that they could welcome Ladislas, said unto Pope John XXIII, "Holy Father, doubt not but that the whole of Rome is ready to die with you. Romans would rather eat their children than be subject to the king of Naples."

On the night of June 7, 1413, Cossa, with thirteen cardinals, the entire Curia, and a combined household of eleven hundred people, albeit with far fewer camp followers on his way out than on his way in, fled from Rome. The next night the city was taken by Ladislas. The main body of the fugitives, less a few of the elderly who had been overpowered by the heat or were too feeble to ride, reached Sutri beyond Lake Bracciano, but Cossa didn't feel safe there. Before morning he set out again with his great baggage for Viterbo, famed for its handsome fountains and beautiful women, where he was told that instructions had been received from his pursuers that they were not to be done any injury.

"I feel more like an innkeeper than a pontiff," Cossa told me. "Two years and two months is hardly an epic period for a pope to hold Rome."

"You will go back again."

"I will never go back. Rome is a provincial pestilence."

His Holiness did not wait at Viterbo for proof that he would not be harmed. He pushed forward with his dwindling household to Monte Fiascone, where he rested until the thirteenth, when he went on to Acquapendente. On the seventeenth the papal caravan reached Siena. Cossa was determined to make his way to Florence and Cosimo di Medici, who had been advised many days before that he was coming and would have the Signoria in a mood to welcome him. But the Florentines refused to receive the papal host within the walls, in strict observance of the treaty with Ladislas. They felt they had not violated the treaty by providing a sanctuary for the pope because he had not arrived with an army, merely his entourage. They allowed him to stay on at the bishop's palace in San Antonio, north of the city about two miles from the Duomo. The day after Cossa arrived, exhausted, at the head of a raggle-taggle horde, word came from Rome that showed how Ladislas would use Italy. He had plundered the city and had massacred priests. The pope's chapel was pillaged, relics were looted, horses were stabled inside St. Peter's, and churches were converted into inns and brothels.

"Cossa, this report is crazy," I said. "Why should he do all that on the fifth time around? He's occupied Rome four times before and his troops behaved like choirboys."

"You deny a report from Cardinal de Chalant?" Cossa said

heatedly. "A respected, wise, responsible old man such as Chalant and you tell me he would lie to me?"

"Yes. Anyway, keep reading."

"Cardinals have been imprisoned!"

"Which ones?"

"He doesn't say. He was agitated. The shrines of the Apostles were profaned!"

"Aaah, some soldier probably had to take a leak."

"I should have left you there. Listen to this—'Wives and holy virgins were violated and the soldiers used sacred chalices for their wine.' "

"That I believe," I said.

On June 26, news came in describing the surrender of Viterbo, Perugia, and Cortona. Cossa ordered the commander of the garrison at Bologna to take Cesena. The force succeeded in capturing Carlo Malatesta's concubine, a very agitated fat lady, but before the winter started, all the southern and central parts of Italy, as far as the borders of Siena, were held by Ladislas.

Chapter 48

At San Antonio Cossa received a dispatch from the marchesa. It said that Sigismund, king of the Romans and of Hungary, and his army were marching north from Venice, through the passes of Austro-Helvetia, and that she would be able to effect a meeting with him at Chur. However, she felt that her own presence would be greatly enhanced if she could have in her company myself, Franco, cardinal of Santa Amalia di Angeli, because it would add credence to her mission in that Sigismund was such a religious man.

"Dearest Cossa," she wrote, "in two hours I will be on my way to Chur to deliver Rosa to Pippo Span. That is the apparent reason. The other reason is—because Rosa is so beautiful and the beloved of his closest friend, and because Maria Louise is beautiful and theoretically available in that John of Nassau has become impotent, I am sure that I will be allowed to have time with Sigismund. In that time I intend to prevail upon him to become the protector of the papacy, for he is a man whose family tradition has had much to do with struggles for Church unity and, of course, he will have every reason to be grateful for your sponsorship, which made him king of the Romans. A certain amount of bargaining will need to be done but I can see that my clearest course must be to move him forward toward a meeting with you where you can impose your will upon him. As soon as I have this meeting with Sigismund, I will spare no moment until I am blissfully content to be in your arms once again.''

I was sent north to Chur at once, with a pitiably small household of only thirty-four people, but there was a need to travel fast through rough terrain and Alpine valleys. As we were leaving San Antonio I am sure other cardinals had plenty to say about the size of my entourage, but you may be sure that I held to my dignity and paid them no heed.

We joined the marchesa's party at the episcopal palace of Chur, which was called, in Latin, Curia Rhaetorum, in the western part of Austro-Helvetia. We arrived at Chur on August 26, 1413, two days after Sigismund's address to the representatives of the six cantons on St. Bartholomew's Day. The marchesa and Pippo Span had been negotiating Rosa's "protection for the future," made so necessary by the general's inability to marry her, by courier. At last the agreement had been sealed. The merchandise was being delivered.

By the agreement, Sigismund was to confer upon Rosa the title of countess of Solothurn when he was elected Holy Roman Emperor. She was to be permanently housed in Prague but was to accompany her protector as he followed his king until there should be any heirs. She was to have a stipend of one thousand florins a year for current expenses, one thousand florins a year against the future, and five hundred florins a year as a clothing allowance. Pippo Span did not haggle over Rosa as Spina had bargained. The general signed the papers instantly and had them returned at once to the marchesa in Mainz by military courier.

The instant the young lovers were reunited, in a small audience room of the episcopal palace, they tried to bolt like horses in a stable fire, but the marchesa gripped Rosa's elbow from behind and inquired about the health of Sigismund.

"He is in splendid form—splendid," Pippo Span said in a strained voice. "He is looking forward greatly to the pleasure of your company—and yours, Fraulein, and yours, Your Eminence," he told Maria Louise and me. "You will be having a memorable dinner with him."

"Where shall we dine?"

"He has taken over the bishop's hunting lodge. He will send for you, of course."

"You won't be there, dear Count?"

"I think not."

"Pity. Well, you and Rosa must have so much to talk about. Please don't let us keep you." Pippo Span and Rosa vanished. They were standing there, then they were gone.

"My *God!*" Maria Louise said. "Did you see the lust on that girl's face?"

"That was real, yearning love—not lust," the marchesa answered sharply.

"They look very much the same to me, then."

"It's all in the mind, dear, of course. Love is actually more subjective than lust, although it may be the other way round. What shall you wear tonight?"

"The very, *very* low bodice, I think." I coughed lightly to remind them that a cardinal of the Church was in the room with them, but they carried on as if I were not.

"Excellent," her mother replied. "Sigismund is a painfully obvious man. His father passed it on."

As they dressed for dinner with Sigismund, the marchesa said, "Tonight you must be the Ice Queen."

"Yes, Mama."

"It is the only way to hold his attention, which is so easy to get. Be friendly—in the way you would show respect to a poisonous snake—but he must understand that you are as attracted to him as a man as you might be to a plate of four-day-old fish."

"Knowing that one day he will turn me into a volcano," Maria Louise grinned.

"Not with this one. You stay solid ice forever with Sigismund. It's the only leverage. He is a fool."

"What else is he like?"

"He isn't *like* anything. He is a fool. Tall, quite vain, about forty-four. The same age as Cossa. All you do is stay as beautiful as you are, play the Ice Queen, and we'll have him trussed up before the night is over."

Maria Louise had forsaken blondeness, so effective in Italy, when she moved to Germany. Now, she wore silver hair arranged as chastely as money around her lovely, bold-boned face, which grouped itself for greatest effectiveness around the thrusting nose that all the marchesa's daughters had received from their mother, and a soft, swollen mouth, which seemed preoccupied with the uses of love-making. Her body, like her mother's, created myths in the minds of men. She was her mother's work of art.

A captain of the Fourth Hungarian Hussars arrived promptly to take us to Sigismund. He was tall and spare, heavily rouged and tightly corseted. As we rode out to meet the king, he told them how he longed to see Italy. He had heard so much about Italy, he said, that he did not think he would be able to control himself when he finally got there.

"You appreciate fine sculpture, then?" the marchesa asked.

"Yes. Ah, I know what you mean."

"You speak good German—for a Hungarian."

"We must, you know. Very soon, Sigismund will rule the empire."

"You will be a colonel before you know it."

He smiled from deep below his mustache. "I would rather be in Italy before I know it."

Rosa and Pippo Span were seated on either side of the ladies when the king entered the room, because he had decided he wanted to be able to single out Rosa at once and observe her, aglow from having abandoned herself upon Pippo. It was a rather small sitting room even for a lodge. Sigismund was dressed in leather with great boots and many straps and a short jacket. His hair was straw-blonde, his beard a parted one, and he balanced such mustaches that the marchesa remarked later to Maria Louise that she feared that hunting falcons had made nests within them. The heroic mustaches distracted somewhat from the mottle of his pudding face, drew attention away from his ever-shifting eyes and the constant licking of his purple pendulous lips.

I sat slightly apart from the others as a matter of duty to my station. The king charged across the room to greet me, all at once playing the heavy courtier, ready to prostrate himself before a representative of holiness. I extended my ring. He kissed it like a lover, then gazed perfervidly into my eyes, saying, "My life shall be given to Christ's work," then, having observed the routine social requirements, turned to the ladies, arms out-stretched, fingers fluttering with eagerness. "How en*chant*ing that you have made your way across the *Alps* to let us see you," he sang. "The mother and sister of our dearest friend's own beloved." The ladies curtsied with stately balance while Maria Louise *did* stare at him as if he were a plate of four-day-old fish. The effect on Sigismund was dynamic. He hovered over them. Maria Louise ostentatiously shook him off, rewarding him with a glare of pale distaste. It was aphrodisiac to Sigismund.

We were served a dinner that balanced massive portions of Hungarian, Bohemian, Austrian, and Swiss food. There were many kinds of dumplings, Tokay wine, smoked meat soup, *Segedinsky Gulas,* which was loaded with lard, sauerkraut, and flour, then *cokoladovy, orechovy,* and *darazsfeszek,* because the king had a famous sweet tooth. I didn't think the food was at all bad. Rosa and Pippo Span were careful to eat none of it. The marchesa held to what etiquette and her figure demanded. The king gorged himself. Maria Louise treated all of the food as disdainfully as she regarded the king, as if it were covered with ants.

"You don't like Hungarian food?" the king asked her.

"Oh, yes." Her look pitied him that he could think that this was proper Hungarian food.

"But this was cooked by the great Georgi Marton, the magician of Buda!"

She refused to comment lest toads pour from her mouth.

"But tonight there has also been Bohemian food and delectable Austrian food." He could not fathom this woman, such a sensually beautiful woman, the kind of woman who had always lifted her skirts and reclined on her back when the turnings of life's byways had brought her to such a monarch, who was so deliciously a man.

"Delicious," she repeated as if reading his thoughts, as if trying not to gag. The hopelessness of it to the king was that he could not be sure whether it was the food or himself that had almost made her gag. Perhaps in order to regroup before attacking again, the king fell into conversation with me, directly across the table.

"Well, Eminence. What is our pope going to do about John Hus?"

"I will inquire about that," I said.

"Well! The man is a brigand of the Bohemian church, one might almost say a heretic, don't you know. His statements concerning the archbishop are really seditious and I really do think the Holy Father is advised to silence the man. He is causing unnecessary problems in Prague and, at any moment now, I shall be crowned king of Bohemia."

"His Holiness is studying the Hus case closely, Majesty," the marchesa said. "And you may be certain of the outcome." She glanced at me in a way that, had I been John Hus, would have had me packing and fleeing.

"Pippo tells me that you are a close—uh—adviser to His Holiness," Sigismund said to the marchesa.

"Hardly that, Majesty. The pope is very much his own man, but because he is such a devoutly religious person, one might say immersed in spiritual meanings and theology, as is the nature of the greatest popes—because I travel so much and he does not travel at all—he sometimes asks me to bring to him my impressions of the people I have met and what they have told me."

"What will you tell him about me, dear lady?"

"I shall tell him how deliciously handsome you are."

Sigismund attempted a chuckle, thinking with righteousness that this beautiful woman's response proved he had not been turned into a turd as her daughter would have it. To present yet another facet of his multihued person he fell at once into gravity at the mention of the Church, and it blotted all intelligence out of his expression. "I am so *terribly* concerned about the Church, Eminence. My father—as history shows us—set his life upon reuniting the Church with the Greeks. The goal of one Church has been my grail. My father is gone from history but the seamless garment of Christ is rent by heinous schism. It is my sworn task to shatter that schism, to unite Christendom under one pope."

When Pippo Span had told him that the marchesa and I were "close" to Pope John, as an instantly reactive opportunist he had cast his mind reflexively to make the political maximum out of meeting us—so he had gulped down some Tokay and had become instantly pious.

"His Holiness is one with you, Majesty," the marchesa assured him. "The Holy Father would gladly give his life to banish the schism from the Church."

Sigismund blinked at her. "He would?"

"A very pleasant climate here at Chur, don't you think, Majesty?"

"Climate? My dear Marchesa! You imply that I was feigning concern about the schism. Please, let me assure you that, if necessary to convince you of the icy seriousness of my intent to destroy the schism, I will open a vein, let my royal blood run into a glass and drink a pledge, which will stake my life against the end of schism."

"I thank God," she said. "May the extremity of the pope's danger hasten your determination."

"How so?"

"Only a great leader such as you, who would fight, even die, for the virtuous unity of the Church, would have the perception to glean how greatly the Holy Father needs a protector, my Sire. He is hemmed in by the ruthlessness of the enemies of the Church. But you can guarantee his safety, for which he would wish to show his gratitude by seeking out your counsels and by joining his spiritual meaning to Christians everywhere with the might of your arms."

Sigismund began to see the greater opportunity. Using the pope as his shield as he hacked his way to the center of the schism, he could with one blow sever the disease from the body of the living Church and lay the victory at the feet of the electors, who had named him king of the Romans, but he sought hungrily to hasten his coronation as Holy Roman Emperor.

"Defend him and protect his beleaguered Church, Majesty," I said to him, *basso profundo,* "and you will be defending all Christendom, for his is the *significant* papal obedience. With his blessed Church no longer a fugitive from pursuing bandits, he would reach out and grasp the necessity to realize your hallowed father's dreams by calling, with you at his side, a grand council of the Church to end the schism. No one may summon such a council except a sitting pope. *You* know the Church must move itself to save itself. A meeting with His Holiness, under your protection, will make that happen. *You* will do it! France has no such desire. She stands by the Council of Pisa, for her obedience is to the papacy of John XXIII. England is indifferent. Spain

and Provence are still true to Benedict. Only *you,* the king of
the Romans, is pledged to this in his heart. All of your people in
the North must assume this glorious task and accept history's
blessing for doing it."

He was stunned by the future. He would sweep the imperial
crown upon his own head and by reason of accomplishing what
no man and no nation had been able to do would be transformed
into the central power and force in all Christendom. Statues by
the hundreds would be erected in his image. Multitudes would
sink to their knees at the mention of his name. This haughty
young woman on his left would whimper to have him possess
her. This was hard politics.

After dinner, although Sigismund tried to place himself next
to Maria Louise, she, with obvious desperation, latched herself
on to me and the king found himself seated across the room
beside the marchesa. Rosa and Pippo Span remained at the
table, oblivious of everything.

Sigismund saw that he had been wandering ahead of his soldiers, like some elder of a tribe in the wilderness, and this
chance meeting with this woman who was so close to the pope
might be delivering to him the key to his future.

"How may I help His Holiness?" he asked the marchesa
guilelessly.

"I would say, Majesty, that the oppression of Ladislas and
the defection of Florence, Anjou, and Siena, has placed the
Church at your feet, as it were. The *chief* difficulty, to achieve
your own *dynastic* dream—that, you, King Sigismund, end this
schism—is to persuade His Holiness to discuss with you the
assembly of a grand council."

"He must come to me for that."

"You are one of several kings, among a dozen other princes,
Majesty. He is the pope."

"My dear Marchesa, I *know* these people. They *hate* councils
because councils mean reform."

"Indeed yes," the marchesa said. "And excepting Italy, the
entire Christian world clamors for reform."

"And you may be sure that Pope John knows that if he does
convoke such a council then he must resign his office, because
there would be no other way to settle it."

"That is why there must be a meeting, isn't it? He would need to be assured by you that such a resignation would only be a matter of form. All three sitting popes would be called upon to resign so that the matter will be settled and one true pope elected. But could you not assure him that this one elected pope would surely be himself? He *is* the pope with the overwhelmingly largest obedience.''

"Look here, my dear—would you say that you had his confidence to the extent of being able to persuade him to call me out to save the Church?''

"He thinks with you about the Church's salvation, Majesty. I would tell him of the depth of your faith and zeal and he would cry out to you.''

"Then you must do so!''

She dropped her eyes and made a pretty scene about searching for words. "But, Sire,'' she said in a small voice, "this is my *work* we are speaking of.''

"What?''

"My business—my livelihood.''

"I don't understand.''

"I thought you knew that over the years I have been privileged to represent such distinguished clients as the dukes of Burgundy and Anjou, the Medici Bank, the chancellor of the University of Paris, indeed, His Holiness, the pope, himself— and a few of the electors.''

"The e*lec*tors?''

"Also, I have undertaken many private missions for the late Gian Galeazzo Visconti, duke of Milan. My clients are men who have need that their most private interests be assembled with those of others with whom it is more suitable that they not be seen.''

Had she come here to solicit his *bus*iness? he thought, outraged. But that could not be so, he told himself instantly, for he had originated everything they had discussed. Best to come down flatly upon this thing. "Are you suggesting that I *hire* your services?'' he asked.

She broke out into such a ripple of sweet laughter that he became confused. "Not at all, Majesty,'' she said.

"Then I confess that I am perplexed. Will you take me through it again?''

"There is nothing *new* here, Majesty. Certain things develop

best secretly. Wherever there seems to be no *apparent* solution
—as would seem to be the case here—where the pope certainly
will not consent to call a council that could depose him—while
at the same time you have no means to convoke such a meeting
—then, under such theo*ret*ical circumstances, the effectiveness
of my sort of special services becomes invaluable.''

"How invaluable?''

"Do you mean—how costly?''

"Well—yes.''

"It is negotiable. Always.''

"Do you assure results?''

"You pay me only when there are results.''

"I will tell you that all this interests me, Marchesa. I therefore
commission you to convince the pope that he must meet with
me to discuss my protection of the Church and his person—and
the details of calling a council. For this I will pay you a retainer
of a thousand florins, and five thousand more to be paid on the
day the pope and I agree to call a council.''

"I see.''

"One more thing, I must control the meeting place for the
council itself. It must be held outside Italy.''

"That is intricate work for a mere thousand florins.'' She
groaned deeply within herself as she thought of the effort it
would require to convince Cossa that such a council—which
would most certainly move to depose him—should meet outside
Italy, his own Italy, where, by numbers of his own clergy alone,
he could overwhelm any vote. She felt certain that the matter of
talking to Sigismund about calling a council at all would be considered treason by Cossa, but she knew, and Cosimo di Medici knew, and Giovanni di Bicci di Medici knew, it was necessary for the common good of the entire European business community, if not for Cossa's.

"A *mere* thousand florins?''

"We have to settle the matter of expenses,'' she said lan-
guidly.

"Ex*pen*ses?''

"Travel. Wear and tear. The maintenance of style. The presents and bribes that will be necessary. All those things must be
a part of our contract.''

Chapter 49

At dawn the next day, the marchesa, Maria Louise, their household of ninety-one people and her colorfully uniformed escort of forty soldiers, my household of thirty-four people, including a somewhat drably uniformed escort, rode out of Chur to travel across the Alps through Milan, where our parties would separate, the marchesa going on to Florence, I to Bologna. Cossa was no longer in Florence, he had returned to Bologna, Malatesta's forces having been driven out of the city by its soldiers and citizens, so great was the force of their economic need for their pope.

I had been instructed by the marchesa just to sit quietly and play the cardinal during the meetings with Sigismund, but that is not my way and I believe I conducted myself with considerable effect. There could be no doubt but that King Sigismund would remember me, even if it did irritate her.

Maria Giovanna has told me, years later, that when the marchesa's household reached Florence her mother bathed and slept for the remainder of the night—from six o'clock in the evening until dawn—sending word to Cosimo through Maria Giovanna, at whose house she was resting, to ask him to meet with her in the early morning. Cosimo came to Maria Giovanna's house shortly after dawn.

The marchesa told him of the outcome of the meeting. "Sigismund has retained me to arrange a meeting with Cossa so that he may persuade Cossa to call a council, which would act to end the schism," she said with more than a touch of arrogance.

"I don't know how you do it, Decima. My father will be *enor*mously pleased."

"You don't really want to know how I do it as long as I get it done."

He smiled. "We have to be sure that Cossa thinks that Sigismund is being drawn into his scheme for the protection of Cossa's papacy."

"I may have done that already. I should think the first shock for Cossa will be when Sigismund tells him that a council must be called to reform the Church—as the only way to dissolve the schism."

"That is a good risk. Cossa is desperate. Ladislas turned him into the papal waif of San Antonio."

"He is a man. He wants to believe in himself, and the basis of his belief in himself is the awe and respect in which he holds his cunning. He will feel—and I will help him along in that feeling —that he can agree to the meeting to get Sigismund's protection then that he can outmaneuver Sigismund when it comes to calling a council."

"You can always point to the Council of Pisa to reassure Cossa. No prince had his way at Pisa. No reform resulted from Pisa. Only cardinals can make reforms and accept the resignations of popes. You can certainly feed all that to him. Cossa knows that he controls the cardinals—or he believes that he does. He will assume that Sigismund will be powerless. He will feel safe."

"I wish he was in different work," the marchesa said wistfully. "I am fond of Cossa. I wish he had stayed in his family's business. It will be hard for him when, once the council gets into full sway, everything is reversed and he loses the cardinals."

"Don't worry about Cossa. The bank will take care of Cossa. Have you found the way to subvert the cardinals?"

"Yes," she said (almost) sadly. "We will need to instruct the bank's inside man at the council—whoever he will be—to organize the nations to isolate the cardinals. Who is our man?"

"Two. D'Ailly and Spina."

"D'Ailly has the eloquence. And Spina, God knows, has the deviousness. All they have to do is to see that the council decrees that only the votes of *nations* can carry any reforms, not any majority of cardinals or Italian prelates. The *nations* must see to it that the three popes resign."

"You really do have a knack for these things, Decima," Cosimo said admiringly.

"There is other business today."

"What else?"

"Ladislas wants to negotiate a loan of one hundred thousand florins so that he can continue his war against Cossa. It is important. Cossa has to be kept stretched on the rack so that he *needs* the protection of Sigismund and so that, because of his fear of Ladislas, he will agree to call a council."

"How did it come to you?"

"From Ladislas to Spina to Rosa."

"Who will negotiate the loan? It must be a secret thing."

"Rosa will go to Naples on her honeymoon with Pippo Span. She has explained that she must arrange for the shipment of her clothing and furniture. Rosa will negotiate the loan."

"Tell her to encourage him to ask for double the amount."

"No. Keep it at one hundred thousand. We don't want Ladislas to be able to crush Cossa. You will need him to call the council."

Cosimo grinned at her. "You are right. Better yet, tell Rosa to negotiate a loan for half as much as Ladislas wants."

Cosimo told me about that conversation three months ago, eleven years after it happened. He was as self-righteous as always, saving the Church from Cossa, its enemy, whom he had put into the papacy, never remembering that what he was saving was the Medici Bank and its branches, so that it could become bigger and bigger until someday it must own the earth.

The marchesa returned to Bologna in two days' time, taking Maria Louise with her. She joined Cossa and me for dinner at three o'clock in the morning in a small chamber that adjoined the working area in the papal palace and paid out to him a series of half-truths and flat lies about Sigismund and why he wanted to meet with Cossa. She told him that the king was obsessed with ending the schism and that he had volunteered that, should such a council demand the resignation of all three popes to restore unity, he would unite the German vote with the Italian to see that Cossa would be immediately reelected.

Cossa cross-questioned her on that point, I thought cynically. "I am sure you pressed hard for that," he said.

"Oh, yes."

"And on Cosimo's orders, I suppose."

"Entirely," she said. She emphasized with greatest coloration that the reason Sigismund wanted to be seen as being the papal protector was to enhance his acceptance as Holy Roman Emperor. Cossa bought all of it and so did I because it was logically and reasonably what we wanted to believe.

She worked with him on the draft of a dispatch to Sigismund, then in Munich, proposing an early meeting. "Now, listen carefully," she told him, "at the meeting Sigismund is going to try to dictate the selection of the site for this council. Rosa and Maria Louise will handle him on that and you may be sure that, in the end, the king will be found insisting on *your* choice of site —which must be Konstanz, in southern Germany on the Swiss frontier, in the province of our dear friend, John of Nassau."

"Konstanz? It has to be held in Italy!"

"No, no. I have sent Maria Giovanna ahead of everyone to acquire options to lease the principal residences and other buildings of the city, as well as all of the inns and stabling, and to secure arrangements with the farmers of the region, on either side of the Bodensee, for all the hay, meat, fish, grain, schnapps, and beer they will produce over the next five years. Everything will be legal and in writing. The deposits can be paid for, if you choose, with a loan from the Medici Bank. A hundred thousand people a year will be pouring into Konstanz and that can mean a huge return on our money. Also—and this is important in terms of what we can earn out of the council—Bernaba and Palo must get to work now organizing the women, the entertainment, and the gaming. We have to control as much of it as possible."

"How much do you estimate we can make if we control the site—beginning right now?"

"Enormous sums. Absolutely enormous. I would estimate in excess of four hundred and fifty thousand gold florins." She was relieved and rewarded. She had been able to switch his mind away from fears about what could happen to his papacy if such a council were called by a simple, earnest appeal to his greed. Sigismund could now have his council outside of Italy. Cosimo could have his Church reform. And she and Cossa could win a huge amount of money. "You must fight with Sigismund, tooth and nail, for the council to be held in Italy, then gradually let him beat you down. That will get concessions from him on other points we will want yet give him the feeling of possessing great power. He *is* a fool, you know."

They turned to where Cossa should meet with Sigismund. "It really can't matter to him," the marchesa said, "he is traveling all the time to keep the people from getting wise to him. I have some people looking at Piacenza, Cremona, and Lodi—but right now it looks like Lodi needs the business that the meeting will generate and I think they'll be happy to pay us five thousand florins for the privilege."

"Then Bernaba should get busy there," the Holy Father said. "But keep this in mind, please. It is quite possible that such a council will ask me to resign with Benedict and Gregory. Once they get me out—no matter what you think—they may not be all that eager to put me back in again. Also, there will be all that talk about reform. I am relying on you and on Cosimo and his father. We have prospered together so I know that it is just as much to their advantage as it is to mine that they make sure that there will be no slips in the plan. With a unified Church there is double the money to be made from this papacy, so burn it into your mind. Before I agree to anything with this Sigismund, I want assurances from the Medici that when the Council of Konstanz is over I will be the only pope in Christendom."

"You have my sacred word on that, Cossa," the marchesa said. It was truly sad, she thought, that he was such a provincial politician. She had really been able to teach him so little. Yet she was fond of him. He was a merry fellow and a great lover. He was cunning and brave and many times the man that all of his enemies were. It was too bad but Cossa was finished.

When I returned to Bologna from Chur, I was shocked at how old Cossa looked. I had not been separated from him for any length of time before this so I had not really been able to notice what was happening to him. His gout was very bad. His hair was white. I remembered it as being gray hair, not like this. He was consuming himself with hatred for Catherine's son and with his constant vision of elusive vengeance upon the marchesa. His fear that Ladislas would drive him out of Bologna rested upon him like a succubus, and undoubtedly was what had him agreeing with such alacrity to the meeting with Sigismund. He was too quickly old and haunted, spent from wandering across Italy; a pilgrim without a pilgrim's faith.

PART FOUR

Chapter 50

On November 26, Pope John XXIII and Sigismund, king of the Romans, made their separate ways to Lodi, a small trading town at the center of a rough triangle formed by Piacenza, Milan, and Cremona. They remained at Lodi with their enormous households for almost five weeks, attracting many travelers, traders, jewelers, moneychangers, barbers, entertainers, gamblers, priests, fortunetellers, and whores. Sigismund opened their meeting by expressing his deathless gratitude to the Holy Father for his potent intercession with the electors. The pope thanked Sigismund for his gallant offer to defend the papacy against Ladislas.

Sigismund was as groomed as a battle charger. His parted beard, his thicket of a mustache, and his brown hair glistened with rare oils as they concealed his sunburned face and diverted attention from his shifty, bloodshot eyes.

They moved around each other like wrestlers seeking an opening. Cossa said to me when the doors were closed in our apartments after the first meeting, "Sigismund is an optical illusion in his way. Those who see him from afar must be moved to admiration by that splendid royal head, that graceful figure, a true king in all his imperishable youth and beauty. The hearts of any distant crowd must fly in exultation when he smiles and waves to them. But when one gets up close, the bright eyes are sunken in caves of many fine lines telling of gross storms of the blood and things that, in the eyes of the pious, could not find pleasure with God. Stand back and admire. Go close and shudder at the wantonness of a wild life.''

There were banquets, balls, and parties, which the marchesa and her daughters organized to exhaust the king, but the reason the meeting was protracted was Cossa's stubborn insistence that the proposed council be held in Italy. The Holy Father's position was that it would be impossible to bring the great body of the Italian Church across the Alps. The king's reply was that he not only had to consider his own archbishops, who were also electors, but also the great princes and lords who would attend such a council from many countries, who had not been able to reach Pisa because of its location, and who were of such vital importance.

As the talking went on and on, Cossa allowed his agreement to be moved gradually northward in Italy, as far as Como. Sigismund's compromises moved his choices southward in Germany, toward the center of the land mass. Frequently, the deadlock was so firm that it was necessary to set the discussions aside while they spoke of resolving the schism, both sides showing extreme piety. Sigismund discussed the invidious disloyalty of John Hus.

"You know, Holiness," he said, "Hus comes by his rebelliousness naturally. He was born at Husinez, near Prachtice, close to the Bavarian frontier, where the racial strife was at its worst. His parents were peasants. By 1401 he was preaching at the church of St. Michael and was made dean of the Faculty of Philosophy, and in 1402 he became rector of the University, then they made him the general vicar of Prague.''

No matter what Sigismund said, it was the way he said it that had the power to put Cossa to sleep. Cossa told me he had never met a man as boring as Sigismund, so that he did not listen to and most certainly took no heed of anything Sigismund had to say about Hus, which was a pity, as it would turn out, because Cossa and Hus, in their own strange ways, had a great deal in common in their views on a pure Christian religion. Hus called the priests of Bohemia heretics because they took fees for confession, communion, baptism; in his sermons Hus said they had "lacerated the minds of the pious, had extinguished charity, and had rendered the clergy odious to the people." Hus was also the defender of the teachings of Wycliffe, a reformer who was anathema to all rulers. Hus was not only a reformer, but a patriot, and kings have reason to be suspicious of patriots.

Gradually, the talk at Lodi would get back to the business of the meeting. Sigismund was certain that the council would demand the resignations of all three popes but that, of course, the College would immediately reelect Cossa. His Holiness smiled wistfully, saying that *must* be so, but until that happened only he was pope, inasmuch as the other two men had been deposed, but that he would preside at all council sessions so that Christendom could be assured of the reform of the Church. Cossa considered that this one fact was his lock upon the council.

The king inquired of his staff if there were no city near the German frontier that belonged to the Holy Roman Empire. Count Ulrich of Teck recommended Kempten in southern Swabia. Count Eberhard of Kellenberg agreed that Kempten would be good. I sat at the pope's right hand and rumbled out my authority in a special voice I had developed for my cardinalate. "As cardinal of Fribourg I *know* this region," I said in tones that brooked no opposition. "I can tell you that Kempten is woefully lacking in facilities for the delegations' troops and for the immense number of travelers that this council will attract." I turned slightly to face the Holy Father. "I would recommend to His Holiness the town of Konstanz, which has the advantage of being situated on the Rhine and on the Bodensee. It has ample housing. King Rupert made his army headquarters there and they found ample shelter and food. Also, everything may be bought there—and at trifling cost."

The king turned his beaming face upon the pontiff, his eyes shining with his good fortune. Konstanz was the very city that Pippo Span had been pressing upon him. Maria Louise had told him all the details about it with tingling iciness. Now the pope's own cardinal had brought Konstanz forward! He had won every point! He would shine through history as the savior of Christendom!

"Your Holiness," he said humbly, "Konstanz, the recommendation of your cardinal, is entirely acceptable to me."

"Is there a bishopric in Konstanz?" Cossa asked me mildly.

"Yes, Holy Father."

The Pope pored over the large map on the table before him. The king guided his eyes with a tracing finger. "Ah," Cossa said. "I see. It is indeed at the center of Europe. Very well. We agree that the council should be held there."

When Sigismund's party had dispersed, when Cossa and I were alone in the large anteroom off the meeting room, Cossa smiled brilliantly and said, "We made ourselves about three hundred and eighty thousand gold florins today, merely as side-money from the Council of Konstanz. You are a cardinal after my own heart." Just as Carlo Pendini's gold had pulled Cossa into the papacy, so did the beckoning of all the money to be made in Konstanz pull him into that destiny.

On December 9, 1413, Pope John XXIII promulgated his bull for the convocation of a general council of the Holy Church to begin on All Saints Day, November 1, 1414, proclaiming that he would be present. On the evening of December 9, Sigismund paid over to the marchesa di Artegiana the fee for her services. Then a contract was signed between them by which he agreed to provide Maria Louise with a town house in Prague and one at Buda, grant her the right to travel with him as his consort when Queen Barbara was not required to appear for occasions of state, made provision for her raiment: jewels, furs, shoes, and clothes, with a guarantee of three hundred golden florins to be paid to her each month and a capital payment of five thousand florins should they separate before the end of the five-year contract. The king's hand trembled with thrift-shock and passion as he signed the document.

"I believe she is coming around to liking me," he said to the marchesa.

She patted his arm. "I hope you will make her very happy," she answered.

Chapter 51

Sigismund was unhurried at Lodi. He was a roving postbarbarian who commanded Hungarian and German killer-rustics and he enjoyed having the pope of all Christendom at his disposal for as long as he wished to protract things. He would come back to Hus, which had had no connection with the agenda of the meeting, because it was an area in which he could seem more knowledgeable about the Church than its pontiff. "Did you know," he would ask, "that the University of Paris has been in correspondence with the archbishop of Prague about John Hus?"

Cossa was agonizingly bored with Sigismund. Frequently he wondered, in his desperate idleness, if Sigismund could be mentally arrested. "Hus?" he answered without interest.

"The Bohemian you excommunicated."

"Oh, yes?"

"For not attending the Council of Rome?"

"I don't remember him."

"As I will inherit the Bohemian throne, I somewhat resented the slur on a future subject. The fact is, the French are certain to make a major thing of Hus at the council."

"Why the French?"

"They are drawn to heresy."

"The business of any council of the Church is the extermination of heresy," Cossa replied. He would not, he knew, be able to stand much more of this idiot's country-fair German accent. The fellow spoke Latin by whining it through his nose. How did Maria Louise put up with him? He must be paying her a fortune. The king, on his side, thought that if he closed his eyes he would have to believe that he was listening to a Neapolitan street hoodlum. Such a majestic language as Latin, as educated Germans and Luxembourgers spoke it, was not intended to be coarsened by the accents of an alley pimp, which was how he heard all Italian speech. How could they have elected a pope who spoke as commonly as this one, except that the College of Cardinals was made up mainly of coarse Italians. "I think I should tell you about John Hus, Your Holiness," Sigismund said. "He is a fellow who cannot accept authority. When he argues for the reform of the Church he is really only objecting to the qualities of his superiors."

"That describes every reformer. You, for instance."

"Hus is also overly patriotic for a priest. Bohemia, which has been ruled by my family for a long time, is divided against itself. It is all a swarm of Czech nobility and peasants against Teuton nobility and peasants. The Teuton peasants, already half-German, are up all night clearing forests and making farms. They work the silver mines. They establish towns. They bring prosperity."

Cossa moaned lightly to himself. Why must this man always sound like a comedian? he thought. "It is getting late, Sigismund," he said. He caught Maria Louise's eye, clenching his jaws and popping his eyes. She moved closer to Sigismund, forcing the king to move his relentless gaze away from the pope, which gave Cossa the chance to close his mind to the king's verbal clatter.

"The entire thing is a hatchwork of ironies," Sigismund said. "My father founded the University of Prague on the models of Paris and Bologna, and the mockery is that that was where Hus learned to concoct his poisons against the Church and state." He was forcing Cossa to face what reform would mean. "Yet Hus has much right on his side. The Church is too wealthy. It has too many prelates. It is corrupt. It is licentious. Simony abounds and the clergy are sucked into depravities. Hus de-

manded reform. You sent Cardinal Colonna to Prague and had
him excommunicate Hus for contumacy—which was begging
the whole question. What *I* seek, as you may well imagine, is to
clear up such despicable rumors about the country I may soon
rule. What we must do, therefore, is have our council examine
Hus for heresy. But to be examined he must get to Konstanz.
To get to Konstanz, I would need to give him a safe-conduct. I
can't do that, however, unless you relieve him of the ban of
excommunication."

It was impossible to tell whether Sigismund revered Hus or
despised him, whether he sought Church reform or would stop
it. The man was the shiftiest kind of fool, Cossa saw.

"Why not?" he said.

"Enough of Hus. We should speak of Benedict and Gregory."

"Who?"

"The—ah—anti-popes."

"Then call them by name—de Luna and Corrario."

"Precisely. I propose to call on Corrario at Rimini. He must
attend Konstanz."

"All that is necessary is that he resign," Cossa said.

"Oh. Well! All *three* popes must resign," Sigismund said
piously. "So that we may begin again," he added brightly.

As Sigismund's force of arms moved out of Lodi, then northward to cross the Alps, the Holy Father returned to Bologna on
the Ides of March, which was the marchesa's birthday. On his
arrival he was given the news that Ladislas had announced in
Perugia that he would sack Bologna and take Cossa as his prisoner. The anxiety in Bologna was so great that the cardinals and
the Curia sent their gold and jewels to Venice for safe-keeping.
Cossa raged at the marchesa even as he sank into the torpor of
Neapolitan fatalism. "You are wasting my life with your
schemes," he snarled at her. "All of these elaborate plans to
draw in the protection of the mighty Sigismund, then after almost destroying me by such a prolonged exposure to the insuf-
ferable boob, two days after he disappears with his army over
the Alps, Ladislas gets ready to attack me. What was the use of
Sigismund but to bring about a council, which not only will lead
to general reform of a perfectly sound institution, but will un-

doubtedly clamor for my resignation as well? Whose side are you on? Ladislas will probably have crucified me in St. Peter's piazza before word can even reach Sigismund that our common enemy has murdered me.''

"There is nothing wrong with your alliance with Sigismund," the marchesa told him. "The fault here is with Ladislas. He is insane. He cannot be allowed to continue his constant wars. The pox has affected his brain."

"Then stop him."

"Cosimo wants him stopped. You want him stopped. There will probably be no Council of Konstanz unless he is stopped."

"We have talked enough about it," Cossa said roughly. "Go to Perugia and see that it is done. Take Palo. Take anyone or anything you need. We should have thought of this long ago. Stop him."

"You are asking me to undergo considerable risk."

"I am only telling you to stop him."

"If I am capable of stopping him at the moment when he brings great danger to your papacy, then it becomes a business matter. Your business is threatened, so you choose me as your specialist to remove the threat. That is worth something."

"I'll pay you three thousand florins."

"Who else can do this for you? Palo? Can Palo as much as approach the king of Naples?"

"How much do you want?"

"It is your papacy, Cossa. You must know how much it is worth to you."

"Five thousand florins!" he snapped.

"Ten thousand."

"Seven thousand."

"Ten thousand."

"You guarantee that I will be rid of him?"

"As always, dear man, that is our understanding. If I fail to provide what you wanted to buy then I cannot charge you for it."

"We are not talking about money anymore. Will you pluck Ladislas off my back?"

"I have a double incentive now, haven't I? You should have thought of this much sooner."

Chapter 52

The marchesa held an open safe-conduct from King Ladislas of Naples, which Rosa had obtained during the time in which Spina had been Gregory's ambassador to the Neapolitan court. She rode in among her bodyguard through Perugia's north gate, beside my own bulky, white-bearded civilian presence, not on that day in my capacity as a member of the Sacred College of Cardinals, to her villa on the outskirts of the city. As we traveled I took occasion to ask her why she had requested me for the journey—that is, I could understand why she would feel that she needed me, but why as a civilian? Why not as a cardinal?

"Because you are a superb actor, Franco Ellera," she said. "And being such a distinguished man yourself, it is all the better for our plan that you play the part of a distinguished man." I understood her.

After two days of resting she sent a note to the local physician, Dottore Ezio Bazoni. "Dear Master," the letter said, "for a short time, it will be my privilege to entertain, as guest of my house, the celebrated physician, Jean-Marie de Valhubert, physician to the king of France and to the duke of Burgundy, as well as being chancellor of the Department of Medicine at the University of Paris. While in Perugia, he has expressed the wish to meet you, hoping to exchange views with you upon the state of the arts of medicine, so I intrude upon your busy life to invite you and your daughter, Elvira, to dine with us in two days' time. I remain, your votary, Decima di Artegiana.''

"Esteemed Marchesa," Dottore Bazoni replied, "the reputation of Jean-Marie Valhubert is esteemed throughout Europe. I am overwhelmed with honor that he should wish to exchange views with me. Although my daughter devoutly hopes to be able to attend you at dinner in two days' time, her duties at the court may prevent this. Your faithful servant who kisses your hand, Ezio Bazoni.''

"It will be useless to have him here without her," the marchesa said to me.

"Perhaps—if you would explain what we are doing?"

"Who is Cossa's worst enemy?"

"Cossa, I suppose."

"No, no—who besides himself?"

"Ladislas?"

"Yes. And the daughter of this man," she held up Bazoni's note, "is Ladislas' lover. Through her, we will remove Ladislas as Cossa's enemy."

"Remove?"

She shrugged. "We do it for Cossa's papacy and to insure the possibility of the Council of Konstanz."

"Why do you keep saying 'we'? This is the first I've heard about it."

"You have a small part to play. Surely you would do that to help your friend? The girl will do everything, actually."

Elvira Bazoni came to dinner at the Villa di Artegiana with her father. She was a tiny, full-bosomed, and wondrously stupid woman of sixteen years, whose masses of dense curls were grape-red. She resembled Ladislas in other ways. She had crafty eyes, sharp elbows, and an astonishing basso voice. Her father had impressed her with the fame of the great physician, Jean-Marie de Valhubert, even though he had never heard of the man. Dottore Bazoni considered that omission to be a normal enough thing for a man who had left Perugia only twice in his life. The marchesa, who knew everyone and everything, had told him who Valhubert was, and if the marchesa said it, that was enough to make Dottore Bazoni drunk on Valhubert's reputation.

As the royal physician I was grave and not forthcoming. I refused to speak of medicine at first, but gradually, as the marchesa drew me out about my travels and my practices, it came out that the circumstances of contemporary life had forced me into preeminence for the treatment of the pox. As I told the Bazonis of treating Pope Benedict, the doge of Venice, and the duke of Burgundy for the pox, Elvira Bazoni became thoughtful and more attentive. Dottore Bazoni became distracted. Immediately after the dinner, the Bazonis apologized that they must leave at once because they were expected at the palace to attend the king.

"Four days in Perugia, one quick dinner," I said. "If we've been assassinating Ladislas it is certainly a long, slow death for him."

"You were marvelous," the marchesa told me. "One more hour tonight and I would have placed the health of my family in your hands."

"But what are we doing?"

"Ladislas has the pox. He has given it to the girl. Her father is treating both of them. You are Valhubert, the great healer of the pox. They'll be back."

Elvira Bazoni arrived in a curtained chair carried by two men late in the afternoon the next day. She asked to see Monsieur de Valhubert. She was veiled. The servant took her to Valhubert's apartment. As the great physician, I was surprised to see her. Words came out of Elvira like boulders crashing down a mountainside. "No one knows it, Maestro, but I am affianced to the king of Naples. There has never been such a whirlwind courtship. He loves me as I love him. Nothing else matters to either of us. But he is sick. He never knew what or who he had been seeking until we found each other. But in his seeking, before we found each other, in the innocence of his need to find me, he came upon—an unclean person. You understand me. It is your holy profession. He caught the pox from that person. But he will not acknowledge it because that would mean acknowledging that it has been passed to me. He cannot bring himself to admit such a terrible thing. Suddenly, without warning, as if you had been sent by God and the angels, you have come to Perugia at the brief moment when he is here. Only you can save him, as you have saved those others. The pox is rotting away the insides of both of us, but he cannot admit that he could ever have been unfaithful to me before he ever met me. He will not discuss it with my father, a doctor as you know. You must cure him, my lord. I want to give him healthy children. Please help us, my lord."

As the great doctor, I walked to the high open windows and stared out at the fountain playing in the patio. I dropped my voice an octave to increase its awful authority and, running my hand through my beard, I said, "I will help you. I will discuss the treatment with your father. He will give the medicine to you. You must find a way to give it to the king."

She took up my hand and kissed it, covering it with her grateful tears.

Dottore Bazoni came to me that evening. He said, "We will never know how to thank you, my lord."

"Dear colleague," I answered him. "They are the victims of their lives. How could I not do anything I can?" I went to my baggage and rummaged about in a small case. I brought a vial to Bazoni. "They are not the first to deny having the pox. This potion will paralyze the guilt that lets the king deny the truth. If he refuses direct treatment, then science has to find ways to persuade him to be treated. Your daughter must put this into his wine and make certain he drinks it. Make certain—absolutely certain—that she understands that there is only enough here to effect one cure. The king must have all of it."

"But my daughter—her own treatment."

"Ah, but she needs no persuasion. She wants sound children. You shall treat her as you will treat him after this medicine has persuaded him that he must be treated."

"I see, I see. Yes. But how can we ever thank you?"

"By serving science," I said.

The marchesa and I, with our escort, departed from Perugia that night within an hour after Dottore Bazoni had left the villa. By evening Elvira Bazoni was dead from the poison and her father had killed himself by opening his veins. A hammock and a chair were prepared for the dying Ladislas. He was carried from Perugia to Rome, to the church of St. Paul outside the city walls, thence to the river beside it, and placed upon a racing galley, which sped to Naples. He died on August 6, 1414. Cosimo di Medici, the seekers for the reform of the Church, and Pope John XXIII were freed of an enemy. I had made it possible for my friend to go forward to Konstanz with his back protected, and the marchesa di Artegiana was richer by twenty thousand florins, including her fee from the grateful Medici Bank.

Chapter 53

The tremendous news swept Bologna that Ladislas was dead and that the papal troops had captured Rome. A hysteria of elation shook the city. Cossa seized upon the opportunity to cancel all plans for the Council of Konstanz. "Rome is returned to us," he said to the marchesa. "At long last, as Christendom expects of him, the pope will reign from the Eternal City. There will be no need to have the council in Konstanz. I have never trusted the idea, because councils breed reformers, but I was threatened by Ladislas. Now Ladislas is dead, so I don't need Sigismund. So I shall proclaim that Konstanz is postponed indefinitely."

"You must go to Konstanz," the marchesa said, grimly.

"Are you deaf?"

"Are you in your dotage?"

"Konstanz is nothing but a trap. They will take everything away from us if we go there."

"You are overexcited, Cossa. You have forgotten that you have summoned the leaders of Christendom, prelates and princes, the great bankers and the businessmen, the owners of Europe, to a great council, which you have long since proclaimed. Even if there were any logic to it—and your notion that Konstanz is a trap is not logical—there is no way to turn such men back now. Whether you go there or remain in Rome, the council will be held."

He stared at her dumbfounded. "I cannot see what could be better for the Medici than to have me firmly on the throne of St. Peter, but I have long since given up trying to keep up with either of you."

"There is four hundred and fifty thousand gold florins to be made out of Konstanz. Have you forgotten that? My share is only ten percent. When the bank loan interest has been paid on the money that bought all the leases for us, you will make nearly four hundred thousand gold florins while you consolidate your position with the princes of Europe."

"You and Cosimo always look out for me, don't you, Decima?"

"You must be very tired, Cossa. You know I would die for you. You know Cosimo is your best friend and surely you can see that only if you preside over every meeting of that council will your interests in the Church be protected. The pope has proclaimed a Universal Council of the Church. It will begin in about three weeks' time. If you are not there, the first thing the reformers will do—and there will be nothing Cosimo or anyone else can do to stop them—will be to call upon the council to depose you."

"But I would be the pope in Rome!" he said hoarsely. "They could never dig me out of Sant' Angelo and all during the months they tried to do such a thing, the people of Christendom would rise up and march upon Rome to bring them down."

"The world is changing," she sighed. "Nations act for their own interests now."

"I cannot go to Konstanz, Decima!"

"If you deny the council, my dearest, there is no way that anyone or anything can help you. Listen to me, my darling. Do you think the princes, who will arrive at Konstanz with separate armies, will care one whit about discussing the affairs of the Church? There will be hundreds of private concerns, which will smother every question concerning the Church. The French will be at Konstanz to secure the conviction of the duke of Burgundy for the tyrannicide of the duke of Orleans. The king of Poland and the Teutonic Knights will merely be moving their conflict to Konstanz. The Swedes will be seeking the canonization of their Brigid. The English king will look for official justification of his newest invasion of France. The count of Cleves and the lords of

Rimini want to be created dukes. Every nation is shouting for the reform of coinage to stop the floods of bad money. The Julian calendar is a complete confusion because it doesn't conform to solar facts. The great imperial towns are groaning under the burden of exorbitant tolls. Sigismund seeks the glory of organizing help for the Greeks against the advancing Turks. The burgesses of Lübeck have risen against their magistrates and have banished them. All of these causes—and many, *many* more—will bring huge sums of money to Konstanz to win their cases. Are you going to turn your back upon such a treasury of gold, in which you rightfully have the lion's share? Europe has so much on its plate that cannot be swallowed, much less digested, that the council will hardly have time to discuss religion, much less the reform of the Church. And remember this, Cossa, Giovanni di Bicci di Medici and his son, Cosimo, have only one cause—the unity of the Christian Church under the papacy of John XXIII.''

Cossa and I sat up half the night discussing what he should do. I read everything wrong. The way I saw it, he had sent me to join the marchesa at Chur so that I could have indirect knowledge of his real plans, which, for whatever reason, he could not discuss with me openly. This, in the end, is what must happen to all such devious people. I am not excusing myself. I had been around Cossa's deviousness for all of my life, so I should have been able to grasp what he really meant even if he didn't know what he meant himself. I decided that he merely wanted me to provide him with reasons for going to Konstanz, which he could store with all the other reasons he had accumulated. I agreed, therefore, with the marchesa that he could not cancel the council that he had had announced from every pulpit in Christendom. Then I said to him, "Konstanz will have its great advantages for us, Cossa. The heads of nations and states and their ambassadors will attend this meeting because their national interests are involved. If you invite him, there is no way that the young duke of Milan can stay away. Either he or his envoys must be there, but if you invite him for special honors then he must go to Konstanz and, once he enters your house there, he will be at your mercy.''

His eyes brightened. He lifted his head high and distended his nostrils. "We will go to Konstanz," he said.

The marchesa left Bologna with Bernaba and a household of 119 people, including 37 of Bernaba's most costly courtesans, collected from Bologna, Florence, Perugia, Parma, Lodi, Modena, and Siena, to cross the Alps to Konstanz to inspect the properties and arrangements that her daughters had optioned to control, and to get Bernaba started on the organization of courtesans, gambling, and entertainment.

Cossa refused to as much as consider starting the journey until it had been confirmed that Sigismund had come to a treaty with the burgomeister and city magistrates of Konstanz that would guarantee his reception in the city with all honor and ceremony, and had set forth in writing the guarantees that no one from any nation or of any rank was to take precedence over him. He insisted that the treaty recognize his full spiritual and temporal jurisdiction in Konstanz for as long as he chose to remain with the council. "They must defend these matters against any citizens or visitors to Konstanz while I am there. My dominance of the council must be assured. The safe-conducts that I issue must be respected. I will not move from Bologna until I have been assured that this treaty has been secured."

The marchesa sent a copy of the treaty from Konstanz. It arrived in Bologna at the end of the third week of September. On October 1, Pope John XXIII left Bologna with a household of 582 people and 619 camp followers. He journeyed down the Panaro River to where it joined the Po, then was floated down the Po to Ferrara, where he rested with the marquess of Este. The papal party moved up the Adige River to Verona. Ahead of them lay the valley of the Adige, through which German troops had marched with the many kings of the Romans on their way to be crowned as emperors in Rome. Farther up the river the great procession halted at the village of St. Michael, where there was a rich monastery. A note from the marchesa, enclosing a letter from her daughter Rosa, from Prague, was waiting for Cossa.

"Dear Mama," Rosa's letter read, "John Hus is the hero of this nation. He is rare among heroes. He has the character of an amiable angel and is perhaps the most lovable man to whom Pippo and I have ever spoken. His kindliness and gentle nature win the love and sympathy and support of even those who first approach him as enemies. Sigismund will make the greatest capital by supporting this fellow in Bohemia against the archbishop and against the Teuton nobility because all the rest of this nation is on the side of Hus.

"His fault, and it is a serious fault, Pippo says, is that he thinks often of wearing the crown of martyrdom. He has withstood his enemies who had cast the foul stain of heresy upon him or who had otherwise maligned him to the pope. He is convinced that if he can reach Konstanz, he will emerge victorious, cleansed of all the foul charges. But he has this evil presentiment that he will never return to Prague.

"Pippo and I fear that Hus may be deluding himself by believing that, once in Konstanz, he will be allowed to hold forth in academic disputation, in sweet reasonableness, with adversaries who will be suddenly less prejudiced and intolerant of him than are the prelates of Prague. He actually thinks that all will be solved by calm and temperate discussion.

"Yesterday, August 27, because he says he is concerned with appearing at Konstanz with the proper credentials of orthodoxy, he nailed a notice to the castle gate, which called upon the king of Bohemia and his counselors to bear witness to his orthodoxy. He petitioned a large number of the Bohemian nobility to appear before the papal inquisitor to ask publicly if he knew of any error or heresy in Hus or if anyone had incriminated Hus before him.

"The inquisitor replied that he had eaten and drunk with Hus, listened to many of his discourses, and in all of his words and works, had found him to be a true Catholic. A notarial instrument was drawn to this effect. It was signed by the inquisitor and copies were sent to the pope and to the Bohemian king. After this three barons in an assembly of nobles asked the archbishop whether he could accuse Hus of any error or heresy. The archbishop is Hus' mortal enemy but he replied that he knew of no heresy by Hus and could make no accusation against him. Because of all this, but mostly because of Hus' extreme popularity with the Bohemian people, Sigismund is determined to take Hus under his protection. He intends that Hus shall enter Konstanz in his train. He has commissioned John of Chlum and Wenzel of Duba to escort Hus to the royal camp. Hus will leave Prague on September 20.

"Mama—this amiable man believes he is in God's special care. He knows nothing of the world and I fear he will fail to follow Sigismund's instructions, and this could be politically most dangerous if he does not join with Sigismund's train and enter Konstanz with it.

"For your reference: Hus tells me he will lodge in Konstanz with a widow named Fida in the street of St. Paul near the Snezthor."

Cossa clumped Rosa's letter into a ball and flung it from him. "Why is the Church cursed with people like Hus?" he asked me rhetorically. "It has thousands of high officers, all trained people—canon lawyers, administrators, and theologians—but an ambitious priest like this one has to get attention for himself, and worse, do it all in the name of sweetness and light."

"If you think he is only ambitious and you want to shut him up," I said, "make him a bishop."

"Maybe ambitious was the wrong word. Worse, Hus is one of those professional saints who thinks he is helping the people by making trouble. He thinks that what he is doing isn't hurting anyone, except that every damned theatrical thing he does leads us closer to Church reform, and all because he's one of those people who want to be loved. Come on, Franco Ellera, get the cards. We'll play a little *tarocchini* and maybe I'll get some of my money back."

The papal household moved in ten-mile steps each day as it ascended the Alps. It stopped at the village of Tramin and so on upward until, on October 15, it reached Meran, ancient capital of the Tyrol, on the right bank of the Passer, where Cossa was greeted by Frederick, duke of Austria and count of the Tyrol, his friend—who was Sigismund's enemy.

Frederick was not only ambitious, he was headstrong. He held fortress castles near Konstanz. For that alone, Cossa saw him as invaluable. He was already in league with John of Nassau and the marquess of Baden, two more of Cossa's rampant-warrior friends. Cossa made a formal treaty with Frederick and gave him sixteen thousand florins to seal the bargain, which made Frederick captain-general of the papal troops with an annual salary of two thousand florins. Cossa wanted to have protection when he needed it and Frederick promised him safe-conduct anywhere against any man. It was probably the worst deal anyone made for himself in the century. With the kind of judgment he had, it is surprising Frederick ever made it beyond the cradle.

The ponderous household struggled up the narrow path of the valley of the Eisak, past Klausen to Brixen. From Brixen the mass of animals and men went up the Brenner to Innsbruck, then the road led west. They climbed the steep valley of the Inn —nine cardinals, thirty-one bishops, and the entire Curia in the train. They kept climbing until they came at last to the chasmatic glacier of the Riffler in San Anton, where they climbed to the Arlberg Pass, over six thousand feet above the seas, through the wild, slanted valley. A work party had cleared the road through the powdery snow. Hundreds of horses' hooves, which had hardened the way for the pope's red wagon, had also pounded it into slippery ice. They were just beyond the little hospice of St. Christopher when the wagon skidded crazily and overturned, sending the Holy Father rolling wildly, over and over, into a snowbank. Six pairs of hands pulled him out. Count Weiler, the papal physician, came running in to see if he were hurt. "My epitaph came to me just as the carriage capsized," Cossa said, grinning broadly. "It shall be 'Here I lie in the name of the Devil.' Not bad, hey, Abramo? Or should I have stayed in Bologna?"

The papal train moved upward again to the valley of Klosterle. From the top, looking far downward, Cossa saw the lake of Konstanz, called the Bodensee, glistening in the distance. Before them lay the city of Konstanz. "They trap foxes down there," Cossa said.

Chapter 54

I can paint an unforgettable picture of that fated city for any Italian who had left the sun behind him as Cossa and I had. A strong wind drove a light snow across the lake. It fell upon the thirty towers and gateways of the walled city of Konstanz, which had a population of six thousand people on the day Pope John XXIII entered the city. Two months later, by the end of the first week of January 1415, Konstanz had twenty thousand people; sixty thousand by the end of February the same year.

While the Council of Konstanz met, the city would be the diplomatic and political as well as the religious center of Christendom. Never before in the history of the Church had the Imperial Chancery and the Roman Curia settled down together, side by side. It was to be a running event that was unparalleled in European history.

Pope John XXIII entered Konstanz on Sunday, October 28, 1414, just after eleven o'clock in the forenoon, from the Monastery of Saint Ulrich, at Kreuzlingen, where we had spent the night. After morning reflection, a procession was formed. Cossa, clad entirely in white like a priest at an altar, was accompanied by his cardinals, archbishops, bishops, and the Curia. He was met at the door of the monastery by the clergy of Konstanz bearing holy relics. Four magistrates conducted the Holy Father to his white horse, around whose neck a great bell was hung, richly caparisoned in scarlet, led by Bartoldo Orsini and Count Rudolf of Montfort zu Scheer, who stood under a canopy of cloth of gold. White horses in red trappings led the way of the procession, loaded with clothing bags, followed by a white hackney carrying a silver-gilt chest with a monstrance in which was the Holy Sacrament. Then followed His Holiness, surrounded by burning tapers. Near him was a priest who scattered coins to relieve the press of the crowds. Behind the Holy Father rode "the man with the hat," a huge parasol on a long pole embroidered with red and yellow. On top of the hat there was a golden knob and on it a golden angel holding a cross in his hand. The hat was so wide that it protected His Holiness from sun and rain. Behind the man with the hat rode the cardinals, two and two, in long red cloaks, with their servants and pages. On their heads were broad red hats with long silken bands.

The procession made its way through the Kreuzlingen Gate then through the Stadelhofen and Schnetz gateways, and along a route that led through St. Paul Gasse and Plattengasse to the cathedral, where it assembled and sang *Te Deum Laudamus*. The bells pealed until vesper time. Cossa passed through the chapel of St. Margaret to the bishop's palace, where he settled in with his senior servants. The cardinals rode on to the houses and inns assigned to them. The marchesa occupied the Blidhaus on one side of the Canon's Court, containing the bishop's palace, facing Wessenbergstrasse.

I liked Konstanz from the moment I entered it. First of all it was a German town, the second such I had set foot in since I was a boy of ten. I thought I had become an Italian in the long process that had followed, but I had not. I was a German and Konstanz comforted me for that.

The city was founded in the fourth century and named after the Emperor Constantius Chlorus. The bishopric was transferred from Windisch to Konstanz in A.D. 560 because the town was placed for cheap water carriage by the Rhine and from the lake, having good roads that approached it from all directions. The lake offered supplies of fish and facilities for the easy availability of flesh, produce, fodder, beer, and wine. The drinking water was pure and the air was healthy—except in winter, where the Italians were concerned. I have never heard so much garlic-scented coughing.

The See of Konstanz stretched from Breisgau to the Allgau, from the Bernese Oberland to the middle reaches of the Neckar. Konstanz was a Swabian free imperial town. Jews were only occasionally persecuted there, a northern fashion. Its permanent citizens were divided into eighteen guilds from which the town council was elected annually.

By the time the full French delegation had arrived, in February, 30,000 horses were stabled in the town and as many as 31 barges loaded with hay and straw were counted in a single day alongside the quay at St. Conrad's Bridge. Thirty-six thousand beds were provided for transient strangers. By day and night the streets were alive with the minstrelsy of the great lords, reechoing with hundreds of fifes, trumpets, and bagpipes. On feast days everything gave way to jongleurs and players, to tiltings, feasts, and processions. Jugglers, pickpockets, whores, lottery operators, jewelers, bakers, barbers, gamblers, pharmacists, cooks, bankers, goldsmiths, pawnbrokers, cobblers, pimps, and tailors from seventy towns in Europe had rushed to this place. Chiromancers foretold. Poets sang. There were 29 cardinals, whose combined households numbered 3,056 attendants. Although the average-size household was 105 people, my own numbered 126 because Cossa forced me to carry 37 waiters who belonged on his staff. There were 338 bishops from everywhere, hundreds of prelates, prebends, protonotaries, abbots, provosts, and patriarchs, and hundreds of learned doctors from every university. One hundred and seventy-one doctors of medicine, with 1,600 assistants, hung out their shingles. Each space was utilized to hold these people and almost every other space—and surely the best of them—was the leased property of the syndicate that Cossa and the marchesa di Artegiana owned.

To Konstanz came 5,300 simple priests and scholars and 39 archdukes, 141 counts, 32 princely lords, 71 barons, and 1,500 knights with 20,000 squires. Ambassadors from 83 parts of Asia, Africa, and Europe attended.

Pope John XXIII was established as head of the council with 24 secretaries, 12 court officers, and a household that had grown to 674 persons, not including 37 waiters.

Work was provided for those without funds repairing the city wall, widening the moat, and mending streets, although there were no urgent repair works to be done. The really poor priests, courtiers, and scholars were enabled to earn money for their living. They were paid eighteen pfennig a day for food and lodging. It was something. During the morning they were excused from work to allow them to get alms from priests, which were amply distributed every day. It was ordered that no one was to mock at these workers or to speak ill of them.

The municipal banking monopoly was not maintained. Through intervention by the pope the bankers of Florence, representing Europe's leading money market, were represented strongly, foremost among these being the Medici Bank, whose manager, Bartolomeo de' Bardi, settled in at the Haus zur Tonnen. The Florentine bankers appeared in Konstanz with great splendor and their luxury was everywhere admired. The principal coins in circulation were schilling and pfennig although prices were fixed in gulden. Each foreign banker had to pay the town six Rhenish gulden a month for carrying on their business. In 1414 the city council reopened its mint, which had been out of use since 1407, and with the agreement of the ten towns around the lake, made pfennig.

Konstanz became the most important place on the map of Europe. There had never been such an important assembly of wisdom and might, of Church and state.

A small army of over twelve thousand whores worked around the clock, the less gifted living thirty to a room, and in baths, and empty wine butts that lay about the streets. There were theatricals. Bishop Weldon of Semley exhibited short plays between courses at banquets that the English held at the Haus zum Goldenen Schwert, showing The Coming of the Three Kings, The Birth of Our Lord, and The Slaughter of the Innocents. There were extravagant Florentine processions. Women who could sing were objects of wonderment. The sermons of Pierre d'Ailly, as well as the official protocols and circular letters of the council and the religiopolitical tracts of Jean Gerson, were disseminated by the thousands. The minnesinger Oswald von Wolkstein confessed in a sweet poem that he had found a paradise in Konstanz:

Women here, like angels wooing,
Beautiful in splendor bright,
They have been my heart's undoing,
They possess my dreams at night.
The fairest fair in dainty dresses,
With jewels are in auburn tresses,
The rose-red lips on blushing faces,
When sorrow trips and leaves no traces.

"So great is the host of the most dainty dames and damsels,"
Benedict de Pileo wrote, "who surpass the snow in the delicacy
of their coloring, that you might rightly say of Konstanz, as Ovid
declared of Rome, that Venus herself reigns in this city."

Venus operated mainly under the name of Bernaba Minerbetti
for the more expensive, high-quality women. She managed 107
of the most costly, replacing them as often as necessary during
the four years of the council. It was an enormous business but
it was buttressed by the marchesa's organization of the jewelers,
goldsmiths, and furriers, who sold the same wares over and over
again as they were turned in to Bernaba by the courtesans. The
marchesa supervised the multilevel accounting, medical, and in-
tramural brokerages of the enterprises' managements, as she did
with the inns, produce, wine, restaurant, and beer business in
Konstanz, over the direct management of Bernaba Minerbetti,
who was assisted by me whenever I could find a moment.

The marchesa also handled the organization of the daily and
nightly information that the women were required to pass along.
This intelligence was pooled, then shared with Cosimo di Medici
—some of it, about thirty percent of it, was shared with Cossa.
Little happened in Konstanz, in the private or secret meetings
of the council or in the caucuses and courts of individual nations
attending the council, that escaped the marchesa's attention.

Because she and Cossa controlled most of the housing in Konstanz, as well as its provisioning, lodging, and gambling indus-
tries, as the armies of pilgrims swarmed along the great trunk
roads they found the cost of traveling increased steadily the
nearer they came to Konstanz. When they reached the town
itself, the prices of food, drink, and lodgings soared beyond any
expectations. Buildings for the accommodation of visitors were

erected around St. Stephen's Church and the Augustinian monastery. The quarters for the more important guests were assigned beforehand; claiming placards were posted, which were removed by the nominated occupant, who then nailed up his own coat of arms outside the dwelling.

The College of Auditors sat three times a week to settle disputes for rightful possession. The charge for a furnished room with a clean bed was one and one-half gulden a month. The linen was changed once a fortnight. Stabling for a horse cost two pfennig a day; his food about eight pfennig. Peace within the city was well kept. When there was a robbery or murder the authorities always made sure that these could only have happened outside the town's walls and, over the time of the council, 560 bodies were found in the lake.

The profits from the uncommon enterprises operated by the marchesa and Cossa averaged 9,300 gold florins a month, never less than 115,000 florins a year, and over 400,000 florins over the duration of the holy congress.

Chapter 55

When Pope John XXIII entered Konstanz, Sigismund was hundreds of miles away at Aix-la-Chapelle, called Aachen by the Germans. Ten days later he was crowned, at last, as king of the Romans, and the Council of Konstanz was being opened by Pope John XXIII, several hundred miles away.

Escorted by Niholas Gara, her sister's husband, Queen Barbara journeyed from Buda to join her husband in coronation at Aix-la-Chapelle. Sigismund had made intricate arrangements to be crowned at Aix on October 21 so that he might appear formally as king of the Romans at Konstanz for the opening of the council. It was his plan to arrive at Konstanz before the pope but there were difficulties. Two of the electors had told him the coronation date would be unacceptable to them so Sigismund had to electioneer from Koblenz to Mainz to Frankfurt to Heidelberg to Wimpfen to Ansbach to Nuremberg, to confer with all electors—"as if I were some little burgomeister accumulating supporters and contributors," listening to the clergy of each city intone the solemn introits again and again. "Behold the Lord cometh with the power and the kingdom in his hand. Let the tribes of the people serve thee and be lord over all thy brethren."

At last it was settled, despite the opposition of the electors of Berg and Brabant, although Sigismund decided to ask the duke of Juliers, the mayor and bailiff of Aix-la-Chapelle, to guarantee his safety with four thousand horse.

The interior of the cathedral where the pope opened the council with a high mass had been altered to accommodate the convention. Here the delegates would deliberate solemnly for the next four years, although all of us thought we would be there for a much shorter time. The large altar in the choir was covered with boards. Next to this altar, next to the small sacrament house, a wooden altar had been built and in front of it rested a beautiful chair to seat the pope when he took the sacrament when celebrating mass, and where he could sit throughout the sessions to be seen from everywhere in the cathedral. In front of another altar called the *Tagmessaltar* a seat was placed for the absent King Sigismund.

As soon as the pope had said the mass on the morning of his arrival in Konstanz, I rose and announced that the opening of the business session would take place on November 3. This was subsequently postponed until the fifth.

My announcement established how earnest the pope was that the council must be considered as a mere continuation of the Council of Pisa at which Benedict XIII and Gregory XII had been declared heretic and schismatic and had been formally deposed. If Cossa could succeed in getting the assembly to follow this view then it had to follow that he must be recognized as the canonical pope.

On November 5, the council went into session without the presence of the king of the Romans, or any of the electors, or any of the ambassadors from the courts of Europe, or any of the nations except Italy, or a single representative of Benedict or Gregory. Cossa was elated. "This is going to be another paper-built Council of Rome all over again," he said to me gleefully. "Everyone who was there today is against Church reform. We can go through all the motions and be out of here in a month's time."

"This is different," I told him. "They're coming from all over Europe. You've got to give them time to get here. They have a lot of traveling to do and a lot of them wouldn't be too upset to miss a couple of weeks of straight masses and processions anyhow."

"What are you saying? This council was built up to the heavens. If they were going to take it seriously they would be here, but nobody cares." I knew that Cossa wanted desperately to believe that. For the first time, I realized how frightened Cossa was; frightened of such a concentration of power around him, frightened of the future.

"We aren't exactly poor," I told him. "We can always retire. Let's see what happens."

He looked at me as if I were getting senile.

Even the people of Konstanz and the few pilgrims who had arrived for the great events were disappointed in the showing. Only 15 cardinals, 2 patriarchs, 23 archbishops, and some 300 minor prelates had passed in swaying procession into the cathedral. This time, when the mass was over, I mounted the pulpit and rumbled out in a profound voice that the first active session of the council would be held on Friday, November 16.

"It is as good a date as any," Cossa told the marchesa as they worked over projections of income at the papal residence, formerly the bishops' palace, across from the cathedral.

"Cossa, get it out of your head that no one is coming to this. The people are starting to come in. Peace has broken out temporarily somehow, so the roads are free from troops and their followers. And the weather is good."

"It was the same two weeks ago but nobody got here," Cossa said insistently. "And it is also winter. The Italians are dropping into sickbeds. Count Weiler says there could be an epidemic. We should capitalize on all that and spread the word as far and wide as we can that it is dangerous to come to Konstanz." The return of his fear that they would charge him, and try him, and burn him, brought on an obsession. He would not listen to anyone who believed that the nations would come to Konstanz.

On November 16, after the mass and the anthem, after the silent and the audible prayers and the litany, which was followed by the benediction and the gospel, Pope John XXIII then preached a sermon on the text, "Speak ye every man the truth with his neighbor; execute the judgment of truth and peace at your gates." At its close he intoned the *Veni Creator Spiritus.* I then stood beside the pope and read the bull that set forth that the work of reform had been postponed after Pisa for three years, when it had been taken up by the Council of Rome, and had again needed to be postponed because of the sparseness of the numbers who could attend because of the wars. The bull did not activate reform but it flatly mentioned reform. The officers of the council were then nominated. The second session was fixed for December 17.

The following day a deputation of cardinals led by Pierre d'Ailly called upon the pope at his palace. D'Ailly complained officially to the pope that he was wanting in correctness and decorum. "Your Holiness, the Supreme Pontiff, cuts masses short. He will not give proper audiences. He avoids the processions, which the people so enjoy. Most of the time he chooses to be jocose."

Cossa stared at d'Ailly, Spina, and his own nephew, his sister's boy, Brancacci, with contempt. He had made the fortunes of these men. They knew that all of the endless ritual movements of the Church were what the Church was to practicing Christians. It was their entertainment! What did it matter to them who performed the movements and intoned the gibberish, except, of course, they enjoyed seeing prelates of high rank doing these things because they could then tell their friends that they had actually prayed with so-and-so, and had been within fifty feet of the pope. By sparing his appearances he was preserving the wonderment value of the papacy, and each time he was absent from the gargled foolishness he was only adding to the value and pleasure of those occasions when he was visible to the faithful. These robbers knew that. Indeed, the people themselves knew the whole thing was a mockery of a past that had been dead for a thousand years.

"You go beyond jocosity," he said to d'Ailly, trying to control his outrage.

"His Holiness must prescribe himself for all the world to know," Spina said gravely, "the certain hours for the recitation of his office, for saying and hearing mass—indeed, my lord, for being shriven—for attending the sick and the dying, and allowing of no emergency to break in upon these hours. The people worship what you stand for. They have come hundreds of miles to see you and to be put at peace by you."

"What do I have cardinals for? You are the so-called church-men. You do some of the work for a change. I am a lawyer, not a priest, and you knew that when you elected me your pope. I am a soldier, not a chanter of rituals."

D'Ailly ground on. "A Roman pontiff is expected to hold secret consistories. Also, it is the customary thing for a pope to maintain the Pagnotta, the public alms collection of everything taken from his table when he has done eating."

"The pope is required to appoint three or four referendaries to inspect all petitions. It is only right," Cossa's nephew Brancacci said.

"If I had turned to the referendaries before appointing you a cardinal because my father requested it, little nephew," Cossa spat at him, "you would still be playing among the catamites of Naples and ignoring that there was a church in the city."

"You, Cossa!" Spina snarled. "We are talking about you who should be holding a public audience after every mass and at vespers three times a week—if only to show that you occasion-ally go to mass and vespers. These are northern people who surround us, they are not complaisant Italians. They send in the greatest bulk of the income of the Church. They have paid over and over again whenever they were assessed and reassessed and they deserve to get from their pope what they have paid for."

"Where lords are slack, the steward cannot be expected to be particular," d'Ailly said smoothly. "A lord should rise before his servants and be the last to bed. Above all, his responses to any event should be couched in kindly terms lest he make ene-mies."

"But you do not heed your own counsel, my lords!" Cossa exclaimed, extending his hands to them palms upward, then clenching these into fists.

"Counsel, Holy Father?"

"Your ancient wisdom about making enemies. You have made a hungry enemy today." He turned to Spina. "You must take care, Spina, lest your reputation among popes becomes as smashed as your nose." He smiled slyly. "We really must have a long talk about that nose of yours someday. I never could believe that story of how it happened to you." He turned to the two other cardinals. "Did you know that thirty-one men once took their consecutive pleasure upon our lord Spina's body, Your Eminences? Now you would not have thought he would have been such a morsel, would you? But that is the typical Sicilian every time, isn't it?''

Spina tottered forward, grabbing at a table in front of him, then standing, leaning upon it with both arms, drawing air into his body in great sucking gasps. His face was blank white with two vivid scarlet spots high on the cheekbones. Intensely white sputum discharged from the corners of his mouth. He tried to speak but he could make no sound. It was an insane tableau, with the Holy Father in his whitest of albs and snowy zucchetto standing amiably before a man who was suffocating with humiliation, beside two gorgeously robed princes of the Church. At last Spina was able to lift a hand from the tabletop, keeping the other there to support himself. He lifted the arm and extended a long, brown, palsied finger at his pontiff, eyes wide with horror. ''You knew Minerbetti!'' he croaked. ''Where is she?''

''Get him out of here,'' the pope said, for the moment recreating the enormous amiability of Boniface IX. ''All of you, carrion, fallen upon the purse of the Church—get out of my sight.''

That evening, as he was finishing with the delight of retelling the story to me, a letter bearing Cardinal Spina's seal arrived. Cossa told me to read it to him. ''It is a cheery message, I am sure,'' he said, ''with which Spina will hang himself.''

''Cossa,'' I read from the letter, ''we can come to an arrangement. You tell me where I may find Minerbetti and I will become your agent inside the d'Ailly faction, which intends to bring you down. I put this in writing. I place all of my future in your hands so that you will know that I must find Bernaba Minerbetti.''

''Jesus Christ!'' I exploded. ''Spina must have lost his mind.''

Chapter 56

Sigismund and Barbara kissed the skull of Charlemagne at the Aix Minster and while the *Te Deum* was sung he lay prostrate with outstretched arms upon the floor with his queen kneeling at his side. Since daylight, processions had filled the streets of the town and, at eleven minutes after nine on the morning of November 8, 1414, Sigismund was crowned king of the Romans by the new archbishop of Cologne. Sigismund himself, wearing an alb and dalmatic, read the Gospel and with visible awe held the great relics in his hands—an undergarment of the Blessed Virgin and St. Joseph's stockings, which he had taken off to swaddle the Holy Infant at the moment of its miraculous birth 1,414 years before.

Maria Louise Sterz was close by Sigismund through his travels and ceremonies. She greatly attracted Sigismund's wife by her distant gelidness but to no avail for the queen. Maria Louise listened and watched everything with seeming indifference and reported to her mother by courier each week.

Dear Mama: December 12, 1414, Frankfurt
    The king and queen made joyous entry into Frankfurt today en route to Konstanz. Then the news arrived that John Hus had ignored the king's command that he attend the council only in the king's train. Sigismund is enraged by

this. He had given Hus a safe-conduct from Prague to Konstanz and now he was told the impossible news that Hus was arrested in Konstanz by the bishops of Augsburg and Trent, in league with the burgomeister of Konstanz, and taken to prison.

Sigismund regards this as a flagrant outrage against his honor. He cannot believe that the bishops surrounded the house where Hus was staying. Sigismund keeps saying that Hus *knew* that his place and his safety were to join with the king's entourage at Spier so that he could journey to Konstanz under the king's protection. The second horrendous mistake was to ignore the king's instructions that he was not to say *anything* except in the royal presence. I tell you, Sigismund is in a hurricane of fury about this, although much of it is playacting. He fears deeply that any business against Hus can grow into a serious political matter in Bohemia and he recognizes that the cardinals have shown their stark intention to keep the power in the council.

Sigismund swears to every newcomer who enters the room that he will have Hus out of jail if he has to break down the prison doors himself. He is certain that Cossa is behind the Hus arrest, in order to embarrass and humiliate him and to place his own possible future accession to the throne of Bohemia in jeopardy in Prague. His people answer him only with their conviction that Hus' arrest is the cardinals' signal that it is to be understood that they, not the princes, must dominate the Council of Konstanz.

Chapter 57

The sworn escort of John Hus, the Bohemian knight, John of Chlum, demanded an audience with His Holiness to protest the Hus arrest. Cossa received him with me as witness. "Holy Father," Chlum said after the blessing was done, "your cardinals have cast John Hus into prison and this is not what your paternity promised."

"I call upon Cardinal Ellera to bear witness," Cossa said. "I have never ordered the cardinals nor anyone to take John Hus prisoner."

"It was an act hostile to His Holiness," I said, causing my voice to emerge as from the bowels of the planet. "They try to force disgrace upon the Holy Father by keeping Hus in captivity."

Chlum ignored me, a massive achievement. He spoke hotly to Cossa. "You endorsed Sigismund's safe-conduct for Hus," he said. "You guaranteed his safety. Is what you offer me now to be considered satisfaction?"

"Hus is my son, as you are. I sought his safety and I still seek it. But what has happened is there for the world to see—he is being used as a pawn in a larger game."

"Order his release!"

"These are delicate times, Chlum. The council is just beginning. I must move carefully."

"You have breached your word," Chlum said harshly. "I shall go through this city showing the king's safe-conduct and your endorsement of it to all who can read. I will nail a manifesto to the cathedral door to charge you with vilifying the safe-conduct and the protection that it granted to Master Hus." He stalked out of the audience.

"Well," Cossa said to me. "This looks like a bad start, but it could be worse. It is going to make far more trouble for Sigismund than it can for me."

I repeated the conversation to Bernaba, who passed it to the marchesa, who shared it with Cosimo di Medici. "I cannot imagine Cossa taking such outrageous conduct from a common knight," the marchesa said sadly. "Cossa isn't the man he was at Pisa. Not mentally or physically. His body has thickened with the weight of the gout and his mind cannot rest long upon any choice he thinks he is making."

"We will help him," Cosimo said, smiling. "Nothing has gone right for him since Roccasecca. Besides, I don't think Hus is heavy on his mind. But he knows already what Sigismund has yet to find out—that the council is stronger than either of them. Hus is the one with the serious problem. Cossa doesn't dare to offend the council."

Despite the commands of the pope and Sigismund's endless dispatches, Hus remained in custody in a cell that was eight feet square by nine feet high under a leaking community latrine of the Dominican Cloister at the edge of the lake. He whole-heartedly believed that some technical error had been made, which would soon be put right. He knew he could trust John of Chlum to do all possible to rectify the error and have his freedom restored.

After a week, Hus fell sick with fever from the oppression of the dripping latrine. The vaguely seen shapes of men came to him in his delirium with extracts from his treatise *De Ecclesia* demanding to know if he had written them. Slowly it came to him that there was not to be the academic discussion to which he had looked forward as he set out for Konstanz from Prague. These men seemed to be preparing to try him, so he rejoiced in the knowledge of the protection of his many friends. Not only were there the multitudes in Prague to whom he had preached, and who loved and revered him as a prophet sent from God, but also there stood in his mind, above all others, the immense figure of Sigismund, who had granted him safe-conduct.

The pope sent his own physician, Count Weiler, to treat Hus and he was soon restored to health. Hus applied for the counsel of a lawyer but this was refused. Under canon law no aid could be given to a heretic, so the preliminary inquiry was conducted by three judges appointed by the pope.

The witnesses the cardinals' men examined were, extraordinarily, only those men who had long held the opinion that Hus' beliefs were heretical. On December 1, the council appointed a commission of greater powers, to deal with the growing charges of Hus' heresy, made up of Piero Spina, Pierre d'Ailly, and Cardinal de Chalant, assisted by a Dominican, a Franciscan friar, and six learned doctors of the law.

Hus' protector, King Sigismund of Hungary, king of the Romans, arrived in Konstanz on Christmas Eve. Hus could hear the great procession go by in the night as the king made his way to the mass at the cathedral, but Hus remained in the underground cell at the monastery until March 3.

Chapter 58

When Sigismund's great train reached Ueberlingen a courier was sent off to the pope to ask him to delay the mass the next morning so that the king could be present at the cathedral. The city council of Konstanz sent ships of greeting to Ueberlingen and ordered that the council chamber be heated. On Christmas Day at two o'clock in the morning most of Konstanz was awake to watch the royal fleet, lighted with innumerable torches, sweep past the island of Mainu and round the corner of the bridge within hail of the Dominican monastery. The enormous party came ashore: the king, Queen Barbara, Maria Louise Sterz, Queen Elizabeth of Bosnia, who was the king's sister, Princess Anna of Würtemberg, who was Sigismund's niece, Duke Rudolf of Saxony, their households, and a thousand drunken Hungarian horsemen. It was bitterly cold. The king was lodged at The House With the Steps near the cathedral but the royal party was taken to the warm council chamber to thaw out for an hour, where they drank hot Malmsey wine and the city presented a golden rose to Sigismund while the prelates awaited their arrival to begin the Christmas Mass in the icy cathedral.

When he was rested and refreshed the king was escorted, under canopies held by local nobles, through the torch-lit darkness to the cathedral, where he was welcomed by the pope under a miter that glistened with gold and precious stones. The procession made its way into the cathedral: the canons of Kreuzlingen, monks of Petershausen and of the Schotten monastery, and the priests of St. Paul, all carrying candles. Members of the three begging orders and schoolchildren led by men carrying the golden poles with the crests of each school; chaplains, monks, abbots, priors, archbishops, and cardinals followed in the train. Behind each cardinal came a priest who carried the hem of his gown. All wore white overcoats and the cardinals had on white, unadorned miters. Then followed the pope's singers, then a priest with the Cross and a priest with the Holy Sacrament, followed by small boys carrying tall candles. I was dressed as a deacon, and walked immediately before my pope carrying a gold cloth held breast-high. Cossa was dressed as a priest, in white, wearing two overcoats and a white miter. Four citizens of Konstanz carried the golden canopy above him. King Sigismund followed with the electors, the queen, the princes, the Johanniter and Teutonic orders, then dukes, marquesses, counts, barons, knights, soldiers, people, and women.

Cossa sat on a throne at the side of the high altar. At his right the king sat among noble attendants who carried the golden rose, the imperial scepter, and the drawn sword. The king had changed into the stole and dalmatic of a deacon to allow himself to take part in the holy office. The Holy Father celebrated the mass but the king read the Gospel. During the mass, the pope blessed the golden rose and formally presented it to Sigismund. After the first mass, hymns were sung. The pope celebrated a second mass, *Lux fulgebit,* then the *Prim, Terz,* and *Sext* were sung until six o'clock in the morning. The third mass, *Puer natus est nobis,* went on until eleven o'clock. After the last mass the pope, Sigismund, eleven cardinals, other prelates, and seven princes climbed the steep flight of stairs to the tower, from whose spacious balcony the pope showed the golden rose to the crowd and blessed the people with it. It was not until well past noon that the congregation dispersed.

"That will fix that son-of-a-bitch, for keeping the entire council waiting for an hour and a half until he was ready to come out to a Christmas Mass," Cossa said to me as we entered the sacristy to change clothes.

Chapter 59

The marchesa and her four daughters assembled at her house beside the papal palace, there being a protected passageway between the two buildings.

"Good *God!*" the marchesa exclaimed as they entered the warm room. "Ten hours in that icy church to watch Sigismund play priest! Three *masses!* Has Cossa lost his mind?"

"Last week you were complaining that he didn't say mass often enough, Mama," Rosa said.

"I must prepare my commentary on Sigi's performance," Maria Louise said.

"He'll need a lot more than that," the marchesa said tartly. "Why—will someone please tell me why—after thirty years did Cossa decide to tell Spina that he knew all about his nose?"

"I'm sure Cosimo will keep Spina far too busy for him to make any trouble about that," Maria Giovanna said.

"Spina is a Sicilian," Rosa said. "He is never too busy for revenge. Never mind Spina. What about Hus? Hus is a holy man, not a politician."

"I agree," the marchesa said. "He symbolizes everything this council is supposed to stand for, but he will not be served by what it says it stands for—Peace, Faith, and Virtue. Also, if a great howl is sent up across Christendom about Hus' heresy that will serve to muffle the fact that as little as possible reform is going to happen here if the cardinals have anything to say about it, which they will not have, you may be sure. The council knows it can safely disregard peace because everyone agrees that it can't be controlled. Virtue is the other word for reform—and that will have to be postponed by common consent. Bringing in reforms would only be throwing out management at the top, and they are that management. The only reform they will allow is the election of a single pope so that business can get on its feet again. Just the same, the stomach of this Church can only be purged by its vomiting away twenty-three cardinals and three hundred archbishops and bishops, and cleansing out the entire Curia. But Faith, the publicly-displayed keystone of their slogan, is more easily arrived at, and the solution to the public badge of the faith of the Church was settled on the day John Hus set out from Prague.''

"The cardinals had best take care," Maria Louise said. "Sigi is *insane* with rage about what they have done to Hus. The Bohemian nobles are all over him. More than a thousand letters have come in from Bohemia, Poland, and Hungary.''

Until the pope ended his meeting with Sigismund at The House With the Steps across from St. Stephen's Church, the king had intended that house to be his lodging place in Konstanz. After the meeting, the king withdrew all of his household to the Benedictine monastery in Petershausen on the far side of the Rhine bridge. I was at that fateful meeting and I watched with growing horror as Cossa began to burn his bridges behind him; all because of John Hus.

When the glorious procession bearing His Holiness came to call on the first day after Christmas, he and the king drank wine from a large loving cup, then, without further pause, the king immediately charged the Holy Father with criminal laxity in the matter of John Hus, provoking Cossa's rage, as much because of his contempt for Sigismund (and all who were not Italian) as for the injustice and recklessness of Sigismund's charge.

"You drunken know-nothing," he said to the king. "Hus was *your* responsibility. You abysmal fool—you thought you would make a golden moment out of Hus when they made you king of Bohemia, if they ever do. Hus was your responsibility. Am I the king of the square-headed Germans who call themselves Romans or are you? Romans! Bearded, drip-nosed, stiff-jointed beer drinkers who make a gypsy Luxembourger their king! You are the King of the Scarecrows, you ridiculous hick. If you knew anything about people or consequences you would have prevented that sanctimonious little bastard, Hus, from coming here in the first place."

"You *dare* to talk to me like that? You—who can't control his own cardinals or any part of the council that you, yourself, have called? You sinister fraud, I was told that you were supposed to know something about canon law. The safe-conduct I gave to Hus was *ultra vires* and can have no jurisdiction in a spiritual case. Even *I* can't shelter a man who was excommunicated by you for contumacy."

"How pleased they will be in your future capital city of Prague to hear that you abandoned Hus for so technical a reason."

"Damn you! Your cardinals and bishops did that! What the hell do I have to say about what people are in the eyes of the Church? *Your* bishops examined Hus and had no hesitation about proclaiming his heresy. *You* are responsible for this dangerous affair, yet you have the brass to suggest that I—king of the Romans, king of Hungary, future king of Bohemia, and next Holy Roman Emperor—should bear the odium of your faithless breach."

Cossa moved closer to the king and patted him on the cheek contemptuously, speaking gently as if he were praising a favorite child. "You are a drunkard, a cuckold, a barbarian, and a fool."

"Am I now?" Sigismund said, leaping away from him. "You debauched and degenerate Italians think you lead the world in knowledge and power but I call all of you the dregs of the earth."

Cossa spat at the king's feet. "Do you suppose," he said, "that you are here with me, enjoying a bit of wine and a revealing chat, because you are a *Luxembourger*? If you were not king of the Romans—a throne that *I* lifted you upon—you would be sitting on the floor at my feet. I only grant you this honor of token equality because of the outrageous misnomer of your title. It is that wild anachronism of your title which has me greeting you as a token Italian and not as a barbarian."

"How unctuous you were when you thought you needed me, Cossa. How you appreciated my great faith, how willing you were to lend me money—what?"

"My bailiff will fling you a few coppers as I leave," Cossa said, turning away from him.

"I will settle with you in good time, my lord," Sigismund said. "For now, we share a boat in rough water. Gerson has drawn up a catalogue of twenty heterodoxies, which he has taken out of Hus' own treatises. What are you going to do about that?"

"Sigismund—I repeat—Hus is *your* responsibility."

"Cossa—look at this squarely—you are forcing me to choose between you and the council—or Hus. If I force his release then the council will be at an end because it would tell the world that the council was not competent to deal with such cases. The cardinals would abandon Konstanz before they could be made a laughingstock. But I have sworn before God that this schism must end, so this council must proceed. The prosecution of Hus will be known throughout Europe to have been enforced by you, because it is a prosecution that must proceed according to spiritual laws, something quite beyond my jurisdiction."

When I was alone with Cossa I asked him the key question, point-blank. "Did you order the arrest of Hus?" I said, having just realized it could not have happened otherwise.

"Of course," he said, smiling. "And when I finish, Sigismund will be chopped down to his proper size."

As I watched Sigismund respond coolly to Cossa's vituperation, suddenly everything became clearer about what was happening and who Cossa's enemies really were. Cossa lost his head and indulged his vile temper, but I am not so sure that it changed Sigismund's intentions. I did not believe that Sigismund, stung by the outrage of Cossa's attack, would be changed from a friend into an enemy. The king was a cold man who was always desperate for money. I am sure he went to Konstanz convinced that he must, in one way or another, persuade Cossa to resign so that the way would be clear to accept the willing resignations of the other two popes, allowing him to take the credit for ending the Great Schism before all of Christendom. If he could end the schism, he could claim the leadership of the empire with all of the resources that entailed. If Cossa had remained his ally the way would have been much more difficult for Sigismund, but now that Cossa had flaunted his authority, had insulted him and abased him before a witness, Sigismund had every reason to carry out his most severe intentions against Cossa, which he did do. Nothing had changed, except that Sigismund now had the excuse to move more quickly.

Chapter 60

At the moment that I realized Sigismund's inevitable course, I saw as clearly what the marchesa was preparing to do on behalf of the Medici, who had everything to gain from Church reform in greater or lesser degree. What they wanted was a single pope who would rule a single Christendom, so that business could proceed smoothly and profitably across the frontiers of the papal obediences that had been imposed upon Europe and that taxes would be reduced to one instead of three. I vaguely understood that the marchesa had been moving against Cossa but I had no conception of how great she had allowed her commitment to become.

"You are doing almost everything wrong," I said to Cossa, "but at least you are doing something. You have flushed Sigismund out from his cover."

"How very nice of you to say that."

"Please, I am developing a thought."

"I can't wait."

"I wondered if you were aware that, deep in her mind, the marchesa has decided that you are finished."

"We have known that, Franco Ellera, for some time, don't you remember?" he said. His face was sad but his eyes had hardened.

"Oh, yes. But she was your shepherdess. She cozened you

and clucked over you. But now she has become uninterested in you. Haven't you noticed that? At the most perilous time of your career, she hardly ever comes near you anymore. She dines with you about once every ten days, not every night as she did when things were being built toward the present peril, and when she sees you talks only about the management of the Konstanz businesses, never about the dangers that beset us.''

"It is a mutual thing. I am uninterested in her," Cossa said. "All we have left in common are the properties here, which are yielding far more than anyone estimated they would."

"Bernaba says she isn't sharing the information with you that she gets from everywhere."

"She isn't the same, I'll grant you that, and it's been a long time since either she or Cosimo brought me any little opportunities. But I don't think it means anything. The priorities are different here. Sigismund and d'Ailly are the ones who have to be dealt with to survive. I may be out of touch with Decima but I control the cardinals and they run the business of the council."

"What about Hus?"

"What do I care about Hus? Hus is Sigismund's political problem. I tolerate everything in Konstanz while I wait for Catherine Visconti's son to ride into the city."

He had spoken of the young duke of Milan almost every day and he had hardly mentioned the matter of the marchesa's indifference, but no matter what he said I knew that in the back of his mind there lived an imperishable intention to make her pay for what she had done to him. There was nothing stabilized about his thinking. He was living in a climate of worry and to offset that he used his standard measure. She was making them a lot of money. Her sudden lack of interest in him should have warned him. They were partners. She had him for a tithe of everything he was squeezing out of Christendom. She knew he would be in danger until the council ended yet she hardly ever spoke about either the council or what she knew his enemies were plotting. I knew they were plotting, and I knew she had made it the first item of her business to know every hourly development of the plotting.

By early January she was coming to dine with him only twice a month, pleading the harsh weather. Cossa could have been a laird in some small castle in northern Scotland for all he entered her thoughts. He was about to be deposed, and when he was, he would be a nonentity. He would talk about buying himself an army but she knew he did not have the energy for that. He would probably return to Naples and interfere with the management of his family's business. That was how she saw it.

Cossa, in his part, had no such plans. After he defeated his enemies, he would live on as pope, cutting away any weak elements that had shown themselves at Konstanz and collaborating with Cosimo on realizing a fortune greater than that of Pope Boniface VIII, head of the Gaetani family, making his own family as important and as permanent as the Colonna had ever been.

At the Feast of the Conversion of St. Paul on January 25, Cossa celebrated mass at the cathedral before all members of the council, then led a procession out into the streets. It was a solemn scene of prelates, their aspergilla clanking, banners, singing choirboys, and cardinals two by two. And lining the streets, the dukes and counts with their attendant squires, ambassadors of Prester John speaking a language no one there could understand, merchants, hungry friars with platters, women with their heads wrapped, mountebanks, fiddlers, and students watched them sway past. While the chanting went on and the censers belched holy vapors, Greeks sold aromatic spices to women with dark hair and darker eyes, and musicians with the lilies of France upon their backs sang to lutes and viols.

The swaying canopies held over the prelates, seen from above, made the procession seem like a multihued silk snake as the two-by-two file of cardinals passed through the tightly packed banks of cheering people. Spina, swaying beside d'Ailly, glanced over the crowd and stared, for a moment, directly into the grinning face of Bernaba Minerbetti. His memory hurtled him backward thirty-six years. He seemed to be staring at a note that had been pinned to his shirt. It said—Spina screamed hoarsely and turned out of the procession, intending to crash through the crowd to get her. D'Ailly grasped his wrist with the strength of an iron manacle and held him in the course of the procession. "Whatever it is, don't think," he said to Spina. "Keep walking. You are a prince of the Church."

Spina was sweated and trembling as he changed his clothing in the vestry of the cathedral. He could only feel the threatening presence of Bernaba Minerbetti. D'Ailly sat beside him and spoke to him soothingly.

"What did you see in the crowd, Spina?"

"Nothing. A delusion."

"A deadly enemy?"

"No!"

"Do you want to confess to me?"

"There is no sin to be shriven. I feel pain but I have done nothing yet."

"You should talk to me about it. That would help you."

"Only I know what will help me," Spina said. He left the cathedral alone, almost disabled to know that Bernaba Minerbetti was in Konstanz. She had gone to Cossa. She had told him everything. She was telling that terrible story about the *trentuno* to everyone. He had to stop her. He had to find her and be revenged on her.

When Bernaba returned to the offices of the marchesa's syndicate she was shaken and her face was colorless.

"Bernaba! What happened to you?" the marchesa asked her.

"Spina."

"What about Spina?"

"You should have seen his face. He wanted to screw me and kill me at the same time."

"I can't believe it! You mean nothing has changed after thirty years?"

"He is the ultimate Sicilian. He forgets nothing. He feeds on anything that has damaged his past. I tell you, he wanted to kill me."

"What can he do? You have the pope and Cosimo di Medici behind you."

"You don't understand, Decima. You didn't see his face."

When I got back to our house in the Engelsongasse and saw my wife's frightened face I crossed the room with two bounds and lifted her up into my arms. She began to sob. "I really caught it today, Franco," she said.

"What happened?"

"The marchesa thought it would be a big joke if I stood in the crowd and smiled at Spina as he went by in procession."

"You didn't *do* it?"

"He saw me. He went crazy. He is going to find me and try to kill me."

"Why does Decima care if Spina ever saw you again?"

"I don't know."

"She had to explain *some*thing."

"She said Spina was trouble for Cossa and it would be useful if we could have a hold over him."

"*We?*"

"I'm telling you what she said."

"I don't understand. How did the marchesa get into this?"

"Franco, get me a glass of wine. I think I caught a cold or something."

When I was sure my wife was asleep, I put on a greatcoat and a fur hat and trudged through the snow to the papal palace to begin the working night with Cossa. I pulled up a chair across the work table in Cossa's study. "Something evil is happening, Cossa," I said.

"Like what?"

"The marchesa told Bernaba that it would be a good joke if Bernaba popped up in the front row of the procession and gave Spina a big smile."

"I saw her out there." It came to him. "Spina? *Spina?*"

"The marchesa told Bernaba that Spina was trouble for you and that we could do with a hold over him."

"What happened?"

"He tried to break out of the procession and go after her in the crowd. Bernaba said he looked insane. He wanted to kill her."

"But Decima knew that had to happen."

"Yes. That is why I say something funny is going on."

"Why would Decima want to set Bernaba up?"

"Well! Think about it. She wants to use Bernaba as bait to get at Spina."

"Why?"

"Ask her tonight. You have to straighten this out, Cossa. We have to protect Bernaba."

"I'll protect her right now. Get an escort together. Bernaba is going back to Bologna." His face was blank. He rubbed his nose and said, "Tell her to leave a note for Decima saying that her mother is dying in Bari and that she had to go there. Before she goes she has to set up the women in Decima's house to watch her and report to you. Send a messenger to the marchesa telling her to be here for dinner at two o'clock tomorrow morning."

"Do you want Palo to head Bernaba's escort?"

"What use would Palo be? He is a specialist. We want Captain Munger of my guard to take care of Bernaba. He is steady and he is dangerous."

Chapter 61

On the day after the Council of Konstanz had held its first session all those weeks before, Cossa had sent a warm letter to the duke of Milan to invite him personally to attend with the other nations of Europe at Konstanz and to dine with him on the second night after his arrival, whenever that would be. The answer came swiftly from Milan. The young duke was highly honored by the pope's friendship and hospitality and was resolved to attend Konstanz during the first week of March 1415.

The news seemed to send a shock tremor through the episcopal palace. It halted the pope's participation in any of the business of the conference until he had gone over every detail of the vengeance he had been carrying in his mind since the moment the news that Catherine Visconti had been murdered had crashed down upon him. He locked himself into a small study with me, Luigi Palo, and Bernaba.

"When he comes here we will have a superb dinner. I thought at first a dinner for twelve or so—many cardinals and some beautiful women—the finest wines—but now I think it will be better if it is a dinner for just three of us—Franco Ellera, the duke, and me—because that will flatter him more and put him more off his guard if he feels that the pope would want to honor him by dining with him so intimately. We will dine in the wine cellar of this palace. Very colorful and enormously convivial for such happy company. And soundproof. We will speak of his mother, of the turmoil in Milan since her death, and of superficial things. We will be charming. We will laugh and I will praise him. Then, when the dinner is done, I will begin to speak more closely about his mother's death''—Cossa sunk his face into his hands upon the table—"then I shall tell him how he is going to die."

"How is he going to die?" Palo asked.

"Palo will break his bones and I will talk to him. Then we will leave him alone for the first night."

Palo grinned.

"On the second night we will begin to open him up and pack the wounds with salt," Cossa said.

"We will have to do it carefully or he won't last through the second night," Palo said.

"It is too much," I said. "This isn't vengeance, this is pleasure, Cossa. You have sickened me."

"What would you do?" Cossa asked me hotly. "Just put a knife in his heart?"

"An eye for an eye," I said. "His mother died peacefully and painlessly. So should he. He should be poisoned slowly enough for you to tell him you have done it and why you have done it and that he is the last Visconti."

"He must suffer!" Cossa shouted.

On the night of the second day after the duke of Milan arrived in Konstanz, he arrived at the episcopal palace with an escort of thirty mounted men and two bodyguards, for his dinner with the pope. While we waited for His Holiness to join us, I explained to the duke that the Holy Father had planned to honor him with a most intimate and unusual dinner, just the three of us in the wine cellar of the palace. The young man was enormously pleased. He dismissed his bodyguards and, when we were alone, I took him into the pope's inner study, a room that had been decorated with fine paintings, furniture, and many books from the Vatican.

Visconti was a tall, pale young man with a large, fierce mustache, wearing light armor. I asked him to disarm himself, but the youth was reluctant. I had to cause myself to become larger-than-life before his eyes. I told him it was an impossibility in such times of upheaval for *any*one to enter the presence of the Holy Father bearing arms on his person. I glared into the young duke's eyes and the youth disarmed himself. I wish there had been a mirror on the wall behind him so that I could have measured my effect, so dominating was it.

His Holiness entered the room. He was quite pale. He had to hold his hands together in his lap to keep them from shaking. He was cordiality itself, if somewhat absentminded about it, but he withheld the blessing. I pressed wine on our doomed young guest, and made little jokes that put the duke at ease. Cossa had agreed to use poison, which Bernaba had obtained from the marchesa, telling her that a woman whose heart was being broken had the need of it.

We had a magnificent dinner in the cellar. At the end of it Cossa said, "I knew your mother."

"She told me."

Cossa's eyebrows shot up.

"She was my closest friend," the duke said. "She wanted greatness from me. She told me that you and she—that you had plans for Italy—that you were going to carry out my father's destiny."

"Then why did you kill her?" Cossa asked him equably.

Perplexed, the young man stared at Cossa, trying to comprehend what he had heard. "What did you say, Holiness? Kill her? *I* kill her? I loved her." His answer was so genuine to me that I was shaken, but Cossa did not seem to hear him.

"You poisoned your mother," Cossa said, "and tonight you are going to die for that."

The young man was a Visconti. He had had enough of threats. His arrogance assembled like a cold wind. "Charge me with the crime," he said contemptuously. "Accuse me directly so that I may understand you."

"I am going to kill you because you poisoned your own mother in the citadel of Milan in order that you might rule."

"I did not need to kill my mother to rule," the youth said, "I am the only duke of Milan, which made me ruler. You blackguard! I have put off meeting you for these years because you were shielding the true murderer."

"What are you saying to me? What monstrous charge is that?"

"You know and I know who killed my mother. But the killer lives on at your side."

"Who?" Cossa cried out.

"That woman—my father's assassin—"

"What woman!"

"The marchesa di Artegiana."

Cossa's eyes changed from burning lights of righteousness to confusion to dismay and then to blankness. He seemed to be witnessing the murder of Catherine Visconti in the tower, and he could see the face of the murderer, a face beyond the young man, beyond the room.

"Assassin of your father?" he said stupidly.

"She poisoned my father at Marignano. Barbarelli knows that. Malatesta knows that. Speak to them. They remain silent because of the protection you gave her."

"The marchesa?" his voice croaked as if in doubt, but his eyes said that he believed this truth. In all of the warnings I had pressed upon him about Manovale, I had never wished this much pain upon him.

"She wrote to my mother and said she bore news from you. She asked to see my mother. I argued with my mother not to see her but she said the marchesa, with Cosimo di Medici, was your close adviser and that she had to be bringing your answer agreeing to lead our armies."

"The marchesa di Artegiana?" Cossa repeated, trying to convince himself.

"My mother received the woman in the tower of the citadel where no one could eavesdrop on them. The next morning I was told that my mother was dead by poison. The woman had gone."

"When she brought the word of your mother's death to me," Cossa said, haggard with grief, "she told me that word had come from Milan that you had locked your mother in the tower and had poisoned her." He held out his hands imploringly. "Why did you not come to me and accuse this woman?"

"Had I gone to Bologna, and had you confronted me with the woman, I would have killed her there. You would have executed me. Or, on that woman's evidence, you would have had me killed as a murderer, my word against the word of your counselor. But I wait for her. She will not escape me. I will have vengeance on her.''

''The vengeance is mine,'' Cossa said dully. ''I will take vengeance for the three of us.'' His voice broke. ''Most of all for your mother.''

When the duke of Milan was gone, Cossa lay upon his back on the floor of the wine cellar staring at the ornate ceiling, unable to move. He breathed deeply and slowly, and tried to think of anything except the marchesa, but that was not possible. He spoke to me in a low, monotonous voice. He could prove nothing. If he accused her she would be warned that she was close to her death. She had tricked him into the papacy. She had robbed him of his right to live out his meaning as a soldier and as the ruler of Italy. She had murdered the woman whom he had cherished, who thought only of his destiny. She was plotting his downfall with Sigismund and the Medici. But the even more bitter and inconsolable thought was that he had lost her on the day he had been trapped into becoming pope. Now she would be gone from him as soon as he could devise a punishment, which would last far longer than a few days of agony, but which would break her, hour upon hour, for all the years of her life until death, when it came, would be a merciful thing.

Chapter 62

All servants on the staffs of the pope and the marchesa, in their separate households, were people from Bernaba's hometown of Bari. She had sponsored them, fed them, clothed them, trained them, and paid them well. They were the friends of her childhood.

Bernaba spent the evening before her flight from Spina going over details of the administration of her businesses with two sharp-eyed courtesans who had been with her for nine years, the Angiorno sisters, twins, which had served them well in their work. She spent well over an hour with her kinswoman, the marchesa's housekeeper, Signora Melvini, wife of the Sicilian mime, Alighieri Melvini, brother of the archdeacon, to make clear how the signora was to organize the staff of the marchesa's household to listen alertly for any and all information, and to record the comings and goings in and out of the marchesa's house, and how to gain access to the marchesa's written correspondence. All information, she explained, was to go to me, each morning and evening without fail.

In the early hours of the morning, Bernaba and I sat together as I wrote her letter for the marchesa. "Distinguished Lady," the letter said, "I have received news that my mother is dying in Bari and is calling for me. Franco Ellera has made all arrangements for me to leave Konstanz at once with an escort and with a safe-conduct from His Holiness. The Angiorno sisters are well-briefed on my duties at our office and they understand to assist you in every way. Bari is a long way but I shall return to Konstanz as soon as this sad experience permits me to get away. I press your hand, Bernaba.''

Cardinal Spina left his residence in the Haus zum Hohen Hirschen, and was carried over the snow in a sedan chair to the marchesa's house in the Upper Minster Court beside the episcopal palace facing Wessenbergstrasse, at eight o'clock in the night of the day Bernaba had fled to Bologna. Signora Melvini showed him into the sitting room where the marchesa awaited him. She rose to greet him warmly. ''Eminence! You dear, dear, old friend,'' she said. ''We see each other so seldom.''

Cardinal Spina was in his early sixties, with the eyes, skin, and relentless expression of a sea turtle. His gaze was steady and dry, his hope not negotiable. There was a pleading urgency that was slipping toward madness in his expression.

The marchesa was forty-three years old. Her hair was quite black now, as if it had never been blonde. Her face was utterly handsome because of the shapes of the bones that made it, but she was no longer beautiful, because her glittering eyes had hardened beyond her control.

''Yes. We have been too much apart,'' Spina said listlessly. ''It is a pity.'' Living with Bernaba's ghost for over thirty years, then having it exorcise itself, had changed his expression. The stealth had gone from his eyes. The whirlpool concentricity that had marked him as an intriguer and that had won him such infamy for his deviousness had been washed out of his face by the force of his concentration upon his need to avenge his honor. The marchesa read these things and was pleased that she would be able to help him. They sat facing each other.

''Well?'' Spina said. ''You sent for me.''

''I can help you find Bernaba Minerbetti,'' the marchesa said.

''Does the entire world know of my shame?'' he cried out.

''No. Bernaba told Cossa and Cossa, seeking my counsel, told me.''

Spina made no effort to cover his jagged desires to rape, murder, and mutilate. ''Where is she?'' he said harshly.

"For the time being she must rest where she is. I want to talk to you about the council."

"Speak out," he said.

"My bank has recommendations to make, which must fall upon the right ears. You have the confidence of d'Ailly, who has the confidence of the French cardinals and theologians and princes, and the bank feels that these hold the solution to the future as it must evolve."

"What has that to do with Minerbetti?"

"What the bank asks from you, Eminence, in recognition of whatever service I may do for you, is that you arrange for Cardinal d'Ailly and a French deputation to request a meeting with Cosimo di Medici in Konstanz."

"How do you know Bernaba Minerbetti?"

"From Bologna. She ran the courtesans there. She went to Bologna about thirty-five years ago with Baldassare Cossa when he went to Bologna to study law."

"Cossa!" Spina shouted. "He was the one! He pinned that note to me! Cossa was the boy who defiled me!" He shut his eyes tightly to impress that image upon his memory. "How do you know this?"

"Bernaba told me."

"Where is she?"

"If you arrange what the bank asks, you will be serving many important ends, Eminence. Your own interest first, of course, before all others."

"You can deliver Bernaba to me?"

"I can either tell you where she is or deliver her."

"How can you do that?"

"Eminence—she works for me."

"In Konstanz?"

"You frightened her badly when you saw her from the procession yesterday. She was so frightened that she fled to Bari. She left me a letter saying that her mother was dying. But she won't go there. Bernaba is almost fifty. Her mother is long dead."

Spina pounded on the arm of the chair. "Then where is she?"

"The bank's needs come first, Eminence."

"I will do it. Give me two days, then the Medici can expect a message from the French."

"Bernaba will be in Bologna in six days' time, but you cannot go to Bologna. You are needed in Konstanz and must be here."

"You will bring her back?"

"If the meeting is held, yes."

"Nothing must go wrong with this," he said.

Chapter 63

After midnight, when she was sure the marchesa was asleep, Signora Melvini left the house at the servants' entrance and made her way through the town to the Broadlaube, five streets away, into Engelsongasse to my house, the deanery of Albrecht of Beutelsbach. I was waiting for her. We sat by the fire and drank warmed wine as she reported Cardinal Spina's visit to the marchesa. When I had heard her story I dressed myself in warm outer garments and we walked to the cathedral area, where she returned to the marchesa's house. I went into the episcopal palace.

Cossa was busy with his chamberlains when I came into the room. He concluded the business and sent them away.

I told him what had been said at the meeting of the marchesa and Spina. Cossa kept his eyes closed as he listened. There was a long moment before he was able to speak. "That is that," he said. "She will not do any more harm."

"She was only after the same thing you were. Always money, Cossa."

"I got them money! I made her rich! I transformed the Medici into Croesus when I transferred the Church's banking to their bank. More than that——" At last he opened his eyes. "She is finished." He clenched his hands before his face in the attitude of prayer. "And it will cost Cosimo, too. Who do we have inside Cosimo's household?"

"No one."

"Use raw gold florins. Have Palo do the bribing."

"Signora Melvini would be better. She knows all the servants in the principal houses here."

"Good. She has two days to have them ready and rehearsed. Her people must be in place in Cosimo's house to report on that meeting. Franco, please do not be distressed. We will protect Bernaba, but you must bring her back from Bologna. She will be *our* bait."

"Where is she to go when she gets back?"

"To the marchesa, of course. Now—in your letter to Bernaba, which must go out tonight, tell her that the marchesa's courier will bring her a message telling her to return and giving a plausible reason. There is nothing to worry about. She will not be harmed. We will destroy them. Please, leave me and send the letter."

Chapter 64

Cosimo di Medici received the four prelates at his small, elegant house, formerly the Haus zum Goldenen Bracken, in the Bruckengasse off the Minsterplatz. Attending him were Cardinals d'Ailly and Spina, of France and Italy, Bishops Weldon and Von Niem, of England and Germany, and Chancellor Gerson of the University of Paris. They were the leaders of the reform party that opposed the papal party in the council. They stood for the reorganization of the Church in its head and its members, for establishing a single true pope, for passing laws that would prevent a future schism, and for complete reform of the Curia. Cosimo had always been happy for them to get their kind of reform as long as he got his: one pope, one obedience.

Cosimo made them welcome. He was forty-five years old, a man of enameled kindness and enforced gentility. He spoke to them. "You may see me, because I am a banker, as being removed from wonderment at the glory of our Church, but that is not the case. I agonize to save the Church and to smash the schism within it, needs that can only be served through reform."

Cardinal d'Ailly reassured him. "If it should seem, dear sir, as if we do not need your counsel in matters of the spirit, the fact is that we must look to you for an explanation of the realities of this council."

There was a low murmuring of approval from the other members.

They were all seated in chairs that described a general circle within the room. Spina breathed shallowly. Bishop Weldon wished for a sweet drink. Gerson, as always, seemed to be assembling his arguments. D'Ailly packed himself into the security of thoughts of how much money this man must have.

"At the outset," Cosimo said, "on the surface, it would appear that I am an Italian."

The prelates smiled at his little joke.

"But before I am an Italian, I am a European, whose interests are alone the interests of Europe—in making Europe strong so that it may serve the Church. Man does not live by the Holy Spirit alone. He must have bread. The stability of the establishment that makes that bread, finances the distribution of that bread, and provides that bread—and I am speaking of the European business community—depends upon the end of the schism and the return of our Church to the leadership of a single pope."

"John the Twenty-third?"

"No."

"You were among his strongest advocates for the papacy at Pisa—and when you persuaded him to accept the papacy at Bologna," Gerson murmured.

Cosimo passed a hand across his eyes. "I could weep for that."

"John the Twenty-third is a godless pope," Spina said. Everyone nodded sadly.

"His godlessness is at the core of the hopelessness of the entire congregation," Cosimo murmured. "If he sees fit not to confess, how should the sheep in his flock respond? If he neglects the mass, what doubts are thrown upon the mass across Christendom? But let me speak out from my own province— Pope John has very nearly bankrupted our Church."

"Nonetheless," d'Ailly said, "he holds the deciding votes of the council."

"That is why we are here, my devout friends," Cosimo answered him. "The method of voting at the council must be changed. If heads are counted according to precedent, then Pope John must win and continue to strip the Church of the glory of God. They have the votes. He has brought an army of Italian churchmen with him for that purpose. The English

Church, however—for one example—is represented by so few delegates that their rights and desires must be banished from any consideration."

"That is all well and good," Bishop Weldon said, "but how else can a council of the Church vote?"

"I have put my best people on the problem, my lord. The council's voting must be done by nations—an equal number of deputies from each nation to have the final decision. The Italians would include under their aegis Cyprus, Constantinople, Bosnia, Turkey, and Tartary. Similarly, the Germans, with whom are united the Bohemians, the Hungarians, Poles, Scandinavians, Croatians, and Russians, would vote as one nation. The English nation would include the Irish, the Scots, Medes, Persians, Arabs, Indians, Ethiopians, Egyptians, and Ninevahns. The French have already amassed over two hundred of their own delegates, and lastly, the Spaniards—who sooner or later must join this council—would also represent Portugal and Sicily."

"But this is a council of the Church, not of nations. The Church must decide what happens in the Church."

"True—and I agree. The secular voters should be there to be used only when the cardinals need them—of course they will not intervene in matters of *faith*. But this plan will save the council from being dominated and controlled by a godless pope. Once control is wrested from him, then, of course, fullest domination will be passed to the cardinals of all nations."

When Signora Melvini passed the word of the meeting to me, I reported it to Cossa. After that, he sat alone, brooding over a plan to prevent his ruination.

At the assembly of the council on February 6, 1415, members of the English and German delegations arose to protest against individual voting and jointly proposed that a fixed number of deputies be appointed by each nation and that the voting rest only with them by national unit. The French ambassador then took the floor and said, "Christendom is essentially distributed into four great nations. These are Italy, Germany, Spain, and France. The minor kingdoms such as England, Portugal, Denmark, et cetera, must be comprehended under one or another of these great divisions." He sat down.

Bishop Weldon leaped to his feet, red-faced with indignation. "A nation, by God?" he exclaimed. "Would for the sake of the strength of Christendom that France were such a nation as England! The English stand at the head of the British islands which are decorated with eight royal crowns and discriminated by five languages. The greater island from north to south measures eight hundred miles, or forty days' journey, and England alone contains thirty-two counties and fifty-two thousand parish churches."

The current victories of the English king, Henry V, over France, added much weight to his argument and he finished boldly. "Let no man forget the testimony of Bartholemy de Glanville, the great scholar of the cultures of the world whose lifetime of studies brought him to the conclusion that there were only four Christian nations: one, of Rome; two, of Constantinople; three, of Ireland, which had long been transferred to the English monarchs; and four, of Spain. Nonetheless and notwithstanding, my country gladly welcomes France into nationhood this day."

On the following day, the French agreed to the national unit voting plan for the council. Nations were to deliberate apart from each other and, when they decided on their resolutions, their deputies were to meet in general session of the council to settle matters. The Italians, massed around the Holy Father for his protection, were powerless to resist. Cossa's hopes were smashed with one blow. There would be three votes to one against him and there would have been four if the Spanish had attended the convention.

Sigismund rejoiced over this new and brilliant ruse, which, in one stroke, had defeated the power of the votes of the cardinals to protect their pope. He knew Cossa was finished. He knew that all the rest would follow naturally. He would be the hero of Christendom and now, at last, it would be impossible for the electors to deny him the throne of the empire. He held a general congregation at which Pope John, all the cardinals, and all the prelates appeared. He reported his negotiations with the Popes Benedict and Gregory, saying that he expected the legates of both popes at the council and that he had promised to meet Benedict at Nice in June. This told everyone in Konstanz that he would not work with Cossa.

As leader of the papal party, I rose to appeal to the authority of the Council of Pisa, which had declared both Benedict and Gregory to be heretic and schismatic. Cardinal d'Ailly took the floor with overweening blandness. He felt that there was some urgency that the cardinals agree with Sigismund, that the essence of politics was compromise, and because the cardinals there present had elected both Benedict and Gregory to the papacy, that the representations of both should be received with the honors demanded. His motion was adopted. Cossa was defeated by his own council. The ground was crumbling under his feet.

Cossa so believed that they were all made of motes cemented into visible bodies that he would daydream of inventing a machine that would disassemble all of the motes in everybody at the council. "They are less than dust," he said to me, "so they should exist and be seen only as dust."

"We'll have to think of something better than that," I told him.

"I will be able to think again when Bernaba gets back here in six days' time. When I settle with the marchesa di Artegiana my mind will be clear again."

Meetings that were unannounced to Cossa began to be held under the seal of secrecy, but he soon knew what happened in them because groups of prelates came to see him every night and he had no difficulty inducing them—if necessary under an absolution—to tell him all they knew of the plotting. He learned that the English and Sigismund wanted him locked in prison. The French were noncommittal. The Italians, a week before so fervent in his support, were now going along with the demand for his abdication.

Out of favor, he was nevertheless acknowledged by the council as the only legitimate pope. He refused to perform publicly the sacred functions of his office, except his function of presiding over the meetings of the council and directing the activities of the council. Although he was thick with gout at forty-seven

years of age, and an elderly forty-seven at that (for I, twelve
years older, seemed far younger, Bernaba often told me), because of his torpid life after so many active years, Dr. Weiler
said, Cossa still bedded the Angioni sisters imaginatively. He
had worked out with pen and instruments, on paper, dozens of
variations on the various sexual positionings and, of course,
these were vastly expanded by his use of twins in the studies.
His other formal audiences were political. But his close direction of the Curia produced steady revenue for himself and his
Sacred College, so there were many who approached the problem of his cession with much reluctance.

Political ceremonies were faithfully performed by him.
Masses opened all council meetings. He solemnly blessed the
people from the summit of his palace. He carried out the canonization of the Swedish Saint Brigid. She had already been
canonized in 1391 by Boniface IX for rewarding fees, but the
Swedes wanted a renewal—and they were to ask for still another renewal four years later.

But Cossa could see the crisis coming. The information was
now coming to him that the marchesa and her daughters were
creating and sustaining a universal feeling by their steady min-
istrations and constant campaigning that the only way to heal
the schism was for all three popes to either abdicate or be deposed. No one ventured publicly to bring forward this proposition. Cossa continued to receive the marchesa at dinner.

They didn't discuss politics anymore. They did not look into
each other's eyes and they talked almost entirely about money.

All at once, Cardinal Spina arose in council and openly demanded that Pope John resign. He was so pronouncedly an Italian cardinal that his exhortation had all the more weight. While
Cossa presided over the meeting, Spina told the council that the
more firmly Cossa was persuaded that he was the true pope, the
more incumbent it was upon him as a good shepherd to make
this sacrifice for his flock. Sigismund took a copy of the speech
and sent abstracts to all nations.

The next day Cardinal d'Ailly advocated the same course.
Although the Council of Pisa had been legitimately convoked,
he argued, and to the election of Pope John XXIII no exception

could be taken, they still had to face the fact that neither of the two other popes had resigned, so that action by all three was advisable. He assured them all that, in counseling Pope John to abdicate, they would not be derogating from the authority of the Council of Pisa, nor, certainly, would Pope John be put upon a level with heretics and schismatics, but they would, instead, confer on him the high distinction of doing honor to Christendom and of showing his own humility by exposing the obstinacy of his rivals.

Nonetheless, he reminded them, whether the pope chose to set the example or not, the council, as representing the Church universal, had the power to depose any pope, legitimate or otherwise, if peace could not be restored to the Church in any other way.

"It is the mockery of my life," Cossa said to me. "I fought as if for my life not to become pope, but no matter what they do, I will not give up the papacy because the marchesa and the Medici have killed to get it for me, and the marchesa killed to preserve it for me."

Chapter 65

Cossa had stationed relays of fast horses all the way north of the Adige to hasten Bernaba's journey. He had teams of people clearing snow in the high passes. "When she gets here," he said to me, "we'll use her to draw Decima in. I have a meeting arranged with the duke of Austria—who took my money and swore to defend me—and the margrave of Baden. They are hard men and they can hold off Sigismund and keep him away from me until I can get out of here."

"Where are we going?"

"We don't have to go too far. We don't have to go all the way back to Italy with a screen such as the duke of Austria can put between me and the council. But when I'm impregnable wherever it is I'm going, let that miserable pack of turncoats see if they have any council without the presence of the pope who summoned it. Whatever they do, if I'm not there it will be illegal. They will be powerless."

"What about the marchesa?"

"I am ready for her now."

"Do you want Palo to stand by to compensate her for her trouble?"

"No."

"What about Cosimo?"

"I have already begun to settle Cosimo. I talked to the provincial of the Benedictine Order. The Order has never had any centralized authority. They have no general superior but the pope. But, because of the Fourth Lateran Council, all of the monasteries of the Order have very strong union. That council also ordered that the abbots of all Benedictine houses should meet every three years to pass regulations, which are binding on all houses. At last I am getting use out of those ten years at the university. Sometimes it is even good to be a lawyer.''

"What does that have to do with Cosimo?"

"The next meeting of the Benedictine abbots comes up in twelve weeks' time. I am going to direct them to organize the parishes of every one of the new water-powered mills that Cosimo is building and not only see that the people raze them to the ground but make sure he never operates factories anywhere in Europe.''

"What about Spina?"

"He's crazy. Anyway, we punished him a long time ago. Maybe we made him the way he is.''

"I am afraid for Bernaba. Palo has to kill Spina.''

"Bernaba will be safe. I promise you that.''

By the middle of the next afternoon, Cossa's two "hard men" had ridden into Konstanz with their troops of horse. Frederick, duke of Austria, contracted bodyguard of the pope, was clad in a uniform of emerald velvet. He was fully armed with helmet, corselet, braces, and greaves of mail, riding at the head of a force of eight counts and eight hundred horsemen. Cossa felt so reassured about his own safety that when Bernard of Baden arrived with four hundred horsemen, he gave the loyal margrave sixteen thousand florins and made a secret bargain with him.

The margrave of Baden was a short man, about thirty-five years old, whose mother had been Maddalena Visconti, which was enough for me. He had thick, black hair, dark, burning eyes and a slender face with a strongly protruding nose. He was bold, hot-tempered, intelligent, sly, and unforgiving—a true Visconti. Even I did not know what Cossa had bought until the night he settled with the marchesa.

"They are planning a coup against me," Cossa told them. "I have to be sure I can get out of the city.''

"We will get you out," the duke said, "and you are welcome to come with me to Austria."

"I thank you," Cossa said, "but I must stay within reach of Konstanz. The council is going to collapse when there is no pope to preside over it. Hundreds of them will go home, but the others will wait here for instructions from me. I am overwhelmed by your support and encouragement. Most of the territory in this region is under your rule, so I think perhaps the best thing will be to allow your troops to take me out."

On February 14, the English nation rose in council to demand that the pope be arrested and held in prison. Bishop Thomas Buckley of Salisbury said he should be burned. Only the opposition of the French, undertaken in part for the sake of opposing the English, prevented this from happening.

Chapter 66

The council now expressed its universal desire that all three popes should voluntarily resign their dignities. Gregory, ninety, was ready to abdicate provided that his rivals resigned and were not allowed to preside at the council. Benedict, eighty-seven, was willing to meet Sigismund at Nice in order to achieve the same ends. The Italian cardinals and delegation became convinced that the pressure of conciliar and public opinion was too great to continue to resist.

Deputies of the nations visited Cossa and hinted at his resignation in vague terms, proposals that, mysteriously, he seemed to receive most cheerfully. To the council's utter surprise he convened a general congregation to begin to carry this into effect by submitting the form that the resignation should take. "If they take this," Cossa told me, "we will not only be buying time, but we will be taking the first giant step on the way to defeating them."

On his throne at the altar of the cathedral as president of the council, in the presence of the king of the Romans, the cardinals, the prelates, princes, and delegations of nations, on February 16, 1415, Cossa called upon me to read the sample draft of the resignation that Cossa, as his own lawyer, had prepared.

"Your most holy lord, Pope John the Twenty-third, here present," I read in a voice that was at once both sincere and thrilling, "although in no way obliged thereto by vow, oath, or promise, yet for the repose of the Christian people, has proposed and resolved of his own free will and accord, to give peace to the Church even by resignation, provided that Pedro de Luna and Angelo Corrario, who were condemned and deposed at the Council of Pisa as heretics and schismatics, also legally and sufficiently resign their pretended popedoms, and in that manner, circumstance, and at a time to be forthwith declared and concluded by a treaty forthwith to be made to this effect by our lord, the pope, or his proctors, and the deputies of the nations."

The council found the formula to be offensive and rejected it. Negotiations for an acceptable form went on, but patience with Cossa was becoming exhausted. The Germans insisted that only the council was the sovereign judge. Bishop Buckley of England said again that the pope should be burned as a heretic. The French demanded that Cossa not merely promise, but vow and swear that he would resign.

On March 1, a general congregation was held at the pope's palace. The king of the Romans and the patriarch of Antioch, who was president of the French nation at Konstanz, and all national deputies were present. The patriarch handed the formula to the pope and asked him to read it aloud. Cossa passed it to me. I rose and read from the document.

"I, Pope John the Twenty-third, in order to secure the repose of Christendom, declare and promise, vow and swear to God, to the Church, and to this holy council, freely and spontaneously, to give peace to the Church by means of my own resignation, and to do and carry this into effect in accordance with the determination of the present council, if and when Pedro de Luna and Angelo Corrario, called Benedict the Thirteenth and Gregory the Twelfth in their respective obediences, shall similarly, either in person or by their legal proctors, resign their pretended popedoms, and even in any case of resignation or death or otherwise, that my resignation may give peace to the Church and extinguish the schism."

Cossa did not comment.

On the next day, to open the second general session of the council, the pope celebrated the mass, then seated himself in front of the great altar, facing the congregation. The patriarch of

Antioch handed him the formula that I had read out the day before. Cossa read it aloud in a loud and sonorous voice. When he came to the words "I vow and swear," he rose from his seat, knelt before the altar, placed his hand over his heart and added, "I promise to fulfill this." He returned to his throne to conclude the formula.

Sigismund made the most of it. He took off his crown and threw himself at the pontiff's feet, kissed them tenderly and thanked him again and again for what he had done for the Holy Church. A *Te Deum Laudamus* was sung. All the church bells in the city broke out into peals of joyous music. The congregation was in tears and everyone believed that, at last, the Great Schism was about to be ended.

Cossa was urged to appoint Sigismund and certain cardinals as his proctors to carry through the abdication. He was supported by the Italian nation when he refused this. His refusal sent Sigismund into such a rage that he ordered the lake and city gates to be heavily guarded night and day to prevent anyone from leaving Konstanz. "He is toying with us," Sigismund ranted. "He has no intention of keeping his word."

On Monday, March 11, he called a congregation to introduce the need for an immediate conclave to meet and elect a new pope for the Church, proclaiming in the most pointed way that he no longer considered Cossa to be pope. John of Nassau arose in wrath and shouted that unless John XXIII were reelected he would recognize no pope, but his worldly character matched the reputation of the Holy Father and lent no weight to the process. At a meeting of the council several days later, Bishop Buckley, speaking for the English nation, again demanded, in the presence of the king of the Romans, that Cossa be arrested and imprisoned, and, again, were it not for the implacably reflexive opposition of the French this would have happened.

Chapter 67

That night, on Cossa's orders, I brought the duke of Austria secretly to the papal palace. Frederick was a tall, fat, florid man of twenty years, still young enough to believe that life was an adventure and that intrigues brought power. He had readily accepted Cossa's money and titles and, in return, had sworn to defend him. The time had come for him to deliver.

"I want to speak to you in an entirely tentative way," the Holy Father said gently. "We must be prepared at all times, even though we may never need to carry out our plans. But that is what leadership is, isn't it, my son?"

"You were twice the commander I could ever be, Holiness. I would give my life to learn from you in all things."

"I bless you for that. First off, I'd like you to get me a boat with a sail and keep it moored in readiness at Steckhorn—that's about five miles down the river, from Ermatingen, they tell me —just past the Gottlieben Castle on the Rhine."

"Oh, I know Steckhorn, Holy Father. Steckhorn is in my dominion."

"Ah. Yes."

"Are you really thinking of escape, Holiness?"

"I cannot conceive that it could be necessary." He paused and gazed sadly at the young man. "Except if the English are able to dominate the council with their threats to burn me. I should have to try to escape then."

"Should such a monstrous thing take place you will ride out of this travesty at the center of my two thousand horse."

"My Cardinal Ellera lives by one rule," the pontiff said. 'If you're always ready you're always glad,' he says."

"Yes. I see. By all means."

"If you will be ready, my son," Cossa said, "all Christendom will be glad."

When the fat young duke had gone, I brought Cossa a large parchment page. "This is what they are circulating throughout the nations today," I said.

Cossa examined the page without reading it. "A fairly expensive job of scrollwork, I would say. How many copies?"

"Dozens. These things are nailed to the doors of every nation's meeting place. And every officer has one."

"Then someone has been working on this little move for weeks. Someone with money to burn. What does it say?"

"Say? Oh, it merely accuses you of every mortal or abominable sin in the books and demands a public inquiry into your character."

"Sins? It was people such as the glossy rats in the council who were so intimately informed of them that they were able to define every mortal and abominable sin in the books. How can they expect mercy? What have they charged me with?"

"Orgies, grand thefts, and the commitment of greater simonies than have ever been bled from Christendom."

"As if I could top Boniface."

"This is serious, Cossa. The misappropriation of Church funds is listed item by item."

"Decima did this. It took money and inside information." He covered his face with his hands. "She must be taken out of my way. She will be here tonight. God give me strength."

He knew that, because this was the last time he would ever see her, she was more beautiful and charming than he had ever known her. But the exterior beauty, I could see, was there only to conceal the form of an ancient witch, long skilled in murder by poison and betrayals by lies. Her long, flame-colored dress had sleeves buttoned to her wrists and a demurely high bodice.

There were jewels in her hair. She was shining and womanly on the outside but a pit of horrors beneath that. He must force himself to understand her as she truly was, I thought. He must see the truth of her and not be cheated by her as she has done to him throughout their time.

Now that he held all the keys to the cipher—her conspiracy with Spina, her murder of Catherine Visconti and her husband, the betrayal by Cosimo, the circulation of the charges against him to the nations—he could admire what a fine actress she was. How long has she pretended with me, he wondered? Did she ever love me? Was she ever my friend?

The marchesa had grown so accustomed to Cossa's taking her for granted as his closest adviser, and to his indifference to what was happening around him or what other people thought of him, that she was sure that he knew nothing about her many-leveled plots to bring him down. But she was also certain that if ever he did know, or found out, he would be the first to understand that it was only business that had set them against each other. She was even more greatly fond of him now, at the brink of his overthrow, than she had been when they had been going up together. She knew, insofar as it could be measured, that if she loved any man, she loved him. She had made Cosimo swear that whatever they or the council might do to him it could not be allowed to bring him any harm. Although she had persuaded Bishop Buckley to cry out twice that Cossa should be burned at the stake, that was merely a tactical position, taken to force Cossa to make a wrong move, and another way to harden opinion within the council. Cossa was her lover and her friend, but the papacy was a business proposition.

The marchesa was fond of Cossa, but she worked for the Medici. The Great Schism in the Church meant nothing to her or to them except that it was bad for business. It was a sad fact to her that Cossa was replaceable; he could have been ten other men. He was pope and he had used his power to move the Church's banking to her employer's bank. He had called the Council of Konstanz to expand and protect that banking. Life was business and business was money and power. When this council was over she was going to use her money and her power to have herself made a duchess.

They sat down to dinner. The marchesa served Cossa from a sideboard. They were alone.

"I've missed you, Cossa," she said.

"We each have our duties," he murmured.

"All this will be over soon."

"Very soon."

"Sigismund has behaved badly. At Lodi he swore to be your defender."

"I can abide Sigismund. He is a bumpkin but I understand him. And, of course, he is an ambitious man."

"But he needs money. I said to myself that if Cossa could lend him the money a new agreement could be reached whereby the total sum of his manner would improve."

Cossa smiled. "Did you talk to him about it?"

"Well, yes. Maria Louise mentioned it to him and he asked her to ask me to ask you for the money."

"You didn't actually speak to him yourself?"

"I did, actually."

"Then he retained you. You represent him?"

She hesitated, but only for a short second. "Yes. Isn't it delicious? That he has to pay me to get you to help him."

"If we had had this conversation before we came to Konstanz, I would say that you were offering me good value, what with Sigismund being eloquent enough to divide the national delegations until, perhaps, they grow tired and go home. But when I see from whom such an offer comes—from yourself, indeed—I see a basket of vipers. I see no woman before me, only a cold and cunning mind, and because you recommend it, I shrink from it with horror."

"Cossa!" she said with bewilderment, "what are you saying?"

"Why did you kill Catherine Visconti?"

She did not hesitate. "Because if I had not you would have turned your back upon the papacy to become a minor north Italian warlord."

"Did you murder Filargi?"

"His time had come. He was old but he was so holy that he could have gone on and on and on when I had vowed that only you should be pope." She pulled her hand across her eyes. "I am so tired. I can't understand it."

"It will be at least ten minutes before you go into a deep sleep," he said. "Your own potion is working on you. Bernaba was happy to procure it for me. Still, there will be enough time for me to foretell your future for you."

"You have *poisoned* me? Foretell my *future*?"

"Remember how you told Spina—just two nights ago—that you doubted whether he—as old as he is and as sick as he is— could ever enjoy his revenge on Bernaba Minerbetti? You could give him to her, you told him, but he would have to get her away someplace, then he would have to follow her wherever that was if he were to have the pleasure of doing the things that he had been planning for her all her life—but that was very complicated, you told him, and perhaps could even be dangerous for him."

"What are you saying, Cossa?" she said with fright. "Cossa! I *love* you. And you are wrong about everything you are thinking."

"Decima—look at this." He produced a scroll from within his garments. He unrolled it, and leaving his chair, held it under her eyes so that she could read it. "It is the letter to my father that you had the stupid Fanfarone forge in my writing. Ah, forgive me. Your eyes may be getting too dim to read comfortably. Let me read the letter to you. 'Dear Papa,' it says, 'you can help me and help the Holy Church by selling this woman at the slave market in Bari to work among the Arab people whose language she does not speak.' It has your deft touch, Decima. It is brilliant. Then you laid out the route the wagons would follow to take poor, drugged Bernaba down the Rhone valley to Marseilles, thence by ship to my father on Procida. Well! You had it all so beautifully thought out that I am going to use that route and your plan for you."

She did not answer him. Her eyes, which had already begun to film over, burned into him. She was not able to move her body any longer but her eyes were alive and they were shocked with horror.

"Stay awake for a bit, Decima," His Holiness said softly. "Just a few more things you must know. I have plans for your daughters as well, although, alas, nothing I could plan for them would be as pitiless as your own notion of selling a friend in the Bari slave market. There won't be anyone alive to search for you. No one will care enough, when your daughters are dead, to bring you back from animal slavery.''

She had fainted. Cossa called for me. ''Are the margrave of Baden and his men in the courtyard?'' he asked me. I nodded, unable to speak.

''I'll want a message from them from Valence and from Marseilles.''

I lifted the marchesa into my arms. ''Bernaba thinks it would be better to kill her,'' I said.

''An easy thing for Bernaba to say, isn't it?'' Cossa said. ''She hasn't lost everything, has she?'' He began to weep and turned away from me. I carried the marchesa's limp body out of the room.

Chapter 68

After going through the marchesa's wardrobe and setting to one side the garments that she felt would be of use to the women working for her outside Konstanz, and after making the best choices from among the marchesa's jewels for herself, Bernaba rode at a gallop to the Petershausen Monastery, having been passed out of the city by order of a good client, the commander of the military garrison, because she was going to the king's headquarters. Rosa was with Maria Louise when Bernaba found them.

"I am worried about your mother," she said to them. "She went to dinner, as usual, with the pope, at one-thirty this morning, but she hasn't returned. Her bed hasn't been slept in."

Rosa and Maria Louise exchanged glances. "Mama has so much to do for His Holiness," Rosa said.

"If it were only that," Bernaba said, "I wouldn't be troubling you. But her bodyguard—eight men—have disappeared. I went to the Holy Father this morning. He is upset about it. The marchesa left him at three o'clock, he said. He had his major domo check the gate. She left with the bodyguard."

"Mama does so much business—"

"A letter arrived when I was with the pope this morning. I think she is being held for ransom."

"Ransom?"

"We must do something," Rosa said. "We'll go to Cosimo. I'll tell Pippo. Maria Louise will bring the king down on them."

"Please, no," Bernaba said with alarm. "The letter told what must be done and if it is done she will be free tonight. They want a great sum of gold. The Holy Father will gladly pay that, he said. He must leave the city, the letter says, and go down the Rhine to the place they have appointed."

"How can he leave the city?" Maria Louise said. "The king has forbidden it."

"His Holiness said—'How can I not leave the city when she is in such danger?' "

"We will go with him. The guards at the city gates will recognize Maria Louise as the king's dear friend," Rosa said.

"More likely they will cheer you as Pippo's dear friend," Maria Louise said. "We must go with Cossa. Mama will need us."

"I don't know about that," Bernaba protested. "His Holiness didn't say anything about that."

"We will not be stayed, Bernaba. With the tournament on today, no one will know we have gone."

The tournament staged by Frederick of Austria at Cossa's urgent suggestion was the most glorious spring festival Konstanz had ever seen. All the houses in the town were closed and everyone but the guards, the sick, and the elderly had streamed out of the city past the Franciscan monastery to the lists on the site of the common ground, called Paradise, on the inner Userfeld.

The lists themselves were sixty paces long by forty paces in breadth. At either end stood the lodges of the combatants displaying their arms, banners, and helmets. Frederick's lodge faced that of the other principal combatant, Frederick, count of Cilly. Facing the center of the lists was the royal stand, provided with semicircles of benches that rose in tiers one above the other, where sat, resplendent in the majesty of the Holy Roman Empire, King Sigismund, a perfect chevalier, so crowd-proud in his bearing and the way it was being received that he did not think about where Maria Louise might have been.

Below the king, on the lowest tier, with the prize of the tourney on the cushion before her, Queen Barbara was leering at the

young Tyrolese knight, Tegen von Villanders, a peacock plume
in his hat and the queen of Aragon's ring in his beard. Gathered
round Sigismund were princes, dukes, and dignitaries of the
empire, with ambassadors and strangers of rank from every
country of Europe and beyond, all glittering in costly garments.
Facing, on the far side of the lists, was the pavilion for the
citizens of Konstanz. Between lay the sanded battleground with
a long barrier to separate the combatants as they tilted at one
another. The tournament began in the early afternoon and would
go on until stars came out in the sky.

When the sisters reached the papal palace they found Cossa
dressed as a groom. He wore gray clothing with a gray shawl
over his shoulders.

"I thank God that you are here," he said. "If I am to claim
your mother, your escort will be sorely needed to get out of the
city."

I was guarding the heavy load of gold packed upon two horses
in the courtyard, disguised as an old priest. When Cossa saw
that the sisters were mounted, he held the halters of their horses
and led them along the street to the south gate, wearing a cross-
bow slung across his back in the manner of a stableboy, while I
led the two pack horses on foot to the rear. We made our way
through the Inselgasse, then out by the Eselthurm, and leaving
the old Benedictine cloister at the rubbish heaps, we went along
the river. There had been no delay at the gate. The officer in
charge had bowed low to the ladies when they showed their safe-
conducts signed by the king. He paid no attention to their stable-
hand or to me.

Cossa mounted one of the pack horses when we reached the
river and I climbed up on the other. We rode past the castle at
Gottlieben to the little village of Ermatingen on the Rhine, five
miles from Konstanz. We halted at the house of the village
priest, who gave us water. We waited. Cossa told the women
that we were waiting to be contacted by the marchesa's abduc-
tors, but he was really waiting for Frederick of Austria.

A messenger named Ulrich Saldenhorn of Waltsew, who was
a servant of the duke of Austria, rode to the lists at the tournament and trotted sedately to Frederick's lodge. He secured his

horse. He went to the duke and whispered in his helmeted ear, "The pope is free." The duke was badly shaken by the news. He had vaguely expected it, always hoping against it, but Cossa had told him nothing and he had given nothing to the plan beyond his moral support. Now that the crisis had arrived it had come at a most awkward time, just as Sigismund had succeeded in undermining the confidence of the duke's Swiss allies. He was unsure what to do. He had pledged his word to the pope and had taken his money but he had the growing feeling that the action would create irreconcilable enmity.

He rode his last bout, against the young count of Cilly for a wager of many jewels, was defeated and unhorsed, and dragged off the ground by his squires. He left the lists without attracting attention. He went into town to his rented house, Zu der Wannen, and sent for his uncle, Count Hans von Lupfen, who refused to come. Instead, he sent his servant, the lord high steward, Hans von Diessenhofen, who delivered Lupfen's flat words that, since the duke had started a thing like this without him, he could also finish it without him.

"Do you have any idea what you have done?" von Diessenhofen said with agitation.

"Is it so bad, Hans?"

"It is worse than that."

"What can I do? I have given my word. I have taken his money."

"What has been begun must be loyally carried through. Here I am, my lord. I am with you." They took three pages with them and rode out to Ermatingen through the Augustiner Gate.

In the course of that evening, the night, and the next morning, the papal household and many prelates also rode out after the pope, until the absence of so many people was reported to Sigismund.

After he had waited for one hour with the sisters Cossa said to them, "Something has gone wrong. They are not coming."

"How can that be?" Rosa said. "They must come."

After another hour Cossa said to them, "Every moment we wait here puts her life more in danger. Only you can help her now. You must go to Sigismund so that his troops may begin a search for her.'' At last the two women were persuaded. They rode off rapidly to the Petershausen monastery. The duke of Austria arrived at Ermatingen over an hour after that. Collecting the Holy Father and his gold-bearing pack horses they rode on to Steckhorn, five miles further down the river, where the sailboat had been moored. It had two rudders and, passing under the old wooden bridge at Stein, it carried them down the river to Schaffhausen. It was long past midnight when they arrived.

Schaffhausen was held by the duke of Austria on mortgage from the empire. Behind the town was a castle, standing on a small hill with a thick ring of walls set with tall bastion towers, where the Holy Father took shelter.

After dawn the next morning Cossa wrote to Sigismund. ''Thanks be to the all-powerful God, my dearest son,'' the letter said, ''for we are now here at Schaffhausen in a free and good climate. We were able to make our way out of Konstanz because the daughters of the marchesa di Artegiana, Maria Louise Sterz and Rosa Dubramonte, love us so well and sought our freedom so bravely (and with your kind safe-conduct). We will stay here well-protected, with no intention of receding from our intention of resigning, doing so in full freedom and good health.''

Chapter 69

At the same time the following morning Sigismund began to collect some idea that the pope had fled Konstanz, because reports kept coming in that many members of the papal household had disappeared. He refused to see Maria Louise and Rosa when they sought audience because he wanted to work on his search for the pope all day. He sent a force to the papal palace in Konstanz to break in and search out Cossa if he was there. When, in the mid-afternoon, a cold, stormy, and oppressive afternoon, Cossa's letter arrived from Schaffhausen, he went wild with rage that the marchesa's daughters had made Cossa's escape possible. "Those women will do anything for money!" he shouted, and sent Hungarian officers to arrest and question Maria Louise and Rosa. Pippo Span was with him, trying to calm him, when a Hungarian captain returned with the confirmation that the two women had escorted the pope out of the city.

"Kill them!" Sigismund shouted at the captain.

Pippo Span drew his sword ominously. His eyes glittered. "Take back the order," he said.

"So!" Sigismund said. "Your woman betrays me and you draw your sword on me. How much did you have to do with that bastard's escape?"

The Hungarian captain did not know what to do with this

change of affairs between his king and his general. He could not decide whether to summon the guard or to fight Pippo Span. The king burned him with a terrible glance. "Guard!" he shouted. Soldiers came rushing into the room and three irrevocable things happened: Pippo Span had drawn on his king, there was a witness, and the guard had been called in to compound the witnessing.

Pippo Span ran the captain through. The guards rushed at him with their weapons. He held them off while he shouted at Sigismund, "How many times have I given you back your life, my dear friend, that you should repay me by killing my woman? How many armies have I saved you and how many victories have I put at your feet that you should deny the loyalty of Rosa?" The soldiers backed him across the room. All at once, Sigismund realized what was happening, that his own people were about to kill his most dear and loyal friend. "Stop! Guard!" Pippo Span was dead before the last word left his mouth.

Two more officers came running into the room. Sigismund stared at them through his blank loss. "There are two women in the cells who have been questioned," he said. "Execute them."

Cosimo di Medici conferred with the cardinal of Ostia about the arrangements for the triple funeral, which was held swiftly the following day. I had returned to Konstanz on Cossa's orders because he wanted a daily report on what the council would be doing in reaction to his escape. I attended the triple funeral.

On the walls in the cathedral were set 134 burning candles, each weighing six and a half pounds. In front of the high altar Cosimo had had a small open house built—eight feet wide, ten feet long, and eighteen feet high. On its roof 400 small candles burned, each a quarter of a pound of wax. The three biers lay under the roof, each covered with golden cloths. Around the small house sat the forty-five servants of the marchesa, Maria Louise, and Rosa, each one wearing a black cloak. Beside each of these stood a soldier of Pippo Span's command. Each one held a burning candle.

The cardinal of Ostia sang the requiem assisted by two cardinals. One sang the Gospel. I sang the epistle. We were dressed as priests but were without vestments. After fourteen days the coffins would be taken out of their crypts to be transported to be buried at the Villa di Artegiana in Perugia.

After the funeral, the two surviving sisters, myself, Bernaba, and Cosimo di Medici went to the House of the Goldener Bracken where Cosimo was staying.

"It is necessary for us to discuss several things," Cosimo said to them in the house. "Everything happened so fast, but it still remains that Rosa and Maria Louise died within a day of when the marchesa disappeared and when the pope escaped."

"Are these things connected?" Helene asked.

"They have to be," Cosimo said. "Your mother dined with the pope, then not only did she vanish but her bodyguard of eight men also disappeared. Why did you go to look for the marchesa, Bernaba?"

"We were going to the tournament together—with Helene and Maria Giovanna—but the marchesa asked me to call on her early because there was a dress that needed fixing and I have the knack for that."

"But you know her. You know that she had, for years, spent much time with the pope. Why such alarm on this particular morning?"

"I knew she wouldn't miss the tournament for anything. I thought of course that she was still with the pope, but she wanted that dress fixed, and as I left her house, I passed the stables. There were so few horses there—so many empty stalls —that I asked the groom if the bodyguard had gone to fetch the marchesa. He told me they had never returned the night before."

"Then you went to Petershausen?"

"No, my lord. I went to the episcopal palace and spoke with my kinswoman, who is the maid for the ladies' apartments there. She told me the marchesa was not there and had not spent the night there. Then I went to Petershausen."

"How do you explain that Maria Louise and Rosa helped the pope to escape?"

"I thought about that for a long time. The marchesa must have gotten a message to them, telling them to help the pope."

"Please don't press Bernaba, Cosimo," Maria Giovanna said.

"She is our friend and my mother's friend. She had nothing to do with this. Sigismund had everyone killed." Her voice broke. "What are you going to do about Sigismund?"

"He is presently beyond my reach," Cosimo said with emotion. "But not forever. He will be repaid."

Chapter 70

From the moment the pope's messenger had whispered into the duke of Austria's ear at the jousting field that the pope had escaped and that he was to join him, the fat young man had begun to feel the freeze of fear. When his own uncle, the famous warrior, Hans von Lupfen, had flatly refused to join him in the adventure he knew that he had great reason to feel terror. When he had seen the expression on the face and in the eyes of such a man as Hans von Diessenhofen, and felt the terrible danger in his voice when he said, so bleakly, "Do you have any idea what you have done?" he had tasted his own doom. But it had become a thing of necessity. What had seemed like a noble action, when he had taken the pope's money and had agreed to protect him, had turned into the possibility of his own ruination, and even his death, but he could not refuse because the pope had rented his honor, as well.

He rode out to the meeting place at Ermatingen sick in his heart, in his stomach, and in his mind. He was barely able to speak to the pope when he found him in the priest's house beside the Rhine, eating quantities of cheese with me and speaking as merrily as if we were all embarked on a rare excursion. They were not alone until the door was closed upon the pope's chambers in the castle at Schaffhausen and the pope, still merry, began to talk to him as if he did not know that he was standing beyond and speaking through a wall of paralyzing dread that separated them.

"Your departed brother Leopold was once married to Katherine of Burgundy and she likes you," was what the pontiff said to him, smiling so sweetly, so charmingly, that the fat young duke was confused as to why he had become so alarmed.

"I don't understand," the duke said with irritation. "Why do you say that?"

"Why? She certainly dealt with you warmly from your brother's estate. She likes you. You can prepare our welcome in Burgundy."

"Burgundy? Your welcome?"

"I am going to Burgundy. I shall rule the Church from France."

"But what do you want from me?"

"Frederick," the pope explained gently, "you are my defender, are you not? You will get me to Burgundy safely at the head of your troops."

"Are you crazy? Sigismund and the nations would take my head!"

"Not a bit of it, lad. The Council of Konstanz is finished. It has no legal head and no legal existence. Sigismund will have many other things to do."

"I have hardly seen you since the night at Meran five months ago! We have only exchanged two messages in the six weeks I've been in Konstanz! You cannot involve me in this terrible thing!"

"Have you forgotten? You took my money in exchange for your own vows to defend me."

"Damn your money!"

"Frederick!" Cossa admonished gently.

"The only reason I agreed to that arrangement was that I was Sigismund's enemy."

"And you needed my help to cope with the enmity of the bishops of Brixen, Chur, and Trent."

"I thought you wanted *moral* support."

"Frederick, you say that you accepted our condition because Sigismund was your enemy. Well? He is more than ever your enemy now. The three bishops have been handled. You have my money. You have one more lofty title and an extraordinary post—Defender of the Papacy—which your descendants will dine off for the next three hundred years. All we ask in return is that you and your troops escort me safely to Burgundian soil. There is no reason to panic, my son.''

"Your Holiness—once you are on Burgundian soil I shall have no position from which to bargain with Sigismund. He will outlaw me for this! He will have everything I own!''

Cossa dropped the silken amiability. His face hardened murderously, making Frederick suddenly doubly fearful. "If you even think you have a bargaining position now, that you can use me as a trading piece with Sigismund, I will have you garroted here, in this room, now—do you understand me?'' he said. "We will stop this nonsense about the value of your word. It is worthless. You will take me out to Burgundy.''

"Holiness—listen to me. It was a mistake for you to escape from Konstanz. You may have had to resign your papacy—yes. I mean, that is the sheer reality of it, isn't it? But the French cardinals and the other moderates in the council who hold the balance between the fanatic English and the Germans on one hand, and the Italians on the other, would make sure that you could resign with all dignity and all due grace. D'Ailly understands these things. He would make sure that your future would be richly endowed. But Sigismund! Sigismund is a barbarian and I shudder to think what it is—right now—that he is getting under way against you.''

"You are not competent to advise me,'' Cossa said. "I hired you to defend me. Are you going to get me out to Burgundy?''

"No, Your Holiness. I can get no one out. How can I get myself out?''

The following afternoon, the thundering news of the pope's flight brought consternation to Konstanz. As if with a single mind, one hundred thousand people decided that the council was finished. The pope's palace was immediately sacked. Italians and Austrians left the town at night, on foot, on horses, in boats, and in terror for their lives. Sigismund's guards occupied every street and square.

At dawn, Sigismund and Duke Ludwig of Heidelberg, pre-

ceded by trumpeters, rode through the town proclaiming that all
was well, that no one was to leave or think of leaving, that all
persons and possessions were safe, guaranteed by the king's
protection. The shops and banks were opened again as before.

Sigismund assembled every conciliar delegate and assured
them that, at the peril of their lives, they would maintain the
council. Slowly his resolution convinced everyone that they
were safe. The town quieted but Sigismund was in a shaking,
tilting, unbalancing fury. He saw his ultimate throne slipping
away from him. He assembled the princes of the empire at Petershausen and impeached Frederick before them while the cardinals met and elected a deputation to be sent to Pope John, to
affirm that nothing should be undertaken to his detriment in the
meanwhile.

The pope, from Schaffhausen, ordered the Curia and the cardinals to join him—under pain of excommunication—within six
days. Some of the Curia left Konstanz. On Palm Sunday, four
of the Italian cardinals, led by Oddone Colonna, fled to
Schaffhausen. On the following day three more arrived, including myself, bringing with me ninety-eight thousand gold florins,
which was Cossa's (and the marchesa's) share of what had been
earned in the past few months by the women, gambling, and
other enterprises that Bernaba had been overseeing for the marchesa.

Outraged by the mass desertions, Sigismund personally nailed
a manifesto to the door of the episcopal palace in Konstanz,
against the pope and the cardinals, charging John with tyranny,
homicide, simony, fornication, and jobbery.

Regnault de Chartres, archbishop of Rheims, was the pope's
first ambassador to the council. He brought a letter from the
pope to the cardinals, which appointed all of the Sacred College
as his proctors to effect his resignation in the case that both of
his rivals died or abdicated. The letter also stated Cossa's wish
to make the journey to Nice with Sigismund in order that simul-
taneous resignations might be effected there, knowing that if he
arrived in Nice Benedict would refuse to resign. Two days later,
a committee of three cardinals returned from Schaffhausen and
reported to a congregation of the council. They advised the

council that it was virtually dissolved through the absence of the pope, who possessed and retained the right to dismiss it when he chose. However, they reported, the pope would promise not to dissolve the council, and he, himself, would remain in the neighborhood of Konstanz, if the Sacred College and the Curia went to him.

Sigismund then addressed the council and told how it would vote. "My soldiers surround this place," he told them. "If you vote to leave Konstanz you will be dragged out to a prison."

It was circulated everywhere throughout the city that the pope's proposals had been scornfully rejected by the council and by the cardinals, so that everyone was able to believe that Sigismund did not at all want to alienate the cardinals because that would have effectively broken up the council.

At the fourth general session of the council, held on Saturday, March 30, 1415, the following resolutions were passed:

(I) The Synod of Konstanz, legitimately assembled in the Holy Spirit, constituting an ecumenical council and representing the Church Militant, derives its power directly from Christ, to whom everyone, of whatever state or dignity, even the pope, is bound to render obedience in all that relates to the Faith or to the extirpation of the schism,

(II) The pope shall not summon from Konstanz, without consent of the Synod, the Curia or its officers, whose absence would entail a dissolution of the council,

(III) All penalties pronounced by the pope since leaving Konstanz against any dependents or members of the council are invalid.

Sigismund resolved to strangle the mockery of his religion, his ambition, and his dignity, done to him by Cossa's flight, with a vengeful and relentless force of statesmanship and logic but, he hoped, mainly by a force of arms that would drag Cossa back to Konstanz by his heels through the mud. The Italian libertine, as Sigismund saw the pope, had almost succeeded in maneuvering him into looking like some foolish outlander who had no more authority than some scullery maid. Even the *thought* of Cossa returning to Konstanz bearing all of the dignity of a reigning

pope filled him with dismayed rage and a blind sense of preven-
tion at any cost. He could see, as the council most obviously
could not see, that Cossa's design was to draw out the negotiations, to vacillate and procrastinate until he could scatter the
council and leave Sigismund standing there like some bewil-
dered bumpkin. Therefore, in protection of his *amour propre,*
that haughty, sky-high edifice from which most history has been
hung, the king stationed guards on the city walls, and posted
armed men along all roads.

There were still desertions by the papal party from Konstanz
to the Pope at Schaffhausen, only thirty miles away. As soon as
they got there they were under the protection of the duke of
Austria, the entire populace of Konstanz was told, so that Sigismund, driven almost mad by frustration, told his armies to deal
with the fat young duke. I withdrew to Schaffhausen once again,
leaving Bernaba behind to observe.

Sigismund summoned Frederick to appear and answer. The
three days of grace had expired and the duke had made no sign.
His treachery to the empire and to the council was so heinous,
as Sigismund daily reminded everyone, that not a voice was
raised in Frederick's defense at any of the assemblies of the
Teuton leaders.

On March 25, Sigismund pronounced the ban of empire
against him. All of the duke's lands and subjects were released
from their obedience to him and reverted to the empire. It was
forbidden to give him lodging or shelter, to provide him with
food, forage, help, or counsel, to keep the peace or to abide with
him. The whole of empire, lords and cities, clergy and laymen,
informed of the ban, were told that all alliances and contracts
with the duke were null and invalid. The duke was outlawed.

By order of Sigismund, sealed letters were affixed to the cathedral door at the upper court, and at the door of St. Stephen's
Church, summoning Frederick before the royal court. The king
demanded of all secular lords, knights, vassals, and mercenaries
that they go to war against the duke's possessions. Mobilization
was ordered in the imperial cities stockpiling food, provisions,
and weapons. The first expedition, made up of troops from
Konstanz, Biberach, Ueberlingen, Pfullendorf and Buchhorn,
Kempten and other places, was sent out against Frederick's

possessions in the Thurgau. The duke's Swiss confederates refused to break their fifty years of peace with his family, but the Tyrol seized the opportunity. Patriarchs, bishops, and counts all produced their claims against Frederick. Within eight days, 437 lords and cities had sent in their letters of defiance. The heavy military operations began on April 2.

On the twenty-eighth, so many Letters of Feud arrived at Schaffhausen that the pope was appalled by their number. He was on his way to the church on Black Thursday when a messenger brought him the news of the mobilization for war. Without hesitation he told the cardinals that each man was to shift for himself. He turned back to the castle. The next morning, when he asked them to join him in flight, every cardinal, including the pope's own nephew but excepting myself, declined. They were frightened of being made prisoners by Duke Frederick, who had sworn to make the pope and his cardinals pay for the war that had been forced upon him.

On Good Friday, clad in his pontifical robes, Pope John left Schaffhausen and rode twenty-four miles that day in a driving rain as far as Waldshut. Ten miles more the next morning got our papal party to the castle at Gross-Laufenburg, in the bishopric of Basel, where the Rhine separates the Jura from the Swabian range.

"We have to decide the way to get out of here safely to France," Cossa said to me over a hearty dinner before going to bed with the Angioni twins, whom Bernaba had been thoughtful enough to send to Schaffhausen for his pleasure.

Chapter 71

Although the council abandoned respect for Cossa's feelings at its fifth general session on Saturday, April 6, he could not have said that the form was not observed. The delegates passed a resolution that read: "Whoever, of whatever condition or dignity he be, even of the papal, shall obstinately refuse to obey the decrees of this council, shall be liable to penitence and to punishment, even though secular aid have to be invoked."

The actual method of punishment of all who had left Konstanz without permission was made over to Sigismund, who was also asked to write to Pope John to offer him a safe-conduct for his return to Konstanz.

At last the Swiss, who had to be threatened with being placed under ban of empire, agreed to take arms against the duke, on the conditions that they might retain every place that they conquered and that the king of the Romans would not make peace with the duke without including them in it. The war could now proceed with brutal surety. Frauenfeld and Winterthur in the Thurgau were taken. The duke of Austria was in despair.

"How could I ever have believed that he was a true pope?" he wailed upon the bosom of his mother, who had been sent in a clamoring rush by the family to persuade him to surrender in the hope that at least something could be saved by negotiations with Sigismund.

"A pope is a pope," she said comfortingly. "How could you know what kind of man he would turn out to be?"

At dawn the following morning, Pope John XXIII crept out of Laufenberg, disguised as a forester, carrying a bow and arrows, and began the journey through the deep snow of the Black Forest to the city of Freiburg. His five faithful friends were with him: Geoffredano Bocca, his cook; Count Abramo Weiler, his physician; Luigi Palo, his squire; Father Fanfarone, his chaplain; and his last remaining cardinal, which is to say, myself, Franco Ellera. On the first night we reached Todtnay in the Weisenthal. The next day we passed Muggenbrunn and made sanctuary at the Dominican cloister at Freiburg in Breisgau, arriving on the night of April 10. Freiburg had been held by the Austrian dukes since the summer of 1368.

Within two days, those of the Curia who had straggled after Cossa arrived in the town and were struck by its beauty and by the elegance of its broad streets and squares, its fountains and runlets. No cardinals came, but there were bishops, chamberlains, and other officers of the court who were still in train.

Cossa sent a letter to the duke of Burgundy, who had been so profuse with his gifts of wine at Konstanz during the winter and who had, so joyously and respectfully, sent a bodyguard to meet him in Alsace. At Konstanz his ambassadors had been in the pope's confidence and they had urged him to race to Avignon, to settle there under the duke's protection. Cossa sent another letter, to the council. It was a message from one combatant to another, which told the assembly that he was still willing to resign but that the war against the duke of Austria must cease and that he, Baldassare Cossa who was Pope John XXIII, must be appointed cardinal-legate in perpetuity for the whole of Italy, with Bologna and Avignon ceded to him, with an annual pension of thirty thousand gold florins, secured on the cities of Venice, Florence, and Genoa, and with perfect freedom from account for any of his actions in the past or the future.

While he awaited replies he showed his gratitude for the loyalties and friendship of the men who had been at his side since he left Procida thirty-seven years before. He bestowed upon his physician, Count Abramo Weiler, now ninety-one years old, the archbishopric of Cologne and the administration of the diocese of Pederdorb. He made his cook, Geoffredano Bocca, and his squire, Luigi Palo, bishops who would rule over Bohemian dioceses and, no matter where they might choose to live, would receive their benefices. He made his chaplain, Father Fanfarone, a general of the Franciscan Order. "I could not do less," he said to me simply, "but you have served me more truly than anyone in my life. Tell me what you want, Franco, and you will have it if it is mine to give."

"I want to go back to Bologna," I told him.

"I am working on that," Cossa answered.

The Swiss overran the Aargau. They took Mellingen and Sursee. Baden was besieged. All the duke of Austria had left out of a vast domain was the Black Forest, Breisgau, and the Tyrol. Sigismund had an army of forty thousand men in the field against him.

Sixteen hours before Cossa's letter reached the duke of Burgundy, the messenger of the Council of Konstanz reached him with Sigismund's version. The duke of Burgundy was a very unsentimental politician who had assassinated his cousin to get where he was. When Sigismund's letter explained that the pope had made a fatal move, which had cost him his place and his influence, he no longer wanted to have anything to do with Cossa, so that, when Cossa's letter arrived, the duke repulsed it with great indignation and dispatched ambassadors to Konstanz to deny any possibility that he would cooperate with the disgraced pope.

"I should have known," Cossa said when he was told of the duke's rejection, "that anyone who would kill his own cousin to get ahead couldn't be relied on."

"Maybe it's the other way round," Franco Ellera said. "Maybe we are the ones who can't be relied on."

"How can you say that? I am the pope. All Christendom relies on the pope." He grinned sardonically. "Look at the deal that idiot turned down. Everything being equal, with the pope making Burgundy the center of the world and the focus of the Church, that would have given him more power than the king of France. But he didn't know what was good for him."

"Maybe we're finished," I said.

"Maybe you're right. Maybe I'm more unpopular than I think. But nobody can discharge a pope. That's the lever we have and I'm going to use it to set us for the rest of our lives."

"What can you do?"

"I have to agree to resign. There is no other way. To persuade me to agree, they have to pay me. It's simple."

"No. We can't win this one."

"Cosimo has all my money and most of the Church's. Therefore we have to get a lock on Cosimo, because money is the big lock he has on Sigismund and the council."

"How do you get a lock on Cosimo?"

"We kill Decima's daughter—Helene MaCloi."

"What is she to Cosimo?"

"Decima, Cosimo's true instrument, is gone. He knows I did that. He doesn't know how or when, but he knows I got rid of her. Two of her daughters are dead. He knows Sigismund wouldn't do anything to harm Pippo Span. What were two women to Sigismund? Pippo Span was his greatest friend. Pippo Span had saved his life twice. So Cosimo has reasoned that I arranged that."

"Cossa, tell me, please. What does all that have to do with Cosimo?"

"He loves Maria Giovanna. He loves her almost as much as he loves that bank. When they see Helene MaCloi dead while they know that her sisters are dead and that their mother is gone, it will come to them that Maria Giovanna is next—unless he does something."

"You mean you disposed of the marchesa, then her two daughters, so that you would be able to handle Cosimo di Medici if it came to that?"

Cossa shrugged. "Cosimo owed me. He wronged me. He trapped me in the papacy but I must have him in the background as my ally if I am to come out of this with anything. Tell Palo to kill her. Now. As soon as he can get to Konstanz. Bernaba will set her up for him."

On April 27, Duke Frederick, prodded and petted by his mother, urged on by his family, and threatened with cousinly violence by Duke Ludwig of Bavaria, decided, at last, to deliver the pope to Sigismund as a peace offering. His troops took Cossa from the outraged monastery at Breisach to Umkirch to meet the deputation of cardinals who set before him the alternatives of honorable resignation or disgraceful deposition. Cossa took a night for reflection, enticing the absent innkeeper's wife into bed with him, but in the morning, he told the cardinals that he was willing to resign but not at Konstanz. He would resign in Burgundy, Savoy, Italy, or Venice—always providing a fitting provision was made for his future.

Twelve guards watched him by day, twenty-four by night, from the end of April in Freiburg. The town was densely occupied by imperial troops. The pope was the prisoner of Sigismund, king of the Romans.

Chapter 72

On April 30, the prelates of the four nations and the secular princes and nobles of the empire and Christendom assembled at the Franciscan cloister in a long throne room where Sigismund stood in judgment. It was an exquisitely staged proceeding. Sigismund stood in the refectory with his back to the door and chatted with the envoys from Milan, Genoa, Florence, and Venice, who looked over his shoulders at the door. While they chatted Duke Ludwig of Bavaria, Burgrave Frederick of Nuernberg, and Count Nicholas Gara appeared at the door, as if the king's meeting with them was merely accidental, leading the saddened Duke Frederick, who kneeled three times at the entrance to the room. When the four men approached Sigismund, he turned casually in the direction of the stares of the Italian envoys. All petitioners kneeled.

"What is your offering?" the king said distantly.

"Here has come for your mercy," Ludwig said, "our cousin, Frederick, duke of Austria. He will submit to your mercy and swear, do, and keep what is said in this letter, which was written here according to an agreement with your royal mercy."

"Relative," Sigismund said to Frederick, "are you really willing to do this?"

The young duke mumbled in a broken voice, pleading for grace humbly.

"I ask the king to pardon him," Ludwig said, "while knowing that, because he has scorned your royal majesty and the council, he hereby makes over to the king's grace and power his body, his land, and his people, all that he has. He promised moreover to bring back Pope John from where the king has confined him, provided, for honor's sake, that no injury befall the pope's body or his goods."

Sigismund held out his hand to Frederick and said, "It grieves me that you have committed this fault."

The young duke's letter was read aloud. Sigismund spoke to the envoys. "You see how one can be mistaken?" he asked them. "You thought that the dukes of Austria were the greatest lords in the German countries of the Germanic nation. Now you see what the king of the Teutons can do. I am the mighty ruler over not only the Austrian princes but over all other princes, lords, and towns."

The duke of Austria swore to and subscribed a deed whereby he made over all of his lands to the king, from Alsace to the Tyrol. He contracted to bring the pope back to Konstanz and to remain himself as a hostage until his promises were fulfilled. Sigismund asked him to swear to that. Frederick lifted his hand. The bishop of Passau gave him the oath, which he repeated in a shaking voice: "I will swear it, keep it, abide with it, and undertake nothing against it."

Sigismund turned away from them again and immediately proceeded with the auction of the Austrian possessions, which went, piece by piece, to the highest bidder. He sent out his delegates in all directions to take possession of the duke's lands. He needed the money.

The Austrian towns in Upper Swabia as well as all towns in the county of Tyrol refused to swear allegiance to the king.

Chapter 73

On May 2 Pope John was summoned to appear before the council within nine days: The summons cited him as a heretic, a schismatic, and a simoniac, and as being incorrigibly immoral. Therefore, on Ascension Day, Thursday, May 9, the envoys from Konstanz arrived in Freiburg to take their prisoner to the council. They were Frederick, burgrave of Nuernberg, and the archbishops of Besançon and Riga, with a troop of 450 horsemen.

Everyone in Cossa's official household had deserted except myself, of course, Count Weiler, Bocca, and Luigi Palo. Father Fanfarone had departed immediately upon receiving his generalship of the Franciscan Order. It was a sorry train for the spiritual lord of Christendom. Cossa received the envoys and promised to accompany them to Konstanz, but the nine days allowed for his appearance elapsed and still he delayed his departure.

The burgrave refused to lay his hands upon the Lord's anointed. "We are only here to protect the escort," he told his military staff. At last the pope agreed to be moved. They got under way on May 19, getting as far as the ancient town of Radolfzell at the end of the Zeller See, where the pope put up at an inn. "We must keep them off balance," he said to me. "The council must become as a flock of chickens in a burning coop. Let them wear themselves out."

As the pope had not appeared within the time allowed, at the ninth general session, on May 13, Cardinal d'Ailly applied to the council that he be suspended, that evidence be taken, and that the process for his disposition proceed. Five prelates were sent to the door of the church and called out for Pope John to appear. They returned to the assembly to say that they had received no reply. A body of thirteen commissioners was appointed to take evidence and, by the next day, eleven witnesses had already been examined. From their depositions it was sufficiently proved that Pope John XXIII had dissipated the Church's goods, had practiced all manner of simony, and had caused scandal and confusion to Christendom, so that he deserved to be deposed from the spiritual and secular control of the Church. There was no evidence of heresy, they said.

A decree of the pope's suspension was read out to the assembly by the patriarch of Antioch.

"In the name of the holy and undivided Trinity—the Father, the Son, and the Holy Ghost—amen. Since we have surely known that Pope John the Twenty-third, from the time of his accession until now, has scandalously misgoverned the Church, has through his damnable life and infamous conduct given evil example to the people, has notoriously by simony distributed bishoprics, monasteries, priories, and other Church benefices, has wasted the property of the Church at Rome and other churches, has neglected all admonition and still continues to oppress the Church, we therefore declare the aforesaid Pope John the Twenty-third to be suspended from all spiritual and secular control, hereby prohibit him from exercising same, and we direct that a program for his deposition be introduced. At the same time, any further obedience to him on the part of the faithful is hereby forbidden."

Helene MaCloi's body was found on the steps of St. Stephen's Church, Konstanz, early on the morning of May 13. Her neck had been broken.

The body was taken to the house of Konrad of Hof, where Chancellor Gerson lived as the guest of two dukes of Lorraine. Her sister, Maria Giovanna, was notified and came at once to the place, weeping, with Bernaba Minerbetti. Within moments

Cosimo di Medici was there. He brought a guard of thirty armed men with him. The family mourned until nightfall.

The funeral was held the following morning. By sundown Cosimo had sent Maria Giovanna and the guard out of the city to Florence. Cosimo did not explain to her what he thought had happened. He told her she was in gravest danger, and that she must, for the love of God and her life, do as he commanded her to do.

Chapter 74

After the examination of many bishops, priests, and curials by the commission charged with investigating Cossa, on May 16, an indictment of Pope John XXIII was presented before the council. Eleven articles concerned his misconduct in Konstanz, mainly having to do with his seduction of wives and daughters. Simony, the most serious charge, occupied twenty-five articles. Three times in the indictment he was charged with the murder of Pope Alexander V. A miscellany from the past was offered, including adultery with his brother's wife, unchastity with nuns and virgins, and sodomy. He was charged with disposing of the 1,460-year-old head of St. John the Baptist, property of the nuns of St. Sylvester, Rome, to an unknown buyer in Florence for fifty thousand gold florins, and with the oppression of the poor, with tyranny extending to sentences of death and banishment, with neglect of the admonitions of cardinals, of the French ambassadors, and of the king of the Romans. All these were written in the blackest ink, but the only article that related to his heresy said that he did not believe in the immortality of the soul or the resurrection of the dead.

Three hundred of Sigismund's Hungarian troops took the pope to the prison in the castle of Gottlieben, a few miles down the Rhine and across the river, where John Hus was held pris-

oner, both under the wardership of the count Palatine, elector
of the Rhine, and one of the two foremost protectors of Pope
Gregory XII. Within one hour of Cossa's arrival at Gottlieben,
Cosimo di Medici was brought into his damp, dark cell and the
warders were sent away.

Cosimo owed Cossa a great debt. Cossa had made the Medici
Bank the wealthiest and most powerful bank in the world. He
had made the Medici lords of the world by working unceasingly
to transfer all of the banking of all levels of the Church to Cosimo and his father. By this one act, Cossa had made the Medici
the princes above all princes in Christendom. "Protect Cossa!"
Cosimo's father had told him, had written to him. "Once he is
brought down from the papacy we must do everything to see
that he is safe and entirely comfortable."

Cossa watched unsurprised as Cosimo entered the place.
There was only one stool, occupied by Cossa. Cosimo sat on
the bed.

"I understood what you meant by what happened to Decima
and her daughters," he said grimly.

Cossa nodded.

"I sent Maria Giovanna away."

"She can be found, I suppose."

"That won't be necessary, Baldassare. You have grievances
and I came here to set them right."

"Good."

"This place is impossible. I have spoken to Palatine. He will
make you comfortable, with your staff and your cook, no matter
where they take you from here. You can have—uh—visitors."

"We mustn't let anyone harm Franco Ellera."

"My dear fellow—he is a cardinal. He is inviolate."

"Good."

"The council will sentence you." He sighed. "If you had only
resigned, what a life you could have had! But that would have
been too uncomplicated for you, I know, so I will see to it that
the sentencing will be as light as possible under the circumstances. They will forget those heresy charges and that false
charge about the murder of Pope Alexander."

"You and Decima killed Alexander."

They stared at each other.

"It will be necessary for you to stay in confinement until the new pope is elected, but I will see that it is extremely pleasant. You will have your friends and your books. You will be better off than merely comfortable."

"How long will they imprison me so?"

"I should say, first, until the new pope is elected. Second, I should think he would want to get himself safely back to Italy before pardoning you."

"How long should that take?"

"There is no way of measuring it. They will all want to discuss reform before they will get around to electing a pope."

"Reform!" he snorted. "What about money for me, Cosimo?"

"Well! You'll have the money from all of the various businesses you and Decima set up in Konstanz. You have your accumulated account at the bank—which includes the gift from Carlo Pendini."

"Bernaba has to have her share of the Konstanz enterprises."

"Why not? But you will have your share and Decima's share."

"I think I deserve to have your share as well."

"You shall have it. Then, when the new pope is elected he will want to give you a respectable pension, won't he?"

"Will he?"

"Be sure of it. I guarantee that. Besides, popes take care of popes for reasons of precedent, don't they?"

"They do when the Medici Bank tells them they must. But he must also give me a dignity. I can't be expected to return to Bologna as plain Signore Cossa."

"I will handle everything. You will never be less than a prince of the Church."

"You are a good friend when you are a good friend, Cosimo."

"Then you won't look for Maria Giovanna?"

"No. They were all such lovely women. Decima was the loveliest."

"What happened to her?"

"I can't tell you that," Cossa said sadly. "But there is one more thing. All of this running I have been doing has only reminded me how old I am. Whatever the council tells the world I am, there is the danger that is what I will always be after I am dead. We wouldn't want that, would we? But I reason that you and your father were very much a part of what my life became.''

Cosimo nodded, silent.

"So I want the respectability of a fine tomb, a tomb of such majesty that it will cast doubts into the minds of Christians unborn, a tomb that will defy time by making them see me in the light of its glory.''

"I will do that for you.''

"Yes, and I thank you. It will be my revenge on the miserable men who will judge me, the Princes of Nothing, who, when they die, will be forgotten almost before their bodies grow cold. I will pay for the tomb and you will see that a great man designs it. Take whatever it will cost out of Carlo Pendini's gold.'' He smiled a most beautiful smile, a sweet, endearing, warm smile, which shared his own joy with his friend.

"So be it, Your Holiness,'' Cosimo answered him.

Chapter 75

Within two hours after Cosimo had left him, Cossa was moved to luxurious quarters in the main part of the castle. As his "confessor" I had been permitted by the warders, after the intervention of Cosimo, to live with Cossa in these apartments. We played cards. We remembered old campaigns. We quarreled genially. Early on while we were there, we got to talking about Hus. Cossa called for the captain of the guard and gave him two hundred florins, with a wink that said there was more where that came from.

"They tell me you have John Hus here."

"Yes, Your Holiness. He is safely locked in a cell."

"Bring him to me, please."

"Holiness! Hus is a condemned heretic. He will be burned to death tomorrow."

"All the more reason, my son. The man is doomed and I am his pope. Bring him to me."

When Hus came into Cossa's apartment from his windowless dungeon he was deathly pale but he looked younger and more serene than when he had arrived in Konstanz. Cossa was older and thicker and more companionable with eternal death. There was a lightness about Hus, a health that seemed capable of taking him beyond death. When he saw Cossa he bowed deeply, without smiling. "Holiness," he said, "what a great day for me."

Cossa hobbled on his gout to a chair and pushed it toward Hus. "Sit, my son," he said. "You have a great journey ahead of you." They sat facing each other in front of a broad window that looked across the limpid river toward the fields where Hus would be burned at the stake the next day.

"Where did it go wrong for you?" Cossa asked him.

"I don't remember anymore."

"The same council condemned me, you know."

"So the warders told me."

"The king spoke of you last summer at Lodi. I canceled your excommunication at Lodi."

"Did you?"

"A woman who used to advise me—a great woman—sent me a letter concerning you, which her daughter had sent her from Prague. It puzzled me."

"How, Your Holiness?"

"Why did you get into political things, Hus? You had a great pulpit. All Bohemia was your congregation. You were the queen's confessor. Everyone praised you. Why did you come to Konstanz among all these ambitious men?"

"The Church needed reform. I wanted to debate what was wrong with the men who disagreed with me and convince them to change their ways. There are evil men in the Church, Holiness."

"No man is evil to himself," Cossa said, solemnly wanting Hus to carry this knowledge to his grave. "There are only pragmatic men who seek to make things work. As Jesus told us— they know not what they do, they only know they must get it done as best they can. Things—certainly enormous concepts such as Christendom—must *seem* to work."

"Is that what you did, Holiness?"

"I was never in all that with them and with you, Hus. I had a different trade. Fate—you would say God, of course—turned me away from where I served well to this for which I cared nothing. You came to Konstanz. I accepted the papacy. We don't belong here so the men who do have cast us out."

"I know there is more than that," Hus said solidly. "God awaits me tomorrow with the explanation."

"Do you want to confess to me?"

"I have confessed with my life, Holiness."

"I can vaguely understand that. Perhaps—all my life—I met the wrong men. That is the hard sentence imposed upon lawyers."

Pope John XXIII was deposed on May 29. He did not appear at the council. Sigismund was surrounded by the princes of the empire, fifteen cardinals, and a shining array of prelates and learned doctors. The decree of deposition was read by the bishop of Arras, assisted by the deputies of four nations, then the archbishop of Riga produced the pope's seal, which was solemnly destroyed under the eyes of the council by a goldsmith.

HISTORICAL NOTE

The Council of Konstanz, which ended in 1418 after three years and six months of existence, also ended the Great Schism in the Church, which had lasted for thirty-nine years, and terminated the 112-year period when popes ruled from France.

Cardinal-Deacon Oddone Colonna was elected as the single pope of Christendom on November 11, 1417, at Konstanz, taking the name of Martin V.

Baldassare Cossa was held prisoner at the Heidelberg Castle from 1415 until 1418, when Cosimo di Medici took up the matter of his release with Pope Martin. For payment of 38,500 Rhenish gulden, made by Bartolomeo de' Bardi, the Medici Bank representative, presumably advanced against Cossa's promissory note, the former pope was released to his jailer, the count Palatine.

While Pope Martin was officiating in the cathedral at Florence on June 18, 1419, Baldassare Cossa appeared before him. Cossa threw himself at Martin's feet, acknowledging him as the true and only canonically elected pope.

On June 23, 1419, Pope Martin bestowed on Cossa the bishopric of Frascati, and on the following Tuesday raised him once more to the Sacred College as Cardinal Tusculanus, with all of the benefices, incomes, and emoluments due to a prince of the Church.

Cossa lived out his remaining days with his faithful friend and banker, Cosimo di Medici, in the Medici house in the Via dei Buoni. He died on December 22, 1419. He was fifty-two years old. Cosimo di Medici commissioned a tomb for Cossa, which was designed by Donatello and fashioned by Michelozzo, and which rests to this day on the right-hand side of the high altar of the Baptistery, the most ancient church in the city, which replaced the Temple of Mars. The bronze figure of Cossa, recumbent and looking to one side, looks out over the Florentine children who are brought there to be baptized.

Franco Ellera lived on in Florence, Bologna, and Rome after Cossa's death. He died in Florence, in Cosimo di Medici's garden, in 1424, surviving his wife, Bernaba, by four years.

Cosimo di Medici died in Florence, the host to the Italian Renaissance, in 1464. At the urging of his mistress, Maria Giovanna Toreton, he sent two consecutive expeditions to North Africa, Turkey, and the Middle East to search for the marchesa di Artegiana, to no avail.

Maria Giovanna Toreton was the last survivor of the group that had secured the Church's banking for the Medici. She died in 1468, eighty-five years old.

No reform of the Church was attempted by the Council of Konstanz.

Richard Condon

November 25, 1982

BIBLIOGRAPHICAL NOTE

The author gratefully acknowledges the contributions to *A Trembling Upon Rome* made by the following texts:

Flick, Alexander Clarence. *The Decline of the Medieval Church.* 2 vol. N.Y.: Burt Franklin, reprinted 1967 (originally printed in 1930).

Gimpel, Jean. *The Medieval Machine.* London: Victor Gollancz Ltd., 1977.

Kitts, Eustace J. *In the Days of the Councils.* 2 vol. London: Archibald Constable, 1908.

Loomis, Louise Ropes, John Hine Mundy, and Kennerly M. Woody, trans. and eds. *The Council of Constance.* N.Y. and London: Columbia University Press, 1961.

Masson, Georgina. *Courtesans of the Italian Renaissance.* London: Secker & Warburg, 1975.

Spinka, Matthew. *John Hus at the Council of Constance.* N.Y. and London: Columbia University Press, 1965.

Ullman, Walter. *The Growth of Papal Government in the Middle Ages.* London: Methuen, 1955.

———. *A Short History of the Papacy in the Middle Ages.* London: Methuen, 1972.

The author also acknowledges with thanks the generous help of Decherd Turner and Dr. Claude Albritton, Jr., Bridwell Library, Dallas, Texas, and that of Mrs. Barbara Johns of Konstanz, West Germany.